Praise for
A December to Remember

One of *USA Today*'s Best Romance Books for Fall
One of *Reader's Digest*'s Best Holiday Books

"[A] delightful new holiday romp . . . A December TBR list must."

—*Reader's Digest*

"If you like families reuniting, small-town romance, celebrating Christmas, and [books that] wrap you in a big hug then this is the book for you."

—BookBub

"The story of the North sisters wraps up at the end like the perfect present. . . . *A December to Remember* will instantly put you in the holiday mood."

—*The Daily Beacon*

"Compelling . . . Delightful, heartfelt."

—*Library Journal* (starred review)

"No one does holidays better than Jenny Bayliss!"

—Amy E. Reichert, author of *Once Upon a December*

"A charming winter solstice treat with *Love Actually* vibes and a hint of bohemian magic."

—Abby Jimenez, author of *Part of Your World*

Praise for
A Season for Second Chances

One of *Buzzfeed*'s Best Books of October
One of BookBub's Best Holiday Romance Books

"[An] inspiring tale of strength, integrity, and self-respect . . . Readers will be enchanted."

—*Publishers Weekly*

"Readers who enjoy laugh-out-loud rom-coms will want to spend a cozy winter evening by the fire with Annie and the residents of Willow Bay."

—*Library Journal*

"There's so much to love about this enchanting story. This lovely, cozy read is perfect for winter."

—*BookPage* (starred review)

"Enormously entertaining, this manages to be escapism of the highest order."

—Minneapolis *Star Tribune*

"Full of quirky characters and a refreshingly mature leading lady, this book will restore anyone's faith that it's never too late for a second chance at love, or indeed, life."

—Sophie Cousens, author of *This Time Next Year*
and *Just Haven't Met You Yet*

Praise for
The Twelve Dates of Christmas

"With its cozy, small-town setting and adorable premise, *The Twelve Dates of Christmas* is the perfect book for anyone looking for a charming holiday romance."

—*PopSugar*

"We can't get enough of this twist on the '12 Days of Christmas'!"

—*Country Living*

"Delightful holiday atmosphere and believable romantic tension . . . By turns tender and hilarious, this adorable rom-com is sure to satisfy."

—*Publishers Weekly*

"Charming . . . This slow-burn rom-com set in a small British village at Christmas will be the perfect cup of tea for fans of Marian Keyes or Helen Fielding."

—*Library Journal*

"Fans of the best-friends-to-lovers and second-chance tropes will savor this."

—*Booklist*

"[A] nice cozy rom-com novel, one with a bit of an edge, a larger meaning, and a satisfying ending."

—Minneapolis *Star Tribune*

"Feels like getting a hug while sitting under a thick blanket with a cup of tea on a wintry afternoon."

—*Refinery29*

Also by Jenny Bayliss

A December to Remember

Meet Me Under the Mistletoe

A Season for Second Chances

The Twelve Dates of Christmas

KISS ME
at
CHRISTMAS

JENNY BAYLISS

G. P. Putnam's Sons

NEW YORK

PUTNAM
— EST. 1838 —

G. P. PUTNAM'S SONS
Publishers Since 1838
An imprint of Penguin Random House LLC
penguinrandomhouse.com

Library of Congress Cataloging-in-Publication Data

Names: Bayliss, Jenny, author.
Title: Kiss me at Christmas / Jenny Bayliss.
Description: New York : G. P. Putnam's Sons, 2024.
Identifiers: LCCN 2024027974 (print) |
LCCN 2024027975 (ebook) |
ISBN 9780593717905 (paperback) |
ISBN 9780593717912 (ebook)
Subjects: LCGFT: Romance fiction. | Christmas fiction. | Novels.
Classification: LCC PR6102.A975 K57 2024 (print) |
LCC PR6102.A975 (ebook) | DDC 823/.92—dc23/eng/20240621
LC record available at https://lccn.loc.gov/2024027974
LC ebook record available at https://lccn.loc.gov/2024027975

Printed in the United States of America
1st Printing

Book design by Shannon Nicole Plunkett

For Jo, who takes care of everyone, with love xxx

KISS ME
at
CHRISTMAS

ONE

THEIR EYES MET THROUGH THE CURLS OF STEAM TWISTING out of their mugs. His were the color of burnt honey, framed by dark eyelashes and skeptical S-shaped eyebrows. Hers were the color of faded denim, and they watched him with the hunger of an alley cat that's just spied a tasty-looking field mouse.

At the other end of the pub—despite only being the third week in November—the Christmas karaoke was in full swing, and the main bar area was swamped with swaying punters trying to cram in another round before the end of "happy hour." The smaller bar in the saloon area was quieter. Couples cozied up in corners or ate at the candlelit bistro tables.

Her phone rang. Emma. She sucked on the inside of her cheek as she debated taking the call and then decided that she wasn't ready to talk about it yet. If she did, she might cry, and she didn't want to cry. She dismissed the call and buried her phone deep in her handbag. Tonight, she wanted to forget.

This was Harriet's second mug of mulled wine, and she was enjoying the taste of cinnamon and star anise and the velvety caress of the hot wine slipping down her throat. The warmth feathered out through her chest in a delicious trickle. The man smiled and one of those skeptical eyebrows quirked a little higher, giving him serious Jack Nicholson vibes. A delightful zing of excitement ricocheted around inside Harriet's sensible knitted tights. She smiled back in what she hoped was a flirtatious way and then wider when he began walking toward her. She could do this; it was just like riding a bike. Right?

"Do you mind?" he asked, gesturing to the barstool next to hers. His voice was moody blues and sandpaper. She nodded and he perched, keeping one foot planted on the sticky carpet. He smelled like sawed pine and cloves. His suit was sharply cut and expensive, the top button of his white shirt undone, tie ever so slightly pulling to the left. He was so good-looking that she had the urge to punch him. This wasn't a normal response, she knew this, but something about this level of attractiveness was sparking a visceral physical reaction inside her. Perhaps she was just horny; it had been a while. She kept her free hand in her lap and instructed it not to make any sudden movements.

"Can I buy you another drink?" he asked.

"Thank you." She furnished him with a cool smile, like she did this kind of thing every night of the week. *I'm doing it! I'm actually doing it. I am the smooth, self-assured woman at the bar; I am goddamned Kristin Scott Thomas!*

"Same again?"

"Please."

The flirting at a distance had come easily, but now that he was here, she felt her bravado scurry away like a spooked squirrel. She was out of practice and drank deeply from her mug of crimson bravery.

He was watching her with an amused expression.

"Slips down easily, doesn't it?" he remarked.

"A bit too easily," she confessed. "That's the trouble

with mulled wine, it tricks you into thinking it's a warm bedtime drink instead of alcohol."

"And is it making *you* feel ready for bed?" His eyebrow quirked up again, so bold that Harriet immediately was indeed ready for bed.

"You're very forward, aren't you?"

His cocksure demeanor slipped, and he looked away as though embarrassed. When he met her eyes again, his smile was shyer but no less potent.

"Sorry," he said, "I had some long-awaited news today and I think I've maybe indulged a little too freely with the mulled wine."

His dark hair was smart like the rest of him, short at the sides and just a little longer on the top, swept up at the front; the lamplight highlighted flecks of gray at his temples. The sounds of a drunk couple doing a convincing rendition of "Fairytale of New York" drifted through the bar.

"It's easily done. Was it good news or bad news?" Harriet asked, taking another deep swig.

The bartender placed two more mugs of steaming wine on the bar. Sexy-eyebrow man handed one to Harriet, and she smiled a thank-you.

"It was both," the man said, picking at a loose thread on the bar towel. "I'm not sure whether I should be celebrating or commiserating."

"Aha, you're experiencing a commiserbration."

"I think you just made that word up."

"But it fits the experience."

"It does," the man agreed. "I potentially put wheels in motion on an endeavor that could make one of my clients an even wealthier woman than she already is and throw me into the path of other wealthy clients."

Harriet raised her mug. "Well, cheers to that!"

"But I wonder if I may have to sell a piece of my soul in the process."

"Souls are overrated." Harriet waved away his concerns. "Cheers!"

They clinked and sipped.

"What about you?" he asked. "Celebrating? Waiting for a friend?"

Her smile flattened.

"Unlike you, there is no ambiguity in my emotions; I am comprehensively commiserating."

"Oh, that sucks. Is it insensitive to ask what happened? You can tell me to mind my own business, I'm drunk enough not to mind."

He looked sincere. Sincerely hot. Was she really going to spill her guts to a stranger with come-hither eyebrows? Yes.

"My seventeen-year-old daughter has been on a school exchange trip for the last three weeks. Cooperstown, in upstate New York. She was due back next week; I was going to decorate the flat ready for Christmas for when she got back home."

"That's sweet," said the man.

"Yeah. Except I got a phone call this evening saying the family have invited her to stay for Christmas."

"Ouch."

"Ahhgghh!" She threw her arms in the air. "I don't know. I mean, I'm happy for her, of course I am, what a wonderful experience, and she's so excited . . ."

"But?"

Her sensible head told her that she was sharing far too much with this handsome stranger, but her wine head was yelling, *Just tell him already, what have you got to lose?* Her wine head won.

"But. This is the longest time we've ever been apart. Next autumn she'll be off to university and . . . I guess I was just trying to soak her up before she goes, you know?"

Good-hair man gave a noncommittal nod. He obviously didn't have children.

"This last three weeks has been a snapshot of what my empty nest is going to look like, and I've got to be honest, I don't like it one little bit. Who even am I without her to look after? What's the point of me?" she shouted, sloshing hot wine down her cleavage. She mopped her boobs with a bar towel and lowered her voice. "It'll be our first Christmas apart. But I want her to do it, she's going to have an amazing time, and I'm so proud of her. Sooooo, I guess I'm commiserbrating too. Sorry—*hic*—that was a lot. More wine?"

He continued to watch her, his face close to hers, his eyes oh so sincere, like he was really listening.

"Does she know how you feel?" he asked.

Harriet laughed. "Don't be ridiculous! She doesn't need to know. I'm not going to guilt my daughter into spending the holidays with me. She was still unsure about whether to accept the invitation, but I know it was only because she was worried about me, bless her. She's a good girl. I told her she absolutely had to stay; I wouldn't hear another word about her coming home."

"That's very selfless."

"That's being a parent."

He flinched infinitesimally, but it passed almost before Harriet had registered it, and she had neither the presence of mind nor the will to chase it up. She didn't know him; it wasn't her job to wonder. Two more mugs of hot spicy wine arrived, and she blew on hers before taking a sip, Christmas dancing on her tongue.

"It's all about consumerism these days, anyway, isn't it? You're probably better off out of it," he said plainly.

"No!" Harriet was aghast. "I love Christmas. I am Christmas's biggest fan. I love everything about it. People are so much kinder at Christmas, have you ever noticed that? For the month of December even the most hardened bum-barnacle can find a little charity in his heart. I love doing all the Christmassy stuff and making it magical for my daughter and my family; I am the Christmas fricking queen! Or at least I was. Now I'm . . ."

"Dethroned?" he added helpfully.

"Surplus to requirements," she sighed. "Christmas feels like a demonic candy cane poking me relentlessly in the ribs."

"So you convinced your daughter to leave you alone at Christmas and then came to a pub that's decorated like Father Christmas's grotto, hosting Christmas karaoke and serving the most Christmassy of all the alcoholic beverages." There was that eyebrow again, being all sarcastically sexy and suggestive.

"Yes, I did," she deadpanned.

"Isn't that rubbing salt into the wound?"

"I am vaccinating myself against the holidays. Building my resistance. By December the twenty-fifth I will be completely immune."

He looked dubious about her logic, but he nodded sagely.

"What about you?" she asked. "Are you a Grinch or a Saint Nick Nut?"

"Are those my only choices?"

"You can add your own."

He pondered for a moment and then said, "I would describe myself as middlingly merry. I like the festive esthetic; I like the way the decorations bring light to an otherwise dark month. And I like that I get time off work. I would say that up to now I've been happy to take advantage of Christmas while not fully partaking." He paused, as though wondering whether to continue. Seriousness fell like a shadow across his face. "But there have been recent unexpected developments in my life that have made me wonder what I might have missed . . . what I might have found if things had been different."

Even through her haze she could feel his regret, see the longing in his eyes and the drop of his shoulders. She could taste it on him, and it had the same bitter tang as her own.

"Regret is the ultimate party pooper." She heard the weariness in her voice. "Its mission in life is to constantly suck you backward into the past, where it forces you to replay all your mistakes on a loop. The only way is forward; you've just got to keep on trying to outrun it, my friend." She smiled lopsidedly and took another drink.

"Spoken like someone who knows," he said. "Have you tried vaccinating against regret?"

"I get my yearly booster shot and live in hopes that one day it will take." *I am so much wittier when I'm drunk. I wonder if there's a way to carry this forward into sobriety.*

He nodded as though he understood. "Sorry." He shook himself. "This got deep all of a sudden, didn't it?"

"I think we're working through the many stages of drunkenness." She smiled.

"What's the next stage?" His eyes had become darker; they glinted with something enticing.

She took a breath and let her eyes drop to his lips, twisted up at the edges in a devilish smile. A dark line of stubble ran along his jaw.

"Dubious decision-making," she answered, licking her own lips.

His smile widened into a full grin as he raised his mug, and Harriet was all in.

"I propose that in the interests of doing justice to this fine evening of commiserbrating, and vaccinating against negative emotions, we continue to drink hot wine until we can think of something better to do."

This time his eyebrow lifted so suggestively that Harriet had to bite her lip to stop herself from biting his. He clocked it straightaway and grinned wider still.

"When you say 'something *better* to do,' do you have anything specific in mind?" she asked, leaning toward him, so that he could smell her perfume and get a better view of her chest. This was most unlike her; the alcohol had released her inner vamp, and she'd be lying if she said her own brazenness wasn't acting as an aphrodisiac. His Adam's apple bobbed as he swallowed hard, and she felt powerful.

He cocked his head and regarded her, smiling wickedly.

"One or two things," he said enigmatically, bending his body and sliding his arm along the bar to move even closer to her. "But I'm open to suggestions."

The sounds of bad karaoke faded to black and the other patrons in the bar melted out of her consciousness, leaving only the two of them in sharp focus.

Oh my god, this is so sexy! Her heart was pinging around in her chest. His hand was on the bar next to hers, their fingers not quite touching, and she could swear she felt static zinging in the sliver of space between. She needed to keep up the appearance that she was a temptress. *What would Kristin Scott Thomas do?*

She looked up, blinking slowly to show her nonchalance, and fixed him with her eyes.

"I'm sure if we put our heads together, we can come up with something to satisfy us both," she purred.

She watched his pupils dilate and wanted to moan with pleasure. Who or what had taken possession of her this evening? In her head Sean Connery's voice whispered, *The name's Wine. Mulled Wine.* Her fourth mug had gone down a treat, settling around her shoulders like a velvet shrug and softening her bones. She smiled at him and felt a warm pleasure as he looked hungrily at her mouth before he raised his eyes to hers again. He leaned in close.

"I'm James, by the way."

His voice rumbled through her body like a train she was running to catch.

"Harriet," she responded breathlessly.

With the barest of movements, she closed the gap and brushed his lips with hers.

"I am delighted to meet you, Harriet," he whispered hoarsely.

She smiled as he crushed his mouth to hers. Stars collided behind her closed lids. A sweet tickling sensation began to build inside her as though she were on the slow climb to the top of a roller coaster. This was exactly what she needed tonight.

Harriet allowed herself to follow that feeling all the way back to his place, where an hour later, shouting in ecstasy, they finally dropped over the edge of the roller coaster together.

TWO

THE FIRST THING THAT CONFUSED HARRIET AS THE FOG OF sleep began to dissipate was the light shining in through her closed eyelids. She had blackout curtains in her bedroom—had she forgotten to close them last night? Her eyes were stuck shut with last night's mascara, and as she unpeeled her top lashes from her bottom ones, the sight of the unfamiliar room caught her momentarily off guard before the events of last night slammed back into her mind like a series of stills being played at top speed on an old movie projector. The images might have been grainy, but there was no mistaking their X-rated nature. *Sweet Magic Mike! What was his name? J. Jake? Jacob? James!* Okay, that was something, at least she had a name. The crumpled sheets in the space next to her were barely warm and she could hear a shower running in the en suite. *Ooh, an en suite! Fancy.* She peered around the room. There was a lot of dark wood furniture and a seascape canvas on the wall; it screamed *well-heeled bachelor with taste.* What was the etiquette these days with one-night stands? She was a bit rusty; it had been ... years. Did one stay for awkward conversation over breakfast or leave quietly and maintain an element of mystique? She fast-forwarded her mind through their sexual gymnastics—feeling slightly smug that she could still bend like that in her midforties.

The problem was that the Harriet who lay disheveled in expensive Egyptian cotton sheets was not the Harriet of last night. The cool, confident woman-about-town with mulled wine sloshing through her veins was a different version of the one who preferred quiet nights in and big knickers and was currently scrabbling about trying to find the estrogen patch that was missing from her left butt cheek. *There it is! Thank God.* She peeled the scrunched patch off the sheet and dropped it into her handbag. James had gone to bed with a woman channeling Kristin Scott Thomas and woken up with Velma Dinkley. She wasn't sure she wanted to deal with his polite disappointment when reality struck home. Better to leave. She could be his "one that got away"; too bad she didn't have a glass slipper to leave behind.

Her phone bleeped and she reached for it on the side table as she pulled herself up to sitting.

LYRA: Can't wait to see you! xx

Who's Lyra? she wondered. And then she looked again. Not her phone. *Oops! In that case, it's not my business to wonder.*

She slipped out of bed and gathered up her clothes, screwing her nose up as she stepped back into yesterday's knickers and dressed quickly. Dammit, she was missing a cardigan. And it was her third favorite. She found her own phone complete with eighteen emails forwarded to her from her boss. She groaned, stuffed the phone into her bag, and slung her bag onto her shoulder. With her shoes in one hand, she tiptoed out of the swanky bedroom and into a very sleek open-plan living area. It was movie-set-chic with a wall of windows that overlooked Foss Waterfall cascading down a rock face before crashing frothily into the River Beck, which ran through the town of Little Beck Foss. This guy must have serious money. And great taste in décor. The shower stopped running, and Harriet stopped admiring the marble kitchen worktop and wondering if he had to buff his gleaming black matching cupboards daily and— briefly noticing the pair of shiny oxblood brogues sat neatly side by side on the doormat—ran out of the apartment, pulling the door closed quietly behind her, saying to herself, *Goodbye, third-favorite cardigan* as she scuttled down the corridor, not stopping to put her shoes back on until she was safely in the lift.

Despite being icked out by her lack of a shower and the inside of her mouth feeling like a suede jockstrap, she felt invigorated by her night of passion with a stranger. Harriet didn't often throw caution to the wind; she kept her caution tied down away from stiff breezes, but when she did let it fly, she did it with style. She smiled to herself.

A bitter wind whipped along the street, tossing a discarded paper cup this way and that along the pavement. People walked with heads down against the cold. Snow was in the air. She could feel its peppermint breath on her lips, and her eyes teared up at the scent of cold pine in her nose. Thick ecru clouds gathered, lying low over the forests of fir trees that covered every hill surrounding the small Cumbrian town.

Christmas had been seeping slowly into shop window displays since the first of November, seamlessly replacing the pumpkins and witches on broomsticks. Now, a snarling mass of festive lights crisscrossed above the main high street in a glittery carnival of greens and reds.

A Christmas tree that reached as high as the church stee-ple stood resplendent in the center of the town, discreetly masking the dilapidated and long-defunct Winter The-ater from tourists.

Until Maisy's phone call last night, she had been itch-ing to get going on Christmas. It was her favorite time of year, and she made a stonking big deal of it. The twin-kling lights all over the town and the overly tinseled shop windows had always made her inwardly—and some-times outwardly—squeal with delight. Until now.

Was it her imagination or was it more Christmassy this year than ever before? Or was it simply that now she wanted to forget all about it because Maisy wouldn't be here? Christmas felt pointless without someone to make Christmas for.

In the three weeks since her daughter had left for the U.S., Harriet had, not to put too fine a point on it, mis-laid her mojo. She'd stopped cooking from scratch after work because what was the point in cooking for one? Instant noodles and microwavable fisherman's pie had become her food staples. It was tough to go from being somebody's chef, chauffeur, revision buddy, best mate, comforter, confidante, and housekeeper to being sud-denly surplus to requirements. The long evenings felt as though she was merely killing time until Maisy came home and she was made vital again. Only of course now Maisy wasn't coming home, at least not until after Christmas.

It wasn't that they had lived in each other's pockets; Maisy had an active social life, and quite frankly Harriet enjoyed the time to herself. But when all her time was time to herself, it rather lost its appeal. Was this what her life was going to be like when Maisy went to university?

Am I Schrödinger's mum? Immaterial until summoned into being by my offspring?

The Salvation Army band were playing "God Rest Ye Merry, Gentlemen" outside the bank, and Harriet had to bite her tongue to stop herself from shouting *Bah humbug!* as she passed them by. *Get a grip!* she chided herself as she threw a pound coin roughly into the charity tin. *This is what you wanted!* Harriet had helped to create a strong, confident woman and she could not be prouder. But she also felt like a discarded hermit crab shell left to drift along the seabed, empty and alone.

It was almost eight when she pushed open the door to her quiet flat. She missed the sounds of her daughter, even if it was only the tinny commentary of whatever TikTok video she was watching. The emptiness was loud, and the space left by Maisy's absence felt cold and dull, like someone had draped a gray filter over her home. Her breath caught in her chest as she remembered that all too soon this sensation would be her permanent flat-mate. She wasn't ready to be retired from parenting. She sighed as she looked around her too-tidy, Christmas-free home. Her intentions of going full Santa's Grotto for Maisy's return had been smashed like a dropped snow globe. She didn't think she could face putting the decorations up now. They would remain in the cupboard under the eaves, and the fancy orange-and-cinnamon-scented candles would stay in their boxes. Christmas was officially canceled.

Her phone pinged. Emma. Again.

Hey, so, I'm guessing after last night's Christmas bombshell you crawled into your cave and ignored my calls. You know you're still welcome here. You're family and my bestie, which makes you double

welcome. Give me a call when you've finished sulking.
Love ya xx

She messaged back.

Hey. No cave for me. Woke up in a sexy stranger's
bed this morning. Think I'm rebelling. Call you later.
Love ya xx

She grinned, knowing this would drive Emma crazy
because she'd be in the middle of getting the kids ready
for school and herself ready for work and she wouldn't
have time to call and get the goss. Her phone pinged
with a voice note, Emma's voice squeaking out from the
speaker.

WHAT!!!!!!!! We need to talk. I need to know
everything! Shit, I'm late. You did that on purpose.
Jordan, take that nose ring out, you know you can't
wear it to school, I'm not having you suspended
again!

There were some mumbled arguments and a distant
bloodcurdling scream, presumably from one of the twins,
enraged that one of her siblings had "stolen" her phone.

Sorry. Kids. Who knew teenagers would be such little
shits? I'm calling you at lunchtime, you better make
sure you're somewhere private, I'm gonna need gory
details! Kisses Mrs.

Harriet smiled. Emma was married to Harriet's ex,
Pete. On paper, the two should never have become friends,
let alone best friends, but she and Emma had found in

each other a kindred spirit, so much so that Pete had often joked that they should have got married instead.

She stood under the shower and hoped the water might wash away some of her hangover. No such luck. Had booze got stronger, or had she become a lightweight?

Harriet and Pete had split up when Maisy was a baby. They'd met in foster care and were childhood friends who became sweethearts almost by default and who should have let their courtship take its course and fizzle out naturally. Instead, they were so afraid of risking the friendship they had come to rely on that they'd had Maisy, hoping that their shared love for their daughter might ignite some passion between them. It didn't. Nobody cheated, nobody said unkind things, they loved each other, just not that way. They co-parented as friends, and—even if they said so themselves—they'd done a pretty good job. A couple of years after their split, Pete met Emma and unsurprisingly, given how similar she and Pete were, Harriet and Emma hit it off too. The rest, as they say, was blended-family history.

Forty-five minutes later, Harriet arrived at work late with freezing cold wet hair, a headache, and the beginnings of cystitis, which had become more frequent; it was one more kick in the hoo-ha beside the long list of things her body had decided to reward her with in her forties.

"Psst! Harriet!"

Harriet turned to see Ali, one of her colleagues on the pastoral care team, violently gesticulating to her from the doorway of an empty classroom. She hurried over to him.

"Cornell is on the warpath. Billy didn't show up for his revision session yesterday and he hasn't registered today," he whispered loudly.

Crap! This was all she needed. Sebastian Cornell was the head of the English department and the pastoral care team. He made sure to milk both of his titles to their fullest, while shirking his responsibilities for both by being an Olympic-standard delegator. He was a permanently outraged human as old-school as his beige toupee. He complained bitterly about the "malcontent youth of today" and seemed to feel as though students were sent here to try him. Billy, one of her charges, had a way of getting right up his snobby nose.

"Are you sure he hasn't just signed in late?"

"Like you?" Ali winked at her, and she poked her tongue out.

"I had a rough morning."

He smirked. "Looks more like a rough night."

"Oh god, is it that obvious?"

"Only to me."

At thirty-five, Ali was almost diabolically youthful-looking, with jet-black hair swept back off his face and large brown eyes sporting obscenely long lashes. He was many a student's secret crush and some of the parents' too. Harriet suspected he had borrowed Dorian Gray's portrait for his attic.

An electronic bell bleeped out the start of first period, and the corridor filled up with students. Ali pulled Harriet into the classroom and closed the door.

"Drinking on a school night's not usually your style. Is everything okay?" he asked.

"Maisy's not coming home for Christmas."

Ali's mouth dropped open. "Oh, babe! That is shit. No wonder you got rat-arsed."

Harriet decided to change the subject before Ali delved further. "I can't believe Billy. Cornell's been looking for a reason to exclude him, and he's giving him the excuse he needs."

"It's not just Billy. I've found three more missing from

the list so far." The "list" accounted for the students on the pastoral team's radar. "Carly, Ricco, and Isabel. I haven't checked the rest of the registers yet, but it's a bit of a coincidence that four of the famous five are all absent at the same time, wouldn't you say?"

Foss Independent was a private school catering to both boarders and day students from all over the world. It had been established by the "old guard" in the early 1900s, back when Little Beck Foss was still a thriving town making hay while the favor of the wealthy shone upon it. The town was still as pretty as ever, but behind the ancient stone buildings much of the prosperity had dwindled and many of the shops on the high street lay empty.

Each year as part of their "leveling-up" scheme, the school took in a certain percentage of students from the town. Harriet was not a particularly cynical woman, but she knew well enough that the scheme was as much about ingratiating Foss Independent with wealthy philanthropic sponsors as it was benevolence. The famous five—so named because they were almost always together—were "level-up" kids living in Little Beck Foss, and they were often at odds with their peers at the school.

Though many of the students came from privilege, it offered them little immunity against the pitfalls of adolescence. The "list" therefore tended to be a long one. Most were teenagers struggling with the transition from child to adult, which could manifest itself in anything from mild depression to eating disorders and self-harm, and everything in between. It was the pastoral team's job to keep these young people safe and help them evolve into well-adjusted adults. It wasn't easy.

Unsurprisingly, a chunk of the list contained the names

of level-up kids, many of whom dealt with added complications such as poverty or unstable home lives. Billy, for instance, carried a lot of weight on his young shoulders and sometimes it spilled over into bad decision-making.

"You think we're looking at a mass truancy?" Harriet asked, ruffling her drying hair.

"Could be. If I've clocked it, it's only a matter of time before the attendance team join the dots."

Harriet bit her lip. "Billy's already skating on thin ice. He can't afford another discipline point. Can you try and keep this on the down low for me, just for a little while?"

"I know that look. What are you going to do?"

"A spot of teen wrangling. If I can find them."

"Are you going to lasso them back to the school grounds?"

"If that's what it takes."

Ali looked at her, and she watched the cogs of his mind whirling.

"Okay, I reckon I can hold the truancy hounds off for two hours. Isabel could do without another demerit against her as well. Where are you going to start looking?"

She shrugged. "Coffee shops along the high street maybe? The park? Any ideas?" She didn't relish the thought of going back out in the cold, but needs must.

"Maybe the falls?"

"Okay, I'd better get going. Call me if there's an emergency."

"I'll try and field Cornell's calls if I can, keep him off the scent."

"Thanks, Ali. I owe you one." Harriet refastened her scarf around her neck.

"But if they pull out a lie detector, I'm giving you up

immediately!" he called after her, and her replying laugh echoed down the corridor.

She was almost home free when she heard her name snapped out like a pinged elastic band. She turned to find Sebastian Cornell marching toward her. The swish of his corduroy trousers sounded like laundry being rubbed hard against a washboard.

"Sebastian." She smiled tightly.

"Billy Matlin is absent . . . again! That takes his unauthorized absences to eleven this term."

"It's not unauthorized," Harriet lied. "He called in earlier, I forgot to put it in the register. He has a dentist appointment."

Cornell gave her an appraising look. *Lying to a senior member of staff, excellent move.* She smiled sweetly. Cornell narrowed his eyes.

"The fact remains, he is a disruptive student who has the rare ability to be just as disruptive when he's not here."

"The world needs disruptors."

Cornell's thread-veined nose flushed a deeper shade of purple. "People like Billy are the reason this country is swirling itself down the toilet!" he spat, before turning and striding away, the sound of his corduroy thighs chafing loud in the quiet entrance hall.

The receptionist gave Harriet a knowing look and stifled a snigger.

"One day his trousers will burst into flames from all that friction," said Harriet.

"I really hope I'm here to see that," said the receptionist, smiling.

THREE

THE MOMENT HARRIET STEPPED OUT THE DOOR, THE WIND started in on her hair again. Luckily, hers was the kind of style that didn't mind a bit of rough handling. Falling just below her shoulders in choppy layers, it had always had a mind of its own; most recently it had decided to start streaking her formerly teak-colored locks in ash gray. She was undecided whether to soften it with some highlights or go full Lily Munster . . . Her phone buzzed: Cornell. She tried to ignore the nervous tightening in her stomach as she pressed decline.

As she made her way to the main gate, she spotted Leo—fifth member of the famous five and Ricco's on-off boyfriend—slip through an arch cut into the perimeter brick wall and in a snap decision decided to follow him.

She kept a discreet distance as she followed Leo up the high street. He crossed the road, hurrying past the café on the corner and several fast-food joints, and then the Salvation Army band who appeared to have great stamina and a limitless repertoire. Suddenly he ducked behind the giant Christmas tree.

Where are you off to?

She tailed him as he walked briskly past the front of the Winter Theater and down the side of the building. She turned the corner just in time to see him squeeze behind a large piece of corrugated iron and disappear through what must have been the old backstage door.

Her phone buzzed again and she checked it. Cornell. Not answering a work call went against her every instinct, but she couldn't risk answering it and have him realize she was off campus. She let it go to voice mail and consoled herself with the knowledge that if it was urgent, Ali would call.

While she waited in the alley beside the theater to see if Leo reemerged, her phone rang with a call from Jules, her liaison with the teen counseling service; there were too few therapists in the area and there was a woefully long waiting list to see them. She kept her voice low as she spoke with Jules, phone pinned to her ear by her shoulder as she scribbled notes. The call ended. Still no sign of Leo. There was only one thing for it.

Checking that the coast was clear, she lifted the corrugated iron and pushed open the peeling red door behind it. It was dark, and she had to use her phone torch as she carefully navigated the narrow concrete stairs littered with old leaves and rubbish. This would have been the entrance for the theater workers, away from the glamour of the front doors. Posters torn and brown with damp lined the walls, and the air was cold and sour with the tang of forgotten dreams. From somewhere farther inside the building she heard muffled snatches of voices and followed the sound.

At the top of the stairs was a corridor which split into three and was signposted *Dressing Rooms*, *Stage*, and *Front of House*. The corridors leading to the former were in darkness but there was a dim light at the end of the one leading to the front of house, and it was this that Harriet decided to follow. Here there was carpet, albeit carpet that had seen better days, and the farther along she walked the more decorative the corridor became. Soon paper posters were replaced by prints in Baroque-style frames, their details obscured by decades of dust. The walls became paneled below and ornately corniced above, and the ceiling height grew and arched. Now she was faced with two more choices, *Lobby* or *House*. She chose lobby and, in a few moments, found herself stepping down a short flight of stairs and out into a wide space.

A cobweb-strewn chandelier hung down from a ceiling that was decorated with swirling roses and twisting thorns. The plasterwork was cracked and chipped, and in places damp patches bloomed in brown frills across the once-white stucco. The light that had drawn her came from dimly glowing Art Nouveau wall sconces; these too dripped with cobwebs. To allow such grandeur to rot felt almost obscene. This was the Miss Haversham of buildings, bitter and disbelieving of its fate.

There was an old-fashioned box office to one side, a cloakroom area, and a dusty concessions stall. To her left were the glass front doors, darkened by the large security panels boarded across them on the street side. On the wall farthest from where she stood was another set of doors, oversized and arched and patterned all over with black lead leaves and flowers, and chained shut with heavy padlocks. Harriet knew that these led into the building next door, which had once housed cocktail lounges and the Winter Restaurant, where patrons could enjoy a three-course meal and drinks before the show. She'd seen old photographs of the place in its heyday: black-and-white images of celebrities dressed in their finery.

In the center of the lobby, a sweeping staircase of old-world glory rose up from the faded red carpet, the kind the Nicholas Brothers might have tap-danced down. At the top it curled away left and right into a balcony, which circled above. Harriet could feel the wanting in the walls, the ghosts of the theater haunting the place. Long-dead faces stared out at her from the picture frames, begging remembrance. Even in its decrepitude, it was breathtaking. A tiny spark flickered deep inside and stole through her bones; she couldn't give the sensation a precise name, but it felt like possibility.

Little Beck Foss had once been the aristocracy's playground. The thundering waterfalls and tranquil lakes offered London ladies a taste of the wild, while dukes and lords enjoyed the hunting and shooting, and the Winter Theater was the place to go for nightlife. Later, when the Bright Young Things found themselves holed up in their country piles with their parents for the holidays, the theater quenched their thirst for culture while its cocktail lounges provided a place for carousing. The partying came to an abrupt halt with World War II, and the glory days never returned.

A high-pitched cackle, which Harriet instantly recognized as belonging to Isabel, pierced the melancholic fug, and she gingerly ascended the creaking stairs and pushed through a set of moth-eaten velvet-covered doors at the top. She found herself on a large balcony looking down over the auditorium.

Cigarette smoke plumed up out of the stalls. Billy was reading aloud from a copy of *A Christmas Carol*, this term's English lit text, a cigarette hanging casually out the side of his mouth, while on the stage Ricco and Carly—holding their own copies of the script which they'd been studying for drama—were acting out the parts. This was all done with a heavy sense of mocking, which—in Harriet's opinion—Charles Dickens didn't deserve. Billy had made his voice plummy while the actors onstage significantly overegged the pudding. Isabel and the newly arrived Leo lounged in the faded seats, legs outstretched and feet resting on the tops of the chairs in the row in front, laughing at their friends. Leo already had his sketchbook out, his pencil furiously scratching at the paper; that kid was never without his sketchbook.

I mean, it's not ideal but at least they're engaging with the subject matter? Harriet was an optimist. Now all she had to do was convince them to come back to school.

FOUR

SLOWLY SHE MADE HER WAY DOWN THE STAIRS THROUGH THE middle of the dress circle. A few of the spotlights still worked and with these illuminating the stage, Harriet was obscured by darkness until she reached the top of the slope where the stalls began.

"You know, we have a theater at the school I'm sure we could arrange for you to use," she said.

Five heads snapped round in her direction. Billy hastily dropped his cigarette into an empty bottle. Ricco and Carly—blinded by the spotlights—squinted in her direction while Isabel—her long black ponytail swinging wildly—had jumped up to standing in readiness to sprint, and Leo, shouting "Shit, it's the feds!" had drop-rolled onto the floor and was peeping up over the folded seat.

Harriet couldn't stop herself from laughing. "Relax, guys, it's only me. And for the record, Leo, we don't have feds in the UK."

"Miss Smith?" Carly asked uncertainly, her hands shielding her eyes from the spotlights.

"The one and only," Harriet replied dryly.

"Shit, miss, you nearly gave me a heart attack!" said Billy. "What are you doing here?"

"What am I doing here? You've got some cheek. What

are *you* doing here? Mr. Cornell is not impressed at your absence, *again*."

"He's never impressed," said Carly, jumping off the stage and landing in a crouch like a cat. She was in the process of growing out a buzz cut, which she and Ricco had both done as a dare, and habitually ran her palms over her white-blond spikes.

The others murmured their agreement. Ricco—whose mum had cried when he'd first shaved his head and said he looked like a gangster—more wisely took the stairs off to the side and came to stand beside Leo, who had relinquished his bad hiding space. "Why does he even teach if he hates kids so much?"

This was a question Harriet had asked herself numerous times, but in the interest of maintaining her professionalism she replied, "Mr. Cornell has an appreciation for literature, which he wants to pass on to his students, and he becomes frustrated when he is unable to do his job properly. He can't do his job at all if you're not in school for him to teach you."

"It's all irrelevant to us, though, miss, isn't it? All this oldy-worldy stuff. I'm not saying it isn't a good story." Carly waved her copy of the play. "A lot of them are, if you can get through the crusty way they're written, but what actual use is all this stuff to us?"

"I think we can learn a lot from literature: social history, opinions of the time . . ." Harriet began.

"How is that going to help me get a job?" asked Isabel. Isabel's family lived in a high-rise on the same infamous estate as Ricco. Her mum worked fiendishly long hours to make ends meet, and Isabel, the oldest, took on a lot of responsibility for her younger siblings.

"I'll grant you that being able to recite passages from a Dickens novel won't help you in an interview, but the qualification that you'll gain from the course will. If you attend classes, that is."

"It's dumb that Foss makes English lit a compulsory A-level," said Isabel. "No other school makes you do it. I don't care about literature."

"You must care about literature if you care about drama; they're intrinsically linked." Bored expressions all round. "Look at it this way—having an A-level in English literature certainly can't do you any harm."

This was met with a unified groan.

Harriet wasn't fazed by this type of sulking; she'd heard it all before. Being on the pastoral team rather than the teaching staff meant that her relationship with the students was more relaxed. She had no agenda, and that meant students tended to be less guarded with her. Her role was often as mediator and always as guardian of their physical, emotional, and mental welfare. And when the need arose, she made sure they got their butts to class.

"Are you going to dob us in?" asked Billy.

"I won't have to because you're all going to come back to school."

Carly had relaxed her stance and stood with one hand on her hip; she was looking at Harriet with a smirk. Of all of them she was the most indomitable—on the outside, at least—a tumultuous home life had ensured that her first response was always attack.

"Does Mr. Cornell know you're here, miss?" she asked.

"No, he does not. I wanted to give you a chance to do the right thing."

"Whoa!" shouted Ricco, grinning. "Nice one, miss. You've gone rogue."

"Good on you!" added Leo, whose bravado had fully returned.

"How did you know we were here?" asked Billy.

"I followed Leo."

Groans of "Leo!" and "Fuck's sake, mate!" from his peers made Leo wince.

"What?" he retorted hotly. "How was I to know Miss Smith was a super spy?"

"That's pretty badass, miss!" laughed Carly.

"Yes, well, this badass needs you to get back to school before you all get slapped with discipline points."

Billy, the only one of them who had remained resolutely in his seat, sparked up another cigarette and asked, "What does it matter? What's the point?"

"Put that out, please, Billy, it's a fire hazard."

"Your mum's a fire hazard!" said Leo.

"That's not even funny!" Isabel sniggered.

"Then why are you laughing?" he retorted.

"Billy, I'm serious." Harriet gave him a challenging stare; she'd never lost a stare-off with a student yet. Sure enough, Billy looked away first, conceding defeat by angrily stubbing out the cigarette in one of the old metal ashtrays attached to the back of the chair in front.

On the outside, Billy was a tough nut. He'd had to be. Most people saw a kid with a bad attitude because that was the persona he projected. What they didn't see was a boy who had spent the biggest part of his life yo-yoing between foster placements and care homes with his younger brother, Sid. Harriet saw through his projection because she'd lived that experience too.

"You didn't answer the question, miss—what's the point?" Ricco picked up Billy's mantle.

"Yeah, what's the point?" parroted Leo, who was always braver when riding on someone else's coattails.

"Look. These exams are a stepping-stone, nothing more, but having the qualifications will make it infinitely easier for you to move on to the next stage of your lives, whether that's an apprenticeship or the workplace or university."

Billy snorted derisively at her mention of university, but she'd included it on purpose. Just because the likelihood of them going into higher education was small didn't mean it was impossible. And sometimes, along with keeping it real you needed to offer nuggets of possibility. If you gave them nothing to aspire to at all, then you were confirming what they already saw as a foregone conclusion and sending them out into the world with no hope at all of charting new paths for themselves. Her job was a fine balance of facilitating positive change and managing reality.

"I know it doesn't seem like it now, but you will regret not using this time to make life easier for yourselves down the line. Everything is going to be harder if you leave the school without taking advantage of what's on offer there. Even if it's just for the sake of making your CV look better, it's a competitive job market and every little bit helps when you're applying for jobs that a hundred other people are also going for."

"I can't imagine you young, miss," said Ricco contemplatively. He clearly wasn't listening to a word she was saying.

"Well, I can assure you that I was, and as someone who is now *old* I am offering you the benefit of my wisdom."

"It's weird how nothing ever shocks you," Billy pondered. "Most teachers would have freaked out about us being here."

"Maybe I've just seen it all before."

"*Done* it all before, more like," Carly sneered, opening a bag of crisps.

Harriet didn't argue. Instead, she made her way to the end of Billy's row and, pushing down the seat pad and scraping off the dust bunnies, sat down.

"Why here?" she asked, waving an arm to encompass the decrepit theater.

"Why not?" Carly challenged.

"Where else are we supposed to go?" asked Ricco.

"You mean besides school?" Harriet asked dryly.

"There is nowhere else," said Billy, snapping open a can of shop's-own-brand soft drink. Harriet saw the truth in his words. There was a run-down mall in the center of the town, but she didn't imagine the security guards would stand for gangs of kids hanging around. Or the park or the forest, not so much fun when it was barely two degrees outside. Not that it was much warmer in the theater.

"We don't only muck about here." Leo was uncharacteristically defensive. "Sometimes we do homework, discuss books we've read. Carly likes to sing on the stage."

"Shut it, Leo," Carly snapped.

"What?" Leo asked, hurt. "You do!"

"Stop trying to be such a tough bitch all the time," Ricco admonished Carly.

"And we discuss stuff, important stuff." There was a defiant note in Isabel's voice. She was a shy girl until it came to the causes she felt passionate about. Harriet had watched her hold her own during debates around LGBTQ+ and other social issues during their tutorial sessions; it was a pity she didn't channel some of that energy into her homework. In another era these kids would have been labeled beatniks.

Harriet nodded. "Couldn't you do all these things in the common rooms at school?"

"I can't sing in the common rooms," said Carly.

"And you can't smoke there," added Billy.

Harriet pursed her lips. "I wouldn't advise it here, either. Aside from you being underage and risking lung cancer, this place looks like it would go up like a tinderbox."

"You would say that, wouldn't you?"

It was pointless to answer.

"Didn't you ever have a den when you were a kid, miss? You look like someone who read the *Secret Seven* books; this is our den, our place," said Ricco, who did not in Harriet's opinion look like someone who'd read the *Secret Seven* books, but who was she to judge?

She checked her phone. Half past ten; most lessons would be on morning break time. She could sneak them back in after. *It wouldn't hurt to stop here for another few minutes.*

"Okay, what do you make of Charles Dickens's Christmas ghost story, then?" she asked.

Isabel groaned dramatically. "Are you going to make us do lessons?"

"I'm not making you do anything. You were already reading the text when I arrived. And Leo said you discuss books here, so . . ." She saw Ricco roll his eyes. "I'm just asking what you think of it."

Carly and Isabel pulled themselves up on to the edge of an old stage block and sat with legs swinging. Ricco and Leo perched a couple of rows down from Harriet and turned round to face her and Billy.

"Bleak," said Ricco.

"Interesting," Harriet mused. "Did you know Dickens wrote *A Christmas Carol* to highlight the plight of child laborers and children living in poverty because he was frustrated by the upper classes' lack of care for anyone below their social class?"

"Some things never change," said Billy.

"Exactly! Britain was in the middle of an economic crisis; people couldn't afford to buy food. Families were starving on the streets. Sound familiar? Maybe not the families starving on the actual streets, but the rest of it—"

"Cost-of-living crisis," said Carly. The slashes at the knees of her faded jeans revealed black fishnet tights beneath.

"If you can call it living," added Isabel, running her tongue back and forth across her lip ring.

"Got it in one. The modern focus is always on Scrooge learning his lesson and saving himself from eternal damnation—which is all well and good—but the backdrop to the story is a whole section of society that was invisible to the people who could actually help to make positive change. Dickens felt that people weren't seeing what was going on right under their noses. The writing might be a bit old-English, but the text resonates down the decades."

Harriet was enjoying herself. She'd been an English teacher for almost ten years before she switched to a pastoral role, but her love of the subject had never dwindled.

"Not much of a ghost story, though, is it, miss?" said Isabel.

"Oh, I dunno," Leo butted in. "Maybe we've just become desensitized to it, you know? Once the Muppets had a go at it, it lost a bit of its horror, but in theory the idea of being alone in a big old house and having a ghost dragging chains and stuff about, well, that's freaky."

"I actually found *The Muppet Christmas Carol* quite frightening when I first watched it," Carly admitted.

"Was that last year?" Isabel mocked.

"Like you're so brave," Billy challenged her.

"Yeah." Carly joined in with a half laugh. "You hide behind cushions when we watch the *Simpsons* Halloween specials, Isabel."

"They are well scary!" Isabel was defensive.

"If you're five," said Billy.

"I think Leo's right," Harriet joined in. "If you try to imagine you've never heard of Scrooge before and then read it with fresh eyes like the people did in 1843, it would have been frightening. I wonder how many people that Christmas felt a bit nervous after reading it, how many unquestioningly supported the idea of workhouses thinking it would never happen to them. I like to imagine it made a few people change their ideas."

"That's because you're an optimist, miss," said Ricco.

"Did you know Dickens was sent to work in a workhouse as a twelve-year-old boy?"

"You are really geeking out, aren't you?" Carly said, but Harriet only grinned and continued.

"But doesn't that make you admire him even more? His dad went to debtor's prison, and Charles had to work ten hours a day to try and pay off the family's debts. How old is Sid, Billy?"

"Ten," Billy replied.

"Almost the same age as Dickens was. Can you imagine Sid working ten-hour days in a factory?" she asked.

Billy picked at a loose thread on his jeans. "Sid can barely put his own socks on. He'd be a liability."

"Precisely. Because he's a child, he has no business being forced to work in a dingy, overcrowded factory. Dickens wanted to shake people up, make them see the wrongness of what was going on right under their noses. He was an activist, and this book was his banner."

Isabel had been playing with the badges showcasing

various causes that were pinned to her jacket, but now she perked up.

"I didn't know that."

"Maybe if Cornell told us this stuff, we'd be more interested in going to his classes," added Ricco.

"You could find this stuff out for yourselves; it's called independent learning. It's what you're supposed to be doing for your Extended Project Qualification."

This received groans.

"Why don't you become a teacher if you like this stuff so much?" asked Billy.

"Because someone has to keep you lot on the straight and narrow."

These were bright kids, but poverty—which in Harriet's opinion was the tenth circle of hell—was like a boulder dropped into water from a great height, the ripples of which reached down through generations. Once you were in it, it was a near impossible cycle to break, and the world was smaller for them than it was for other kids their age.

She thought about Maisy and her extended exchange trip. How, before she'd gone out and got drunk last night, she'd called Pete and they'd pooled their money to send extra funds out to their daughter to see her through the holidays. Harriet had never been rich, and, on her salary, she wasn't likely to be, but God willing, Maisy would never experience the kind of hardships faced by the famous five.

"I don't need a babysitter," said Carly, who was as self-sufficient as she was self-destructive. What that girl didn't know about bad choices wasn't worth knowing.

"No, you don't. But I do have a duty of care toward you, making sure you are safe and helping you to get the most out of school. Neither of which are possible when you're hiding out in an abandoned theater. And on that note, it's time to come back to campus."

The famous five mumbled and grumbled but began to retrieve their bags all the same.

The double doors at the back of the theater slammed open with a smack and everyone jumped and turned toward the noise. Two police officers stood in the doorway.

Oh, bugger!

"We've received a complaint that there are trespassers on this property. Can I ask you all to accompany my colleague and me down to the station, please," said the taller of the two.

Harriet pushed her shoulders back and addressed the officer. "Hello, Officer, we were just leaving, as I think you can probably see. Is it really necessary to take us to the station? I promise we won't come back."

"I'm afraid that's not up to me, Ms. . . . ?"

"Smith."

"It's out of our hands, Ms. Smith. There has been a complaint, and the owner of the building has asked that steps be taken."

Harriet glanced back at the faces of her students. Their youthful bravado had evaporated, and they suddenly looked their ages. She made a decision.

"The children are here under my instruction. They had nothing to do with breaking in. I thought it would be good to show them the inside of a theater as part of their English literature and drama studies. It's my fault they're here."

"Miss!" Billy protested.

She shot him a warning look.

"No, Billy, I appreciate that you're concerned about me,

but this is my fault, and I should face the consequences. You must all go back to school immediately—I absolutely mean it! Officers, please don't make these students suffer because of my poor judgment."

Both officers looked at her skeptically.

"So you're the ringleader, are you?" said the shorter of the two, one eyebrow lifted so high it disappeared under the rim of his helmet.

Harriet nodded emphatically. "Yes, Officers, I am."

He shook his head in resignation and glanced at his colleague, who shrugged.

"All right," he said. "Ms. Smith, if you would like to come with us. The rest of you, make yourselves scarce and don't let us catch you in here again. Do I make myself clear?"

The students mumbled their assent.

"Go on, then, off you go." He gestured to the door and the famous five shuffled quickly along the aisle, murmuring "Sorry, miss" and "Thanks, miss" as they passed her. At the top of the stairs, the taller officer held the door open for them and then followed behind to be sure they left the building. Billy looked back once and bobbed his head at Harriet.

"Back to school!" Harriet shouted after them.

She fired off a quick message to Ali: Found the FF. I'm being escorted to the police station. The kids are on their way back to school, please find them and sign them all in. Don't tell anyone I've been collared by the fuzz!! She smiled thinking of Ali's face when he read her message, then slung her bag over her shoulder and climbed the steps to meet her fate.

"Okay, let's get this over with. Am I under arrest?"

The officer smiled. "No, you're just helping us with our inquiries."

"What's the difference? I'm new to this whole being-on-the-wrong-side-of-the-law thing. Are you going to handcuff me?"

"No, Ms. Smith."

That was something at least.

"Will my place of work be informed?"

"That's entirely down to you."

"That'll be a no, then. I'm not sure the school will look too kindly on their pastoral team leader being accused of trespassing."

The other officer returned, and they walked single file—Harriet in the middle—back through the dim corridors and out into the alleyway.

"Can I ask, why did you do it?" asked the taller officer, helping her into the back of his car.

"Take them into the theater?"

The officer shook his head.

"Take the fall for them."

Oh.

"Is this off the record?" she asked.

"For now," he said, settling himself into the front seat.

"They don't need a black mark on their records. They already feel like the world is out to get them, and I don't want to prove them right."

"I wish I'd had a teacher like you when I was at school."

"Did you need one?"

He swiveled in his seat to face her.

"Can you see the color of my skin?"

She nodded. "Point taken."

FIVE

IT WAS A LONG TIME SINCE HARRIET HAD BEEN INSIDE A PO-
lice station, and the experience was flinging memories at
her that she would rather forget. Her palms were sweating and her stomach was a knot of anxiety. She discreetly
eyed the other occupants and wondered what they were
here for. She tried to make herself look hard, but her flo-
ral cardigan was undermining her. *Why do I feel so guilty?
It's not like I've robbed a bank or anything. We were discussing Dickens, for god's sake!* She pulled her cardigan
more tightly around her.

A smiley officer with an East London accent took her
details and assured her that someone was on their way
to talk with her. Then she was led into a waiting room
that resembled a dental reception area, with out-of-date
magazines on a low coffee table and a water cooler with
annoying cone cups in the corner. She sat up straight on
the edge of the green sofa, her hands clasped in her lap.
Should she call a solicitor? Did she need one? Pete was
the only solicitor she knew, and she really didn't want to
call him.

After ten minutes Harriet had all but thought herself
into a prison sentence; the prison library would be the
safest place for her, she decided, and maybe she could get
some of her fellow inmates interested in reading . . . Her

spiraling thoughts were halted when the door opened and a plainclothes officer walked in. The officer took her details again and listened as Harriet repeated and embellished her initial lie about cajoling the students to accompany her in breaking into the theater so that they could experience the environment firsthand . . .

The detective's expression was dubious, but she accepted Harriet's statement and got up to leave.

"Ms. Evaline Winter—the owner of the Winter Theater—has instructed me to let you know that her solicitor will be along presently to speak with you. After which, as far as we are concerned and provided Ms. Winter doesn't want to press charges—"

"Charges!" Harriet blurted. "Oh my god! Do you really think she'll press charges? Son of a nutcracker, I'm going to lose my job." Her mind began to spiral again; would she be allowed to take her own pillow to prison? She didn't think she'd be able to sleep on prison pillows.

"In all honesty, I don't think it will come to that," said the detective kindly. "It would be more trouble than it's worth. But wait and see what the solicitor has to say. In the meantime . . ." She picked up a magazine, frowning at the date, and handed it Harriet. "Take a look at the fashion must-haves of 2016 and try not to panic."

"Thanks," she replied weakly. Could this day get any worse?

She was on her second cone of water when the door opened again.

"Hello, Ms. Smith, I'm . . ."

Oh, you have got to be kidding me!

James—of last night's excellent drunken sex—rocked back on his heels. Well, damn, he was even more devastating in the daylight. She'd consoled herself that her attraction to him was more than likely due to her mulled-wine-tinted glasses, but now she was sober and the light of day was cold as hell, and he still looked like temptation personified. Her heart pounded in her chest. She smiled hesitantly, wishing she hadn't left so abruptly that morning, and quickly necked the last of her water.

The door swung shut, bumping against the brown leather messenger bag that rested against James's left hip. He recovered himself, rearranging his expression into one of professional disdain.

"Ms. Smith. My name is James Knight. I am acting on behalf of Ms. Evaline Winter, owner of the Winter Theater. I am here regarding a breaking-and-entering incident at one of her properties earlier today."

He was wearing another most excellently tailored suit. She wondered if he had a walk-in wardrobe full of them, and it occurred to her that if she'd stuck around this morning she might have found out. He pulled one of the low armchairs opposite the sofa toward the coffee table and lowered himself into it. He looked uncomfortable. She smiled at him.

"Well"—she tried to catch his eye and adopted a jokey tone—"'breaking and entering' makes it sound much worse than it actually was . . ." James remained unmoved, his gaze cold as the clouds that scudded across the wintry sky outside. She continued to blather on in the hopes of causing a crack in his demeanor that would reveal the man she'd met last night in the bar. "I mean, technically, I didn't break in at all—there was a flimsy piece of corrugated iron covering an already open door. Someone long before me had done the actual breaking in; mine was more of a squeeze-through and enter, if you will."

Nothing. The spirit of Kristin Scott Thomas had well and truly deserted her.

"The semantics of the crime do not interest me, Ms. Smith. A crime was committed. And by your own admission, you are answerable for it."

"Yes, but—"

"Ms. Winter would be within her rights to press charges," he went on.

This went beyond mere professionalism; he was being downright rude. Had her abrupt departure this morning dented his ego?

"Listen, about this morning—"

"Not the place, Ms. Smith." He didn't look up from his papers, but he did gesture toward the mirror with his Montblanc fountain pen. She glanced up at the mirror in the ugly frame and then it registered. *A two-way mirror! No wonder he's being cool.*

"Riiiight." She gave him an exaggerated wink, which he pointedly ignored. After a moment more of scribbling in his leather-bound notebook, he raised his head and speared her with a look dead-on. A sudden flashback to those eyes boring into hers last night as she lowered herself down onto . . . "Holy Moses!" The words exploded out of her like an involuntary spasm before she could check herself. Her cheeks burned. She tucked her hair behind her ear and cleared her throat, adding more quietly, "How much longer do you think we'll be here?"

The left side of his mouth quirked up infinitesimally. It was the first indication she'd had that he wasn't an AI robot. But just as quickly the micro-smirk disappeared.

"Ms. Smith, I have been instructed by my client to inform you that no charges will be pressed, provided you clean up the mess on my client's property made by you and your accomplices."

"I didn't make any mess! The place was already a

poop hole when I got there—god only knows how many people have broken into the place before I did."

"Try not incriminate yourself further, Ms. Smith."

Embarrassment, indignation, and shame made a sickly brew that swirled in her stomach.

"Oh, for god's sake, take the stick out of your bum for five seconds and act like a human!" she snapped, and regretted it instantly. Used to being quite far up on the moral high ground in any given situation, Harriet was well out of her comfort zone, having pulled a Cinderella disappearing trick, engaged in an Inspector Clouseau–style pursuit, and been seized by the old bill, all before lunch.

He didn't bat an eyelid. Clearly this was not the first time he'd been confronted about his bum-stick.

"I'm afraid my client's terms are non-negotiable. Clean up the mess or face charges."

"And when do you suggest I clean up a whole theater? I work full time."

"That is not my problem."

Well, she thought, *at least I'll be busy during the holidays.*

"Fine. I'll clean your client's dingy old theater." *And I'll make flapping sure those pesky kids help me do it.* "Can I get out of here now?"

"Just as soon as you've signed the initial agreement, you are free to go. I will draw up a more formal contract and have it ready for you to sign tomorrow. You will be contacted with regard to the time and place of the meeting in due course. This is just for our insurance. We wouldn't want you sneaking off without so much as a by-your-leave." He looked at her, his face a mask of blank disinterest, but his turn of phrase was a shot fired in her direction.

Yep, he's hacked off that I left without saying goodbye.
Hypocrite. I wonder if "Lyra" knows I slept over?

James slid a piece of paper across the coffee table for
her to sign. He handed her a pen and she scribbled her
name. This guy was really pressing her buttons and not
in a good way anymore. Her mind filled with memories
of his mouth on her body, long fingers exploring . . . *Stop!*
Stop thinking about it. This man is the enemy. I will not be
turned on by him. Name signed, she held the pen out and
he took it, his finger brushing hers. Sparks zipped through
her. *Traitor!* she told herself.

They stood at the same time, the coffee table between
them. Harriet looked up at him to find him staring
straight at her. She stared back. The space between them
was charged. She could feel the energy, like if she leaned
in it would prickle her skin or suck her into a vortex. She
didn't know whether she wanted to throw a chair at him
or kiss him. He held her gaze for a moment more and
then nodded.

"Goodbye, Ms. Smith."

"Goodbye."

And he left.

SIX

HARRIET COULDN'T TAKE HER FRIEND'S LUNCHTIME CALL FOR obvious reasons, which meant that Emma, unable to contain her need to know everything that had happened from the night before up to and including Harriet's stint in police custody, arrived promptly at seven p.m. with a Chinese takeaway, two liters of cranberry juice, and a bottle of D-mannose. A friend bearing cystitis remedies was a friend indeed.

"Howdy, jailbird! I want you to know that I was fully ready to hide a chisel in a loaf of banana bread to spring you from the clink." Emma beamed. "Ooh, it smells gorgeous in here."

Harriet always had candles burning for when people came over; she was known for her cozy ambience.

Emma marched into the sitting room with the white plastic takeaway bags dangling from her hands. She was petite, swore like a sailor, and wore her dirty-blond hair in a pixie cut which suited her heart-shaped face. Harriet was barely five foot six, but when she stood beside her bestie she often felt like Hagrid.

"Where are the decorations? You're normally the first person I know to get your Christmas groove on."

"Oh." Harriet tried to act casual. "I haven't had time to put them up yet."

"You want me to help you? We could do it after we eat."

"No, no, it's fine. I'll probably put them up at the weekend when I've got a bit more time," she lied.

Emma nodded and took the bags through to the kitchen.

Harriet hadn't had the energy to go back into work after the police station. She'd made a quick call to Ali, who confirmed that all the students were present, correct, and looking decidedly sheepish, and demanded the skinny on what had gone down. Then she emailed HR, claiming she had a migraine and needed to take the afternoon off, and came home, where she collapsed on the sofa. She was not a woman prone to calling in sick, even when she was actually sick, but today had been exceptional.

Despite her supposed migraine, Cornell had called her three more times before the end of the school day. The first was to ask her to put together a phased-return plan for a student who had been absent with anxiety; the second was to chase a report he'd delegated her to write on his behalf to the governor's board; and the third was to ask where his stapler was. One of these days he'd delegate himself right out of a job.

Over tumblers of cranberry juice and bowls of vegetable chow mein, Emma extracted as much information as she could about Harriet's night with James and her brush with the law.

"So, do you like him?" Emma asked, slurping up a long brown noodle.

"I did last night, and then I didn't, and now I don't know."

"But you fancy him."

"He is irritatingly hot, in a high-end-funeral-director kind of way."

"Right."

"But he's mean. He knew I was freaked out with the whole police thing, but instead of being compassionate, he was petulant. What a baby! Sure, I behaved immaturely, but I'm out of practice at waking up in a strange bed. I haven't had a one-night stand since I was thirty, and believe me when I tell you, I don't look as good when I wake up as I did when I was thirty."

"Me neither. It takes my face at least an hour to de-crumple and that's if I haven't been drinking. Throw a few glasses of vino into the mix and my skin looks like I've slept in a food dehydrator."

Harriet waved her fork in agreement. "Exactly. And my eyes were puffed up, and I hadn't brushed my teeth for obvious reasons before I went to sleep. When I got home, I found a hair like a hog bristle poking out of my chin. So I was basically a horror show. It would have been like waking up with a gorgon."

Emma spluttered into her cranberry juice.

"You never know, he might have been beastly too. How old is he?"

"I don't know, late forties? But it's different for men, isn't it?"

"Not in the morning. Pete looks like he's been dead in the water for two days when he wakes up."

Now Harriet laughed.

"You're so mean. James Knight probably wakes up looking like a catalog model. I think he might be made by Mattel."

"Or is the reason he jumped up and rushed into the shower because he looks like Leatherface before he's moisturized?"

"I'll never know now, will I?" Harriet plucked an escaped bean sprout out of her cleavage and threw it into her mouth. "How is it I always manage to get food down my tits? It's like a disorder."

"Nah, I'm the same. I found a corn flake in mine when I took my bra off the other night. It must have been in there since breakfast. My bra is the adult equivalent of one of those baby bibs with a catcher tray."

Harriet lived in a flat above the local library, which never ceased to make her happy. Her sitting room had high ceilings, picture rails, and large sash windows that looked out over the park. An original cast-iron Victorian fireplace dominated the living room, and above it hung a modest flat-screen TV. Facing each other on opposite sides of the fireplace were two sofas covered in William Morris print scatter cushions. Harriet and Emma had a sofa each, the fire crackling between them and Miss Marple gently sleuthing—regardless of being ignored—on the screen above.

"Have you got his number?" Emma asked, smooshing a whole prawn cracker into her mouth.

"Nope. I didn't think to get it last night, and I was too annoyed at him to ask today. And I left a cardigan at his place."

"Which one?"

"Third favorite."

Emma sucked in a sharp breath. "I'm so sorry. At least it wasn't first favorite."

She sighed. "I suppose." Her first-favorite cardigan only came out for very special occasions. "Oh god!" A fresh wave of humiliation washed over her. "What must he think of me? First, I behave in the exact way that I've always sneered at men for, and then I get caught trespassing."

"Who cares? It's done now and there's no reason why you should see each other again."

"I guess. Although he did say I'd have to sign another contract." Was it weird that she kind of did want to see him again? He was the first man she'd really gelled with in a long time. If only she hadn't panicked this morning, things might have worked out differently. She might have stayed for breakfast and then called in sick at work (to be fair, this was unlikely) and they'd have spent the day together (even more unlikely) and she'd never have known that her students were AWOL or followed them into that cursed theater . . .

"I hope you're going to make those students help with the cleanup."

"Yes, I flapping am!" She hesitated for a moment, wondering if she should share the thoughts that had been brewing ever since she'd stepped into the crusty old foyer. As her best friend poured her another glass of juice, Harriet decided that Emma would tell her outright if this idea was good or straight-up bananas. "I've been thinking about them, the students—"

"How to disembowel the little shits and get away with it?"

"After I'd thought about that. They need a place, you know? Somewhere they can hang out."

"Like a youth club?"

"Yeah, kind of. Some place that's only gently supervised but safe."

"Okay."

"I mean, if I'm cleaning up the theater anyway, maybe I could propose something to Ms. Winter, ask her if she'd consider letting us use it. It's not like it's being used for anything else. They could put on shows, start a glee club . . ."

Emma snorted.

"No, seriously," Harriet protested. "These kids would

like that! Given the chance, they like reading and drama, they write poetry—angry, sweary poetry, but poetry all the same. I could get speakers in, inspirational people to give talks about careers and charities they could get involved in . . ."

"I'm not disagreeing with you, but isn't that what school is for? There must be after-school clubs."

"Yes, but they're filled with the kinds of kids you'd expect, and that isn't these guys. But for all their raging against the machine, I believe they want what any teenager wants: to find a place where they fit. And I think I could give it to them. I'm talking about a community space, not just for kids from Foss Independent, but from all over. Ms. Winter might be happy to have it useful again."

Her friend nodded and hummed, letting Harriet spill her thoughts out across the space between them. When she stopped for breath, Emma speared another floret of broccoli in oyster sauce and asked, "Have you ever met Evaline Winter?"

"No," Harriet admitted. But how bad could she really be?

Everyone knew about the theater magnate, but few had been acquainted with her. She resided in the manor house that overlooked the town. Her father, Fitz-William Winter, had famously squandered the Winter fortune, and when he died Evaline inherited the estate and all its debts. Unlike her father, she had a head for business and had not only settled all his debts but grown the Winter assets to ten times what she'd inherited.

"Well, I have," said Emma, her lips pursed in distaste. "She's a hard-nosed cow-bag and she's got a finger in every pie in Little Beck Foss, and none of those fingers contain an ounce of community spirit."

"She might feel differently once the place is cleaned up a bit. I thought I might try to set up a meeting, run it past her."

"You've really thought about this, haven't you?"

"Do you know what they were doing when I busted them?"

"Drinking vodka and smoking?"

"Half right, I think it was a bit early for vodka." She took a sip of cranberry juice. "They were reading Dickens. The novel and the play."

"Okay. I didn't see that coming."

"Exactly, nobody does. It's easier to make yourself fit into the suit you've been pegged for than to try and break out of it. These kids have got bigger things to worry about than trying to change people's minds about them."

She was thinking about Billy, how he looked out for his little brother, how he worried about the system pulling them apart. And she was thinking about Zoe, her own personal ghost, the bright, clever girl who could have been anything she wanted if only Harriet hadn't let her down.

Emma looked hard at her.

"Don't take this the wrong way, but sometimes I feel like you're still trying to atone for what happened, even though you had nothing to do with it."

Harriet waved it away. "It's not about that." It *was* about that. She'd been too busy, too tired, and she missed the signs. She pushed the memory away and met her friend's stare. "This could make a difference."

"I believe you. Just do me one favor, before you go rushing into opening a community theater. Make sure this isn't another knee-jerk reaction to Maisy's announcement, like your one-night stand with *James*." She said his name in a husky whisper. "'Cause, you know if you're really suffering with empty nest syndrome, you can take some of my kids."

Harriet laughed, knowing Emma was only half joking. Her teenage kids' hormones were hell on wheels. When she'd had Taylor and then the twins—Jordan and Phoebe—with only eighteen months between them, everyone had told her that the hardest part would be the first three years. When the kids grew into their teens, Emma had suddenly realized that everyone had been lying to her.

"Maybe there's a little bit of empty-nest panic to it," Harriet confessed. "But under no circumstances do I want your kids."

Emma groaned exaggeratedly. "What kind of husband's ex-girlfriend are you?"

"The sensible kind."

"You'll still come to us, though, won't you? For Christmas, I mean. As far as Pete and I are concerned, this year's just like any other."

Harriet, Emma, Pete, and their combined children spent every Christmas together, alternating households each year.

"But it isn't, is it? Maisy won't be here."

"But we always do Christmas together."

"Because we didn't want Maisy to miss out on Christmas Day with her parents and siblings—"

"And because we love you! The kids will really miss you if you're not there. You know they like you better than me."

"Only because they don't live with me," said Harriet, smiling.

"And when my little shits decide to ditch Christmas with the olds, I'll still be expecting to spend it with you. We'll start a Christmas rejects club."

"I don't know. I'm not feeling very festive at the moment. I just . . . I feel adrift. This is what it'll be like permanently soon. I've been a parent for almost eighteen years; I don't know how to be only me."

"What do you mean, 'only you'?"

"You know what it's like—you spend your whole life putting them first, always thinking about what will make them happy, cozy, safe, better. What am I if I'm not parenting?"

"Oh, you mean besides being an intelligent, educated woman with a career and an excellent best friend."

"I know all that, I'm talking about mum-me."

"You're still a parent. Maisy's always going to need you. Especially for money."

"Yeah, but I'm not ready to be retired from active parental service."

"Fuck me, I dream of being retired from active parental service. This is how my exit from the house went tonight. Me: 'Bye kids, Dad's in his office if you need anything. Love you.' Them: 'Where's my basketball kit? I'm hungry. Where's the remote? Can I have twenty quid? There's no bog roll!'"

Harriet laughed. "You'll miss it all when they're gone."

"I promise you I won't."

"Let's have this chat in five years' time and we'll see how you feel then."

Emma flopped dramatically to one side, her face buried in a Larkspur patterned cushion.

"Five years! Is that how long I've got to wait until they leave home? FML!"

When Emma left, Harriet turned up the volume on the TV to drown the quiet. Then she went round and blew out the scented candles. *No point leaving them burning just for me.*

SEVEN

HARRIET WALKED INTO HER TUTOR ROOM AT 8:15 A.M. FOR morning registration to find the famous five already waiting quietly. This was clearly a concerted effort on their part; usually students wandered in between 8:35 and 8:45 a.m. in various states of bleary-eyed lethargy—the famous five were particularly prone to lateness. But not today. The rest of the class had yet to arrive, and those already gathered looked either contrite or sheepish. She took a seat behind the desk.

"Good morning," she said in what her daughter termed her *bright but dangerous* voice.

The students shifted uncomfortably in their chairs; Billy was captivated by something inside his rucksack. Leo looked pensive as he scribbled away in his sketchbook. Even Carly seemed unsure of herself.

There followed various offerings of "Morning, miss," in voices significantly smaller than usual. She let them stew. Finally, Billy asked, "Are you in trouble, miss?" at the same time as Ricco asked, "Are we in trouble?"

All faces pointed at her.

"It wasn't the best afternoon I've had, sitting in a police station." They had the good grace to look guilty. "But I wasn't charged with anything"—she watched their shoulders sag with relief—"on the proviso that I clean up the theater. And by that, I mean clean up the mess that I didn't make."

She let that sink in.

"That's not fair!" Isabel exclaimed.

"No, it isn't. That's why you're going to help me." She gave a sweet smile with just a hint of don't-mess-with-me attitude.

Five mouths dropped open. One or two made a feeble attempt at protest, but she caught their eyes, squinting her own in challenge, and their voices dried up.

"When are we supposed to do it?" asked Billy.

"After school and weekends, I should think. It ought not to take too long; from what I saw the mess was mostly superficial. It'll be like litter picking but with the benefit of being inside."

Cue groans and profanity. She didn't say anything. In her job you chose your battles with care.

"We didn't do all of it." Ricco sounded hard done by.

"Yeah, it was already a skank-hole when we found it," added Isabel.

"I'm sure it was. But *we* were the ones who got caught trespassing."

They had no answer for that.

"She can't actually make us do it," Carly said, smirking.

"No, I can't. But if you're not prepared to take responsibility for your actions, then I'm not prepared to keep covering for you."

"When do we start?" asked Billy, his voice thick.

Her phone vibrated on her desk, and she glanced at the screen.

UNKNOWN NUMBER: Ms. Smith, the finalized agreement of which we spoke yesterday is now

ready. Please meet my client outside her property,
the Winter Theater, at 12:30 p.m. today. Regards,
J. Knight

Her first thought was *Cripes!* Her second was *Will he
be there?* Quickly followed by *Cripes!* again. The possibility that he might be at today's meeting had nothing whatever to do with her decision to wear the rust-colored
shift dress that suited her skin tone and the lipstick to
match. She felt the eyes of her students upon her and
quickly scrabbled through her brain to recall what they
were talking about.

"As soon as I get the go-ahead, I'll let you know," she
replied to Billy.

"Can you not tell our parents about this?" Ricco
asked. "I mean, I'll tell them what I'm doing but just not
why, if that's all right. I promised them I'd stay out of
trouble, after the last time, and I don't want them to have
anything else to worry about, you know, what with Dad
and everything."

Ricco's dad had a chronic illness and couldn't work;
he probably wouldn't work again. His mum worked long
hours as a carer. They were good people stuck in a sad
situation.

"What about health and safety, miss?" piped up Carly.
"Insurance and stuff. From a safety perspective, we might
not be able to go into a derelict building." Clearly Carly
was looking for legitimate ways out, which made a refreshing change. Carly did have a point too. She'd ask at
the meeting.

"Health and safety didn't appear to concern you when
you broke in repeatedly and spent countless hours in
there illegally," Harriet countered.

Carly shrugged. "Yeah, but that was before—"

"Before you got caught? Or before you realized there would be consequences for your actions?"

"UUURRR!" Ricco laughed. "She's got you there, Carly."

Carly turned to him with her eyes squinted. "I'm trying to get us out of having to do free and illegal labor—what are you doing to help?"

"We can't get out of it," said Billy flatly. "We were there. We should help to clean the place up."

"I agree with Billy," Leo added timidly. "We can't make Miss Smith do it by herself, not when she took a bullet for us."

Ricco nodded. "Yeah, we owe her."

The rest of the group made pained noises of assent, and then the other students began to filter into the common room and the discussion was dropped.

....

The snow was the light, dusty kind, as though someone in the clouds were tapping it through a fine sieve. It settled on Harriet's hair and coat and made the busy street look even more Christmassy as it fluttered past the overhead fairy lights. The snow-capped forests of fir trees that flanked the hills around the town looked like cake decorations from down on the street.

Usually this would have filled her with a childish glee, but this first snow of the season served only to remind her of all the fun she wouldn't be having. Well-meaning people kept telling her that the empty-nest feeling wouldn't last forever, that she would grow to cherish her independence and that the time she did spend with Maisy would become "quality time" rather than the mundanity of everyday life. But most of this wisdom came from couples who had gone on to redefine their relationships in their new, changed landscape. Maybe she should get cats.

Her phone rang in her pocket; it was Pete.

"Hey, Pete, what's up?"

"Emma says you've got a meeting with Evaline Winter today."

"That is correct. I'm on my way to it now. Took an early lunch."

She heard Pete pull in a deep breath. He did this when he was measuring what he was going to say next, carefully lining up his words to best effect before speaking.

"She's a bit of a slippery fish. A pike, with a large bite radius—metaphorically speaking, of course; I've never known her to actually bite anyone. But there's a first time for everything."

"If you're trying to warn me about something, could you be a bit more specific, please?"

"Em told me that you've got ideas about turning the theater into some sort of community youth club."

"So?"

"Just be on your guard. Evaline Winter is an astute businesswoman, and she isn't famed for her philanthropical ventures. The reason she's got so much money is because she's very good at keeping it for herself. I say this as a solicitor who's had more than one run-in with her professionally."

"Really? How have your run-ins gone?" Harriet was curious. Before yesterday, she'd never crossed paths with the wealthy widow.

"She owns a lot of properties in the area, private rentals and the like; she's quick to sue for missed payments but less proactive when it comes to maintenance and building regs."

"I'm clearly having a slow brain day, you're going to have to spell it out for me. What exactly am I on my guard for?"

The theater was coming into view as she hurried along the pavement. A limo with blacked-out windows had already pulled up outside the front.

"She isn't going to give anything away for free. If she lets you use the space for your students, look for the catch because I promise you there'll be one."

"She's already got me for cleaning services."

"Yeah, well, that'll just be for starters. Strictly off the record, the woman's a shark."

"You are really feeling those marine-life analogies today, aren't you?"

"I'm serious, Harri. Be careful."

Pete was the only person who still called her Harri.

"All right, all right, keep your hair on. I'll stay alert." She paused and then asked casually, "In your dealings with Ms. Winter and her impressive bite radius, have you had much contact with her solicitor?"

"James Knight?"

"Yes, I think that's his name." *Act casual.*

"He's one of those steely types. Gives nothing away and then clobbers you at the last minute with some hidden clause or other that collapses your case. He's a good solicitor, just not very personable; that's probably why he heads up the business side of the practice and leaves family law to the other partners."

"Right. Good to know."

"Well, that was all, just wanted to give you a heads-up. Good luck. I'm sure I'll hear all about it from Em later. Oh, and listen, I get that you're feeling a bit weirded out about Maisy not being around for the holidays, but we'd still love to spend Christmas with you. You were my family before any of the kids came along, you always will be."

She smiled down the phone. "Thanks, Pete. Did Emma put you up to that?" She knew Emma would have been bending his ear about it when she'd got home last night.

He gave a chuckle. "A little bit. But it doesn't make it less true."

She pressed end call and took a deep breath. She was ready.

EIGHT

HARRIET STOOD OUTSIDE THE THEATER WONDERING IF MS. Winter was already inside. The front doors were still boarded shut, and she couldn't imagine someone of Evaline's age and social stature squeezing past the corrugated iron covering the backstage entrance.

Behind her, she heard the whine of an electric window motor and turned to see a white-gloved hand with gray fur trim reach languidly through the limousine window and beckon her over. Harriet bent to look inside. Evaline Winter was sat back in her seat, making no effort to lean forward. There was an empty seat beside the elderly woman, which seemed to be reserved for a cream beaded minaudière bag with a gold chain, and on the seat next to that was another figure, too shrouded in darkness for Harriet to see more than a pair of long, slender legs clad in expensive suit trousers and the same oxblood brogues she had admired yesterday morning in James's apartment. Her stomach gave a yip of excitement despite her better judgment and Pete's warnings.

"Miss Smith, I presume?"

The woman's voice was icy and aristocratic, and it snapped Harriet out of her thoughts.

"Ms.," Harriet replied automatically.

"Please be so kind as to join me in the car so that we can talk."

"Oh, okay. I thought we'd be meeting in the theater."

"Don't make me keep this window open any longer than I need to. I am not in good health."

"Right, sorry, yes. Shall I get in this side?" She gestured to the door, but the hand flicked her away.

"Other side!" the woman snapped.

Harriet jumped to attention. As she dashed around the front of the car to reach the other side, her boots slipped on a patch of dusty snow on top of an ice puddle and with a most unladylike exclamation of "Son of a cluck bucket!" she was sent sprawling across the long bonnet of the limo, emitting a guttural "Oof!" sound. She peeled her cheek from the polished paintwork and looked in through the windscreen to see a chauffeur staring back at her with one brow arched quizzically but no other signs that this wasn't an everyday occurrence for him. He wound his window down.

"Would you like some help, madam?" he asked politely.

"No, thank you. I can take it from here."

"As you wish."

Pushing up with her palms, she gingerly maneuvered herself off the bonnet, hoping that her coat buttons wouldn't scratch the paintwork. When her boots were back on the ground, she bent over, keeping her hands flat on the bonnet, and crab-stepped her way around to the door on the far side. Before she opened it, she straightened up and pulled her shoulders back. *Maybe they didn't see me slip?* Grateful that the interior was dark enough to hide her blushing cheeks, she climbed into the car, taking one of the seats opposite Ms. Winter and James, and pulled the door shut behind her.

James's lips were compressed to invisibility and his

eyes squinted with the effort of not laughing. He sat rigid, looking everywhere but at her. Clearly, they had seen her splat over the bonnet.

Ms. Winter, however, was less amused. She wore a gray fur ushanka hat that matched the trim of her gloves, the ends of her short white hair curling around the brim. Intelligent, beady eyes glared out at Harriet from beneath it.

"Is this your first time getting into a car, Ms. Smith?" she inquired coldly. "You appeared to struggle with the concept."

James stifled a squeak that sounded like someone letting the air slowly out of the neck of a balloon. His compressed giggle was infectious, and she wanted more.

She lifted her chin. "No, Ms. Winter. I was practicing my Bo Duke bonnet slide technique."

James turned pointedly to the window, his eyes squeezed shut, his shoulders shaking. Harriet had to bite down on her own lip to stop herself from joining him. Evaline Winter's visage remained glacial.

"Mr. Knight, kindly contain yourself. Ms. Smith, do not be facetious," Evaline snapped, and just like that all good humor was sucked out of the car. She left a beat—presumably for them to think about what they'd done—before saying, "You broke into my property."

"Well, I mean, technically—" Harriet began.

"That wasn't a question."

"Oh, right."

"I would be quite within my rights to charge you. But my legal counsel rightly advised that this would only hit your pocket."

Harriet glared at James, but he was busy rifling through papers in the briefcase open on his lap. His glee had dissipated completely. Ms. Winter continued.

"And I have always found that people acknowledge the consequences of their failings, or in this case misdemeanors, best if they are forced to atone for them. It seems only fitting that you clean up your own mess."

"I certainly wasn't the first person to break in—"

Ms. Winter removed her gloves and held up one gnarled hand for silence, gold rings heavy with diamond clusters and precious stones wedged over swollen knuckles, arthritic fingers bent at painful angles.

"By all means furnish me with the names of your co-conspirators, Ms. Smith. I would be delighted to include them in the punishments." She gave a slow blink that felt like a challenge, and Harriet knew she'd been snookered. Ms. Winter cocked her head ever so slightly to the side. "No?" she asked. "Nobody you'd like to implicate?"

Harriet remained quiet. Seething. Her phone pinged loudly in her bag once, then again, then five more times in quick succession.

"Sorry," she muttered, pulling it out of her bag. She glanced at the screen and saw several texts from Cornell and a voice note from Ali. Her stomach squeezed. "I'm sorry," she said, holding the phone to her ear. "I just need to address these to make sure there's not an emergency."

Ali's message was about lunch and a glance at Cornell's texts informed her they were simply more requests for her to do his work. Reluctantly, she turned her phone to silent and put it in her bag.

"Are we interrupting your social life?" Evaline's voice was snide.

"No, it's work. I'll deal with it later."

Evaline regarded her coldly. "My solicitor has been kind enough to draw up a contract. You are welcome to have it looked over by your own counsel, but I can assure you that it is completely legal." She held her hand out to James, and he passed her a set of documents fastened with a paper clip. "In lieu of pressing charges, this contract will be signed by you and me and witnessed by Mr. Knight and my chauffeur."

"Is all of this really necessary?" Harriet asked.

"What assurances do I have that you will keep your side of the agreement if I don't have it in writing?"

"You have my word." Harriet gritted her teeth.

"The word of a woman who trespasses? I don't think so, Ms. Smith. Mr. Knight, would you be so kind . . ." She gestured to the side of Harriet's seat.

James leaned over and slid a small tabletop up from inside the door and flipped it down across Harriet's lap. She could smell his aftershave, neroli oil and patchouli, and beneath that his shampoo, notes of fresh mint and eucalyptus so clean and crisp she wanted to breathe him in like a blue-sky morning. The scent transported her to his bed, his head between her thighs, her hands gripping fistfuls of his crisp white sheets. She swallowed and tried to steady her racing heart, pushing the thoughts from her mind. As he locked the table flat with a click, James looked briefly up at her with the intensity of a person trying to convey something of importance. She looked away, pointedly. When he sat back in his own seat, the dispassionate glaze of professionalism had returned.

Evaline slid the contract onto Harriet's table and snapped her fingers. The sound was weak, soft, unlike the resolve of this formidable woman. But James set to as though she'd cracked a starter pistol; he reached into his briefcase and pulled out a pen, which he placed in Ms. Winter's wrinkled palm, and she placed it on top of the contract.

Harriet's hand hovered over the pen. If she was going

to do it, she had to do it now, before she signed the paper-work.

"I will sign. But before I do, I have a proposal that I'd like to put to you." She wished her voice sounded less halting, but this formidable woman made her feel deeply nervous, and with James there watching too, it was very much like being stuck in one of those dreams where she turned up to work inexplicably naked.

Evaline's stare was withering.

"Do you feel as though you are in a position to be making proposals?" she asked.

Before this meeting, Harriet had been pep-talking herself with things like *Find a common ground. Appeal to her community spirit. She's a person, you're a person, you're both just people.* Now, however, she realized the futility of her reasoning; at this point she wasn't even sure Evaline Winter was human. Her eyes darted to James, who had suddenly become engrossed in a spreadsheet. He didn't look up. Okay. She could do this. It was now or never.

She cleared her throat.

"I'm sure you are aware of how little there is for young people to do in the town. The cinema has closed down, the bowling alley is now a charity shop warehouse, and even if they were still open, a lot of the kids in the town couldn't afford to use them. Your theater is sitting empty. What if it could become a community space, a place where the young people of Little Beck Foss could meet, away from negative influences? Supervised, of course. I'm not talking about a free-for-all. We could utilize the layout for drama, singing, a theater group; we could have book clubs and table tennis, art classes . . ." She was ram-bling, her ideas spilling out and falling over one another, but she dared not take a breath and risk being cut off.

"Maybe the school would pay you a rent to allow students to perform their creative work . . ."

"And I would allow all this why, exactly?" asked Ms. Winter, her tone a knife edge.

Was her idea not self-explanatory? James had begun writing furiously in his leather-bound notebook, the scratch of his pen loud in the frosty silence.

"Because it would help people. Young people in your community. And it wouldn't cost you anything. I'm already going to be cleaning the place up anyway, it may as well be used—"

"Perhaps I don't want my family's theater to be used as a den for miscreants, Ms. Smith."

Harriet bristled. "It wouldn't be a 'den,' and the kids I'm talking about are not 'miscreants.' And I'm sure your father would have preferred the theater to be used for the creative arts than left crumbling like a forgotten mausoleum."

Ms. Winter's green eyes flashed, like a snake readying itself to strike.

"Sign the contract, Ms. Smith."

Harriet lost her cool. "But it's empty! It's just sitting there like a big unloved blot on the high street!" Evaline remained unmoved, so she tried appealing to her ego. "With a little TLC, your theater could be a vital resource for the whole town. You could help change the fortunes of young lives and secure a legacy as a beloved philanthropist. A double whammy, with very little effort on your part."

Evaline regarded her steadily, her lips pursed. James passed her the book he'd been writing in, and Harriet watched the old woman's eyes scud back and forth over his notes. When she'd finished, she handed the book back to James without acknowledging him or his scribblings. She rubbed the pads of her thumbs and forefingers on each hand together as she ruminated. Harriet's spirits rose. She was getting through to her.

"Perhaps we could help one another, Ms. Smith."

In her mind Harriet punched the air and shouted *In your face, bum weasel!* at James.

Evaline continued.

"I have been working toward a private sale of the theater for some time. Most recently there have been two offers on the table, both of which, to coin the phrase of my associate here, have been 'lowball' due to the condition of the building. Therefore, I have been left with two choices: one, demolish the theater and sell the land; or two, renovate the building to make it more appealing to potential buyers. Suffice to say, I have decided upon the latter."

Harriet frowned.

"Wait a minute, if you're planning to renovate the place anyway, then why I am being made to clean it?"

"One must pay for one's crimes," Evaline replied simply. "My legal counsel"—she gestured to James with a limp flap of her hand—"has suggested a counterproposal for you. There are some influential theater companies who have been waiting for me to sell up or die; thus far I have disappointed them on both scores. Now is the time for me to dangle the carrot, so to speak."

"You've lost me, I'm afraid. What does any of this have to do with me?"

"It's very simple. Any property for sale benefits from some staging—excuse the pun—to help buyers see its potential. Here is where our individual concerns diverge. You may use my property for your little community project, on the proviso that you have a production ready to perform on the stage in time for an open house viewing I have arranged for December the twenty-first. It is a theater, after all—buyers will be trying to envision it in working order, and what better way to facilitate that than by providing them with a live production, the first in more than half a century." She smiled as she warmed to her theme. "In fact"—she tapped a finger to her shriveled, lipstick-caked lips—"why not raise the stakes by opening the performance up to the general public? That ought to stir up some of that 'media interest' you're always so keen on, Mr. Knight, don't you think?"

James looked up questioningly at Evaline just as Harriet barked out an incredulous laugh.

"What?"

"Are you hard of hearing, Ms. Smith?"

Before Harriet had the chance to answer, James put in, "If I might interject. Ms. Winter, this is a bold proposal with multifaceted considerations; it would be prudent to take a little time to consider. I only meant to have some window dressing on the stage, as it were—"

"No." Evaline cut him off. "My mind is made up. Ms. Smith can have her little community project and provide some entertainment for my open house on the twenty-first. Call the media. Tell them that the Winter Theater is reopening for one final night."

"Evaline, please, be reasonable, the logistics alone—"

"Mr. Knight, I pay you so that I don't have to consider logistics. Make it happen."

James looked as though he wanted to argue further, but Evaline flicked open a mother-of-pearl compact mirror and checked her reflection, signifying that the subject was closed.

"But." Harriet glanced pleadingly from Evaline to James and back again. "But what you're asking is impossible. Nobody could put a production together that fast. The twenty-first is"—she counted on her fingers—"just over five weeks away. Not even a professional company could pull that off. I have zero experience."

"Then this will be a sharp learning curve for you," Evaline replied, snapping her compact shut. She regarded Harriet down her long Roman nose.

Harriet pulled her shoulders back in defiance.

"Let's say for argument's sake that I agreed to your pie-in-the-sky demands. What happens to my group if you do manage to sell the building to a theater company?"

Ms. Winter opened her mouth to speak, but James beat her to it.

"I would imagine the new owner would be only too happy to encourage community amateur dramatics groups. Theaters are businesses, of course, but they are fundamentally supporters of the arts. I see no reason why the two concerns couldn't thrive concurrently."

His employer looked less than pleased, but she pressed her lips together and turned an approximation of a smile to Harriet.

"I'd need some assurance." She was remembering Pete's warnings about slippery fishes. "Something in writing to say that the community can still use the theater after it's sold, something legally binding that the new owners would have to honor." Harriet tried to sound as demanding as Evaline. This palaver was by no means what she'd envisioned, but equally maybe this was her chance to put her pipe dreams into practice; perhaps the universe was throwing her a bone.

Again, James answered before Evaline had a chance to speak.

"I'm sure there could be a clause written into the sale that would protect your rights on that score—"

"Your choices are limited, Ms. Smith," Evaline bit out, slicing through James's conciliatory gesture. "I can still decide to press charges, drag this out through the courts. It would take less than an hour for my contacts to furnish me with the names of each student who trespassed alongside you. Oh yes, I know you weren't alone. How secure is your job at Foss Independent School? You work in pastoral care, I believe. A worthwhile vocation, I'm sure. I understand that you answer to one Sebastian Cornell. How would he react, do you think? Is your position strong enough to want to find out?"

This was too much. *Screw you, Evaline Winter, and screw you, James Bum-Wipe Knight!*

"You can't blackmail me! I will not be a pawn in your seedy little real estate games."

Evaline continued as though she hadn't spoken. "I'll have my solicitor draw up a fresh contract for you to sign." She whisked the original contract away from Harriet and tore it in two. "One that covers our new agreement. A Christmas production to be performed in front of a live audience on the twenty-first of December."

It was like being squeezed by a boa constrictor; every objection she made only caused Evaline to coil tighter. There was no air in the car. She couldn't think straight. *What have I got myself into?* She could feel herself getting hotter and hotter, a prickling heat rising up through her body. If she didn't get out of this car right now, she was going to spontaneously combust.

"Clean your own damn theater!" she exploded. She wrenched the handle of the limo door too hard and kicked it open with her boot. She was boiling with outrage and embarrassment at having been so perfectly snookered, even after Pete's warnings. Evaline did indeed have a large bite radius, and she'd bitten her right on the bum.

She climbed out into the freezing afternoon—leaving the car door disrespectfully open—and was grateful for the rush of cold air after the stuffy interior. Evaline's lily of the valley perfume had permeated her hair, and that only made her angrier as she stomped off along the road, slipping every couple of steps on the new snow and muttering obscenities. People gave her a wide berth as she stormed along the pavement. The Salvation Army band pulled in a collective breath as she stamped past them: "Weeeeee wish you a merry—"

"Bah humbug bah humbug bah humbug!" she shouted, so loudly that one of the band members dropped his cymbal, which crashed to the ground, making a baby cry and a dog bark. She stomped onward, slipping again and only saving herself by swinging on a lamppost.

Someone was calling her name, but she didn't turn. The footsteps behind her became louder.

"Harriet! Ms. Smith. Harriet, wait!"

She kept her head down and plowed on until the expensive shoes of James Slimeball Knight blocked her path. She stopped walking and stamped her foot—not her finest moment—and let out a strangulated growl of frustration that caused a cyclist to swerve as he rode past her.

"What? You are a stinking, flatulent beast! I don't want to talk to you. Go back to Miss Haughty-Pants and tell her to stick her contract up her shriveled bottom!"

James was looking at her with wide eyes.

"Flatulent?"

"Arrrrrggghhhhh!" she roared. James took a step back.

"Is that the 'long-awaited news' you were celebrating the other night? That her ladyship was finally going to sell the theater? You big capitalist cow testicle!"

"Look, can we just talk for a moment? Believe it or not, I want to help you," said James.

Harriet laughed mirthlessly. "Help me?" she shouted. She noticed James looking from side to side as people walked by, gawping and stifling giggles. She wasn't usually one to make a spectacle of herself, but she was steaming mad, and she didn't know what to do with it. "You call blackmailing a person *helping*?"

"Technically it isn't blackmail . . ."

Harriet felt her eyes bulge; James must have seen it because he held his hands up for calm.

"I think your ideas for a community space have merit."

"You mean leverage." She smudged her hands along her cheeks to wipe off her tears of frustration.

"I promise you, I didn't know Evaline was going to spring a whole Christmas production on you. I had in mind a talent show or a skit, a bit of window dressing for the potential buyers as they toured the theater. I had no idea she'd escalate it to a full-on bonanza."

"So it was your idea? That's what all the scribbling in your little pocketbook was about?"

"It's actually an Aspinal of London journal . . ." He must have seen that she was about to go nuclear because he added quickly, "But that's neither here nor there. Look, I think that your proposal for a safe space for teenagers to hang out is inspired, and I admire your altruism. In my line of work, I don't meet many people whose motivations aren't profit based. I promise you, I was trying to be helpful, though I realize it has rather backfired."

She squinted her eyes to study him more closely. He

looked genuine. But then, he was a lawyer. Weren't they trained to lie convincingly?

"Will she really press charges if I don't play along?"

He took a moment to consider. "I could probably talk her out of pressing charges by appealing to her bank balance. But it wouldn't cost her anything to ask for a meeting with the dean of the school, which—"

"Could cost me my job," she finished for him.

He nodded.

"How can you work for someone like that?" she asked.

In all honesty she'd had no idea what kind of man he was when she'd slept with him, so she shouldn't feel disappointed in him, and yet she did.

"She's my firm's biggest client. It's my job, my sworn oath to defend her interests, whether they be personal or business."

"That's such a cop-out," she snorted derisively.

"It's my job. What do you want me to say? When all is said and done, you were in the wrong. As far as the law is concerned, you are the perpetrator of a crime, and my client is the victim."

She shook her head in disbelief, stepped around him, and carried on up the street. The snow was getting heavier. The high street was full of people: mothers pushing pushchairs laden with bags and stressed-out toddlers, people out of the office on their lunch breaks, drunks on the benches outside sandwich bars hoping for a little charity.

James caught up with her.

"It may not look like it, but I'm offering you a lifeline: a chance to do something that I can see you're passionate about. I know it's not ideal, but the world is built on compromise. If you agree to her terms, I will do my utmost to ensure that a clause is written into any sales negotiations that will secure a space for community ventures going forward. Please."

He looked so earnest she almost believed him. Almost. The black limousine pulled up beside them to more curious looks from passersby. The tinted window wound slowly down.

"Mr. Knight," came the cool voice from the interior of the car. "I am not in the habit of having to chase down my employees. I trust the matter has been settled?"

James looked at Harriet. "Has it?"

"Do I have a choice?"

"There is always a choice."

"Ah yes, the proverbial rock and hard place."

"You have until tomorrow lunchtime to decide." Evaline's bored voice drifted out of the perfumed car. "I will have Mr. Knight draw up a second contract. I look forward to seeing the fruits of your labors." She left a beat and then added with languid frustration, "Mr. Knight, when you're ready."

James handed Harriet his card. She glanced down at it and then back up. Did he actually think she was going to call him? After this?

"In case you need to discuss . . . anything," he said hesitantly before walking around to the other side of the car. How was he not slipping in those fancy brogues? Maybe they came with built-in snow chains on the soles.

"Until tomorrow, Ms. Smith." Evaline's voice held the gravel of someone who had smoked all their life.

The window had whirred shut before Harriet could think of a reply.

The car purred away, and heads snapped round to stare at it as it glided down the shabby high street. Harriet shivered, her fingers slowly freezing around the small card. What in the world had she got herself into?

....

Harriet was eating dinner that evening when Maisy FaceTimed. In the blurry background, she could make out a huge real Christmas tree with blinking lights. Somewhere close by the sounds of a whisk scratching against a china mixing bowl and squeals of laughter made Harriet's heart squeeze. Missing her daughter was a visceral sensation, an ache running through the center of her bones, a hollow ringing like her ribs had been struck with a tuning fork. Someone else was Christmas baking with her daughter. She pasted herself back together and forced a ringmaster smile.

"You look ready for Christmas."

Maisy grinned back. "Yeah," she said, panning the phone around so that her mum could see the decorated sitting room. "We're making a gingerbread house and sugar cookies. Polly's an amazing baker. She's won the Cooperstown gingerbread house contest four years in a row."

Harriet tried not to hate Polly, the perfectly lovely woman taking wonderful care of her daughter, with her perfect baking skills and perfect house. Mariah Carey began to sing about what she wanted for Christmas and a girl's high-pitched voice joined in the chorus badly. Maisy laughed.

"That's Savannah, she loves Christmas music."

An unseen voice called out, "Hi, Harriet! I love you!" Savannah was the same age as Maisy; she'd stayed with them in Little Beck Foss last summer as part of the school exchange program.

"Love you too, Savannah!" Harriet called back. All this jovial togetherness was shredding her heart. Their merriment highlighted how quiet her home was. Her carefully curated soft furnishings and tasteful pictures felt like a stage with no actors to bring it to life.

Polly, Savannah's mum, said, "Let her be, honey, she needs to spend some time with her mama."

Perfect flocking Polly and her perfectly clucking loveliness! thought Harriet peevishly.

"Pan round and show me the sitting room." Maisy pressed her face up close to the screen, squinting to try and see around Harriet. "I want to see it all decorated. I've told Polly and Savannah how we're always the first to have our decs up and ours are always the best. Did you get the tree out yet? Did you manage to put it up without me?"

Harriet looked around her naked sitting room, the fancy orange-and-cinnamon candles still boxed; she'd probably use them as gifts. The only nod to the coming season was an early Christmas card from her foster parents, Sue and Gil, down in Surrey.

"I . . . I haven't had time to put them up yet," she lied. "Had a lot on my plate."

Maisy frowned. "Oh, okay." The disappointment in her voice made Harriet's organs deflate. "I guess I'll show Polly when you've done them. Speaking of plates," her daughter continued, "is that beans on toast? For dinner?" Her voice was thick with incredulity.

Harriet shifted slightly, feeling judged and hoping Polly wasn't listening. "It's a healthy meal. Beans count as one of your five-a-day."

"What were you eating the other night when I called you?"

"I don't recall," Harriet lied again.

Maisy gave her a hard stare and said, "It was a Pot Noodle." She pursed her lips in a way Harriet recognized as one of her own signatures of disapproval.

"So?" Harriet asked.

"So, why are you suddenly eating like a student?"

"Oh, you know what it's like, I'm tired after work, I don't always feel like cooking."

"But you *always* cook after work. I have never known you not to come home from work and start foraging in the fridge."

Maisy was right. She loved cooking. She'd get in from work, put on some music and cook while she and Maisy shared the details of their day. Or if Maisy was out, she'd listen to an audiobook while she prepared their evening meal. Somewhere between waving Maisy off at the airport and now, she'd lost the motivation. Suddenly it felt less like winding down after a long day and more like a chore to be got through before she could finally switch on the TV and lose herself in someone else's drama.

"I've been having a big meal for lunch at school, that's all." She hadn't. "Now did you call me to critique my dinner or was there something else?"

"Something else. How did your meeting with the old theater crone go?" Maisy settled herself cross-legged on an expansive armchair strewn with Christmas cushions and waited expectantly.

Harriet finished her beans on toast while she filled Maisy in on the day's events and then carried her plate and phone into the kitchen to wash up.

"So, when you boil it down, you got the deal that you actually wanted."

"Yes, but it's all on her terms."

"I guess. It sounds cool, though, hanging out in an old theater. I'd have loved to have somewhere like that when I was their age."

"That was only a year ago."

"Still counts. Maybe if me and my mates had had

somewhere to hang out, we wouldn't have had to freeze our tits off drinking cheap wine in the park on a Saturday night."

"Please don't tell me these things. Oh my god, Maisy!"

Maisy laughed. "Like you didn't do the exact same thing when you were my age."

She had her there.

"This could be good for you, you know. With me not coming home for Christmas and everything. It'll help with the pining."

"I am not pining for you."

Obviously, she was pining.

"Dad says you're pining."

"Dad's a dunderhead."

Maisy snorted. "Will you still go to Dad and Emma's for Christmas? It's their turn to host."

"I don't know. I haven't made any firm plans yet."

"Mu-um!"

"You worry about planning your own fabulous Christmas with Savannah and stop trying to micromanage mine."

"I'm worried about you."

"Don't be. I'm fine. I'm the parent, remember?"

"I can't stand the idea of you sitting by yourself eating baked beans on toast for Christmas dinner."

"I promise I won't eat baked beans for Christmas dinner."

"I just want you to take as much care of yourself as you take of other people."

As an independent woman with a solid career, a comfortable home and fifteen years' successful single parenting in the bank, Harriet had always considered that she took rather good care of herself, but these last few weeks had given her pause.

By the week after Maisy had left, she'd lost the will to plump the cushions on the sofas and even her bed, and she had always prided herself on her cushion plumping. Suddenly all the things she'd done daily for decades seemed pointless and she'd realized that she'd built her home almost entirely around her daughter's needs: the soft throws in the basket by the fire for when Maisy wanted to snuggle under a blanket and watch telly, the constantly brimming biscuit barrel for when Maisy got peckish, the posh bottles of bubble bath for when Maisy wanted a hot soak in the tub. Without Maisy there to enjoy it, it was simply staging.

Harriet smiled. "You don't need to worry about me, love. Honestly, I'm fine. But you're right, this community thing will be good for me, and it'll be good for the students—they just don't know it yet."

The FaceTime ended and in the silence her world became two-dimensional again, her sitting room flattened like a photograph in a magazine.

No! She stood and brutally chopped two of her cushions into plumped perfection. *I will not wallow.* If anything, it was for the best that Maisy was away, because Harriet was going to be busier than ever this Christmas. *I will agree to Ms. Bossy-Knickers's unreasonable demands, and I will create a safe space for the youth of Little Beck Foss, whether she likes it or not.* With a simple twist of her fingers, she deadheaded her orchid on the way to the kitchen and flicked an errant baked bean out of her cleavage and down the plug hole from ten paces. She nodded, satisfied. She was going to boss the schnitzel out of this thing!

NINE

"YOU WANT US TO WHAT?"

"No! No no no. Not gonna happen. No."

"I can't even look at you right now, miss."

"What have you got us into? You're supposed to be the adult. This is some childish BS happening right now and I am not equipped for it."

"H to the E to LL, NO!"

The disgruntled students were crammed into Harriet's broom cupboard of an office. Outrage was thick in the air. She'd lured them away from the canteen at breaktime with offers of takeout gingerbread lattes and toasties, which had cost her a small fortune. Unfortunately, not even barista coffee and grilled cheese was enough to disguise the poop sandwich she was serving them as the main course. When bribery had failed, she'd tried appealing to their interests, but they still regarded her with suspicion. Ali was sitting in, mostly for moral support, but thus far he'd barely been able to get a word in sideways.

"The part about having somewhere to hang out is good," said Leo in his usual diplomatic way. "I like the sound of the book club, and, Carly, you'd be great in a glee club." Carly shrugged but accepted the compliment. "But putting on a play, in front of people, well, that's . . ."

"Crap on a cracker, with a side order of crap and a big fat crap shake to wash it all down," finished Ricco. He was wearing cerise eye shadow today, which was a tough shade to manage, but he pulled it off.

"You are actual drama students!" Harriet huffed. "How can you be so against the idea of performing?"

"I took drama to learn about the writing process, not to be an actor," said Billy.

"I'm not afraid of the stage," Carly said, looking at her nails. "I like performing, but I don't like being made to look like a dick, and this sounds like it's going to make us look like dicks in front of the whole town."

She made a good point.

"And how are we supposed to learn a whole play in five weeks?" asked Isabel.

"You won't need to learn it; you already know it." This was her trump card. "We'll do *A Christmas Carol.*"

Ricco sighed dramatically.

"Oh my god! This is why you should never talk to teachers like they're actual people!"

Harriet couldn't help but laugh. "But you *do* know the text. Between you, you've studied the book and the stage play. That's half the battle won."

"You see!" said Ricco, gesticulating wildly. "Evil, I tell you!"

"We do know it, though," Leo piped up.

"Whose side are you on?" Ricco asked him.

"What's in it for us?" asked Billy.

Good question.

"Well," Ali chimed in. "You're all starting your Extended Project Qualification soon, so maybe there's a way you could use the experience to earn some marks toward it?" He looked at Harriet and smiled warmly. *And that is why I flapping love you!* she thought. EPQs were accepted grade currency for universities, colleges, and workplaces, and they were a great way to bump up a shortfall in exam results. The promise got the famous five's attention.

"That is a brilliant idea!" she said. "I'll speak to the coordinators; we'd just need to tweak your existing proposals to focus your projects through a theatrical lens. Billy, your proposal was a study of Irvine Welsh, so it wouldn't be a stretch to make it a compare and contrast between the worlds created by Welsh and Dickens. Carly, yours is about social politics, so that's an easy fix, either switch it to Dickensian social politics or compare it like we did at the theater, with today's cost-of-living crisis and wealth inequality. Leo, I'm not sure how we'll make your dissertation on Edvard Munch work off the top of my head, but we'll find a way . . ."

"He designed the sets for Ibsen's *Ghosts* play," said Ali. All eyes swiveled in his direction. He shrugged. "I have a master's in art history. Among others."

"Good lord," Harriet said, impressed. "Well, there's your connection, Leo."

"How many degrees have you got?" asked Billy.

"Five," said Ali proudly. "Two bachelor of arts degrees, plus the two master's and a PhD."

"You're overqualified, mate."

Ali looked crestfallen. Harriet would massage his ego later.

"I hadn't thought about my EPQ yet, so I could make it about the process of putting on a stage play?" Ricco suggested.

"Perfect!" Harriet felt the familiar teaching endorphins zipping through her. "It could be a study of bringing a classic novel to life on the stage and why the old stories still resonate today."

"Bloody hell, miss, did you just come up with that?" asked Carly.

Harriet grinned at her.

"Do me next," said Isabel, who had her legs draped across Billy in a clumsy attempt at flirting, about which Billy seemed none the wiser.

"Okay, your idea was . . ." She ran through the many proposals she'd had dropped on her desk for perusal before they reached Cornell. *Ah there it is, how could I forget!* "'Is Barbie a Feminist Icon?'"

Billy spluttered derisively, but Isabel ignored him and nodded expectantly.

"Maybe we could tweak it so . . ." *Come on, brain, don't fail me now!* "What about 'Does Dickens Write Feminist Characters in *A Christmas Carol*'?"

Isabel side-eyed her. "Where's Barbie?"

"I can't fit Barbie into Victorian England off the top of my head, but if you can find a way, write a proposal and I'll happily consider it. So, are we all agreed that we will put on a stage production of *A Christmas Carol*?"

"Will you go to prison if we say no?" asked Billy.

"I'd like to think not." Though she wouldn't rule anything out where Evaline Winter was concerned. "But it would make my life a lot easier if you agreed. And . . ." She left it a beat. "You are the reason I got caught up in this mess in the first place. Plus, using it as experience for your EPQs will legitimize your being at the theater, and therefore your parents and guardians are less likely to ask why you are suddenly spending your free time there."

"So the old woman corners you and then you corner us," said Carly.

"Pretty much."

"All right," said Billy. "If we earn credits toward our EPQs, I'm in."

Harriet felt a wave of relief. "Great!"

"We're going to need way more people," said Carly matter-of-factly. "We don't even have enough for the cast, let alone stage management."

This is progress. We're talking about logistics. Harriet felt . . . excited?

"I could possibly help you there," said Ali. "My aunt Prescilla is part of an amateur dramatics group in Great Foss, they might be willing to get on board. Or at least give you some pointers."

"You are just full of surprises!" Harriet laughed. "That would be great. Would you mind asking her for me?"

"Of course," he said, smiling. "They might have their own Christmas production to perform. It's a bit short notice. But you never know . . ."

"Ultimately, the choice is yours." Harriet appealed to her students. "I can't force you to do anything, nor would I want to. I am happy to go to the drama department and see if any of your fellow drama students want to get involved. I'm sure the extracurricular drama club would jump at the chance to showcase their skills."

"Oh, I'm sure the drama club would lose their shit with excitement," Ricco drawled with a double helping of snark.

"Right!" Carly agreed, giving him a high five. "They'll be all over this like fake tan. They're such a bunch of wannabes."

"So, you don't want me to enlist at the drama department?" Harriet asked. "You said yourself, we could do with the extra hands."

"They'll take over, miss. Like they always do."

"Yeah!" Ricco was up and out of his chair, spinning on his glitter high-tops. "This is our punishment, and they can't have it."

"Yeah!" parroted Isabel.

"Wait, so now this isn't crap on crackers with a side order of crap?" Harriet inquired.

"Oh, it's still a crapfest," replied Ricco. "But it's *our* crapfest."

....

"That went better than I expected," said Ali when the students had gone back to lessons and he and Harriet had sneaked outside so that Ali could vape. "They didn't even seem too pissed off about spending their Friday night cleaning the theater."

"It's amazing what a guilty conscience can do."

The sky was making a half-arsed attempt at snow, spitting out flakes intermittently. Harriet's hair was frizzing in the damp air.

"And a spot of bribery," he said.

"Hmmm."

Ali's eyes went suddenly wide, and he stuffed his vape back into his pocket and waved away the popcorn-scented cloud above his head.

"Harriet!" Cornell's voice boomed across the courtyard. "A word, please."

"For heaven's sake, what now?" she muttered as she watched him stride toward them.

"Ali, is it really professional to be flaunting your nicotine addiction in full view of our impressionable students?" he asked when he reached them.

Harriet made a show of looking around the empty courtyard.

"I think he got away with it," she said.

Cornell glared. "Not the point."

"I'll catch you in a bit," said Ali, sloping back in

through the double sliding doors, looking like a naughty schoolboy.

"What can I do for you?" Harriet asked. "I've got a tutorial in ten minutes."

"Not here," Cornell snapped. Melting snowflakes left dark marks on the shoulders of his tweed jacket. "My office. Now."

"You do know I'm not a student, don't you?"

"Your behavior often gives me cause to wonder."

Cornell marched back into the building toward his office. He was annoyingly tall, like a beige flagpole, which meant Harriet had to practically skip to keep up. A vein pulsed purple at the side of his head and his jaw was locked so tight she imagined his teeth squeaking under the pressure. She wondered what could have got him so wound up.

He sat in his chair and swiveled round to face the window, so that his back was to her. Harriet closed the door to his office and took the seat across from the desk. His office was considerably larger than hers, lined with bookcases and choice pieces of antique furniture. It oozed the ambience of a person who feels that their position is secure until retirement.

She shifted in her chair, waiting for him to speak. She could see his fingers tented in the reflection of the window.

"I do not appreciate my staff going behind my back," he said finally.

"I'm sorry?"

"You should be. I had a call from Evaline Winter. She's on the governing board of the school, did you know that? She holds a lot of influence."

Harriet did not know that. A queasy wave washed

over her. This was what her daughter might describe as a "squeaky bum" moment.

"What did she want?" She kept her voice even, but her brain had declared a code red alert and activated the melodramatic thoughts protocol: *Do I get redundancy money if I get the sack? I'll have to sell my flat to help make ends meet, get another job, what job? What if I can't get another job? Maybe I could live in a caravan, how much are caravans? I'll live in a field, forage for food, cook nettle soup, I'd need gloves to deal with the nettles, I'll need a cauldron, have to learn to make fire. I'll be like the bird lady in* Home Alone 2 *. . . bull-phooey, he's talking . . .*

"To advise me that you are planning to produce a play in the old theater with some of our students, and that you and she had discussed making the space a student 'community hub.'" He made air quotes around the last two words.

That sneaky cow! She was making it impossible for Harriet to back out of their agreement.

"I have to wonder why you felt it necessary to do this in secret," he continued, barely contained seething in his voice. "She also called the dean. He is delighted. Your endeavors will be charted in the next newsletter. It smacks of an underhandedness that I can only assume was meant to ingratiate yourself to the governing board and perhaps grease your ascent up the career ladder."

"I can assure you, Sebastian, that nothing could be further from the truth . . ."

He swiveled so quickly to face her that she wondered if he'd given himself whiplash. "You will not have my job," he spat.

"I don't want your job. I don't even want to be putting on a play; it's really all a big misunderstanding . . ."

"How so? Please elucidate."

Cornell glared at her, his nostrils flaring so wide that she could see the hairs poking out of them like spider legs. His jealousy that—in his mind at least—she had been singled out by Evaline and the dean was so strong that his blood was almost certainly a violent green.

She opened her mouth to speak but realized that there was no way to tell him how she had ended up in this predicament without implicating the famous five or telling him that she had spent Tuesday afternoon at the police station, or that she was being blackmailed by an evil theater crone. She closed her mouth again.

"Fine," he snapped. "Keep your secrets. But know this." He leaned forward and pointed at Harriet. "I will be watching you. If your work is affected, if you take time off, if the students involved fall behind with their homework or attendance, if this extracurricular production causes you to shirk your duties or drop the ball even once, I will slap you with a disciplinary before you can say *Macbeth*!"

Harriet sat up straight in her chair and met his eyes. "I think you know me well enough to be assured of how seriously I take my responsibilities to the students under my care, Sebastian. *I* do not 'shirk,' and I certainly have no intention of dropping the ball on anything."

Even as she said the words, she wondered how she was going to keep her many balls airborne. Half the emails she dealt with daily were forwarded on from Cornell, who seemed to think that correspondence was beneath him, and she had no doubt that he would make her life even harder now.

Cornell sat back in his chair.

"It wouldn't be the first time you gave up, couldn't cope."

It was a low blow, but she had grown used to them

from him. Everyone—including Cornell—knew that had she not changed jobs from the English department to pastoral care, she would have been head of the English department by now instead of him. Undermining her was how he eased his discomfort at being second choice. Hiding inside his large skeleton was a small, frightened man with a porcelain ego.

"We both know that isn't what happened. I expected better from you." She didn't, but it sounded good.

"How dare you!"

"If we are done here, I have work to do, as you well know, since most of it is yours."

She left Cornell in his office, his mouth flapping with outrage, but her triumph was short-lived, as the reality of her situation bolted itself to her shoulders like a concrete cape. Outside forces were backing her into corners.

She checked her phone as she rushed to make her tutorial meeting with her Year 13s. She had three messages from Ali:

What did Cornell want? Tell me everything!!

Do you need me to take your tutorial?

Would you like the good news or the bad news?

"For flap's sake!" she muttered, hitting dial as her office came into view. "Hey, what's up? Give me the bad news first."

"The famous five have gone AWOL again. They must have left straight after break."

"Give me strength!" She blew an exasperated breath up to the ceiling. *How did someone get a gummy bear to stick up there?* "Okay, now the good news."

"Caramel brownies are on the lunch menu in the

canteen? Sorry, I didn't have any good news as such, I just didn't want to give you only bad news."

She laughed despite feeling like she was being pulled under the sand by her ankles.

"Okay. Thanks for letting me know. Leave it with me."

....

Despite the promise of caramel brownies in the canteen, Harriet decided she needed a big fat barista coffee from the café in town and made her way out of Foss Independent, registering the incessant ping emitting from her phone as fresh emails forwarded from Cornell poured into her inbox. She hadn't managed to find any of the famous five, and of course none of them answered her calls or texts. If only she could covertly stick tracking devices to their rucksacks.

As she wandered past the rows of hellebores in the flower beds that lined the path to the exit, a familiar car parked in one of the visitors' spaces caused her to groan aloud. She considered trying to scuttle past, but even before the thought had fully formed, the back door clicked open and James Knight rose up fluidly before her. He was wearing a navy blue double-breasted military coat over his suit today. She noticed the line of dark shadow where he had shaved and how it defined his jaw. Then she recalled his five o'clock stubble grazing her throat as he kissed his way down her body. "Holy moly!" she gasped out, pressing her thighs together.

"Ms. Smith?" he inquired. "Is everything all right? It is lunchtime. We have a meeting scheduled?"

Of course. Lunchtime. The deadline on her decision that wasn't really her decision at all and a contract that would be the bane of her life for the foreseeable. Her run-in with Cornell earlier and subsequent mission to locate her incredible disappearing students had pushed the theater to the back of her mind.

"I'd assumed it was a done deal after your client ratted me out to my boss," she challenged.

"I'm sorry?" James's mask of professionalism slipped.

He doesn't know, she thought.

A voice crackled with age rose out of the dark car.

"I do not 'rat' people out, Ms. Smith. I was merely ensuring my position and, I might add, securing yours at the same time."

Harriet looked at James, and he shrugged ever so slightly as though in apology.

"Do get in, the pair of you," Evaline barked out. "You're letting all the warm air out!"

Harriet rolled her eyes and climbed into the car, slamming the door shut. Today Evaline was wearing a felt cloche hat in claret with a rose on one side and a coat in the same color. She didn't bother to make eye contact with Harriet.

"May I?" James asked as he reached to pull the tray across her. Harriet nodded and tried not to breathe in his cologne. She was cross with absolutely everyone and she didn't want to be aroused by a deliciously scented scoundrel.

James sat back and pulled a sheaf of papers from his briefcase, which he handed to Evaline. Evaline took them, eyed them lazily, and passed them across to Harriet.

"Please sign this most recent contract, which accounts for your additional responsibilities, and I'll leave you alone to get on. I'm sure you're very busy." She made it sound like she was doing Harriet a favor.

Harriet scanned the paperwork. It was all straightforward enough: *sign here to sell your soul to Krampus.*

"You'll notice that I've put in a paragraph pertaining to the 'gentlemen's agreement' with regard to a community-use clause being added into any sales contract going forward," said James.

His careful choice of the words "gentlemen's agreement" was not lost on Harriet; she was sure Evaline would not have approved a contract bearing anything more substantial. The old phrase *Promises are like pie crust, made to be broken* swam through her mind, but it was better than no agreement at all.

"What happens if for some reason I can't get the production performance ready in time?" she asked.

"Then you'll be in breach of contract," said Evaline simply.

"But what does that mean? It's not like you're paying me. No money is changing hands, so technically if I am unable—"

"I can sue you for breach of contract," Evaline finished. "And I will. But let's not get into all that unpleasantness. And you won't be without help; Mr. Knight will be with you every step of the way to ensure that you deliver."

"What!" Harriet and James blurted.

Evaline's countenance remained unmoved.

"Obviously I want to ensure that my theater is being treated with respect, and I'll need to know that the production is on schedule. The only way to ensure this is to have a person on the ground, as it were."

James angled his head away from Harriet and lowered his voice. "Evaline, please. I have a full workload, your interests need my attention. I have other clients. I don't have time to act as a glorified babysitter—"

Harriet's hackles rose. Evaline cut James off with one raised hand.

"All taken care of. Your partners at the law firm were very supportive of what we are trying to achieve here and were only too happy to give you the coverage you need. I will expect detailed weekly reports, and it might be handy if you keep a journal of the day-to-day to ensure that nothing slips your mind. I know how you like to jot down ideas." She grimaced like an angry Yorkshire terrier.

"Evaline, I really must protest in the strongest terms—"

"It is done, Mr. Knight." She turned her attention back to Harriet. "Do sign the contract, Ms. Smith, time is ticking on for all of us."

Harriet finished reading the new contract and signed it. She handed it back to James, but Evaline took it instead, saying, "Thank you. You may both go now, and I look forward to seeing the Winter family theater brought back to its former glory one last time."

Harriet marveled at how she had managed to make what was essentially a posturing project to snare buyers with a side order of blackmail sound like the fulfillment of a dear old lady's final wish. She supposed that was how Evaline would be spinning it for the media too, drumming up interest and creating a buzz that would make her crappy old theater seem like a ripe investment.

Evaline pushed a button on the side panel of the car and said, "Austin, would you mind seeing our guests out?"

The driver opened first Harriet's door and then James's and ushered them both reverently out into the school car park. James clutched his briefcase to his chest with an expression of disbelief as the limo reversed slowly out of the space and pulled out onto the road and away.

Harriet watched the limo disappear around a corner. "I probably shouldn't, but I feel so much better now that Evaline has screwed you over too." She didn't need to look at James to know that he was glowering.

"I don't know anything about the theater," he mumbled. She wasn't sure if he was talking to her or not.

"Neither do I, really. I've read a lot of plays, but I've never produced one. Still, before we worry about that, we've got to clean the place up."

"We? I didn't make any mess. I won't be cleaning anything. I don't understand how this has happened." He gazed along the road where the car had been, looking genuinely flabbergasted.

"Perhaps Ms. Winter felt like you needed to find some Christmas spirit?"

"I have plenty of Christmas spirit, thank you very much!" he snapped.

He was still looking down the street as though the limo might return for him any moment with Evaline leaning out of the window cackling *Gotcha!*

"This is ridiculous. Unbelievable. Incomprehensible..." he continued to mutter.

"Outrageous?" she offered, tapping her chin. "Ludicrous?" When he glared at her in response, she added, "Oh, I'm sorry, I thought you were seeking synonyms."

He straightened his jacket. "You cannot begin to conceive how disruptive this little venture of yours will be to my life." James's voice was so peppery it got right up Harriet's nose.

"*My little venture?* You're not the only person who's been thrown into this, you know. It's going to disrupt my life too."

James sniffed and turned away from her.

"Oh, of course! Your life is so much more important than mine."

He whipped back round. "Don't put words into my mouth. I wasn't casting aspersions on your life. I have nothing more to say to you."

"Clearly you reserve your charm for picking up women in bars."

He had the audacity to look offended at this. "Are you accusing me of being a player?"

"If the oxblood brogue fits," said Harriet, making a show of glancing distastefully down at his shoes, even though she secretly liked them very much.

The wind had picked up and flurried snowflakes in their direction. Students hurried past them, off to find food in their lunch hour. James looked down at his feet.

"What have you got against my shoes?"

"It's not your shoes that are the problem," Harriet replied in her most condescending voice.

James shook his head. "Let's start again, shall we? Would you like to grab a coff—"

"No thank you!" she said, cutting him off. *That mercurial nonsense might work with your usual conquests, but not with me, pal! Be a jerk or be a gentleman, pick a personality and stick to it.*

For a moment he looked a little hurt, and Harriet didn't like the way it made her stomach twist. But he quickly recovered himself and fitted the mask of self-assurance back over his features.

"Well then, I suppose I'll see you at the theater tomorrow?" he said.

"I suppose you will. Bring your rubber gloves."

She turned on her heel and stomped away along the slushy path. *Is he still standing there, watching me walk away? I could turn around, but then if he's looking he'll know that I was hoping he was still looking. But I really want to know! No. Actually no. I don't care. He is stroppy, and I have quite enough actual teenagers to deal with. But it would be cool if he was watching me . . .* It was a relief when she finally turned the corner and that particular inner monologue was rendered moot.

TEN

THE FOLLOWING AFTERNOON, HARRIET WAS GATHERING THE things that she would need for the big theater cleanup. Last night she had created—with their permission—a WhatsApp group for her and the famous five called "The Bah Humbugs," which she thought was inspired, but which had only received a series of groaning memes in the chat. Still, they had all promised to meet her at the theater at half past five, which she counted as a win.

It was almost dark already, cold too, and she could do without spending her Friday evening cleaning, but this was going to be her life for the foreseeable, so she might as well resign herself.

Usually, she would still be at school at this time, trying to catch up on admin or having meetings with parents—the hours of free labor that anyone employed in education had to work to maintain any kind of balance! Ali, kind soul that he was, had forced her to delegate some of her load to other members of the team so that she could leave on time. Still, a niggle of unease squirmed in her stomach.

When her doorbell rang at four fifteen, she was surprised to hear James's voice crackling through the intercom.

"Hello, Harriet? It's James. Knight. I think we got off

on the wrong foot yesterday. I'd like to clear the air before we get to the theater."

She froze. Many conflicting emotions buzzed around inside her torso, all of them sending confusing messages to her brain. When she didn't say anything, he added, "May I come up?"

"Oh. Yes, of course." She pressed the door release. She couldn't very well say no when he'd clearly come here as a conciliatory gesture. She didn't want to appear churlish. Also, it was kind of thrilling to have a handsome man at her door.

"You live above a library," he said when she opened the door to her apartment. He was holding a poinsettia plant with a red ribbon in one hand and a bag in the other.

"Yes," she agreed.

"That's very cool."

She eyed him to see if he was making fun, but he seemed genuine. "Thank you. I think so too. It's wonderfully quiet." She arched an eyebrow.

He smirked. "I'm sure it is." He held out the bag to her. "You left this at my apartment."

Folded neatly inside was her third-favorite cardigan. *Welcome home.* She smiled.

"And this"—he held out the plant—"is a peace offering."

"Thank you. That's very kind of you." She placed it on the console table. It looked rather lovely with its crimson petals and dark green foliage.

Dammit, he's like good cop/bad cop all in one package!

"Now I think it's customary for you to apologize too?" he said.

"Too? You gave me a plant, you didn't apologize."

Her phone rang; she looked down and then back up at James. "Sorry, it's the parent of one of my students, I have to take this. Come in." She invited him into her hallway and slipped into the sitting room, closing the door behind her to take the call. Five minutes later, she came back into the hall.

"Sorry, where were we?"

"I can't remember."

"Is that what you're wearing?" She eyed his suit.

He looked down at his suit as though seeing it for the first time. "I came straight from the office."

"Are you planning a more directorial approach to cleaning up the theater?"

"Are you always this rude to people who bring you gifts?"

Great! I'm an ungrateful cow. Well played, Mr. Knight.

"I'm just a little confused. You have a whole Jekyll and Hyde thing going on, and I'm struggling to keep up."

"Right," he said. "Yes, I can see how I might be coming across. My apologies, I find myself out of my comfort zone. I'm not accustomed to wearing more than one hat at a time, as it were."

Presumably he was referring to his bedroom and business hats.

"Ours has not been a traditional 'get to know you,'" she agreed.

Harriet didn't usually let men into her home, not unless she'd been dating them for a while, vetted them fully. It was a rule that had allowed her flat to remain a haven for her and Maisy. She'd never wanted her daughter to have to worry about getting up in the morning to find a strange man sitting at the breakfast counter. A few men had passed the test and made it into the inner sanctum over the years, but most hadn't, and she had always been pleased, when those relationships inevitably came to nothing, that she'd kept her sanctuary free from drama. And here she was breaking her own cardinal rule by letting in a one-night stand.

Her front door opened into a generous hexagon-shaped hallway that housed a console table—on which the poinsettia sat—a mustard clamshell chair, a white-painted French armoire for coats and shoes, and doors that led off to all the other rooms.

"You have a lovely home," said James.

"Well, it's not as swanky as your waterfall apartment, but I like it."

"I'm surprised you can recall my apartment, you ran out of it so fast." His sarcasm took her by surprise.

"Was that a dig? Or an accusation?" she asked.

"That was a statement of fact."

Okay, we're doing this, then. She had assumed "clear the air" meant sweep it under the carpet and start afresh; apparently not. Harriet pulled her ninth-favorite cardigan on over her eighth. She was cleaning a theater—this was not a time for best knitwear.

"I thought you'd be grateful not to have the entanglement. Isn't that what most men want?" she asked honestly.

"Why would you think that? I thought we'd hit it off." He sounded hurt. He sounded like she'd sounded after similar encounters.

This made her fluster. She wasn't used to this kind of role reversal, and it caught her off guard.

"We did. It. It was . . . great," she stammered. "But I'd assumed it was a onetime thing. Aren't men usually champing at the bit to get rid of their conquests?" Her words came out snippier than she'd intended as previous experiences sprang to her mind. There was nothing more demeaning than being given the cold shoulder by a lover while their sweat was still damp on your skin.

"*A conquest?*" His features contorted in chagrin. "Is that what you thought was happening? Like I'm some lowlife predator?"

This was too much.

"Don't act so pious!" she snapped. "You can't tell me you went out that night looking for a life partner. We both knew what we were getting. You don't get to sleep with me and then slut-shame me for not expecting a promise of marriage afterward. That's just another fudged-up form of sexism."

He stared at the ceiling.

"You know, women like you make it harder for men like me to do better."

Wow!

"*Women like me?*" Her high horse was rearing up on its hind legs. "What kind of *woman* am I like, in your humble opinion?"

James, clearly playing his words back in his head, shook his head and held his hands up. "I'm sorry. That came out really badly."

He at least had the grace to look horrified.

"Yes, it did. For a lawyer you are surprisingly careless with your words."

"Please, can I explain myself?"

"I don't know. You can give it a try." She folded her arms.

"What I was trying to convey, badly, is that I have been careless with women's feelings in the past . . . I have been careless with people full stop. The fault is mine entirely. I'm trying to do better, and part of that is not being the type of man who sleeps with someone and then ghosts them."

Heavens to Betsy! How could she argue with that?

"And instead"—Harriet spoke slowly, choosing her words—"you feel like *you* got ghosted?"

"I'm not saying I didn't deserve it; what goes around comes around and all that. And please understand, I am not suggesting that you owe me anything. I have the utmost respect for you. This is my personal journey, and I have no right to drag you along with me. But I thought we'd connected on more than merely a physical level. I'd hoped that might continue. And then I came out of the shower . . ."

"In my defense, I kind of thought the whole being-in-the-shower thing was my cue to leave. I thought I was doing you a favor."

"Why would you think that?"

It was on the tip of her tongue to say that she'd looked at his phone and seen a message from someone called Lyra, but she felt like admitting to reading his private messages might make things worse.

"Because in those situations, in my experience, that's what men usually want. Easy breezy, no strings."

James looked at her. He took a breath in through his nose, his lips pressed together as he listened. *Good crikey, if only men knew how sexy they are when they actually listen.*

"You're right. Obviously, I can't speak for other men, but for myself I have been guilty of being that person. Which is why I was hoping to do things differently this time. With you. I am trying to create more meaningful connections. Granted, inviting you straight into bed wasn't exactly taking things slowly, but I had hoped that our night together might be the beginning rather than the whole story." He looked embarrassed. "I can see now that that's not your responsibility."

Harriet puffed out a breath. She was, as a rule, cautious of meaningful connections, because once made she was all in. It was one of the reasons she'd found it so easy to keep Pete as a genuine friend. She originated from loose connections, her roots severed when she was removed from neglectful parents at three years old and placed into the care system. It had made her scrupulous with her choices and fearlessly loyal to the people she did let in. But she wasn't about to divulge any of this to a practical stranger, so she summoned her humor shield.

"I mean, I am all for personal growth. Like, 'You go . . . guy.'" She reached forward awkwardly and gave him an encouraging bump on the shoulder. "My job is encouraging people to be the best version of themselves. But it is unfair for you to suddenly change the fundamental rules of the one-night stand as we know it and expect me to just instinctively know. That sort of societal restructuring requires a memo, at the very least."

James's face cracked into a smile. "Duly noted."

"We have a real problem with getting our wires crossed."

"Something to work on." His expression was serious, but his eyes held a kindness that began a thaw somewhere deep inside her.

"Are we good?" Harriet asked. "We're going to be working together for the next few weeks. I don't want you to experience wrath every time you look at my face."

He laughed then, and it was easy with unmistakable relief. "We're good," he assured her. "I'm sorry about the way I was in the police station too. There's professionalism, and then there's being an arsehole."

"I'm not used to being in trouble with the law. You could have been the friendly face that I needed."

"I know. Sorry. You took me by surprise. I'm not good with surprises."

"No shizzle."

"Which brings us to yesterday and another surprise sprung, where I behaved like a recalcitrant child, again. I apologize for that too. I will add 'not being a dick when caught off guard' to my list of things I need to work on."

His earnestness caught *her* off guard. She couldn't help her smile and found herself feeling shy under his frank gaze. It felt like she was meeting him for the first time, which was ridiculous, considering they'd already had very uninhibited, drunken coitus.

"Apologies accepted. And I'm sorry for any miscommunications that made things harder than they needed to be."

They stood awkwardly in the hallway; a hug was too intimate, but a handshake felt too formal. In the end Harriet broke the tension.

"Come through, I just need to get my bag of cleaning supplies."

"Mine are in the car," he said.

She led him into the sitting room, where he stopped abruptly with a crease in his brow.

"What?" she asked. Was he judging her interior design skills?

"You've got no Christmas decorations up," he said, confused.

"Oh." She hadn't expected that. "Well, I mean, it is only the middle of November."

Never mind that she wouldn't be putting decorations up in December either.

"Yes, but in the pub, you said you loved Christmas. If

I remember correctly, you described yourself as the 'Christmas fricking queen.' You told me you were always the first person you knew to get their decorations up. So I'm wondering why Christmas's biggest fan doesn't have a single piece of tinsel hung."

He remembered that? She hadn't expected to even see him again, let alone have him remember the things they'd talked about.

"Oh. I, um." James Knight had an uncanny way of dissolving her bull-whoopie. She sighed. "I can't see the point."

He frowned at her. "Go on . . ."

"Why make all that effort if there's no one here to appreciate it?"

"You'll be here."

She rolled her eyes. "You don't get it." How could he possibly understand, living in his penthouse apartment, a high-flying career man? He'd probably only ever had to put himself first, selfishness coming as second nature. And why shouldn't he? She could understand how that would work for him, but her life was different; her life was built around being a parent.

"Has it always been just you and your daughter?"

Her wary side reminded her that they weren't drunk anymore; the rules were different now. And yet she found herself drawn in by his open expression, compelled to answer.

"Since she was two. Pete, my ex, is very present in her life, our life. His wife is my best friend."

She enjoyed James's surprise. People were always surprised. Or skeptical. But mostly surprised.

"That's very . . . I don't imagine that's very common. I know lots of adults but not so many of them that behave like grown-ups. You must all be very sensible."

She smiled. "I don't know about that. Pete and I simply weren't in love. Then he met Emma, and I guess we both fell for her. It's not that surprising, really. Pete and I are very similar, that was the problem, we were more like siblings than partners."

"You consciously uncoupled, like Gwyneth and Chris. I'm impressed."

"Actually, they did it like us." She gave a wry smile and went into the kitchen, where she stuffed a roll of black sacks and some rubber gloves into a large shopper with several litter-grabbers she'd borrowed from school. "What about you? Any significant exes? Kids? I assume you are single?" she fished.

His brow furrowed.

"My history isn't quite as clean-cut as yours. Or as amicable. I have an ex-wife who doesn't speak to me. I met her when I lived in the U.S. I was twenty-six. We got married, I put my career first, she felt neglected, rightly so. I wouldn't give up my career progression for my marriage, and after three years she called it. She met someone else. Last I heard, she was happily married with a couple of kids, a dog, and a house in the burbs."

Was there a hint of regret in his voice?

"You're probably imagining that I'm full of regret for what could have been."

"Are you?"

"I am sorry that I made her feel unloved. That, I do regret, but you can't reach your late forties and not have things you wish you'd handled differently. I don't regret the effort I put into my career. I've built a good life for myself."

There was something else behind the unapologetic sentiment. It felt like he was holding something back, a sadness; she could feel it hiding in the spaces between the truth. He was being careful with his words, but it was the ones he didn't say that sounded loudest to Harriet.

The sex between them had been easy, but getting to know someone took work. They were, technically speaking, middle-aged, and had naturally acquired some baggage that would take some unpacking. Of course, they didn't need to share their stories. They could work on this project as colleagues. But Harriet couldn't ignore the rising desire inside her to know absolutely everything about James Knight.

ELEVEN

UPON FURTHER INSPECTION, THE MESS IN THE THEATER wasn't as bad as she remembered. But the sheer dilapidation of the place meant that they could litter-pick for a year and it would still look like the opening scene for a zombie apocalypse movie. Stale cigarette smoke and dust hung in the air, mixed with the earthy scent of damp chair fabric and dirty carpets, and with no windows in this part of the building and the ventilation system out of action, there was little chance of things improving soon. The enduring chill that clung to the old bones of the auditorium kept it from feeling claustrophobic, but it felt like a place outside the normal rules of time.

Harriet hoped the act of cleaning would keep her warm and was glad she'd fitted a jumper beneath her cardigans.

"Are you sure you don't want to go home and change?" she asked.

James was using a litter-grabber to gingerly maneuver a takeaway coffee cup into a black sack hung on the back of a music stand. He stood out even more than usual in the shabby surroundings.

"It's fine. This suit was due to be dry-cleaned anyway."

Harriet pulled a face.

"I saw that," he said. "What is it?"

"Nothing."

James continued to look at her. Waiting.

"It's just. I'm trying to imagine what you look like when you're not dressed in formal attire. I can't imagine you not in a suit."

He speared her with a look.

"You've seen me at my most informal, Ms. Smith."

She instantly flushed, remembering his taut body hovering above hers, the heat of his skin as their naked bodies crushed together, moving in the rhythm of lovers, her hips pushing up to meet his. *Get a* grip! she told herself, wiping the back of her hand across her forehead. His mouth twitched into a smile.

"I—" Her voice came out as a strangled croak, and she cleared her throat. "I meant, I can't imagine you slopping around in a tracksuit." *Is there a heater on in here?* She shrugged off one of her cardis.

"You see me more as a smoking-jacket-and-silk-pajama-bottoms sort?"

She burst out a laugh. "I didn't, but now I have a very clear image of what that would look like."

"And?"

"I think you could probably pull it off."

He shook his head, smiling, and went back to filling his black sack while she concentrated on clearing the dress circle of sweet wrappers and other detritus, screwing her face up in disgust at the number of used condoms she had the misfortune to find. *At least they're practicing safe sex?*

She considered what James had said in her flat. Had she met men who claimed they wanted to do better? Not often, she concluded. Plenty felt that they deserved points for being up-front about the fact that they were only interested in sex. Many assumed that simply professing themselves to be feminists would get them laid, and ninety percent of those thought that feminism was something to do with burning bras and taking their jobs.

Did James's quest for betterment mean that he was genuinely looking for something deeper? Or did it simply mean he intended to be more courteous after one-night stands—breakfast and a handshake before parting? Had he really been hoping that their night together might lead to more? She sneaked a glance his way.

He was classically tall, dark, and handsome, albeit in a buttoned-up sort of way. Yes, he walked around like he had a rod up his bottom and he was quick to judge, but equally, she noticed, quick to apologize and learn from his mistakes, and that was an attractive personality trait. However, he was essentially acting as her parole officer, and this was a strike against him. As was the mysterious Lyra, who could be significant or a family member or friend. *The odds are even thus far; I guess we'll just have to wait and see*, she thought.

Half an hour later, a maintenance team composed of at least forty people wearing boilersuits in blues and dark green arrived and immediately took up stations all over the building to begin the task of reinforcing, replacing, securing, and the general fixing of the countless things that creaked ominously in the dilapidated theater.

Harriet finished up another work call and turned to James.

"It's a bit late for them to be starting a job, isn't it?" she asked.

"You can talk—you don't seem to finish work at all."

He looked pointedly at her phone, which had managed to interrupt every conversation they'd had at least once since they'd arrived. She bristled.

"I have a demanding job."

"Indeed, you do." The heavy quiet of the theater had been replaced with the hammer and whirr of tools. "With so much work needing to be done in such a short time, Evaline gave me the go-ahead to instruct an around-the-clock maintenance team." He speared an orange peel in the orchestra pit and added, "It's for insurance as well as for the renovations. She doesn't want to be sued when a student falls through rotten floorboards or gets squashed by a sandbag because the ropes on the rigging system have perished."

"She's all heart."

"It's an expensive window-dressing exercise, but Evaline is hopeful that showing the theater in its best light will encourage the right kind of buyer."

"Does she care who buys it? Does it matter?"

James considered. "I had always thought not. Her relationship with this building is complicated, and I had thought she'd be glad to be shot of it. But when we received a generous offer for the land from a company that wanted to raze the theater to the ground, she turned them down, even though it was the best offer we'd had on the table in years." He stood and looked around the empty stalls as though suddenly remembering where he was. "Forgive me, I've said too much. I'm not usually so free with my clients' personal matters. Please, can we strike all that from the record?"

"As you wish, Mr. Knight. Sustained!" She'd known that binge-watching *The Good Wife* would come in handy one day.

James turned away, smiling. She heard his low chuckle as he moved along the stalls. She liked making him laugh.

"Why is she really making me clean the place up

when she's obviously got professionals on the payroll? Does she honestly believe her own rhetoric?"

"Evaline is a powerful woman, and she maintains that power by ensuring that no one is in any doubt about who is in charge."

"So essentially this is me being in detention."

"Correct."

"How come you got put into detention with me?"

"I've been asking myself the same question."

"And why sell now? It's been closed for almost half a century—why the sudden rush?"

James paused and leaned back against one of the seats.

"Shouldn't your students be helping with this?" He waved an empty share bag of crisps like a flag.

He was evading her question. She could push, but it would be unfair if his silence was due to client confidentiality.

"They will." *I hope.*

"If they show up at all."

"They will." *They'd better!*

"Your faith in them is rather endearing. Especially after they scarpered and left you to take the blame."

"That isn't how it happened." Harriet would have expanded but for the shouts erupting from the foyer.

She and James hurried out to see what was happening.

"Miss! They won't let us in!" Carly was brandishing a mop at two burly maintenance men.

Harriet aimed a self-satisfied grin at James before stepping forward.

"It's okay, they're with me," she said, unable to squash the pride exploding in her heart as she saw that all five of them were there.

"Told you," Billy grumbled at the men. He was holding a can of Mr. Sheen at his side, a yellow duster poking out of his pocket.

"It's discrimination." Ricco puffed out his chest.

Harriet flapped her hands to shush them. "They're just doing their job," she reasoned, pushing Carly's mop down into a more passive position. "You don't exactly look like a traditional cleaning crew."

Leo—who had blue hair today—looked down at his oversized hoodie and acrylic-paint-splattered work boots and shrugged. Isabel—in a short bomber jacket and boyfriend jeans—jutted one hip out and rested her hand on it, drawling, "So judgmental!"

"I can vouch for them," said Harriet. But the men only eyed her dubiously.

James stepped forward just as a wall of a man in a yellow high-viz jacket joined them.

"Mr. Knight," the foreman exclaimed. "Surprised to see you here." He was a broad, balding man in his early sixties, with deep laughter creases around his eyes and the booming voice of a no-nonsense Yorkshireman used to being heard and obeyed. Harriet liked him instantly.

"Not as surprised as I am to be here, I can assure you," he replied. "Good to see you, Ken. These people are with me," he said, gesturing uncertainly to the students. "They are helping with the cleanup. And this is Harriet Smith." He turned to her and smiled politely. "She is the students' teacher and responsible adult, and they are her charges. Harriet, this is Ken—Ken is the site manager and general head honcho around these parts."

Ken nodded and shook her hand.

"Community service thing, is it?" he asked, giving a side nod to the famous five.

"Something like that," Harriet smiled. "We'll be putting on a Christmas production for the town, one last hurrah for the theater before it becomes, well, whatever it becomes." She tried to make it sound as though she was in control of the situation. If she said it with enough conviction, maybe she'd believe it herself.

"Will you now? Well, I wish you luck with it, I genuinely do. This old building deserves it before it's overrun with fat cats."

"Right, well, lovely to meet you, Ken, I'm sure we'll be seeing a lot of each other these next few weeks." She gave him a grimace, and he laughed. "We'd better make a start."

"Fair enough. In you go. But stay off the stage until we've made sure it's all secure. I don't want any accidents on my watch," Ken warned, wagging a finger at the students.

"On that point we are in agreement," said James, holding out his hand for the man to shake. "We'll be keeping a close eye on them, don't you worry."

Ken and his colleagues disappeared through the double doors to the old cocktail lounges, and Harriet turned to her students.

"Thanks for coming, guys."

"Did we have a choice?" asked Billy.

"No, you didn't." She smiled. "This is Mr. Knight; he'll be helping us with our endeavors."

James became rictus stiff. The students trained their eyes on him, waiting, daring. *Don't show fear*, she wanted to urge him. *Any sign of weakness and they'll eat you alive!*

Finally. Stiltedly. He stepped forward as though addressing a jury. "It's a pleasure to meet you all. Please call me James. Ms. Smith speaks very highly of you. I am here to help in any way I can to make this venture a success."

Oh dear!

The students were staring at him with a mixture of

disdain, distrust, and scorn. They said nothing but managed to make their nothing sound more aggressive than words ever could.

"Okay, then!" Harriet declared. Using her arms in the way one might guide a flock of chickens to their henhouse, she ushered the students up the main stairs, which brought them out onto the balcony overlooking the theater below. She glanced back at James bringing up the rear and gave him a sympathetic smile.

"What are you planning to mop, Carly?" asked Ricco, sniggering as Carly—dressed in a camouflage boilersuit and Doc Martens—twirled the mop like a baton.

"I don't know yet, do I?" she retorted. "It's called being prepared. What did you bring?"

Ricco pulled a Dustbuster out of his rucksack and gave her a smug smile.

"The battery will run down before you've done a flight of stairs," said Billy glibly.

"And what are you going to do, Billy? Polish the stage?" Ricco retorted in a derisory tone.

"Tess said there'd be a lot of wood." Billy was defensive. "She said it would freshen the place up."

Tess and Arthur were Billy and Sid's foster parents. They were good people—they'd certainly had a calming effect on Billy—but they were well past retirement age and Harriet worried about what that might mean for the boys down the line.

"Tess is right," Harriet intervened. "This place definitely needs a freshen-up. Everything you've brought will be useful. There's a lot to do, and it's going to take a joint effort. And no, Ricco, by 'a joint effort,' I do not mean that we ought to smoke joints."

Ricco smirked. "It would make the time pass quicker, miss."

"The only highs will be elevated heart rates and soaring community spirits."

Isabel—who took a Cleopatra approach to eye makeup—snickered. "I love you, miss, but you are well square. Are you sure you're not Amish?"

"Not in those jeans," said Ricco, chewing his cheek.

"What's wrong with my jeans?" Harriet asked.

"Nothing's wrong with them, per se," answered Ricco. "But they are way too tight to be Amish."

Harriet found herself smoothing her hands down over her bottom and thighs self-consciously. Isabel saw and said, "Not tight in a bad way, miss. They look good on you. Bums are in."

Leo made agreeing noises. Out of the corner of her eye, she saw James's mouth twitch with a smile.

"Right. Thank you, Isabel." Harriet straightened her back; she needed to remove her bottom from the topic of conversation.

"I've never seen you in jeans, miss. You look kind of hot. Don't you think so, James?" asked Carly.

James's smile faltered and his cheeks darkened.

"Yes," he agreed stiffly. "Very nice. Practical."

Harriet held her hands up. "Let's leave the subject of my jeans behind, shall we?"

"It's your behind that started it," Isabel quipped. This earned her high fives all round.

"Thank you all!" Harriet used her "final" voice and the students quieted and waited for her to continue. "Now, we need to take a methodical approach to this cleanup. So we'll start at the top of the theater by the exits; each person picks a section of seating and works their way along and down each row until they reach the orchestra pit." She handed each of them a black sack and a litter-grabber and pointed them toward the stairs.

"I've got to pick Sid up from football club today," said Billy, "but I'll come straight back after. Sid can help, he loves a bit of litter-picking—they do it at school all the time."

"Of course, that's fine, Billy; Sid is most welcome. Why're you picking him up and not Tess or Arthur?"

Billy shrugged. "I just thought it'd make a nice change for Sid."

Harriet nodded, but her internal antenna pinged an alert.

"This is going to take forever!" Ricco complained, as he leaned over the balcony surveying the stalls below.

"Not forever, Ricco, and please don't lean too hard on the balcony until we know it's safe. The quicker you snap to it, the quicker we'll get it done."

"Ugh! Yes, Mum!" he groaned, starting down the stairs with the others following suit.

"Sorry about that," she said when she and James were left standing on the balcony. "They're high spirited."

"No, I'm sorry. I've not had much to do with teenagers, not since I was one myself, and I seem to remember being rather awkward and unpleasant most of the time."

Harriet laughed. "I think most of us were unpleasant teenagers, if we're honest with ourselves."

"They like you." James peered over the balcony at the scattering students below as they took their positions.

"They're used to me, that's all. They're good kids." She smiled as she listened to their bantering shouts below.

"You say that a lot."

"Do I?" She gave a self-conscious half laugh. "I suppose I'm used to having to defend them. God knows somebody needs to." Zoe's face swam into her mind.

She felt James watching her and plastered a smile on her face. He studied her for another long moment.

"That's why I went into law. Originally," he said. "To help people. Somewhere along the way, I appear to have stopped using my powers of persuasion to defend the defenseless and instead protect the interests of people who already have too much." His own thoughts seemed to drift then as he stared into the black mouth of the empty stage below, and she wondered where they took him.

"Is your career one of the areas in which you are striving to do better?" Harriet ventured tentatively.

He continued to look down when he answered. "Yes, I think it is. I was—" He hesitated. "I was moved by what you said in Evaline's car, about wanting to create a space that would benefit the community. The idea got me thinking in a way I haven't for a long time. I suppose this is all my fault, really." He gestured around the auditorium. "I rather got us into this mess. Perhaps this is what a midlife crisis looks like."

"Isn't that supposed to involve buying a fast motorbike and dating women half your age?"

He smiled. "That's what it says in my middle-aged-man handbook, yes."

"Have you ticked either of those things off your list yet?"

"I've never been much into fast vehicles. I don't like to feel out of control." He left a beat before continuing. "And I find I'm rather more attracted to women who have lived a little, preferably ones who consume mulled wine like it's about to be rationed."

Now it was Harriet's turn to flush as she tried desperately not to smile. The blood in her veins seemed to pick up speed, and she felt suddenly very alive.

"And for the record," he added, tearing off a fresh black sack from the roll Harriet had been handing around, "you do look hot in those jeans."

He left the words hanging in the air and took the stairs briskly down into the theater. Harriet shrank into the shadows and leaned her back against the wall, trying to control her breathing. What the heck-fire was happening to her? It was like being fifteen again. She bit her knuckles to stop herself from squealing and then bent over and jogged fast on the spot for a full ten seconds, pumping her arms at the same time to try and expel some of her excitement.

"Everything all right, miss?" Billy looked alarmed and confused. "I just came up to get more bin bags."

"Yes, yes, everything's fine. I was just warming up. You should always warm up your muscles before you start a workout." She did a couple of clumsy lunges to illustrate.

"Right."

Billy tore a bin bag off the strip and left without another word. She rolled her eyes at herself.

Downstairs she heard Ken's beefy laughter mixed with James's more conservative expression of merriment. Though he was out of sight, she knew exactly what James would look like in that moment. His deep-set eyes would twinkle as though a lamp had been switched on behind them, high cheekbones pushing them almost to slits, lines fanning at the corners like sunbeams. When he smiled, the deep lines that ran from either side of his nose to the corners of his mouth were accentuated, lending him a mischievous appearance that was very much on the right side of sexy. Against her better judgment, she found herself wanting to memorize all of James's expressions.

TWELVE

JAMES HAD BEEN UNABLE TO HELP WITH THE CLEANUP AT THE weekend because of "prior commitments," which he'd made no effort to expand upon. Harriet, however, had no weekend plans and so spent much of it at the theater. To her surprise, she found she liked being in the thick of all the bustle as the old building was systematically stripped back and reborn. Plus, it beat staying at home and dwelling on how empty it was. The famous five had popped in to lend a hand at various times around their weekend jobs and familial responsibilities, even though Harriet hadn't asked them to, and she'd been pleased to see them. Perhaps the old building had bewitched them too.

On Monday evening after a shower to de-grime, she flopped down onto the sofa just as Ali called.

"Hey, how's it going at the Hammer Horror theater?" he asked.

"Making progress. We finished clearing the rubbish in the auditorium today."

"And the famous five showed up for duty?"

"They did. Actually, they've been brilliant. Some of the stuff we were clearing was pretty grim, but they kept at it."

"Maybe if we throw some rubbish around the study halls, they'll be more likely to show up for class."

"It's something different, I suppose. A change of scenery and all that. Plus, you know there's a buzz about the place with all the maintenance teams there hammering and drilling and their radios blaring. It feels like we're a part of something."

"And how is the handsome specimen that is James Knight?"

"He is by turns surprisingly thoughtful and a completely closed book."

"I found his profile on LinkedIn. He does look like he would have hidden depths," said Ali dreamily.

"Yes," Harriet responded. *But is he going to let me dive into them, or will he continue to mine my secrets while keeping his buried at the bottom of the ocean?*

"And?" Ali persisted. Gossip was his drug of choice.

"And what?"

"Are you a thing?" he pressed.

"I don't think so."

"But you find him attractive."

"Anyone with eyes would."

"You're so cagey!" he said exasperatedly, and she laughed.

"Did you call your aunt Prescilla about the am-dram group yet?"

"I did, they're called the Great Foss Players. She's given me the number of the director, one Gideon Clarke. Got a pen handy?"

"A director, that sounds promising." She scribbled down the number he gave her.

"Don't get your hopes up, we're not talking team Julian Lloyd Webber here."

"They'll be more professional than anyone on team Humbug, that's for certain. Thanks, you're a star. I'll give him a call tonight. How were things after I left? I feel bad leaving work early."

"You're not leaving early; you're leaving at the time you're paid till—it's called clocking off. You're so accustomed to doing free overtime every day that you've become conditioned into thinking it's normal."

Harriet rubbed her temples. "Things are going to get missed." She couldn't bear the idea of somebody falling through the cracks because she was distracted . . . again.

"They won't. The rest of the team have all promised to pull their weight, except for Cornell, of course."

"Of course. Did Saffron get her personal statement finished after I left?"

"Finished and sent."

"And what about Harvey's university application?"

"Completed."

"I called the food clinic about Aurora's new meal plan three times today, and each time it rang off the hook. We really need a response on it," said Harriet.

"Leave that with me, I'll chase them tomorrow. That reminds me, Susan said Cornell dumped all his parent/guardian-teacher consultations onto you, is that true?"

"Yes, it is, he sprang that particular delight on me just as I was leaving this afternoon. It's retaliation because he thinks I went behind his back with Evaline Winter to score brownie points with the dean."

"Why didn't you say no? You've got your own consultations to do."

She had been asking herself the same question all evening.

"Well, I guess he's so good at delegating his responsibilities that I know his students better than he does, and their guardians too. So it makes sense for me to do them, rather than have him sat in front of them simply reading out my notes. The least the kids on our list deserve is to know that we give a turd about them."

"You should suggest that to the dean as the new school slogan: 'Foss Independent: We give a turd.'" He laughed at his own joke.

"Thanks for helping me out, Ali, I really appreciate it. I'll thank the rest of the team for stepping up too."

"Wellll . . ." He stretched the word out. "It's not that we're helping you out as much as we are doing the jobs that we're being paid for. You're always so busy being the queen of fucking everything that you kind of take on our work too, and we let you do it because we are flawed humans. Essentially all that's happening here is a righting of the scales."

She frowned. "Oh." *Is that true?*

"You're kind of a control freak, Haz."

"Am I?"

"Yeah. Sorry. I mean, I totally get why. It's that kind of job, the kids on the list are in our care and it's easy to get obsessive. But equally—and forgive me if I've mentioned this before—I have two degrees, two master's degrees, a PhD in counseling and psychology, and five years of Harriet Smith pastoral care boot camp under my belt. I know what I'm doing, as do we all, apart from Cornell, who must surely have been made head of department due to a typo."

Harriet laughed. Ali consistently reminded her how qualified he was if she tried to micromanage him.

"You make me sound like a right bossy-boots," she said.

"I only want you to see that you can rely on us. Let us do the job that you employed us for."

"Have I ever told you how amazing you are?"

"All the time. I only stay in this job for the adulation."

....

The call ended and Harriet's worries were somewhat relieved, aside from learning that everyone on her team thought she was a control freak. She looked down at the number from Ali's aunt. *Now's as good a time as any.*

She tapped the number into her phone and waited.

"If this is a sales call, I am not interested," a sonorous voice boomed out, "and I will hang up in three, two, one—"

"Oh, wait! No, no, don't hang up, I'm not a cold caller, Mr. Clarke. I was given your number by Prescilla's nephew about a possible drama collaboration . . ." She spoke very fast, hoping he wouldn't cut her off.

Silence filled the air for a handful of seconds, and she wondered if she'd lost him.

"A collaboration?" The man rolled his tongue around the *r* like a tiger purring.

"Yes!" The relief was evident in her voice. "It's all rather short notice, but I'm hoping you can help us. We're putting on a production of *A Christmas Carol* and we are short on numbers, and to be honest, we could do with some advice from experienced dramatists such as yourselves." By the tone of his voice alone she could tell he was the sort who required flattery.

"And who, might I ask, are you?"

"Oh, ha! Yes, sorry. My name is Harriet Smith."

"And the name of your society?" His boredom dripped through the speaker.

"My society? Oh, you mean our group! Um, we are a collective from Foss Independent School."

"Students!" His tone was so scathing he might as well have declared *Excrement!*

"Yes. Bright young things, full of enthusiasm and talent just waiting to be unleashed." Was she hamming it up too much?

"And how many *students* make up this collective?"

"Five."

"*Five! Five*, you say?"

"I was hoping you could add to our numbers."

"You want the Great Foss Players, an amateur dramatics society renowned in several counties for their professionalism, to add to the numbers of a *school play?*"

Oh, well, now he was just being rude.

"Not a school play, no. Our venue is the Winter Theater, and our production will be a one-night-only performance of *A Christmas Carol* by Charles Dickens in front of the dignitaries and townsfolk of Little Beck Foss." She didn't know if there would be dignitaries there, but it sounded like the kind of bait Gideon might go for.

Incoherent blusterings ensued before Gideon Clarke rediscovered his voice.

"Preposterous! The Winter Theater has been defunct for half a century!"

Aha! Gotcha!

"It is being refurbished as we speak, Mr. Clarke." She echoed his superciliousness. "And my students— handpicked by Ms. Evaline Winter—will be the first and possibly the last actors to tread its boards under that name."

"Ooh-ahh-brrrr-hoho-ahem." He was spluttering like an old generator. "Well now, that puts a different slant on things."

"I thought it might."

"Harriet, was it?"

"Yes."

"Please call me Gideon."

"Okay."

"Leave it with me. It will be a huge imposition, of course. The Great Foss Players are much in demand, especially during the season of goodwill to all men. But I will see what I can do. If it is within our power to assist in bringing this production to fruition, then we are bound by the sacred code of thespians to help."

Every word he uttered boomed.

"Thank you," said Harriet.

"Have you approached any other dramatic societies for assistance?" he asked.

"Not yet," she confessed.

"Bravissima!" he boomed. "I'll be in touch!"

And with that, the line went dead. *I think that went rather well*, she complimented herself, and headed for the kitchen, where a delectable three-course meal of a packet of crisps, a carton of instant noodles, and two mince pies waited.

THIRTEEN

BY TUESDAY THE TWENTY-FIRST OF NOVEMBER, JUST ONE week since Harriet had discovered her students in the crusty old theater, the building now resembled a work in progress rather than one awaiting the wrecking ball. The stage had been fixed and declared safe, and almost all the ropes, rigging, and sandbags, bar those holding up the curtains, had been removed. The bulk of the maintenance team now focused their expertise on the main lobby and backstage areas. You couldn't go ten paces without finding someone wearing a toolbelt and wielding a hammer, tape measure, or drill. Paint fumes drifted out from private dressing rooms and public bathrooms, while the lobby smelled like burnt varnish and sawdust as the handrails and balustrades of the main staircase were sanded down.

Delittering the theater had instilled the famous five with a sense of personal investment in the space, which Harriet hoped would help their motivation in the weeks to come. She had brought in an old travel kettle, tea bags, and coffee and set up a makeshift breakroom in one of the recently painted dressing rooms. The original old mirrors, patchy with oxidization, still lined one wall with the dressing table running beneath them. The names of long-forgotten performers were scratched into the wood alongside the stains of old greasepaint, the waxy tang of which still lingered in the air.

Ken had informed her that the carpets would be replaced sometime in the next week. But some of the original features were salvageable. A team of professional upholstery cleaners dotted the auditorium, dressed like Ghostbusters with heavy packs on their backs as they steamed fifty years of dust and dirt out of the seats. The whirr of their machines echoed around the space. The chemical freshness of upholstery shampoo had all but eradicated the pungent perfume of stale beer, tobacco, and urine.

"I think it might be better if we work in one of the dressing rooms for now," Harriet said over the ruckus.

"Ahh, miss, it's too cramped in those rooms," moaned Isabel.

"The paint fumes make me feel dizzy," agreed Carly.

"Yeah, but it's too noisy in here," reasoned Leo.

"It's even worse in the foyer," added Ricco. "It sounds like the chain saw massacre."

Harriet puffed out a breath. "Well, where, then?"

"What about the basement?" Billy asked.

Harriet frowned. "There's a basement?"

Billy shrugged. His friends eyed him with curiosity; clearly, they didn't know about the theater basement either.

"It's under the stage," he said. "It's kinda hidden."

"Wait a minute. How do you know about the basement, and I don't?" Ricco looked hurt.

Billy shuffled on the spot.

"I used to come here sometimes before, at night."

"Weren't you frightened, by yourself? In the dark?" asked Isabel. "I would be. This place is creepy enough in the daylight, I only hung out here because of you guys."

He looked down at the cigarette burns on the carpet. "Buildings don't frighten me . . ."

Harriet felt her chest constrict. Once again, she was reminded of how tenuous some kids' safety ropes were, how reliant young people were on the adults who were meant to protect them, and what could happen when those adults let them down.

"Okay, then, Billy, lead the way. Wait, it's not dangerous, is it?" Harriet asked.

"Define 'dangerous,'" Billy replied, grinning.

Harriet shook her head. "You kids will be the death of me."

She fired off a quick text to James, letting him know where they would be, and then followed Billy up the steps onto the stage, then into the left wing, where it was darker. Billy flicked on his phone torch as they walked gingerly through the space and squeezed single file past stacked wooden stage blocks, eventually reaching a narrow staircase—hidden from view unless you knew where to look—that led down into darkness.

"This is some *Phantom of the Opera* shit," mumbled Ricco.

There was no need to whisper and yet they spoke in hushed tones as they tiptoed down the rickety stairs. The door at the bottom was unlocked and Billy pushed it open, causing a gust of cold, musty air, with more than a hint of old weed smoke, to whoosh past them up the stairs.

"Did I mention I'm claustrophobic?" Leo hissed as the step he was on let out an eerie creak.

"It opens out, once you get inside," Billy replied. He flicked a switch on the wall and a line of naked bulbs swinging from the ceiling sputtered to life.

"Holy shit!" Carly breathed.

"Sick!" Ricco was grinning ear to ear.

Though the ceiling was low—held up by wooden pillars reinforced with steel—the space itself was wide. By Harriet's calculations it ran beneath the stage and stretched all the way to the back of the building. It had obviously been used for storage over the years. Dust-covered packing crates and stage props were stacked up against the walls. A few feet away from the door, almost hidden by an old bedstead, was a chair she recognized as belonging to the cocktail lounge, a stack of books and toppled beer cans on the floor beside it—Billy's, she presumed. She glanced around. It looked safe enough, structurally at least, but she couldn't be sure it wasn't haunted.

"Leo, are you okay with this or would you rather we found somewhere upstairs?" she asked.

He looked about him, keeping a tight hold of Ricco's hand, and took a deep breath as though testing himself within the space.

"I'm all good, miss." He nodded. "Can we keep the door open?"

"Of course. And we can leave at any time if you change your mind."

Billy dragged a sandbag across the floor and used it to prop the door open, then moved to a nearby packing crate, flipped up the lid, and began handing out rolled rugs and scratchy wool blankets.

"To sit on," he said when faced by quizzical expressions.

So they did. Harriet checked her phone. No signal. She breathed through the electric zip of anxiety that having no signal induced.

"It does have a touch of torture chamber about it," Ricco commented, sitting cross-legged on a tartan throw.

"God, Ricco!" Isabel admonished, shuddering. "Don't say things like that!"

"I've got beer," said Billy, producing a four-pack from behind the chair.

"Yes!" shouted Carly.

"No!" said Harriet.

"School's over, this is our free time," Ricco grumbled.

"You are still in my care and underage," Harriet replied firmly.

Billy put the beers down on a crate. "We can drink them when we go out for a smoke," he said, like this was a reasonable compromise.

Harriet let it drop for the moment. To be honest, she wouldn't say no to a glass of wine right now. It had been a hell of a day. Two of the pastoral team were off sick with a stomach bug, and a truant student had been caught snorting speed in the bus station toilets. She'd be writing reports in bed again tonight.

Despite the cavelike atmosphere, the basement was comparatively quiet, and they quickly fell into discussing the bare essential—due to Harriet's constant reminders of "shoestring budgets"—sets and props they would need. She had spent her lunch break googling production necessities and had made lists accordingly.

"It would be cheaper and easier if we could paint old sheets to use as backcloths rather than trying to find wooden boards large enough and then having to shift them between scenes," said Harriet. "The rigging will be all new, if we can work out how to use it."

"I think you'd need to sew a few sheets together to make it large enough," Carly said ponderingly.

"Yes, you're probably right." *I'll just add it to my list of things to do, shall I? I can sew them with my toes while I use one hand to write up my reports, the other to email*

*parents, and if I stick a feather duster up my bottom, I can
dust the shelves at the same time!*

She could feel herself sinking into the depths of de-
spondency when Leo asked quietly, "Can I design them?
The stage backdrops?" And just like that, her head broke
the surface, and she was buoyant again. It was what she
had been hoping for, but she had known better than to
ask. Leo was skittish and terrified of failure. If she'd
asked him outright to oversee their scenery design, his
knee-jerk reaction would have been to refuse. She'd
needed to wait for it to be his idea, his choice.

"I know every scene." He proceeded to pitch his
ideas—as though it were necessary. "I can picture what
each one looks like in my head. The dingy fireplaces, the
leaded windows behind Scrooge's desk looking out onto
the snowy street scene. The Cratchits' kitchen. The roofs
over the city when he's flying with the ghost. Look." He
pulled his sketchbook out of his bag. "I've been working
on them. See. I've only done six so far, but I already know
what the others will be, you know, if I'm allowed to do it.
And I could easily copy them bigger onto sheets or whatever." He opened the sketchbook and handed it to Harriet, and she took it, smiling warmly at him.

She looked at the pages. *Whoa!* She knew Leo had a
talent; his work was plastered all over the art studio walls
in the school. He was the art teacher's most prized student, and his most frustrating. It was one of the reasons
Harriet tried so hard to keep his attendance up; he had
the potential to study in one of the best institutions in
the country—Goldsmiths or the Royal College of Art,
even—but he'd need good grades and references and a
clean record to get an interview.

She turned the pages with reverence. Leo's world of

graphite lines and careful finger-smudged shadows was alive with movement.

"Leo, these are incredible," she said, noticing the blush blooming in uneven patches on his pale cheeks. "I can't think of a better artist to design our backcloths. You are now our art director."

"Really, miss?" His whole face was now a mass of magenta splotches; beneath his blue hair, his natural coloring was pumpkin orange, and like most redheads he didn't blush by halves.

"Absolutely. Think how this will elevate your EPQ! You can examine your own experiences alongside your study of Edvard Munch's set designs. I could speak to Mr. Norton too, see if you can use your backdrops as part of your A-level submission . . ." *Calm down! You don't want to spook him.* She took a breath. "Do you mind if I show the others?"

He shrugged, seeming to fold in on himself. "Yeah, no, it's fine, whatever."

She passed the book to Carly, who began to coo over them, and Isabel leaned in closer to her so that they could share the pages between them. Ricco scooched over to where Leo was sat on a checked wool blanket, his knees pulled tight into his chest and his head resting upon them. Ricco knelt in front of him and gently hooked a finger beneath Leo's chin, lifting his face so that their eyes were level.

"I told you they were good, didn't I?" His voice was soft, so different from his usual gregarious tone. "You've got this."

Harriet watched them, her heart doing little backflips of joy. They were good for each other. Each boy hid from the world in his way but was made braver by the other's temperament. Ricco was loud and outrageous as a means of keeping people at arm's length. By contrast, Leo was taciturn. Unlike Billy, whose quiet was usually brooding, Leo's reticence—like Ricco's vivacity—was a protective mechanism; he folded himself small and pulled himself inward, making himself invisible to all but a chosen few.

In the process of averting his eyes from his friends' tender moment, Billy had become fixated on a large packing crate in the far corner. Isabel looked up from Leo's sketchbook and saw him.

"I swear to god, Billy, if you're about to pull some Blair-Witch-in-the-corner shit, I'm outta here," she said, following his gaze.

"No, it's not that. I've just remembered something, from when I first came down and had a bit of a scout about . . ." He stood and began walking in the direction of the crate.

"What is it?" Harriet asked, getting up to follow him. The light didn't reach very far and the corners were rendered gloomy lumps in the shadows.

"I'm going to pick up Sid again today, but I'll only be gone for half an hour or so and then we'll be back." Billy didn't make eye contact as he led the way to a packing crate and stopped. "In here."

"Billy, are you sure everything's okay at home? You collected Sid yesterday and Friday."

"It's fine," he snapped, and then adjusted his tone. "It's not a big deal. It saves Tess a trip."

Harriet tried to read his expression, but his face was in shadow.

"Give us a hand?" Billy was smacking his fist under the lip of the wooden lid to loosen it.

Harriet did the same on the other end and together they pulled off the lid, coughing as dust motes swirled around them. She peered over and looked inside. Lying one on top of another were long rolls of pale, canvas-like fabric.

"I didn't really think about what they were at the time." He gave a shrug. "I didn't know I was going to be forced into being a drama nerd. I was hoping I might find something I could sell. Or a body." He grinned.

"Eww, Billy! You morbid little soul. Here, help me pull one out."

Grabbing an end each, they heaved out the roll nearest the top of the crate and laid it on the ground.

"I really hope this is what I think it is," she said.

"Me too."

She used her boot to shove at the roll, which unraveled like a giant scroll along the ground. It was, as she had hoped, a backcloth. It was somewhat yellowed with age and a little brown around the edges, but it was unused, and it was exactly what they needed. It must have been stashed there and forgotten when the theater closed down. It was miraculous that it hadn't been nibbled by mice or moths, and thankfully the crate had saved it from the worst of the damp. They pulled out another three, to be sure, and they were blank too and in equally good condition. Harriet felt as though they'd been given a gift from the gods. And she wouldn't need to sew anything with her feet.

"Leo, your blank, slightly stale canvases await you," she said, grinning.

Leo hugged his sketchbook to his chest and smiled.

FOURTEEN

THE ORNATE DOORS IN THE FOYER THAT LED TO THE DEFUNCT restaurant and cocktail lounges next door had been opened up, and work had begun in earnest on those sections too. The old kitchens were ripped out and were being replaced with new stainless-steel fittings, while the bar and restaurant areas were treated with the same sensitivity as the theater proper as restoration works began to bring them back to their former splendor. Clearly, Evaline had confidence that her efforts would attract buyers with big bucks.

With teams working around the clock, the old buildings quickly became their own village; faces became familiar, starting with nods and smiles and moving on to greetings and conversational snippets as they passed each other in the corridors.

On Wednesday evening, as she drew near to the giant shimmering Christmas tree in front of the theater, she saw great rolls of red fabric being ferried into the building. New curtains. She smiled, excited, and dodged between them, taking the stairs two at a time and pushing through the main double doors to the balcony just in time to see the old stage tableau curtains—which pulled up into swags revealing the players—collapse heavily down from their invisible tracks in a sea of languidly rippling fabric the color of cranberries. They landed with a muted *flump* on top of all the other curtains, which helped to reveal and conceal the magic of the stage and now lay discarded across the boards. These last and largest drapes released a cloud of dust into the air that rolled out into the auditorium like a gray sea fog.

Though she knew that none of this renovation was for her or the famous five, in moments like this it felt like it was *all* for them. It was thrilling to think that they would be the first people to put on a show here in fifty years, that theirs would be the first faces behind the new drapes, the first feet on the newly polished boards, the first voices to carry out into the resuscitated auditorium. Of course, it was terrifying too, but all troughs had their peaks, and these moments helped to temper her exhaustion as she worked all day at the school and then all evening at the theater.

She couldn't see the famous five, but Leo's loud sneezing echoed around the auditorium. The dust was an acrid twang in her nostrils, and she didn't think they could realistically work here this evening.

"Harriet!" Ken's voice snapped out. He came up behind her just as she reached the three teenagers who had taken refuge from the dust in the farthest corner of the dress circle. She turned to see Ken hanging on to the back of Ricco's jacket with one hand and Carly's sleeve with the other. Ricco's jaw was jutted out in indignation, and he kept trying to wriggle out of Ken's meaty grip.

Carly spat, "Get off me!"

"I caught these two smoking a joint out the window of the downstairs toilet."

Harriet's good-mood bubble popped. She glared at them. *Give me strength!*

"I'm sorry, Ken, it won't happen again," she said pleadingly. *Please don't call the police . . . or the school!*

Ken released his grip on the pot-smoking duo. Ricco shook himself and schlepped over to the rest of the students, throwing himself into a seat in the stalls with a face like thunder, but Carly flicked a double bird and shouted, "Fuck this shit, I'm outta here!" and started walking toward the side exit.

"Carly!" Harriet shouted.

"I'll get her, miss," said Billy, leaping to his feet.

"I've got this, lad," said Ken. "Oi! You! Carly!" he boomed. "You walk out that door and you're off the team. D'you hear me? Everyone gets one chance to screw up and this was yours, but if you leave now, you're barred. There's no coming back."

Harriet put her head in her hands. She felt sure Carly would keep on walking; that girl spited herself more than anyone else ever could.

"Come on, Carls," said Billy. "Don't be a dick."

"We need you!" Isabel called.

"What about our duet?" Ricco added.

Carly had reached the door.

"One chance, Carly," said Ken, only slightly booming. "Make the right choice. Stay and be part of this team. Everyone wants you here. Don't blow it."

To Harriet's astonishment, Carly turned back and looked at them.

"You're not the first person to make a mistake, lass," said Ken. "It's how you deal with them that counts. Come back over here and take the bollocking that I'm about to dish out to you and your mates and then it's done. Over. We never need to talk about it again."

Harriet held her breath; she knew the warring emotions that would be colliding in Carly's head. *Come back!*

Harriet willed her. Carly took a step toward the group, then another and another. Her hands in her pockets, her head held defiantly high. She reached them and sat down between Ricco and Leo. Leo reached both his arms around her and pulled her tightly to him. "Thank you for staying," he said quietly.

Ken nodded, and Harriet waited for her heart to return to normal speed.

"Okay then, now we're all present and accounted for," Ken began. "This is technically a building site and as such is under my jurisdiction, and I do not tolerate drugs being consumed on my site. Do I make myself clear?"

"Absolutely." Harriet nodded emphatically.

"What about the rest of you?"

They each mumbled their understanding. Ricco looked sullenly up at Harriet and added, "Sorry, miss."

"All right," said Ken. "That's the end of it, as far as I'm concerned, but cross me again at your peril." He puffed out a breath that seemed to instantly dispel his displeasure. "Blimey, it's dusty as a spinster's bloomers in here— why don't you take the kids into the cocktail lounge to work this evening. We can't do any more in there until the new wall plaster's dried, and it'll be a darn sight quieter than it is here."

"Thanks, Ken." She smiled at him. She wanted to hug him, but she held back. He rubbed the back of his neck and made a dismissive *pft* sound.

"Well," he growled, "all that dust's no good for their young lungs."

Ken carried on down toward the stage and began to bellow orders at his team, and five sets of eyes bored expectantly into Harriet's face. She met each of them in turn.

"Okay," she began in her quiet but dangerous voice. "I

think we can all agree that was a stupid thing to do and that 'it' and all variations of 'it' will not happen again."

"Are you going to dob us in?" asked Ricco.

If the same situation had occurred at school, she would have been duty-bound to report them. But this was after hours, and they were not representing the school. Ricco's dad smoked medicinal cannabis to treat his chronic pain, and though he would doubtless be annoyed with his son, the chances were that Ricco had swiped the joint from home in the first instance, which rendered it a somewhat gray area. And as for Carly, her stepmum had left with her younger brother last year when her dad had lost his job, and his functioning alcoholism became the nonfunctioning kind. No good would come of telling him.

She let out a long breath. "No. I'm not. But this is your one and only pass. You heard Ken. I need all of you with me if this is going to succeed."

Ricco nodded. "Thanks."

Carly, who still had her head on Leo's shoulder, mumbled, "Yeah, thanks. Sorry."

"Okay," said Harriet. "I am officially drawing a line under this incident. As far as I'm concerned, it's done, put to bed, and we don't need to visit it again. Now let's get out of here."

"I was hoping to make a start on the first backcloth tonight." Leo sniffed and sneezed again. "The only space big enough to lay them out flat is the stage."

"At the rate this crew works, I doubt it'll take longer than a couple of days to replace all the rigging and hang the new curtains, and then it'll be all yours," Harriet said.

"There won't be any need for backcloths if we don't start rehearsals soon," added Isabel, worrying at her black-painted fingernails. "I'm not gonna make a twat of myself in front of everyone I know."

"Too late," Billy smirked. Isabel punched him in the arm.

"The work we've done so far is all relevant." Harriet tried to sound confident even though she'd started checking her phone hourly for news from Gideon Clarke. "It's important that we familiarize ourselves with the way in which the play is structured. And then there's the language; it's no good simply reciting the lines. If you don't understand the meaning of what you're saying, your cadences will be off."

"Who's that up there with James?" asked Carly, who clearly hadn't listened to one word Harriet had said.

"Maybe he's brought his mum along," Ricco sniggered.

"Looks like Cruella de Vil," said Isabel.

Harriet followed Carly's pointing finger up to one of the royal boxes overlooking the stage. James looked down and gave her a halfhearted wave. Sat next to him was Evaline, a pair of opera glasses held to her eyes. *Oh god, had they seen all that play out?*

"That is our patroness," said Harriet distractedly. "The theater owner."

"I wonder what she wants," Carly said.

"To wear your skin like a coat," Ricco quipped, and the others snickered.

"Um, you guys go on ahead, and I'll meet you in the cocktail lounge. If anyone tries to stop you, tell them it was Ken's idea." Harriet shooed them off and began to make her way to where Evaline observed them from on high.

"Good evening." Evaline's voice scratched as Harriet pushed through the curtain into the box. The stale reek of old dust was stronger here, closer to the stage, and for once Harriet was glad of Evaline's overpowering lily of the valley perfume.

"Hello," Harriet replied. She steeled herself. "How long have you been here?"

"Just long enough to catch the end of Ken showing the students how to project their voices," said James quickly. Holding her gaze and nodding imperceptibly at her. "An impassioned speech from *Romeo and Juliet*, if I'm not mistaken?"

Harriet wasn't sure she had ever wanted to jump a man's bones more. She smiled brightly and hoped her legs wouldn't give way with relief.

"Yes," she replied. "The Prince of Verona, Act One, laying down the law."

"As I thought," James replied.

"Yes, yes, but what about the new curtains?" Evaline snapped.

The new curtains had completely slipped Harriet's mind.

"Oh, we're all so pleased about them." Harriet hoped she was effusing the right amount of gush. "It's very generous of you."

"I wasn't going to bother, but Mr. Knight convinced me that since everything else was being necessarily replaced, I might as well 'go the whole hog.'"

Harriet felt sure that was the first time Evaline had ever uttered such a phrase.

Down on the stage, people lined up in a row and began moving forward as one, slowly rolling up the old curtains like a giant roulade. Backstage—which was visible to all now that the curtains were gone—was occupied by a swarm of maintenance people climbing up and down tall stepladders, the tops of which were hidden by the wooden painted pelmet that framed the stage. Ropes like thick jungle vines hung loosely down and coiled on the stage boards waiting to be made useful again.

"It's very kind of you," said Harriet. "We appreciate it."

"It isn't kindness, it's business," Evaline barked.

"I wonder, have you thought any more about securing a spot for the community in any contracts for sales going forward?" Harriet asked.

"No."

"No, you haven't, or no, you won't?" she pressed.

"I take it that was your cast?" Evaline gestured with her opera glasses at where the famous five had been sitting.

James gave Harriet a look, which she conjectured to mean *Don't push it*. She gave him the benefit of the doubt, but she'd take it up with him later.

"So far, yes," said Harriet. "We're hoping for some new additions soon."

Evaline's mouth turned down in distaste. "I must be going. It's Cook's night off."

"Of course." James nodded. "What's on the menu this evening?"

"Risotto. It takes time to make it right and you know how I like to eat at eight o'clock sharp."

"You're making it yourself?" Harriet blurted, incredulous.

"I like to cook. You seem surprised, Ms. Smith."

"Oh. No. I mean, yes. I mean. It's only that I wouldn't bother making something like risotto just for myself, I'd probably buy one that I could microwave."

Evaline stared at her hard and when she spoke her voice was flint. "Am I, in your opinion, not worth cooking for?"

Harriet swallowed. "No. That's not—"

"But you do appear to be suggesting that the effort to cook good food should only be undertaken when there is someone else present, and that a person who has no one but themselves ought not to bother."

Evaline had pinned her absolutely.

"I was just thinking about myself, really, about how I don't tend to cook if it's only, well, me. My daughter's been away, and I'm still getting my head around it."

"*Only?*" Evaline exclaimed. "*Only you?* 'Only' and 'me' are words that should not be used together. Being alone does not make a person less worthy of good things. *I* deserve to prepare myself delicious food, whether that be a risotto for supper or a soufflé for breakfast or both. *I* refuse to curtail life's little enjoyments because I am without a companion. *I* am worth the effort, and *you* should feel the same way about yourself, young woman. Don't live your life as though you are only a shadow without other people to validate you. Validate yourself!"

Harriet opened and closed her mouth a few times saying, "I, I, I," but she had nothing.

James, seeming to sense that she'd had her mind blown by their haughty benefactor's words, stepped in. "Evaline, would you allow me to escort you safely home?" he asked.

"I don't need to be seen home, safely or otherwise. I'm not an invalid," she snapped.

"Of course." James, in Harriet's opinion, had the patience of a saint. "In that case, I'll join Harriet and the students in their endeavors."

"You can help me down the stairs." Evaline narrowed her eyes. "Or would you have me fall down and break a hip? That would keep me out of your hair for a while, wouldn't it? Perhaps I'd break my neck and save you any more bother."

It was incredible to Harriet that someone could be so insightful and such a cow-bag all at the same time. James's eyes rose to the gold-painted ceiling of the box, and she knew he was counting to ten in his head as Evaline stowed her opera glasses in her handbag and, using her two sticks, creaked herself up to standing. She wobbled and listed to the left, and Harriet put her arms out to steady her but got a stick jabbed into her shin for her troubles.

"Don't fuss so!" she snapped. "I can do it."

"You are a tempest of contradictions!" Harriet snapped back without thinking. "You're either so frail that stairs could kill you or you are indestructible—which is it?" She rubbed her leg.

Evaline grinned, making her thick pink lipstick crack.

"So, you have got a backbone after all. Perhaps James was right about you."

Harriet cast a quizzical glance at James.

"I only said you had what it takes to make this project work," he said, trapped between Evaline's and Harriet's gazes.

"'Gumption,'" Evaline croaked out. "That's the word he used. I didn't believe him. But, well, we shall see. James." She held out her arm. "Till we meet again, Ms. Smith."

....

The group had settled themselves at a pasting table in the cocktail lounge and were discussing Ebenezer Scrooge's motivations and how he came to be so hardhearted when James joined them.

"Could I have a quick word?" he asked, catching her eye.

"Of course."

"Ooooh!" Carly said in a singsong voice.

"Old-person love is kind of cute," said Leo, smiling.

Harriet shushed him as she stood to leave. *Old-person love indeed!*

They pushed through the saloon doors and out into the corridor, where a man wearing a Nike cap backward and over-ear headphones was expertly layering plaster onto the wall, while a woman in dungarees was painstakingly reconstructing a section of broken cornice.

"I'm sorry about Evaline," he said, when they were out of earshot. "She speaks as she finds, and she generally finds a lot to speak about. She can be a bit much."

That's an understatement!

"As much as I hate to admit it, she's got me pegged. She's astute, I'll give her that much. Thank you for, you know, not ratting me out to Evaline about Carly and Ricco's little indiscretion. I assume you heard it all."

"I got the gist," he said. "Thankfully, Evaline had turned down her hearing aid because of all the building noise."

"I guess I caught a break on that one."

"I imagine Evaline would have strong views on recreational drug use, especially in her theater," said James. "You would likely have lost any chance at a community space going forward. Unlike Ken, she doesn't give second chances. She barely gives first chances."

"I honestly don't know how you tolerate her."

"This may sound hard to believe, but she grows on you." He pulled a face like even he couldn't believe what he was saying.

"Like skin tags," she deadpanned back, and he laughed.

"More like a wallpaper that at first you think you'll never get used to until after a while you find you've grown quite fond of it."

"Hmmm. I think it'll be a long time before I feel any kind of fondness for Evaline Winter."

"Well, anyway, I'm sorry that she gave you a hard time. If it's any consolation, it means that she likes you. If she didn't, she wouldn't bother."

"Tough love, huh?"

"I think tough is the only language she knows. This theater was her father's whole world and there wasn't much left over for his only daughter."

"That's sad."

"He had no time for her when the theater was thriving, and then when things started to go downhill he became a recluse, shut himself away from everything and everyone."

"Including Evaline," Harriet guessed.

"He sent her away to school. It needn't have ended in the way it did. The theater could have kept going on a smaller scale but he refused to open it up to local productions, preferring to have no show at all than what he deemed as beneath him. His snobbery was the death of the place, and eventually the death of him too. Evaline blames this place for ruining her father. She's worked tirelessly to rebuild the Winter family fortunes and left the theater to rot."

It was hard for Harriet to picture Evaline as a girl, desperately trying to get her father to notice her. "I guess letting a bunch of student dramatists loose in her dad's hallowed theater is one way of giving her old man the bird."

He laughed.

"You could be right. Fitz-William had a lot of offers for the building when the theater closed. He even had one from an Italian casino owner who wanted to extend his empire and he felt Little Beck Foss was the place to do it."

"Really? Here?" Harriet was incredulous.

"Las Vegas wasn't much more than a dusty little railroad town before the casinos went up. Maybe this guy thought he could do the same here. It's all academic anyway, because Fitz-William turned down the casino and all the other offers, even though Evaline begged him to sell up. This place is her own personal ghost."

"Well, now I just feel sorry for her," Harriet harrumphed.

"Don't. She's a difficult, spiteful, selfish woman, and I say that as someone who genuinely likes her. There are plenty of people who've had it a lot worse than Evaline who have seen their way to be far nicer humans. But her history helps me to understand her, and that in turn enables me to represent my client's interests to the best of my ability." He checked his watch. "I have to make a call, but I'd like to join the group afterward if that's okay?"

She smiled and said that it was. He was a conundrum. His emotional intelligence was very attractive. But his willingness to work for a woman so wholly unpleasant gave her pause. Then again, he was a solicitor, that was his job . . . and then her phone chimed with a call from a parent, and her contemplations were pushed to the back of the queue.

FIFTEEN

BY THURSDAY EVENING, HARRIET WAS BEGINNING TO FEEL the pressure. Four weeks from today there would be a theater full of punters expecting to watch *A Christmas Carol* on the stage. She still hadn't heard back from Gideon's Great Foss Players. And her quest for costumes had been a bust; Cornell had got wind that she'd been sweet-talking the drama department technician for wardrobe loans and had sent her a snitty email.

It felt like too much of her time was spent putting out small fires instead of concentrating on the blaze. Today was a case in point: she'd attended four compulsory departmental meetings and proxied for Cornell in three others because he declared them to be a waste of his time. Most often her presence was merely an exercise in box-ticking, and she was always left with a bubbling undercurrent of frustration at having to neglect the more practical elements of her job.

Now she was sitting on a chair on a stage listening to a bunch of teenagers and a grown man bicker like toddlers in a sandpit. She was tired, cold, and hangry. The four cardigans over her pinafore might have been made of chiffon for all the good they were doing, and the fearsome draft around her ankles was making her long for Jane Fonda–style leg warmers.

"I didn't make the rules," said James when Ricco threw his arms in the air dramatically. "We'd have to pay a licensing fee for the copyright to *A Christmas Carol* the musical, which takes it off the table. End of."

Thus far he had managed to successfully shoot down all their ideas without a hint of positive reinforcement. He would really benefit from the "unconditional positive regard" workshop she and Ali had arranged for the last professional development day at Foss.

"Let's not be too hasty," Harriet interjected. "Ricco, I like your idea of introducing a musical element; I'm sure there must be a way around it. I don't think we need to take singing off the table entirely."

James rolled his eyes. "Of course you don't. God forbid you agree with me."

Harriet ignored him and picked up her phone to search theater licenses. The bickering continued around her.

At least Leo was happy. He had spread one of the backcloths out across the freshly mopped stage and was diligently drawing out the images from his sketchbook. He expressed himself via his hair color and his artwork, which was preferable; the last time his emotional dam burst, a chair had gone through a window.

"You're a lawyer." Ricco looked accusingly at James. "You must know about loopholes. Isn't that how you keep rich white people out of prison?"

Oh gawd, here we go again! She scrolled down the government website to the section she needed.

"Dude! Nice burn," said Billy, holding up his hand, which Ricco gleefully high-fived.

"That is both presumptive and offensive, and I will not dignify it with a response." James's tone was condescending.

"*I will not dignify that with a response,*" Carly mimicked

in a voice so laden with snobbery that Harriet had to stifle a snicker behind a cough. She felt James glaring at her.

"Found it!" She held up her phone triumphantly. "Evaline will need to acquire, if she hasn't already, a public performance license if she wants the theater to be fit for purpose. So, while I don't think we have the time to get a whole musical under our belts, you could choose a couple of songs that would fit with the play, and we would be covered by the theater's license."

Phew! Another crisis averted. Although James was looking at her like she'd just wiped a bogey on his suit trousers.

"Ooh, Kate Winslet sang 'What If' for one of the animated versions. I've learned all the words to that one already!" Carly was bouncing on her chair. Her mood this evening was the complete opposite to that of the night before.

"Yeah, that's a good one," agreed Ricco. "I know it too. Done my Chazzer Dick homework!"

"I'm not sure we should nickname one of Britain's finest writers Chazzer Dick," said Harriet.

"Nicknames are affectionate, miss," offered Isabel.

"I trust that after all this you can actually sing?" James's tone was snippy; he was clearly still smarting after Ricco's last remark.

"Oh, I can vouch for that," Harriet jumped in quickly. "They sang a Taylor Swift duet in the Foss end-of-year talent show, they were incredible."

"I love that you're such a Swiftie, miss," said Leo, looking up from his backcloth.

"I cannot deny that Taylor Swift has my whole heart," Harriet said, smiling.

"Are you a Swiftie, James?" Isabel asked.

He looked discombobulated. "Um, I'm not sure I know much of her work."

Bless his misguided life.

"I'm not singing," said Billy.

"Me either," added Isabel.

"You don't have to. Nobody needs to do anything they don't want to," Harriet assured them.

"Except put on a play," Billy grumbled.

"Precisely."

"Excuse me." A short woman in a leopard-print hijab stood at the bottom of the stage steps. "I'm looking for Harriet Smith."

"That's me," Harriet said, standing. "Can I help you?"

"I'm rather hoping you can. Could I possibly steal you away for a few minutes? It's a community matter."

"Oh, um . . ."

James stood and said, "I ought to leave now anyway, I've got some work to do."

"Me too," said Isabel. "My mum's working nights this week, I've got to put my brothers to bed."

"I'll walk you home," said Billy. And then to dispel the catcalls from Carly and Ricco, he added, "It's on my way anyway."

"I didn't mean to break up your meeting," said the woman. "We can arrange a time that suits you better."

Harriet smiled at her reassuringly.

"No need, we were about done here anyway. Would you like to get a drink? There's a bistro along the way that serves coffee all evening."

"Sounds perfect." The woman smiled broadly back at her.

"I'll just grab my coat from the dressing room, and I'll be with you."

James followed her backstage. "Why do you always side with them?" he asked as they walked the corridors.

"I don't."

She did.

"Demonstrably, you do."

She chewed the inside of her cheek. "Well, somebody needs to be in their corner."

"What about my corner?"

"I think you fill your own corner just fine."

They reached the dressing room, and Harriet wrapped her scarf around her neck.

"But it undermines me, and it only succeeds in further pitting them against me. How am I supposed to build any sort of rapport with them when you behave like their gatekeeper?"

"To be honest, James, I've seen very little evidence of you trying to build any sort of connection with them."

"I saved their bacon last night!"

"Yes, you did, and I am grateful to you for it, but I'm talking about personal connections, letting them know that you're on their team."

He looked ready to shoot back something defensive, and then he seemed to change his mind.

"I want to be on their team." The anger had gone out of his voice, leaving behind a kind of dispiritedness. "I want *them* to know that I'm on their team. But I can't seem to judge it right, I keep putting my foot in it. And if I'm being completely honest, they, well, they . . ."

"They scare you a bit?" she said softly, making sure to catch his eye so that he knew she wasn't mocking him.

He grimaced. "I hate to admit it, but I think maybe they do a bit. They're so unpredictable. I never know what's going to come out of their mouths next. Or what they're going to do. One minute it's all singing and dancing and the next they're punching walls, literally."

She laughed as she pulled her coat on. "But you're a solicitor. Surely you must work with unpredictable people all the time?"

"I deal with adults. I can read adults, they're straightforward, they may think they're complex, but I can break them down and see how they tick. These guys . . ." He rubbed his jaw, which was well into five o'clock shadow. "They're all over the show, I can't get a handle on them."

She shrugged. "That's teenagers for you. Look, they haven't been set in stone yet, they're still figuring themselves out. Did you know that a teenager's brain goes through a literal process of reconfiguration? They are not only physically changing but neurologically too. Imagine having to deal with school and peer pressure and exams and family and all that other stuff, all while there's an illegal rave happening inside your brain."

She pulled on her bobble hat and adjusted her hair in the mirror. James watched her reflection intently, his eyes studying her face as though seeing her again for the first time. She turned back to him.

"Okay," he said, nodding as though answering a question only he could hear. "What do you suggest I do?"

"Try to relax around them. And then just accept that you've bought a one-way ticket for the banana express and lean into it. It's the only way."

"Right. Banana train. Got it."

She finished doing the buttons up on her coat. "And I'll try not to be quite so gatekeepery around them."

"Thank you."

....

The famous five had scarpered by the time Harriet got back to the auditorium, and James had left through the newly replaced back door, leaving the mystery woman alone on the stage.

"Sorry about that," Harriet said, throwing her bag over her shoulder.

"No problem at all, I was just marveling at this interior. I've never been in here before. I'm Hesther, by the way."

"Good to meet you, Hesther." She shook her hand. "It's a pretty awesome place, isn't it? I'd never been here until a week ago and now I feel like I live here." She chuckled. "But it is beautiful. Especially now that the repairs are properly under way, it's like Sleeping Beauty waking up. Come along then, I could use a treat."

The bistro was situated halfway along one of the narrow alleyways off the high street. Its bay windows were bowed with age, the little square panes of glass so thick you could see neither in nor out. Flower-shaped sconces glowed amber on the rough plastered walls, and candles flickered on the tables. There wasn't a straight wall or floorboard in the place, and each table was fine-tuned by pieces of cardboard wedged under the legs to stop them from wobbling.

They ordered two bowls of French onion soup, and each nursed a steaming cup of decaffeinated coffee—it was after seven p.m.—while they waited for their food to arrive. Hesther was a striking woman. Her dark eyes were defined by black liquid eyeliner with perfect flicks at the corners, and a bright purple lipstick enhanced her heart-shaped lips.

"You've probably heard that the community center

had to close all its spaces?" said Hesther. The community center had designated meeting rooms dotted throughout Little Beck Foss.

"I did." *This town!* she thought. *Always cutting back the resources most needed.*

"Well, it's left some of the groups out in the cold, literally. I run a group for refugee women, a safe space where people can meet and cook together and make new friends, you know, just find some sense of community in a new country. We like to share food. The familiar flavors can be a great comfort, especially for those living away from loved ones. We run a few courses alongside to help with their English-speaking skills and give them the tools they need for entering the workplace if that's what they want. Anyway, I've been looking for a new place to set up camp and I was told that you might be able to help us."

Harriet took a sip of her coffee as she considered. Technically there was plenty of room. And Evaline had agreed in principle to her idea for a community hub. And Hesther's group was a part of the community very much in need of a home. Would Evaline agree? Probably not. Would Evaline need to know? Maybe not?

"How many of you are there?" she asked.

"Usually about twenty, give or take. Sometimes they bring their children."

"Do you know what? Yes, absolutely, the more the merrier. It's a bit like playing musical chairs—there's a lot of shifting between spaces depending on where the maintenance teams are, and it gets pretty noisy, you heard that for yourself. But it's friendly and we'd be honored if your group would share the space with us."

Hesther's smile was wide and joyful. "Thank you. You don't know what it means to these women."

"Don't thank me, I don't own the building; I'm pretty

much squatting there. But if you don't mind squatting alongside us, then you're very welcome. I can't guarantee that it's a long-term solution to your problem. The owner might feel differently to me, but what she doesn't know . . ."

"Ah yes, the infamous Evaline Winter." When Harriet eyed her curiously, Hesther continued, "Some of the women in the group live in her buildings, and let's just say the property maintenance companies in her employ don't deserve their title."

"Oh." She had heard something of this from Pete, and now here too. She would speak to James about it; surely he couldn't condone such negligence. "I'm sorry to hear that."

"It isn't your fault. I am learning that is often the way with landlords who own multiple properties: they're quick to buy the buildings up at auction but slow to maintain them on a day-to-day basis."

"Well, one thing you can be sure of, the team renovating the theater is excellent and very supportive of us being there. I'm sure they'll welcome you too." She was thinking of Ken's bonhomie, how it infused every space he inhabited.

"You are a lifesaver," Hesther enthused.

Harriet laughed. "Hardly. Can I ask, who pointed you in my direction?"

"A solicitor. Mr. Knight. I emailed his law firm to ask if we had any rights with regard to community areas. Unfortunately, we don't, no surprise there. But he very kindly wrote back to me and told me to come and find you. He said if anyone would help me, you would."

Harriet's blood became honey in her veins. She wasn't sure why, but knowing that hers was the name on the tip of James's fingertips warmed something inside her.

"Funnily enough, Mr. Knight—James—was the man you met at the theater."

"Really? Oh, I wish I'd known, I would have liked to thank him in person for his help."

"Never mind, you'll be seeing plenty of him, he's at the theater almost as much as I am. I'm glad he pointed you in my direction. Come whichever days work best for you and your group. I'm only there in the evenings— aside from weekends—because I work during the day, but I'll give you my number." She scribbled it down on a napkin and handed it to Hesther. "And if you let me know when you'll be coming, I can alert the maintenance teams."

"Evenings would probably work for us too, most of us work during the day. I get the feeling you stay busy too; Mr. Knight outlined your project in his correspondence."

Harriet laughed the maniacal laugh of overworked and underappreciated women everywhere.

"Rather too busy. But there's nothing to be done about it. And it's only another few weeks until the end of term, and then hopefully I won't be quite so tired."

Only *a few more weeks! Lawks! By the time this is over I'm going to need a cruise, shares in a sensory deprivation tank, and an intravenous ginseng drip to aid my recovery.*

Hesther was looking at her with concern.

"Is your employer being supportive?"

This time her laugh was a harsh bark. The pile of paperwork on her desk plus the extra that Cornell had delegated her way felt like a mountain on the verge of an avalanche.

"No. They are not."

"Could you ask to take some leave?"

She thought about her empty flat and a lonely Christmas. *Schrödinger's mum.* At least when she was working, she had a purpose.

"To be honest, I don't mind keeping busy at the moment. You know," she said, stirring her coffee, "the maintenance team just put a brand-new stainless-steel kitchen in one of the restaurants at the theater. I'll ask Ken, but I'm sure he wouldn't mind if your group used the kitchens."

"Who is Ken?"

"Oh, he's the site foreman. He shouts a lot, but it's all bluster. He's sort of taken my students under his wing, a bit like a granddad who scolds them and looks out for them all at the same time."

"I think we could all do with a Ken in our lives." Hesther smiled.

"I think you're right."

"Thank you," said Hesther, suddenly serious. "It will mean a lot to my group. It's hard to start all over again in a new country, especially when English isn't your first language and your accent sets you apart. A little kindness goes a long way."

Harriet felt a twinge of guilt for complaining about being tired and lonely in her warm and safe life.

"I'll be happy to help you all settle in." A thought occurred to her. "If your group would like a project, we're in need of hands to help us paint up some sets and backdrops. We have an excellent artist in our midst, young Leo—blue hair," she added for clarification, "who has designed all the backdrops and is working on drawing them onto the backcloths. We could really use some extra hands to help us paint them . . . once I find some paint . . . and brushes. We're what you might call a ragtag outfit." She covered her face with her hands and let out a tired huff. "What am I doing? I'll be honest with you; I'm making it all up on the fly. To say I'm out of my depth would be an understatement."

Hesther gave her a knowing look. "I'd never started a community group before this one. I'm a receptionist at a dental surgery, not a social worker. But here I am. Some people follow a calling and some, like us, stumble into one. Consider us part of your team. Put us to work. It'll be like the art therapy I'd love to provide if money weren't an issue," she said with a wry smile. "But I'm guessing you know all about that."

Harriet nodded in sympathy. "Unfortunately, I do."

Hesther clapped her hands together as though to dispel any gloom, a sunshiny expression on her face.

"I can't wait to give the group the good news. One of our members was an interior designer in her old life, I'm sure she'd love to stretch out her design muscles."

"What does she do now?" Harriet asked.

"She works for a cleaning firm, cleaning offices. We have a former cardiologist who does the same." Her smile slipped. "These women held up the sky in their old lives; here they are invisible at best and targets of xenophobia at worst. I can't magically change everybody's mind about them, but I can help make it easier to survive here."

Harriet felt like she understood Hesther on a cellular level; she saw her own driving force mirrored back at her.

"I get it," she said earnestly. She placed her hand over her heart in an effort to make Hesther feel her sincerity. "I don't have the right words to explain myself, but I honestly get it."

Hesther smiled at her with wise eyes.

"I know that you do. I saw it the moment I clapped

eyes on you with your students." She grinned. "Mr. Knight knows it too."

Later, after she'd cleared her work inbox for that day, she lay back against her pillows, replete with French onion soup and good conversation, and thought about Hesther and her women's group. She realized that her ambitions for a community space went beyond the needs of her students. Everyone deserved a safe sanctuary, no matter their age or station in life, and she would challenge Evaline and whoever bought the place to ensure that the Winter Theater reserved a space for anyone in Little Beck Foss who needed it.

And then she remembered what Hesther had said regarding Evaline being a crappy landlady. She wasn't surprised where Evaline was concerned, but she'd expected better from James. She set a high bar for herself, and she would be doing herself a disservice if she lowered it simply because he had a very nice face and had given her two orgasms on the night they'd met. He had become her new favorite sexual fantasy and she was loath to part with it, but she couldn't in all good conscience continue to perv over him if he was complicit in his client's dodgy dealings. Words would need to be had, and the sooner the better.

SIXTEEN

IT HAD SNOWED AGAIN IN THE NIGHT AND LITTLE BECK FOSS positively sparkled on Friday morning as Harriet made her way to school. The huge Christmas tree outside the theater had fully come into its own now that its bauble-laden branches were also slathered in thick white snow-flakes. The newly restored glass doors at the front of the theater were open, and she could see the frenetic activity inside, hammering and sawing sounds drifting down the path toward her, and she suddenly wished she were headed in there instead of to work.

Her phone rang as she reached the school grounds. It was Emma. She swished at the powdery snow on a low wall and sat down.

"Hello you, what are you up to?" she asked.

"I'm getting ready to take my parents Christmas shopping," Emma replied.

"Cripes. Good luck with that."

"We're taking the train, which means I can drink a bottle of wine at lunch to ease the pain."

Harriet laughed.

"I'd rather be spending the day with your parents than at Foss."

"Blimey, work must be bad! Listen, I need to book you up in advance. I've been working on a marketing campaign for a small vineyard down south who want to expand their sales reach into the north—sustainability, vegan wines and smaller carbon footprints, et cetera . . ."

"What an eco-warrior. You are to booze what Greta Thunberg is to the rest of the planet."

"I know, there'll be a special place in wine heaven for me. Anyway, my campaign caught the eye of an art gallery in Penrith, and they've ordered a few crates for their upcoming exhibitions. As a thank-you-slash-bribe the winery has acquired a couple of tickets for me to the opening night of an up-and-coming young artist's exhibition next Thursday to take some pics for their website. Fancy it?"

"Who's the up-and-coming artist?"

"No idea."

"Doesn't Pete want to go?"

"I haven't asked him. I'm asking you. Pete's had nonstop Christmas dinners with clients for the last fortnight; he can stay home and give his cholesterol levels a break."

"I'll be at the theater."

"Leave a bit early! I'll pick you up from there at half seven. Even you are allowed to take an evening off."

"I've got so much to do—"

"Which is exactly why you should come out with me. It's not good for you to spend every single night in your Scroogy flat working till your eyeballs fall out."

"If I don't work until my eyeballs fall out, I'll get behind. And my flat is not Scroogy."

"It is too. The only excuse I'll accept is if you've come up with a cunning plan to seduce James that night."

Harriet snorted. "I have not. He wants to take things slowly. He is determined to get to know me better first. He used the word 'meaningful.'"

"What a bastard."

"Right!"

"So come with me. It's just one night. I'll drive, you can drink free wine, and we'll look at some art and get cultured."

"Like kombucha."

"Yes, and kefir."

"All right, I could do with a change of scenery."

"Yay! That was way easier than I thought it would be. I had a whole layered strategy of guilt and emotional blackmail ready."

"Oh, I'm sorry, do you want to use it anyway? I promise to react receptively."

"No, it's fine," she said in a voice laden with mock weary. "I'll bank it and keep it for next time. Waste not, want not."

"And that is why you are the queen of sustainability."

....

Eight hours later, Harriet banged the snow off her boots and pushed through the theater doors to be greeted by smells of fresh paint and sawn wood. The lobby renovations were almost complete. The plaster moldings on the ceiling had been painted back to their original white, and now a woman in a blue boilersuit stood on top of a scaffold tower painstakingly applying gold leaf to the ivy and the edges of the rose petals.

"Good afternoon to you, Harriet!" Ken called as he trotted down the staircase. "Or should I say good evening, it never feels right to me that night falls before teatime in the winter. Still, this too shall pass and before you know it there'll be Easter eggs in the shops."

She smiled. "Hi, Ken, how's your day been?"

"Not too bad. I'm doing the late shift today, so I spent the morning with my grandkids. Ooh!" He held up his hand. "I've got something for you, wait a mo." He disappeared through one of the doors behind the box office and came back wearing a big grin and carrying a large canvas tool bag, which he handed over to her.

It was heavy, and when she looked inside her heart grew two sizes. It was full of paintbrushes and fat tubes of black and brown acrylic paint.

"You are an angel!" she squealed, dropping the bag and reaching her arms around the burly man to hug him.

"Get away with ya." He laughed good-naturedly as she released him.

"Leo's going to be delighted," she gushed. "They all are. Thank you!"

"Aye, well, those that work hard deserve a helping hand in my book. Speak to Caz, she's working in the cocktail lounge this evening; she's got a load of paint for you. We had a bit of a scout around the warehouse last night, there's always paint left over from jobs. It's mostly half tins, odds and sods, and I can't vouch for the colors, but they're yours if you want them."

"This is . . ." She couldn't find her words; they seemed to be circling her heart in a dance of gratitude. "Thank you, Ken. This means such a lot. It's a huge help, I really appreciate it."

"Well, you know what they say," he said as he began to stride away. "It takes a village!"

It certainly does!

....

The snow had triggered high spirits in the group. Everyone was feeling particularly festive, even more so after Harriet had given them the gift from Ken. Leo was wearing a Rudolph jumper with a glittery red pompom nose under a pair of paint-splattered tartan dungarees and had dyed his hair holly green. He was kneeling on a length of backcloth, drawing a giant replica of his sketch of Mr. Fezziwig's Christmas party.

"We have also been gifted some tins of paint. It should be enough for us to get started, at least," said Harriet as Billy and the others inspected the bag of brushes.

"Can I paint too?" asked Sid, who was spending the evening with them because Arthur had a hospital appointment. Harriet tried not to be worried; it was normal for older people to have niggling health problems, it didn't mean anything.

"Course you can, Sidney!" Leo ruffled the boy's hair, and Sid grinned like a chimpanzee.

"It's still a lot to do, though," said Billy, eyeing the other eleven rolls of fabric stacked up nearby.

"Well, we may have some help with backdrops and other things if we're lucky. Remember Hesther, the woman who popped in yesterday? She runs a group for refugee women and they're going to be sharing the theater with us. They are keen to be involved with the behind-scenes stuff."

"That's so cool," said Isabel.

"I think I know who they are," said Ricco. "They helped out sometimes at the old-person coffee mornings my granddad used to go to at the community center. They brought in snacks; one of them makes the best baklava I've ever tasted."

"I hope they bring their snack skills with them," said Carly.

"I've got raisins!" said Sid, holding out a small box of them for Carly.

"You keep them, Sid. But thanks." Carly smiled at him.

Sid had been adopted as everyone's little brother, and

they looked out for him and kept him in line accordingly. He had dark eyes like Billy and appraised everyone with the same intensity, which could be construed as confrontational if you didn't know them better. Harriet knew this was simply the brothers' way of taking the measure of people, seeking out those they could trust.

"Right." Harriet clapped her hands. "Let's sit and discuss what our next steps should be."

"I've got some ideas for scenery," said Isabel. "I reckon I know where we can get our hands on some free stuff."

This made Harriet a little nervous, but she smiled and said, "Okay, let's have a chat about that."

"What shall I do?" asked Sid.

"You will be an important part of the theater team; we need to know what you think of our plans," Harriet told him.

Sid grinned up at her, one front tooth missing. It was impossible not to adore him, and she felt a bit sad that in a few short years, all that childhood glee would likely be replaced by the same teenage scowls his brother wore.

James arrived as they were setting up chairs on the stage around Leo working on the floor. She'd say this for James, he didn't shy away from a challenge. Harriet found that she looked forward to seeing him, enjoyed the burst of butterflies in her stomach at the first sight of him and the way those same butterflies settled into an easy peace in his prolonged presence, stretching and sunning their wings. But today those wings were lacking some of their luster. She was still troubled by the notion that he might be ignoring Evaline's shoddy approach to building management.

"Um, guys, I just need a quick word with James about . . . acoustics. Talk among yourselves for a minute." None of them needed to be told twice. She motioned to

James to follow her, which he did with a curious expression on his face.

She led him to the back of the dress circle and turned to face him.

"How much do you know about Evaline's private lettings?" she asked without preamble.

He frowned. "It's not my area. I deal mostly with her investment interests."

"Are you aware that she doesn't take good care of her properties? This one notwithstanding."

He rubbed his chin. "What are you getting at?"

"I've heard things, from two sources now, which suggest that she isn't as good a landlady as she could be."

He looked awkward. She folded her arms. "I mean, sure, I've heard mutterings, the odd complaint here and there, but I'm not privy to the ins and outs—like I said, it's not my area. I can tell you categorically that she isn't breaking any laws—she's meticulous on that score—but other than that I don't get involved with that side of things. I have a full schedule of my own to contend with, and now a theater production to monitor too . . ."

Harriet pinned him with a hard stare, the one she used to crack her toughest cookies at school. The one that asked, *Are you absolutely certain about that?*

"What do you want from me?" James asked. "I only work for her. Surely an employee isn't responsible for all their boss's business decisions. Do you take issue with the dean of your school about all his adjudications? Why are you looking at me like that? It isn't my area . . ."

She raised one eyebrow and continued to stare.

"Okay, fine," he said, relenting. "I'll look into it. I'll do some digging and if I don't like what I find, I'll flag it. Are you happy now?"

She rewarded him with a small smile. "I think 'happy' is too strong a word, but I am satisfied. Thank you."

James shook his head and muttered, "You should have been a prosecutor," under his breath.

"You're the one who said you wanted to do better."

"And it seems you're the one who's going to make sure I stick to it."

"Are you annoyed that I brought it up?" she asked.

"No. I'm *embarrassed* that you brought it up and *annoyed* at myself for not chasing it sooner."

"Sometimes things get pushed to one side when we're busy. It's easily done."

"I don't imagine you let anything slide, no matter how busy you are."

The splinter in her heart smarted, like it always did, reminding her of irreparable things.

"Catastrophic failure is a good motivator." The words were out before she'd had time to check them, but when she saw his look of concern, she pushed a smile onto her face and walked briskly back to the group before he could ask more questions.

....

James sat opposite Harriet, sandwiched between Billy and Ricco, a well-used copy of the book held loosely in his hands, long fingers turning the browned pages, one ankle resting on the opposite knee. Today he had swapped his suit for a black cable-knit sweater, dark blue jeans, and a pair of chestnut-colored Chelsea boots. He looked surprisingly at home discussing Charles Dickens. She wished she didn't find him quite so nice to look at.

"The movie *Scrooged* with Bill Murray did it really

well," James suggested, which to Harriet's delight was met with enthusiastic agreement from Ricco and Carly.

"I agree. What did you have in mind, Billy?" Harriet asked.

"We were thinking maybe we could do a modern-day version, you know, keeping the dialogue the same, but really changing it up like Baz Luhrmann did with *Romeo and Juliet*," Billy suggested.

"Certainly not!" A deep baritone voice echoed around the theater.

Everyone on the stage turned to see a man in a tweed cape with matching trousers and a bright green shirt protruding from his cape flaps striding down the middle aisle. A gaggle of equally colorful characters followed behind him.

"I cannot control what happens behind the film camera lens, but the purity of Dickens upon the stage will not be polluted on my watch!" the man continued. He stopped abruptly halfway down the aisle and held up his hand for the people behind him to do the same. Harriet was getting strong *Toad of Toad Hall* vibes. He looked to be well into his seventies, though his hair—thick and swished to one side à la George Michael during the Wham! years—was the color of canned pineapple.

Harriet recognized his pitch and condescension from their phone conversations.

"Mr. Clarke," she called, standing and making her way to the edge of the stage.

"Please." He smiled graciously and opened his arms wide to encompass the whole stage. "Call me Gideon."

"Gideon." She smiled back, hoping he couldn't hear the snickering from behind her. "Thank you for joining us."

"Where there is drama, there are the Great Foss Players!" He swept down into a low bow, his cape flaps flopping forward, then straightened and turned to the people behind him, presenting them to the group on the stage with a flourish of his wrists. They in turn bowed in an exaggerated way that gave the impression of being here to serve while assuring everyone present that they in fact only deigned to be here as a kind of theatrical rescue party.

"Great!" Harriet smiled widely.

"May I first draw to your attention the distinct lack of wheelchair access," said Gideon. "It wasn't at all ideal for Mallory to have to wheel herself through three miles of corridor to reach the auditorium."

"Oh gosh, yes, of course, you're absolutely right. So sorry about that, Mallory." Harriet addressed the woman in the electric wheelchair, who was dressed in layers of autumnal-hued knits, with chopsticks holding up a barely contained bun of gray curls on the top of her head. "Ken is working on getting the lift up and running again as soon as possible."

As she said this, two members of the maintenance team arrived carrying a ramp to fit against the stage.

"Ken thought you might need this," one of them said jovially as her colleague helped her to clunk the ramp into place. They gave a cheery wave and a "Tally ho!" and left the auditorium.

"Okay." Harriet smiled, feeling relieved; the last thing she wanted to do was alienate one of the actors who'd come to help them. "Let me introduce you to the team," she said, and she went around the circle calling out each student's name while gesturing toward them. The students mostly scowled at the newcomers, though Isabel managed a halfhearted wave and Leo gave a side nod from his position on the floor.

By this time Gideon had skirted around the orchestra pit, his cane—seemingly more accessory than necessity—tapping on every stair with a metallic clack as he ascended the steps to the stage. Once atop it, the rest of the Great Foss Players looking up in hungry anticipation, he flapped one half of his cape back over his shoulder and waved his cane around the circle of chairs.

"And who, if any, of you have theatrical experience?" he boomed. Isabel quaked visibly, and Billy slid farther down in his chair. The others raised their hands with varying degrees of confidence.

"They are all studying drama, theater, and English literature, or variations of the arts," said Harriet when no words from her students seemed forthcoming. "So they are familiar with stage plays in general, and they each have an excellent grasp of this particular text. They are all keen to be hands-on with the process, aren't you!" She smiled benevolently at her students, who, under her encouragement, seemed to find their voices again. Carly, Ricco, and Isabel sat straighter as they responded with more confident yeses. "And Leo has designed our backdrops; as you can see, he's a talented artist."

Gideon viewed them down his long nose, and his eyes flickered over Leo's backcloth.

"And who is this?" he asked, pointing his cane at Sid, who grinned back at him like a cartoon cat.

"This is Sid, Billy's younger brother and honorary member of the team," Harriet said.

"Do you want to be on the stage, young man?" Gideon boomed.

"Okay," Sid replied, completely unaffected by Gideon's posturing.

"Good. Well then, it seems we have found our Tiny

Tim, at least." He eyed the rest of the group with a distaste that made Harriet nervous.

"They all have a good knowledge of each character's
lines, so whichever part they get, they'll be ready, won't
you, guys?" She nodded enthusiastically at her students.
"We've spent the last week really knuckling down on
character motivation to get inside the soul of the play."
Perhaps this was overkill, but she wanted Gideon to
know that her kids were serious and up to the task. "Carly
and Ricco are super keen to perform the 'What If' song
during Scrooge's encounter with the Ghost of Christmas
Past."

Ricco sat up straighter but was quickly cowed by the
probing glares of the Great Foss Players.

"Hmmm, we'll see," Gideon snapped, eyes aglow as
they roved around the group, taking in Isabel's facial
piercings, Leo's green hair, and Billy's beaten-up boots.

Harriet saw them through Gideon's eyes, knew the
conclusions he would be leaping to, and her protective-
ness sprung up like a forest vast and deep. Gideon continued in his pretense of an appraisal, but she realized
with a sinking feeling that he'd made his decision even
before he'd hung up from their phone call.

"Perhaps there will be parts for them," he postured.
"Perhaps not. This is not a school play. We will be performing before a real audience of theatergoers. Ours will
be the first voices to grace these hallowed halls in fifty
years!" he boomed dramatically. "We will be making *history*! We cannot afford to give parts to *just anyone*, not
when we have real actors in our party. Grace played a
plague-ridden hag in a History Channel docudrama,
and Douglas has twice been used as a cadaver in *Silent
Witness*." The two actors in question preened under the

praise. "But we will have need of stagehands and dressers and the like—rest assured your protégés will be put to good use."

Harriet's hackles rose. "With all due respect"—her voice was clipped—"while I bow to your superior knowledge of the stage, I asked you here for your help with our production, not for my students to be ousted."

Gideon looked at her as though he'd just sniffed her fart. "My dear woman . . ." he began, condescension lying heavily on the word *woman*.

Harriet clenched her fist. Gideon continued.

"This is a professional theater, hallowed ground to those who are called to tread the boards. It requires, no, it *deserves* actors who can do this stage justice, and the Great Foss Players are seasoned performers. We have performed in such productions as . . ."

Gideon lost his train of boast as James stood, unfolding himself to his full height, which was a good foot taller than the thespian. Gideon quickly recovered his stately posture, and when James held out his hand, he took it as one might handle a dead frog.

"My name is James Knight. I am acting as representative for Miss Evaline Winter, owner of this theater." His voice was smooth and commanding, and Harriet wondered if anyone anywhere had ever resisted him when he turned on the full Knight charm offensive.

She imagined him using that voice to ask her to undress while he watched her from an armchair, legs crossed, suit on, stare intent, his fingers tented as he watched . . . Something deep in her core gave a delightful zing, and she had to pull her mind back out of her knicker department before she started noticeably salivating. *Not the time or place, keep your head in the game. Is it hot in here?*

Gideon's whole persona had changed. Suddenly he was all overly white teeth and graciousness.

"Delighted, dear sir, delighted, I am sure. May I say on behalf of the Great Foss Players just how overwhelmed with profusions of gratitude we are that the great doyenne of the theater herself has decided to resurrect this once-great house of the arts to its former glory."

"You may," James replied coolly. "I should inform you that under Ms. Winter's strict instructions, Harriet Smith is to act as director of the production; she is, for want of a better term, the top banana."

This was news to Harriet, who couldn't feel much less like the "top banana" if she tried. But she appreciated James drawing a line in the sand. Gideon opened his mouth to protest, but James added, "This is nonnegotiable. What Harriet says goes. And I am sure that a devotee of the arts such as yourself will appreciate how vital it is to encourage new blood into the theater. These young people are bright and determined. To turn away enthusiastic fledglings is not only counterproductive to the cause but also self-destructive."

Oh my! Harriet had never wanted to throw her knickers at a man more. *Champion me, it'll score you some points; champion my kids, you're likely to score a home run!*

Gideon's arms were windmilling, as though he was physically backtracking, and he grinned emphatically to show his strenuous agreement. "Of course! Of course! So true! It's like I am always saying to my company." He gestured behind him. "We are but guardians of the craft, sages waiting for willing vessels such as these that we may pour forth our years of wisdom until their cups are replete."

Judging by the expressions of the rest of the Great Foss Players, gathered below the stage, this was not something that Gideon was "always saying" to them. Harriet had googled the am-dram group and knew that they mostly performed in their local Scout hut, with occasional productions playing at the Great Foss town hall. It must have felt like quite a coup to have a whole theater dropped into their laps with only a handful of teenagers and a member of support staff standing in the path of their ambitions. But Harriet had no intention of being railroaded by anyone, and neither did James. As Ricco had so eloquently put it, this was their crapfest, and nobody was going to muscle them out of it.

SEVENTEEN

INTRODUCTIONS WERE MADE—AS WERE SNAP JUDGMENTS—on all sides. The average age of the Great Foss Players was sixty-five to the famous five's sixteen, and the divide was stark. One or two of the more maternal figures made an effort to engage the five and were rewarded with enthusiastic responses from Ricco and Isabel. Grace, an upright woman wearing tweeds with an air of a dog trainer about her, got off on the wrong foot with Billy by picking Sid up on his use of the word *ain't*.

"What are you, the vocabulary police?" Billy snarled.

"I was simply correcting his usage, there is no need to be rude."

"Rude is picking on the way someone talks."

"In my day, we respected our elders!"

"In my day, you have to earn it."

"Insolent boy!" Grace expostulated.

Billy merely glared at her with a bored hostility, which raised her hackles even further.

"Billy, can I have a quick word?" Harriet asked quietly. He shrugged and followed her to the side of the stage. When they were out of earshot, she said, "I know it's hard, but please try not to antagonize the other actors."

"She started it, snobby cow."

"I know, but equally you are quick to take offense. You need to learn to rise above these things or you'll have raged yourself into a heart attack by the time you're thirty." Billy made to protest, but she cut him off. "Please, for now, let's give her the benefit of the doubt. We've literally just met these people. They're probably as wary of us as we are of them."

"Is this how it's going to be from now on? You taking their side all the time?"

"That is not what I'm doing, nor will I. You lot are my top priority. But in the interest of actually making this production, we need to work together and that means swallowing down some of our annoyances."

"Right. We'll just let them walk all over us, then, yeah?"

Harriet narrowed her eyes at her charge. "All I'm asking is that you take a breath before you speak. They have experience that we need."

Billy grumbled but grudgingly agreed to try. Harriet could feel a hot flush rising up through her body, prickling over her collarbone and up her throat. *Not now!*

As more chairs were ferried up onto the stage, widening the circle, Harriet excused herself and sought refuge in the makeshift coffee room to gather herself. She ripped off her first and second cardigans as though they were on fire, followed by her cotton Liberty print scarf, which felt like boiling lasagna sheets draping over her décolletage. Leaning on the counter with one hand and fanning herself with a copy of the play with the other, she looked up at her reflection in the mirror. A crimson-faced version of herself stared back, her throat puce and glistening. She was out of her depth with this play malarkey; Gideon's arrival was liable to shine a spotlight on her ineptitude. Was she really up to this? Every part of her was sweating, even her earlobes. She hiked up the hem of her long linen pinafore dress and began to fan beneath it—no lady-garden anywhere deserved to be this hot.

"Ahem!"

Harriet whirled around to find Toad of Toad Hall himself standing in the doorway.

"Sorry to disturb your, um, ruminations," he said, rubbing his hands together.

She pulled the book out from under her pinafore and went back to fanning her face, which was now blushing on top of sweating.

"No need to apologize, I was simply taking a moment to regroup."

"Ah, yes. Good idea. I was wondering how you intend to proceed?"

"Oh. Um." *Gawd! I don't clucking know!* "What would be your suggestion?"

"Far be it from me to tread on your delicate little toes," he wheedled.

His slippery charm was making her nauseous. She pasted on a smile and imagined vomiting on his shoes.

"Please, tread away."

"Well, if it were me," he began faux humbly, "I would begin by putting together the cast. Really, nothing can progress until we know who within the production is who. The scenery and even the costumes can get away with being stylistically barebones, but the cast must be fully flesh."

She shuddered at the way he rolled his tongue around the word *flesh*.

"Right. Yes. Let's do that," she agreed.

"Excellent!" The hand rubbing went into overdrive. "Let's get this show on the road . . . or should I say, the stage!" He chortled. "Come, come, good woman, Charles Dickens awaits us!"

"You go on ahead, I'll be out in two minutes."

Gideon bowed and left the room. Harriet pressed first one and then the other cheek against the cold brick wall for a full minute each before heading back out to the stage.

....

Gideon clapped his hands, and the chatter around the circle quieted. Leo had left his drawings to join them. The famous five sat close to each other, but Sid had plonked himself between two doting women—Odette, whose long white-and-smoky-gray plaits did not look like they belonged with her impossibly smooth complexion, and Prescilla, who wore a pale-pink-and-mint-green sari with a granny square cardigan and held a Chanel handbag on her lap. These women were hell-bent on pinching Sid's cheeks and feeding him chocolate eclairs; his gleeful expression implied he felt he was winning at life.

"Time is of the essence, good people," Gideon began. "Therefore, auditions will be held tomorrow morning at eleven o'clock sharp! Mallory!" He held out his hand, and Mallory pulled a clipboard out of a voluminous carpetbag and handed it to him. He took it without thanking her and waved it in the air. "Here is the signup sheet. Use it, please. No slot, no audition. The cast list will be ready to view on Monday evening and will be non-negotiable."

Harriet raised her hand. "Just one moment, please, Gideon. Tomorrow is Saturday and my students have jobs and commitments on the weekends; morning auditions may not work for them."

Gideon looked affronted, as though he couldn't imagine anything more important than auditioning. Before he could formulate a comeback, she addressed her students.

"Guys, would early evening auditions work better for you?"

"I could be here by six," said Billy, and Carly and Leo nodded in agreement.

"I finish at six but could get here for half past?" said Ricco.

"I could do half five," Isabel said, her hand half raised when she spoke, as though she were in class.

"That's settled, then." Harriet gave Gideon her warmest smile. "Why don't we start the auditions at four o'clock for those who can do earlier, and the f—"—it was on her tongue to say *the famous five* but she stopped herself just in time—"five others, six if Sid wants to attend, can come later."

Gideon made some throaty noises but agreed.

"Fine. Auditions to begin at four p.m. tomorrow."

"Who decides who gets which part?" asked Isabel.

Gideon smiled cordially. "Myself, Harriet, and James . . . er, may I call you James?" He looked at James, who nodded. "I thank you." He gave a small bow and smiled wetly. "We will have the final say over the casting, but in the interest of democracy, anyone may voice an opinion and be assured that it will be considered."

Isabel nodded and Gideon carried on speaking.

"In addition to acting parts, I suggest we have four members of the chorus, taking alternate lines of narration throughout each act. It gives the narration a wonderfully otherworldly feel, as though a host of departed ghosts are looking down and chronicling us mere mortals below."

There were murmurs of agreement, and Harriet was pleased to see the famous five nodding.

"Why don't we do a read-through now, with all of us

present?" asked Harriet, keen to keep this feeling of harmony going.

"An excellent idea!" Gideon crooned. "Perhaps, James, you would be so kind as to read the role of Scrooge . . ."

"Oh, I won't be in the play," James protested.

"You don't need to be, this is merely a chance for us to bond through the words of Dickens. The theater is a sacred space, and we must become intimately acquainted with both the literature and each other if we are to dwell in its bosom."

James nodded and shifted awkwardly in his chair. Sid sniggered loudly at the word "bosom," and Grace tutted. Billy sucked in a breath, but Harriet caught his eye and he let it out in a huff.

"Now if we could have . . . you." Gideon pointed at Ricco. "Yes, you, young man . . ."

"This is Ricco," Harriet said helpfully when Ricco said nothing.

"Excellent! Ricco, if you would read for Mr. Scrooge's nephew, and I will be one of the 'portly gentlemen,' if you, Douglas, might read for the other?"

Douglas, a man with jowls like a British bulldog and a pair of round-rimmed spectacles balanced on the top of a sparse yet unrepentant comb-over, nodded with enthusiasm.

"And perhaps, I don't see why not, in this day and age. Yes, then." Gideon was a man who spoke out his inner monologue. "Perhaps, you, Carly, my dear, would like to read for everyone's favorite underdog, Bob Cratchit?"

"I don't have to be Bob in the actual play, though, do I?"

"No, Carly." Gideon gave her a grandfatherly smile.

"All right, then."

"Marvelous. Now for the chorus, I suggest we travel

clockwise around the circle, with all those who have not been assigned a character reading one sentence each of the narration. And last but not at all least, Grace, would you please be the voice of the stage directions?"

Grace gave a self-satisfied nod.

After a brief rustling of pages, the stage went silent and Gideon, using his cane as a conductor's baton, signaled that they should begin.

Marley was dead: to begin with.

There is no doubt whatever about that.

And so they went around and around the circle. Harriet felt a shiver down her spine. Gideon was right, having all their voices speak the lines in their different tones and accents was powerful; it lent the prose an almost religious quality. She could imagine how it would feel to be sat in the audience listening to their incantations fill the auditorium. For the first time since she'd been hurled into this crazy endeavor, she could believe they'd actually make it to the stage.

EIGHTEEN

"I FEEL LIKE A JUDGE ON *BRITAIN'S GOT TALENT*," JAMES LEANED in to whisper in her ear during auditions on Saturday afternoon.

It was dark in the stalls where they were situated just beyond the orchestra pit. Harriet was sandwiched between James and Gideon. On Gideon's other side was Mallory, dutifully taking down all of Gideon's notes like a court transcriber.

"You would be Simon Cowell, I presume?" Harriet queried.

"Clearly, I would be Amanda Holden," James shot back. "I am always quick to put people at ease."

She snorted. "Where was your inner Amanda Holden when I was being held at the police station?"

"That was different. It was taking all my effort not to keep visualizing you naked."

Harriet blushed into the darkness, feeling stupendously pleased.

"I expected more professionalism from you, Mr. Knight," she teased.

"I dare anyone to act professionally when being faced with the person who blew their mind and shagged their brains out the night previous."

"Oh!"

"Shhhhh!" hissed Grace, who was sitting two rows back.

"I blew your mind?" she asked. She pressed her thighs together and did a few sets of Kegels. It couldn't hurt to be prepared in case it ever happened again.

"In every way, Ms. Smith."

Holy shish kebabs!

On the stage, Ahmed graveled out Ebenezer's words. *"And the Union workhouses? Are they still in operation?"*

"Louder, please, Ahmed!" called Grace, who had adopted the self-appointed role of theater critic.

Mateo, a man who favored a *Miami Vice* style, had sidled into the row in front of Harriet and turned in his seat to speak to her and James.

"Hiroshi, my husband, is up next. He was a professional dancer, years on the stage. Mostly ballet but he dabbled in interpretive dance, did quite a few pop videos in the eighties, big names too, he worked with Kate Bush."

"Wow! Really? I probably watched his videos on *Top of the Pops*," said Harriet.

"Most likely," Mateo agreed. "He teaches now."

"Dance?" James enquired.

"He teaches a Jazzercise class at the Great Foss sports center, but he gets on the stage whenever he can."

"Next! Hiroshi, you're up!" Gideon's voice blared out beside her, making her jump.

"I'm so nervous for him." Mateo held both his fists to his mouth. "He really wants this!" He swiveled in his seat and began clapping and whooping as his husband took to the stage. Harriet kept craning her neck, looking for Isabel; she'd told Harriet last night that she wanted to be in the play, and she didn't want her to miss her chance.

"Who are you looking for?" James whispered.

She bit her lip. "Isabel. It's gone six, she said she'd be here early."

"Maybe she's slipped in through the back?"

She nodded but couldn't help feeling antsy. Isabel was so nervous she'd asked Harriet to run through her audition piece with her before she went on. She let out an anxious sigh and shifted in her seat.

Hiroshi had dressed in a long black cloak with a hood that covered his face for his audition for the role of the Ghost of Christmas Yet to Come. Prescilla, seated at the side of the stage, fingers poised over an electric keyboard piano, began to play Mussorgsky's "Night on Bald Mountain" and Hiroshi started to dance.

"Oh my god, he's terrifying!" Harriet whispered, awed, as Hiroshi slithered across the stage on feet so light it was as though he floated above the boards. There was a menace to his movements as he taunted and stalked his invisible prey.

"I'm having *Chitty Chitty Bang Bang* child catcher flashbacks," James mumbled.

Mateo leaned his head back and hissed, "We met him once, wonderful dancer!"

When Hiroshi took his bow, hearty applause snapped out from both stage wings and everyone in the stalls.

"Thank you, Hiroshi!" called Gideon. "Once again we are humbled to have your talent in our little gang." Then he leaned toward Harriet and James. "I don't think there'll be any dissension if I give him the part, will there?"

"He's got my vote," Harriet said.

"No arguments here," added James.

Gideon nodded, contented, and tapped Mallory's book, saying, "He's got the part. Put his name in."

Isabel arrived at half past six, with Billy and Sid in

tow. Harriet's relief was short-lived when she noticed that Isabel was a bit unsteady and more than once, she leaned a little too readily on Billy.

Oh no, she thought. *Maybe it's just the nerves . . .*

"And which part will you be auditioning for today, young lady?" called Gideon.

Isabel squinted past the spotlights trained on her. Harriet's stomach was a snake pit of nerves.

"Um, I wanted to try out for Bob Cratchit." Her voice sounded hesitant, and Harriet wondered if anyone else could see her swaying. "I waz-gonna-do-the-ouse-scenes . . ." She slurred the last few words together, and that was when Harriet knew for sure.

Silly, silly girl! Harriet quickly extricated herself from the stalls and made her way silently toward the stage, waving furiously at Isabel, but Isabel was too dazzled by the spotlights to see her and continued to sidestep left and right, occasionally stumbling into Billy, whose lips were pressed so thin with tension he looked like he might shatter.

"Billy!" Harriet hissed, but Billy appeared to have become stage-struck.

"Read on, Isabel!" Gideon encouraged.

"Um, would it be okay if Billy read the part of Mssscratchit?" Isabel asked. She covered her mouth and let out a loud belch. "He helped me with my lines."

"By all means," said Gideon, completely oblivious to the disaster waiting to happen. "Our Ms. Cratchit needs a scowling spouse as a counterbalance to her sunny disposition, and young Billy would appear to have scowls in spades."

Harriet heard the titters of laughter as she raced onto the stage to wrestle Isabel off it, just in time for the girl to vomit red wine all over the newly varnished boards.

Isabel swayed for a second, eyes wide with horror, and then fled from the stage in drunken zigzags and a flood of tears. Billy followed, with Harriet hot on their heels, leaving the squawks of disgust and outrage ringing out behind her.

Harriet turned onto a dim corridor and saw Billy barring Isabel's exit despite her heartfelt protestations. Billy acknowledged Harriet with a nod and Isabel turned, her face streaked with mascara and foundation, and puked again.

"Oh, sweetie." Harriet opened her arms, and after only a second's hesitation, the stricken girl collapsed into them and sobbed.

"I'm. Sorry," she hiccupped into Harriet's fourth-favorite cardigan.

Harriet sighed and rubbed her back. "What were you thinking?"

"I. Was. Nervous. I thought it would hellllp . . ." The end was lost to a slurred keen.

"Did you see how much she drank?" she asked Billy.

He ran his hands over his head as he sidestepped the pool of vomit. "I only saw one bottle. She'd already drunk it all by the time we met her. That's why we were late. I thought maybe if we walked for a bit, you know, it might sober her up."

One whole bottle of red was more than enough to floor a sixteen-year-old as slight as Isabel. Harriet hoped she'd thrown it up before she had a chance to get alcohol poisoning.

"Let's get you into the dressing room and get some water down you." Harriet turned with Isabel still curled into her like a baby bird and walked haltingly back along the corridor.

"I've ruined everything," Isabel wailed. "I really wanted the part! And I've got sick on your cardigan!"

"Never mind. It's not my favorite."

James met them as they reached the dressing room, his expression serious.

"Everything all right?" he asked tersely.

"Well, we've reached the remorseful stage of inebriation," Harriet replied, folding the still-lamenting Isabel into a chair and handing her a bottle of water. She knelt down beside her. Billy stood to one side, managing to look even more uncomfortable than usual.

"I'd better go and check on Sid," he said.

"Was this your doing?" James flared at him.

"He had nothing to do with it!" Harriet snapped. "Isabel is plenty capable of making her own mistakes." She looked at Billy, who was staring at James with such hatred she thought fire might shoot out of his eyes. "It's okay, Billy, I've got this, you go and find Sid. And maybe see if anyone on the maintenance team has any sawdust for the mess."

This caused Isabel to howl anew. Billy shoved past James as he left the dressing room.

"You can apologize to Billy when you see him again," Harriet said tersely without looking at him. She put an arm around the sobbing girl and Isabel leaned into her.

James stared out the empty doorway. "I'm not going to apologize for asking a question."

"You didn't ask, you accused. He's not a defendant in one of your prosecutions, so don't treat him like one."

"It's not Billy's fault." Isabel sniffed. "He tried to sober me up."

Harriet glared at James, lips pursed in the universal

expression of *Told you so*. James pulled his shoulders back, and she watched agitation scudding across his face.

"Right. Is there anything I can do here?"

Isabel pulled her face out of the crook of Harriet's neck and looked up at James with big watery eyes. Her face was pale and blotched.

"Can I still audition?" she asked in a small, sorrowful voice.

Harriet could almost see James's stiff upper lip eroding under the force of Isabel's pitiful gaze.

"Are you sure you want to?" Harriet asked her.

Isabel nodded, still looking at James. "If I'm allowed." The hope in her voice was heart-wrenching.

Harriet met James's eyes in a challenge. "Well, there's something you can do: use your powers of persuasion to fix it so that Isabel can audition."

James looked as though he wanted to argue but thought better of it and left the room.

Forty-five minutes later, Harriet ushered a freshly rehydrated and somewhat shamefaced Isabel back into the auditorium by the side door. All evidence of her stage faux pas had been eradicated. The only clue was the faint scent of disinfectant lingering in the air.

As they made their way over to the stalls where the panel and acting hopefuls sat, it occurred to her that she hadn't seen Ricco or Carly yet. She hoped they hadn't succumbed to the same nerve remedy as Isabel.

Up on the stage, Destiny took a bow and everyone clapped.

"An immaculate performance, good woman!" Gideon shouted. "I have never seen a more agonized Jacob Marley. Thank you, Destiny."

Gideon shined his pen torch on his notes and scribbled some more. James looked up and saw Harriet. He didn't smile, nor did she, but he nodded once in acknowledgment and leaned across to speak into Gideon's ear, causing Gideon to beckon Harriet over, while James excused himself. She watched him head toward Billy and wanted to follow, but Gideon was already speaking.

"Is the young lady ready to audition?" he asked tentatively, glancing around her at Isabel, who was hanging behind her like a nervous puppy. "James has explained that her unfortunate incident was the result of an overzealous dose of Dutch courage. I hazard to say that only someone for whom the role was deeply important would go to such a length to quell their nerves. We have time, if she would like?"

"Well?" Harriet asked her. "Would you like to try again?"

Isabel looked very small as she nodded. She was probably still a bit tipsy, and she was deathly pale but, Harriet reasoned, sober enough to go onstage if that was what she wanted. Billy came to join them, as did James. Since neither of them were glaring daggers at each other, Harriet hoped James had done the right thing.

"You still want me to read with you?" Billy asked.

"Yes, please. I'm sorry. About earlier." Isabel cast her eyes around to encompass all present.

"Nothing that hasn't been seen or done before, my dear," said Gideon. "Richard Burton would be proud of you. When you're ready."

Billy and Isabel made their way to the stage, and Harriet took her seat. Sid plonked himself down beside her, and James settled beside him. They regarded each other over the top of Sid's head.

"I jumped to the wrong conclusion," said James.

"Did you tell him that?" She didn't want to mention

Billy's name with his little brother sitting in the chair beside her.

"I did."

"Don't do it again."

"I won't."

It was hard to stay angry at someone so quick to take responsibility for his actions. Plus, he had smoothed the way for Isabel to have a second chance at auditioning. Harriet was wise enough to know that any kind of relationship required equal amounts of goodwill and forgiveness if it was to succeed.

"Thank you." She smiled at him, and he smiled back.

"Ready when you are!" Gideon called.

Billy cleared his throat and haltingly began to read the part of Mrs. Cratchit. But Isabel, high on being given another crack at the part and the relief of knowing that the worst had already happened, spoke loud and clear. Every syllable was perfectly enunciated; every nuance and cadence in the words of Bob Cratchit was executed with precision. And at the end of her audition even Grace, with all her censorious hubris, had nothing negative to say. The applause was enthusiastic, and Harriet hoped that this would be the moment people associated with Isabel.

"And so, we have our contenders for the parts of Roberta and Mr. Cratchit!" Gideon boomed. "Magnificent!"

Billy held his hand up to protest. But his objections were lost as Carly and Ricco barreled down the center aisle, rucksacks swinging wildly, shouting, "We're here! Don't stop the auditions!"

They brought in the refreshing scent of cold evening on their clothes and generated enough electric excitement to recharge the battery on a flat Tesla.

"We've put together a set list that we think could

really work," Carly shouted from the stage while Ricco handed a folder of music to Prescilla. "We've only properly learned three so far, but if you want more, we have loads of ideas."

"Hmmm." Gideon's expression was dubious. "I am not yet sure that singing has a place in this particular production . . ."

"Please, Gideon," Harriet entreated. "Give them a chance. Hear them out."

He flapped his arms in the air. "Okay, so be it. Sing on, yonder duo! Convince me!"

Prescilla gave Carly and Ricco a very enthusiastic thumbs-up, and Harriet thought maybe under those nice manners she was a bit of a dark horse.

Prescilla played the opening notes to "Underneath the Christmas Lights" by Sia, and Carly and Ricco began to sing, Carly's alto having the slightest amount of scratch to Ricco's clear tenor. Their voices echoed around the auditorium like a lament, a call to all the ghosts who resided in the walls. Harriet heard the doors being pushed open and bodies filling the aisle behind them and the balcony above as the maintenance crews were drawn into the auditorium.

"Brava!" Gideon shouted as he stood in ovation as they finished. "Magnifico! Stupendo! Fantastico!"

Harriet worried he would run out of Italian compliments. Applause filled the theater.

Carly and Ricco took a bow.

"You said you had more," Gideon almost panted with desperation.

"You want another one?" asked Ricco, shielding his eyes against the lights.

"I've never wanted anything more!"

Carly ran over to Prescilla for a brief confab before

taking her position back at Ricco's side. This time they sang "What If."

When they finished, half the maintenance crew were sobbing into their mugs of tea. Harriet was a mess. She could tell from the amount of black all over her tissue that she had no mascara left on her lashes. James's mouth hung open, and even Grace was silenced.

"Sold!" Gideon enthused loudly. "It would be a criminal offense of the gravest kind not to share your talents with our audience. Your voices are in the show!"

Harriet jumped up and down whooping and punching the air as more tears streamed down her face. These kids were amazing, all of them, and her heart was full and overflowing for them.

Ricco, skin glistening in the heat from the lights, stepped to the edge of the stage.

"We were thinking, maybe for the end of the play, that we could sing 'Put a Little Love in Your Heart,' and that the whole cast could join in?"

"Sing it to us, dear boy, you and the lovely Carly, sing on!" called Gideon. "And let us see how it will sound."

It sounded every bit as good as the ones before, only this time the energy was super high, positivity pulsing around the stalls. It was the perfect end to the auditions, and as they poured out of the theater, calling their goodbyes along the dark snowy streets, everyone was filled with the sense that this could be the start of something exceptional.

NINETEEN

GIDEON HAD PROMISED TO BE AT THE THEATER ARMED WITH the cast list by four thirty on Monday afternoon. The famous five and the Great Foss Players had gathered early accordingly and when he still hadn't arrived by five o'clock, tensions began to fray.

"We can't be expected to practice with only half a stage available," Grace grumbled.

Leo flushed and bent lower over his backcloth, continuing to outline the Cratchits' kitchen hearth in black paint while keeping stolidly silent.

"Where do you suggest he does them?" Billy challenged.

"I really don't care where he does them so long as he's not cluttering the stage," she whipped back.

"Yeah, well, it's not up to you, you're only here because of us," Billy snapped.

"Okay, okay, let's not say things we may later regret," Harriet interceded. "We have a whole theater in which to practice."

"There is only dried milk in the dressing room," complained Douglas. "It tastes bloody awful in tea."

"Anyone who wants to donate a drinks fridge to the cause is welcome to," said Harriet.

Geez, they're worse than the kids! She could feel her own tension rising.

"Why can't *you* just tell us who got which parts?" Isabel asked. "You were involved with the decisions."

"I was, but Gideon was very clear that the revealing of the cast list is a rite of passage for actors, and he wanted to be the one to do it. I don't want to steal his thunder or mess with any theatrical traditions that might bring bad luck to the production."

"Any news on when the lift might be ready?" asked Mallory.

"I'll check with Ken later. I'm sorry it's such a pain for you."

"At least I've got to know my way around, I suppose." Mallory shrugged.

"Harriet, there is no toilet paper in the ladies' toilets!" Destiny announced, hands on her ample hips.

"Okay, I'll sort it." Harriet tried to remember where she'd stashed the toilet rolls.

"And don't put more of that dreadful economy stuff in there!" said Prescilla. "It's worse than useless."

Harriet bit her lip, thinking about the twenty economy toilet rolls she'd already purchased.

"Technically not my job to keep the toilet rolls topped up," she said, forcing a smile.

"We've run out of sugar!" shouted Ahmed.

Give me strength!

Her phone pinged with a message.

CORNELL: I need you to write me a report with regards to Alejandro's situation for a meeting I have with his parents in the morning. On my desk by 9 a.m.

Sugar Honey Ice Tea! She'd be burning the midnight oil again tonight.

"You could give us a clue, miss!" Ricco complained.

"Oh, don't you start," Harriet snapped.

"Oooooooh!" singsonged Carly.

Harriet bit her lip and folded her arms. Then she felt a warm, soft arm wrap around her shoulders, and Odette whispered, "You are doing a fine job," in her lyrical Mauritian accent. "Some people are happiest when they're moaning."

Harriet felt some of the tension ease out of her shoulders.

"So this is them living their best life?" she asked, as Grace began to loudly critique the new drapes before moving seamlessly on to complain about Billy's dirty boots.

"Sometimes having their voices heard is the closest people come to knowing they still exist. It doesn't matter if the attention is good or bad."

"You are a wise woman." Harriet leaned her head on her shoulder, and Odette squeezed her tighter. It was very soothing; Odette smelled like baked bread and lavender.

She laughed and Harriet was jiggled in her embrace.

"I am an old woman," Odette corrected her. "And I am very nosy. Nosiness is an underrated tool for understanding the human condition."

"You should come and work with me at the school."

"Oh, no thank you, I'll stick with monitoring the big kids."

It was at that moment that Carly and Ricco decided to bust out a rendition of "'tis the damn season," and Mateo, who had been quietly reading beside them in the stalls, slammed his newspaper down and angry-crab-waddled along the aisle away from them.

"I'm going to make you a nice cup of instant coffee," said Odette. "Why don't you come with me and choose a treat from my handbag?"

Harriet laughed and gratefully followed Odette to the dressing room.

Gideon arrived fashionably late, looking very pleased with himself as he was swamped by eager would-be actors. Ignoring their questions, he glided to the orchestra pit and stuck the cast list to one of the pillars. Harriet could feel self-importance pulsing out of him like a weather front as he stepped back to let eager eyes scan the printout. Thankfully, everyone appeared happy—aside from Billy, who hadn't wanted a part—with their assigned roles, and there were yips and shouts from young and old as they found their names on the list.

Isabel was cast as Roberta Cratchit, and Sid, no surprise, was Tiny Tim and also the boy at the end of the play who buys the turkey. Billy was given the role of Mr. Cratchit, a stay-at-home dad, which, to Harriet's surprise, he didn't point-blank refuse. Grace was the Ghost of Christmas Past, Hiroshi—of course—was the Ghost of Christmas Yet to Come, and Odette was the Ghost of Christmas Present. Destiny was to play the part of Jacob Marley. Ahmed had the lead as Ebenezer Scrooge, while Carly would play—and sing—as Belle, and Ricco would double as Scrooge's nephew and young Scrooge. Members of both groups were also allotted smaller bit parts to cover crowd scenes and townspeople and read the narration.

It was the first time she had seen the famous five and the Great Foss Players bond in any meaningful way. The genuine handshakes and back pats of congratulations from both sides were heartwarming to see. With roles now assigned, the energy in the auditorium had morphed from fraught to impatient to get started. For all their high-maintenance ways, Harriet felt grateful for the new additions to the production.

Hesther and her women's group arrived just after six o'clock with another group—who definitely were not women—in tow. Harriet was waiting for them in the foyer. Carly and Ricco, who had volunteered to give Hesther's group a guided tour of the building, stood beside her. The others were in the auditorium being individually briefed on their characters' motivations by Gideon, while Mallory—a West End choreographer before she retired—gave lessons on how to own the stage and capture the audience with one's body. This had gone down like cat poo in a slipper with Billy, whose whole body, when Harriet had left him, appeared to be curling in on itself with cringe.

"Harriet!" Hesther beamed, dusting the snow off her jacket. "Gosh, the weather's really turned, hasn't it? As you can see, we've brought some friends." She motioned to the gaggle of men lurking near the doors. "But first, I'd like to introduce the refugee women's group." She motioned to the women standing in an awkward huddle in the foyer, several of whom held foil trays covered in cling wrap. "I won't bombard you with names right now, as there's quite a few of us, but suffice to say, we are all terribly grateful to you. And we can't wait to get stuck in with your set designs! We've brought a few treats to say thank you."

"My goodness, thank you, you are going to be very popular! Why don't you pop those down." Harriet gestured to the old concessions stand. "We can carry them through after you've had a look around your new hangout. It's so lovely to meet you all, please make yourselves at home." She smiled at the women. "Carly and Ricco here will give you a quick tour, show you where the toilets are and teas and coffees, that sort of thing. If there's anything you need, don't hesitate to ask me. I don't guarantee I'll have the answer, but I'll certainly try my best. I've spoken with Ken, the site manager, and he's asked us to keep to the auditorium after six thirty, as they've got new fixtures and fittings being delivered and the foyer will be busy."

The women nodded, smiling hesitantly.

"Thanks, Harriet," said Hesther, clapping her hands together. "And now I'd like to introduce one of our fellow groups made homeless by the local council's budget cuts. This is the Lonely Farts Club. Josef, this is Harriet, she's, well, I suppose she's sort of the community coordinator around here."

Harriet tried her best not to look as wrong-footed as she felt. She also noted two walking sticks and a walking frame. *We really need to make this place more accessible!*

"Lovely to meet you, Josef," she said, smiling. "I think 'community coordinator' sounds a bit grand. I'm simply borrowing the space for the time being and subletting it without the landlady's permission." She grinned.

Josef was a slightly stooped beanpole of a man in his late sixties, with soft blue eyes and gray hair swept back in a way that accentuated his widow's peak. He wore a knitted sweater vest over a checked shirt and beige chinos.

"Ah! A bit of a rebel with a cause, are you, that's what we like! Delighted to finally meet you, Harriet." He shook her hand enthusiastically. "We've been hearing all sorts about your endeavors. The Lonely Farts Club are, as you can see, all men of a certain vintage, some of us widowers, some singletons by choice or circumstance, but all of us alone in the world apart from each other." He smiled and went on to introduce each member. "We have Ernest, retired estate agent; Harry, who likes to keep his hand in at building; and Dhruv, an exceptional carpenter." Dhruv gave a small bow. "Then there's Winston, former engineer and full-time tinkerer; Kingsley, our resident tailor; and then me, retired baker, although one never truly retires from baking."

The Lonely Farts nodded and chuckled in agreement.

"My waistline can attest to that," Harry said, patting his stomach.

"Gosh!" Harriet's cheeks ached from smiling. "Well, you are all very welcome." *What's one more group in the mix. It could be fun!*

"We don't expect a free ride," added Josef jovially. "We'll earn our keep, so put us to work wherever you need us. We may be old farts, but we're willing!"

"You may well regret offering your services, I will have no qualms about roping you all into our dramatic endeavors." She meant it. "Please, make yourselves at home." She turned to Carly and Ricco. "Right, you two, have you got your tour guides' hats on?"

"We're ready, miss," said Carly.

"I was born ready," added Ricco.

"Of course you were, Ricco. Now, Ken says the best place to start is next door with the restaurants and cocktail lounges, as they'll have deliveries arriving soon and it'll be off-limits after that."

"Got it," said Ricco. "Okay, everyone!" He stood straight as all eyes fixed on him and began to wave his arms like an air steward giving safety instructions. "If you'd like to follow Carly and me, we will be your guides for today; please keep together at all times and don't feed the maintenance crews."

There was a smattering of laughter as the two groups fell in behind Ricco and Carly. The Lonely Farts and the women's group mingled together, clearly happy to see each other and chatting among themselves.

When the door swung closed behind the last person, Hesther said, "I'm sorry to ambush you like that. I promise it wasn't intentional. I got a call late last night from Josef asking if you might help them too, and he sounded so desperate. I know it's cheeky, but they have nowhere else to go since the council repurposed their meeting space and, well, it's so easy for people to slip through the cracks, isn't it?"

"Honestly, don't give it another thought. This place is plenty big enough for us all and we might as well use it while we can. Perhaps if we root ourselves in firmly enough, the new owners will feel compelled to let us stay."

"By the way, I need to thank you. I don't know what you said to Evaline over the weekend, but it worked."

"I'm sorry, you've lost me," said Harriet.

"Several of the women in the group were visited this morning by surveyors who noted down all the repairs that needed doing and promised that the relevant trades-people would begin work by Wednesday. It seemed like too much of a coincidence after our conversation the other evening, so I assumed it must be down to you."

Harriet tried to play down her delight but was sure it must be written all over her face.

"I can't take the credit for that, I'm afraid. But I think I know a man who can."

As Hesther went off in search of the tour groups, Harriet took a moment to bask in the warm pleasure of knowing that James had done the right thing. He must have pulled some powerful strings to get things moving so quickly, and dug into the Winter coffers too. She wondered how Evaline had reacted.

Harriet could hardly wait for James to arrive. Right now, she wanted to wrangle him into a storage cupboard and show him her appreciation.

Her ardor was swiftly cooled, though, when she reentered the auditorium. *What in the Charles Dickens?*

"I said, leave her alone," Billy hissed through gritted teeth. Isabel stood at his side looking uneasy.

"If you're going to threaten me, at least have the gumption to look me in the eye." Grace's stance was combative; she stood with her legs as wide as her sensible tweed skirt would allow, arms crossed tightly across her chest. She was blocking the aisle.

"How am I threatening you?" Billy asked.

"Everything about you screams 'thug.'"

"What did you call me?"

"Don't give her the satisfaction," Isabel implored, and then added, "Miserable old cow!"

"Now, now, let's not descend into name-calling," Ahmed pleaded.

Harriet hurried down the stairs. She noted Gideon sitting in the front row doing absolutely nothing to smooth things over.

"What is going on here?" she asked.

"An altercation about enunciation," Douglas explained helpfully. "Grace may have been a little overzealous in her critiquing of Isabel's performance."

Harriet felt James fall in beside her; she could smell the cold evening trapped in the fabric of his overcoat.

"A little?" Prescilla asked incredulously. "Like Gordon Ramsay gets a *little* worked up in *Hell's Kitchen*."

"Oh, shut up, Prescilla!" Grace snapped. "The primary function of an actor is to convey the dialogue to the audience, and this girl mumbles like she's got a mouth full of cotton wool."

"Um, Grace, I think you need to understand that Isabel isn't a trained actor; we're all very much learning on the job, and you can be a little intimidating." Harriet tried to sound placating. "I think if we can show one another a little kindness . . ."

"Ah, the snowflake generation strikes again!" Grace sounded triumphant.

"It's not about being a snowflake, it's about being reasonable," Harriet countered.

"I'd rather be a snowflake than a fascist," Billy added.

Ye gads!

"You can't go around calling people fascists, Billy," said James.

"Oh, come off it!" Billy shouted.

"James is right," said Harriet. "Grace, you're out of line too."

"Me!" Grace exploded.

"That's it, take his side!" Billy snapped.

"Not everything is about taking sides," said Harriet wearily.

"I think we all need to take a step back and give one another some room," said James.

"You take a step back!" Billy shouted.

"Not helping, Billy," Harriet warned.

"And this is what we're left with, a generation with egos so delicate they can't take constructive criticism." Grace refolded her arms, self-satisfied.

"Sometimes your constructive criticism sounds like bullying," said Prescilla.

"Nonsense! And as for their disrespectfulness, well, I blame the parents!" Grace announced, sucking her cheeks in triumphantly.

Oh, bum-swizzles! Now she's done it. She waited for the explosion. *Three, two, one . . .*

"Fuck you!" Billy roared, turning away and storming back down the aisle, Isabel trailing after him.

"Come back here!" James shouted, making to follow.

"Don't shout at him!" Harriet grabbed his arm, stopping him in his tracks. "Leave him be."

A howl ripped through the air as Leo jumped to his feet and began kicking everything he could see—a bucket, his rucksack, the bag of brushes; he grabbed a can of open paint and threw it over the backcloth he'd been painstakingly working on.

"Shut up! Shut up! Shut up!" he screamed, pulling at his hair before dashing off the stage.

"Oh, well, that's just bloody marvelous!" Harriet exploded.

"You see," Grace said, satisfied. "Snowflakes."

Harriet rounded on her.

"No! Not snowflakes. Billy doesn't have parents, he's spent most of his life in care, so forgive him if he's a bit sensitive when someone uses something stupid like 'I blame the parents' as a stick to beat him with. And Leo, for reasons that are none of your business, becomes stressed by aggressive altercations. You know nothing about these children, or what they've been through. Now, if you're done issuing judgments about people you don't know, I'm going to go after my students."

Harriet walked away quickly before she said something she'd really regret.

"How was I to know?" she heard Grace say sulkily.

....

She found Leo in an empty dressing room, carving his name into the desktop that ran below the long mirror with a pencil. He stopped, looking guilty, when she walked in and sat down next to him.

"It's okay," she said. "You're not the first person to leave their mark." It was true, the desk was covered all over with names.

"I'm sorry," said Leo.

"There's no harm done. You really kicked the crap out of that bucket, huh."

He rewarded her with the ghost of a smile.

"Did you do your breathing?" she asked.

"It didn't work."

"It's probably the newness of everything making it hard to focus."

"I guess."

"Don't give up on it, it's helped before. You are allowed to remove yourself from any situation that makes you feel threatened."

"I thought if I concentrated on the drawing, I could handle it."

"How do you feel now?"

"Better. Stupid."

"You're allowed to feel any way you want, but in my opinion, you're not stupid. I'm glad you feel better. Would you like me to call your mum?"

"No, I want to stay, if I'm allowed."

"Oh, excuse me, I don't mean to intrude," came the gentle lilt of Odette's voice in the doorway. "But I always carry a few little treats in my bag, and you look like someone who could use a treat."

She bustled into the room and opened her bag wide to show the contents. Harriet glanced at Leo, who looked as awed as she felt; it was a tuck shop in there. Small tubs contained flapjacks, chocolate bars, nuts, raisins, biscuits, and a miniature Battenberg cake.

"Go on now, help yourself," Odette said encouragingly. And when Leo chose a small bag of cookies and muttered a thank-you, she rubbed his head, kissed her teeth, and said, "And when you're done, you come on back outside and work on those drawings of yours. I'll make sure there's no more trouble, don't you worry."

Harriet had no doubt that she would be as good as her word.

"I ruined my backcloth," he said, jamming his fists into his eyes to hide his tears.

"Well now, I had a little look before I came to see you and it's really not as bad as you might think," Odette soothed.

"Really?" he asked hopefully.

"A little Jackson Pollock flourish is all, nothing we can't work into the picture if we put our heads together. Hmmm? How about it? Why don't me and you go see what we can do?" Odette's voice was gently persuasive, and it worked its magic on Leo.

Thank you, Harriet mouthed to Odette as the older woman made to chaperone Leo back to the stage. Odette smiled and winked in return.

Harriet took herself off to the bathroom to gather herself before going after Billy and Isabel. She checked her phone.

CORNELL: Don't forget that report. 9 a.m.

CORNELL: Smoked bacon.

CORNELL: That wasn't meant for you.

CORNELL: The dean wants an update on the Christmas prize-giving. Where are you on that?

Prize-giving! She groaned out loud. With everything else going on, the end-of-year student awards ceremony had completely slipped her mind. She'd sent out emails to teachers to ask who they'd like to nominate but hadn't chased them up. *Maybe I should just give up sleeping. How long can a person actually go without sleeping?* She was considering getting hit by a slow-moving car, nothing too serious, just enough that she could spend the next few weeks in hospital and miss Christmas completely, when she heard voices outside the door.

"I apologize for shouting at you. I was out of line."

It was James's voice. Calm and reasoning.

"Don't worry about it." Billy, sulky.

"She picks at everything, all the time," came Isabel's voice. "I mean, all the time. She's got it in for Billy, he can't do anything right."

"And you give as good as you get," said James.

"I'm not just gonna take it, am I?" Billy mumbled.

"I think it's fair to say that your personalities clash."

She heard Billy's derisive snort.

"I'm not going to ask you to rise above it because that puts the onus on you and relieves Grace from any responsibility, and I believe there to be equal fault on both sides. But I will ask both of you to try and keep the peace and resist falling into name-calling. Does that sound fair to you?"

At a pause, in her mind's eye Harriet could see Billy, seething, wanting to shout and rail, but James's calm gave him nowhere to point his anger.

"Fine," said Billy. "But if she starts—"

"Understood," said James. "Maybe take a few minutes, walk it off, and then come back when you're ready."

Mumbled responses followed, and she heard Isabel's voice talking softly, growing distant. Harriet opened the bathroom door and James turned, his expression pensive.

"I didn't know you were in there," he said.

"I didn't want to interrupt."

"You heard?"

She nodded. "You handled that well."

He sighed and rubbed his face. "After the fact. It would have been better if I hadn't exacerbated it in the first place."

"But you made it right. That's what counts."

"I have a lot to learn about teenagers."

"I don't think I could respect anyone who didn't think they still had things to learn," she said honestly.

"You really are a good person, aren't you?"

She smiled. "You arranged repairs for Evaline's private lets," she said.

He gave a small nod.

"I investigated her rentals portfolio and found it wanting. I orchestrated a change of buildings management agency accordingly."

She smiled. He'd listened and he'd heard, that was worth a lot.

"You're a good person too," she said.

"How's Leo?" he asked.

"He'll be okay."

"They're complicated, aren't they?"

"Aren't we all?" she replied.

....

When she got home, she changed straight into her pajamas, made herself a big mug of hot chocolate, and climbed into bed with her laptop to start her report for Cornell. Today had wrung her out, left her limp with fatigue. She was no stranger to burning the candle at both ends, but at this rate she was going to need a much longer wick. The only upside to being so busy that she'd practically had to start scheduling pee breaks into her day was that she didn't have time to dwell on the Maisy-shaped hole in her home.

TWENTY

HARRIET PUSHED OPEN THE DOORS TO THE THEATER ON TUES-
day evening in a state of obliviousness. She had arrived
on autopilot, barely noticing how the gray woolen clouds
obscured the stars, or the carol singers around the giant
Christmas tree handing out flyers advertising the Winter Theater's one-night-only production of *A Christmas
Carol.*

Her mind was so consumed with work and all the
jobs she hadn't finished today that when Ken boomed
out her name, the surprise of it almost caused her knees
to buckle.

"Flippin' 'eck, lass! Didn't you see me waving at you?"

She blinked a couple of times and reacquainted herself with her surroundings.

"Sorry, Ken, got a lot on my mind." She rubbed her
hand across her forehead as though she could wipe away
her distraction.

"You can't go on like this much longer. Something's
got to give," he said kindly.

She laughed lightly. "My sanity, probably."

He regarded her, frowning, and then said, "Come on,
I've been saving the inaugural trip for you." He ushered
her toward the lift.

"It's working!" she exclaimed.

"We're about to find out." Ken grinned.

He pressed the call button, and the ornate doors slid open to reveal an exquisitely Art Deco interior. Suddenly she was wide awake.

"Oh my god, Ken, I think it's the most beautiful lift I've ever been in!"

He stroked his chin; one eye twitched in a half wink, which was as close to crowing as this hunk of Yorkshireman was likely to get.

"I reckon people with mobility issues ought to experience the same pizzazz as the ones who take the grand staircase."

"They certainly will." Her first thoughts were for Mallory and the Lonely Farts, and then she recalled Evaline painstakingly tackling each stair and was shocked by the surge of affection she felt for the old battle-ax.

"We're putting in another one in the foyer next door that'll reach the cocktail lounges and restaurant," said Ken. "And one backstage—that one'll be a no-frills affair, but it'll get the job done."

"Wonderful. It'll certainly cut down Mallory's mileage. I can't believe the changes to this place in such a short space of time. Your teams are miracle workers."

"Hard workers, at any rate," said Ken. "I reckon another week or so and we'll be close enough to done that we can finish the rest during slightly more respectable hours."

"I bet they'll be pleased about that."

"Their other halves will be, that's for sure."

The lift doors opened, and she waved back at Ken as she stepped out into the auditorium at the bottom of the main stairs.

Yesterday's dyspeptic atmosphere had been replaced by a can-do humor that would have made Santa's elves proud. Several of Hesther's group had settled into painting the backdrops with Leo. Farahnoush, who had worked in design in her former life, was in deep discussion with Billy and Harry about the sets. Down in the orchestra pit, Ava and Dhruv had already begun work on building Scrooge's four-poster bed frame with wood castoffs from Ken. It was a recipe for bedlam but somehow both new groups seemed to fit right in, and the camaraderie levels were high. Harriet hoped their positivity might be enough to dilute the animosity brewing between the famous five and certain members of the Great Foss Players.

"Heartwarming, isn't it?" said Josef when he saw her watching. "Everyone pitching in for a cause greater than themselves."

"It is. It makes me feel quite emotional."

"I feel it too." He placed his hand over his heart. "In here. I'm inclined to think our assemblage was no accident."

"You think we're dealing with kismet?"

Josef smiled in a way that made him look both wise and impish.

"Something like that. Ernest has left two of his famous fruited tea loaves in the coffee room for everyone to help themselves."

"That's very kind of him."

"He's a kind man."

From above their heads came a crackling sound, and then "I'll Be Home for Christmas" began to play through the speakers dotted about the auditorium. Josef clapped his hands delightedly.

"That'll be Winston, he said he could get that old sound system up and running again, and bless my soul, he's gone and done it."

Harriet pushed away the pang of longing for Maisy induced by the music and asked, "Have you got plans for Christmas?"

"Absolutely none." He grinned.

"Oh, I'm so sorry . . ."

Josef laughed and slapped his thigh. "Why are you sorry? I'm Jewish!"

"Oh!" Harriet laughed too, mostly with relief. "Well, that's all right, then."

From the balcony above, Winston called for Josef's assistance and he hurried off, still chuckling, and Harriet made her way over to Billy. She'd seen her students at registration this morning but had been holed up in her office for the rest of the day.

"Billy, can I have a word?" she asked as he hurried past her with a list in his hand.

His expression was pained, and she could tell he really wanted to crack on.

"Farahnoush has got me on a scavenger hunt to find bits and pieces for the sets. I need to track down a desk and a random door for the Marley door-knocker scene . . . and a bowl for 'gruel.'" He shrugged at the last word.

"It won't take long. Please."

He gave a beleaguered sigh. "All right."

She led the way down to their makeshift coffee room backstage, having already messaged Grace to meet her in there under the pretext of organizing a baking roster.

Odette and Grace had brought along homemade shortbread and cookies to Saturday's auditions, and Hesther's group had arrived yesterday bearing a variety of snacks; Zahra's tray of jalebi, sticky with honey and cardamom, had gone down a storm with the famous five. And now there were Ernest's fruited tea loaves too. Clearly baking was a great way for people to bond, and

Harriet was keen to harness that momentum, but she was also aware that if only the same few people were baking with ingredients bought out of their own pockets, resentments could quickly build. Hence, a roster and a kitty.

Technically, though, this was an ambush, as became clear when Billy walked in behind Harriet and saw Grace polishing the mirror above the dressing table top. James sat on a chair with a copy of the *Financial Times* held in front of his face.

"Nope!" said Billy, and he immediately made to leave.

"Not so fast!" said Harriet, hooking his hood with her finger.

"What is this?" Grace demanded, dropping her cloth into the sink.

"An intervention," said James, smoothly folding his newspaper as he stood and moved to block the door and any further escape attempts. There was something in the way James moved his body, at once both languid and purposeful, that made Harriet think she could happily spend a day simply observing him maneuver through the spaces he inhabited.

She was happy to see him here. They had concocted this little ruse via emails sent back and forth while they both navigated their day jobs. She'd been surprised by the uptick in her heart rate every time she got an email notification, the thrill of seeing his name pop up in the header and the smiles that came to her face. It had added some much-needed pep to an otherwise relentless day.

Grace blustered while Billy locked himself inside his protective metaphorical sarcophagus.

"You two got off on the wrong foot. I don't know why, and I'm not interested in who said what when. But it needs to end now," said Harriet. "We have to work together whether you like it or not, so say your pieces to each other and then put them to bed and start over. And just so you know, this is not optional. I am in charge of this project, and I will have to ask you to leave the production, Grace, if this situation can't be remedied. Okay? Who wants to go first?"

Grace's expression was like sucking on a lime. Billy's remained impassive. After checking her nails several times, Grace snapped, "I'll start, then, shall I? I don't apologize for the things I said about your boots because you *were* traipsing mud across the stage."

Harriet raised her eyes to the heavens. This wasn't sounding much like an apology yet. Billy was looking ready to have his go.

"And I don't understand why you youngsters think it's okay to dress like you found your clothes at the bottom of a well, there's no effort. It doesn't instill any kind of self-respect or make others inclined to respect you, either." She took a breath and raised her chin. "I realize I come across as brusque. I spend a lot of time alone and I get out of the habit of being personable; I will try to be more friendly. And I'm sorry for the things I said yesterday, I didn't know your circumstances. It was thoughtless of me." Grace smoothed her skirt and sat down, ankles crossed, staring intently at her hands clasped in her lap.

"Thank you, Grace." Harriet turned to Billy, whose jaw was so set his teeth must surely be aching under the pressure. "Billy, is there anything you'd like to say to Grace? Now is your chance."

Billy's eyes were laser beams trained on the linoleum as though he wanted to melt through it.

"I don't like being judged and I don't like Sid being judged, either. People like you just decide whatever you want about people like me, and you don't care if it's true or not. Being old doesn't automatically give you the right to be respected, it just means you've lived a long time, not that you're a good person. I'm sorry that you're lonely, but that's not an excuse to give everyone else a hard time."

Oh boy! At this point, Harriet wasn't sure if this intervention was making things better or worse. James's expression was one of trained professional blankness.

"You're sorry that I'm lonely?" Grace's voice was small. Her clasped hands had tightened, whitening the papery skin across her knuckles. "Do you understand what it is to be an aging woman? To be all alone in the world and be a woman that society has deemed past her prime?" She faced Billy, her expression a challenge. "Of course you don't. How could you? I am invisible. I am the invisible woman. When I walk down the street, people look right through me as though I'm not even there. When I'm in the supermarket, nobody pays me the slightest bit of attention. Age has stolen my identity. I am powerless. I live with the knowledge that if I disappeared tomorrow no one would notice. I don't want respect because I'm old, I want to be acknowledged as a member of the human race."

Harriet's heart grew heavy. It was hard to believe that someone as prim and upright as Grace could feel invisible. Silence choked up the small room.

"Billy?" Harriet touched his arm in encouragement. "Is there anything you would like to add?"

His brow furrowed even deeper than usual.

"Yeah, all right," he muttered as he cleared his throat, daring a look at Grace. "Me and Sid have been through some stuff, but we have each other. I feel lonely sometimes, but I'm not actually alone, if that makes sense. But I do understand about being powerless. I've had no control over my life, still don't really, not till I'm eighteen. Till we went to live with Tess and Arthur, I never knew where we'd be sent next or how long we'd get to stay there, or if it would be better or worse than the place we were at before; a lot of times it was worse. I've felt invisible for most of my life."

Harriet swallowed hard to push down the lump in her throat. She turned to James and saw that he was struggling to keep his face neutral.

Grace looked up at Billy and nodded. "You and Sid don't deserve to feel invisible," she said.

"Yeah, well, nor do you," he mumbled in reply.

Grace cleared her throat tentatively. "Perhaps we could begin again, you and I, with a little more understanding on both sides. I'll try if you will."

It seemed to Harriet that for the first time since she'd met her, Grace was actually acting her age.

"Sure," Billy agreed. He turned to Harriet. "Can I go now?"

"Yes, of course." She smiled at him. "Thank you for talking with us and for your honesty."

"Didn't really have much choice, did I?"

"No, I suppose not."

He made to leave, and James stepped to one side to let him pass. In the doorway he looked back, glancing between the floor and Grace, teenage awkwardness leaching from his every pore.

"I'll see you around, Grace, yeah?" In the absence of a smile—Billy didn't dish out smiles often—he squinted his eyes at her in a kind of friendly way, and she nodded back in acknowledgment.

"Yes, I'll see you around, Billy." She gave him a diminutive smile, and then he was gone like a rabbit at a dog race.

....

Back in the auditorium, rehearsals were in full swing despite the hammering, sawing, and drilling and half of the stage being taken up with people on all fours painting backdrops. Gideon, cape flung back over his shoulders to reveal a blue velvet waistcoat with embroidered fish motif, was in his element as he readied the actors for a read-through of Act 1, Scene 2.

"Now then, Isabel, you will be farthest away from Ahmed on the stage because you are shivering beside your one measly lump of coal, warming your hands against a candle as you work."

Isabel took her chair and placed it as far away from Ahmed as the painters on the floor would allow.

"Splendid!" His compliments were aggressive, like a sergeant major yelling out orders. "Let us have the narrators for this scene gathered in a loose semicircle between Scrooge and Roberta Cratchit as though you were a group of carol singers. Mallory, darling, could you arrange them, please, they look like they're waiting for a bus. Yes, you too, Leo, if you could leave your canvas for a short while, that's it, and Ricco be ready to enter stage left. Odette, you will begin. Annnnnnnd action!"

"*Once upon a time—of all the good days in the year, on Christmas Eve . . .*"

Harriet stood a little way up one of the side aisles, hidden in the shadows, surveying the action across the auditorium as she sipped a well-earned decaffeinated tea. James came to stand beside her.

"I think that went as well as could be expected," he said.

"Let's hope they each keep their end of the bargain."

James nodded and then observed, "Gideon is a man of great passions."

"He is indeed." Harriet smiled into her mug.

"Would we describe him as eccentric, I wonder?"

At that moment Gideon took to the stage bellowing, "My dear people, you must let the theater take you over! Feel its passion! Give in to its siren song!" He threw off his cape and flung it at Mallory—who caught it with practiced ease—and broke into a spirited rendition of Eminem's "Lose Yourself." The incongruity of a sexagenarian man wearing plaid trousers while rapping in a perfect Queen's English accent startled the entire theater into silence.

"Yes," Harriet said, failing to stifle her giggles. "I believe we would."

....

Harriet tried to cap rehearsals so that they finished no later than seven thirty each evening; any longer than that and people were simply too tired after a full day at school and work that tempers became likely to fray. It also gave her an outside chance of keeping on top of her day job.

Since she'd begun at the theater her evenings had followed a pattern: get home, peruse the fridge for a microwave meal, set up laptop on the sofa, TV on low for background noise, work and eat, hope Maisy might call, fall into bed exhausted and not be able to sleep. It wasn't exciting, but there was comfort in its predictability.

On Wednesday evening, she'd just finished a very satisfactory microwave lasagna when her doorbell buzzed. It was James. Suddenly she was very awake. The thrills zipping up from her toes to her head made her light-headed; this was a lot for a Wednesday. She buzzed him in and quickly gargled some mouthwash and applied a swish of lip balm before he knocked.

She took a breath and opened the door—and realized she was still wearing her fluffy slipper socks with smiling sloth faces on the toes. James smiled sheepishly at her and then looked down at her feet.

"They look cozy," he said.

She felt her cheeks redden. "I don't like drafts on my ankles."

"They work well with the apron."

Oh, for god's sake! She'd forgotten about the Wonder Woman apron.

"I didn't want to get lasagna down my dress, tomato is a trial to get out. I'm a very practical woman."

"You made lasagna?"

"The good people at Aldi made it. But I microwaved it."

He smiled like a crocodile.

"Can I help you with something?" she asked.

"Actually, yes, you can. May I come in?"

She noticed for the first time the large paper bags at his feet. She opened the door wider and stepped aside for him to enter.

"These are for you," he said, laying the bags down on the table in the hall.

She gave him a dubious side-eye.

"Take a look." He gestured that she should open the bags. "And try not to look like I've asked you to dismantle a bomb."

Cautiously she opened the bags. The first contained two wooden nutcracker dolls, one in a green uniform, the other in red. The second bag held a large snow globe on an ornate base. She pulled it out of the bag. Inside the globe was a perfect village scene surrounded by fir trees, with thatched cottages and a bridge over a frozen lake where a boy and a girl in bobble hats and scarves skated. Protruding from the base was a key, which Harriet turned, releasing a tinny musical-box version of "Dance of the Sugar Plum Fairy."

"Do you like them?" he asked, a hint of nerves in his voice.

"They're beautiful!" Harriet whispered; her voice came out hoarse and she cleared her throat. She looked up at him. "But why?"

"I thought some decorations not associated with your Christmases with Maisy might ease you into enjoying the season for yourself. And if it's not too presumptuous, I thought perhaps I could help you put your Christmas decorations up." He smiled at her.

"That's a lovely offer, but I'm not doing decorations this year."

"I thought you'd say that, and I'd really like it if you would reconsider."

"Why?"

"Because I get the feeling that you do a lot of things for other people, but you don't pay yourself the same courtesy. Your daughter is lucky to have the kind of mum who spins the magic of Christmas up around her. I wonder if in her absence you might need a friend to help you spin some of that magic for yourself."

She was trying very hard to keep herself from unraveling into a sad heap of discarded ribbons on the floor.

"That's really thoughtful," she managed.

"Think of me like festive methadone; I'm not Maisy but I'd like to try, in some small way, to fill the gap in your Christmas, if you'll let me."

She hiccupped out a strange sob-laugh and felt mortified that she was coming apart like this in front of him.

When he spoke again his voice was a gentle hum that unfastened her final knots. "It's okay to be sad that you won't be with your daughter this Christmas. But it's okay to enjoy yourself too."

A blizzard of emotions twisted and swirled inside her chest: an aching sadness at reaching the end of this chapter, and the cavernous uncertainty as she stood poised to turn to the next page. She had made Maisy her home, and now she was suffering from the worst homesickness of her life.

Her tears were sudden and profuse, and she didn't protest when James folded her into his arms. He held her while she cried herself out; the steady rise and fall of his chest and the weight of his arms around her were a lighthouse leading her back to shore.

"I'm not usually a crier," she sniffled into his nice smart coat.

"You're lucky," he spoke into her hair. "I cry all the time."

"Do you?" she sniffed.

"I realize that must be hard to imagine beneath my cool exterior, but I am known for bawling my eyes out at the John Lewis Christmas adverts, and those videos of dads coming home from the army to surprise their kids for the holidays; man, they get me every time."

She chuckled wetly into his chest and when she pulled back, in dire need of a tissue, he had one ready. She blew her nose too loudly to be attractive, but after the sloth socks and the Wonder Woman apron and the ugly crying all over his coat, she figured that ship had sailed. It came as a surprise, then, when she looked up at him and he swiped away the last of her tears with his thumbs, his hands cradling her face, before he pulled her back into his arms and kissed her so fervently that her toes went tingly.

Kissing James Knight was every bit as good as she remembered, and she would have been more than happy to let things progress to their natural conclusion, but after far too short a time, he pulled away and smiled at her.

"Where do you store your Christmas decorations?" he asked.

....

James helped her to fit together her very expensive, very tall fake Norwegian spruce, which—while beautiful—was a total ball-ache to assemble. She had dispensed with her apron and made them each a mug of hot chocolate with marshmallows and candy cane stirrers; if she was doing this, she was going all in.

"These look rather fancy—are they part of your festive embellishments?" James asked, picking up one of the orange-and-cinnamon candle boxes.

"Oh, no," she said, setting their mugs down on coasters on the coffee table. "I bought them to make the place smell Christmassy, but now that Maisy won't be here I'll not bother. Just leave them boxed."

He frowned but didn't argue, replacing the box where he'd found it.

"Your decorations are very you," said James as he helped her to tie an assortment of festive ornaments into the thick garland of faux evergreen foliage that they had laid over the mantelpiece. The two nutcrackers stood sentinel on either end; ivy and fir tree branches twisted around their shiny black boots. "I mean that as a compliment. They seem curated somehow . . . loved," he said, turning a ceramic Father Christmas ornament in his fingers. "They suit your home. They suit you."

He looked up at her and smiled and she felt like he really saw her. That didn't happen very often.

"Thank you. They are loved. I suppose they're kind of an anthology; my and Maisy's Christmases are all wrapped up in the tissue paper with them." She could stop there and it would be enough, but something about the way James listened made her want to keep talking. "I was afraid that if I got them out, all the happiness trapped in their fabric would become polluted with my melancholy. That probably sounds stupid to you."

James's expression was contemplative as he tied two glittering turtledoves onto a fir branch. When he'd knotted the golden thread, he stood back.

"It doesn't sound stupid at all. Although I don't think you need to worry in that regard. Your home and the life that you've built here with your daughter is full of warmth, I felt it the first time I was here. I feel it now. And I think your happy memories are so deeply embedded here that they won't be destroyed by a bit of wistfulness." He raised an eyebrow at her teasingly, and she gave him a playful shove. "But I have to ask you, what inspired you to purchase this?" He held up a hand-painted *Beetlejuice* bauble and she laughed.

"Each year my foster parents would buy me two tree baubles from places we'd been or ones that I liked in a shop, so that by the time I left home I would have a box full of my own decorations, each with their own memories. I went through a big Lydia Deetz phase."

"You grew up in the care system?"

"I did."

"That explains a lot."

"Does it?"

She could see in his face that he wanted to ask more

questions, but instead he said, "That was very thoughtful of your foster parents." He picked up a Windsor Castle bauble and turned it in his fingers.

"It was. It was their way of helping me to build my own personal history because I didn't know my parents. Every one of them holds a piece of me at a moment in time. And then I carried it on with Pete and Maisy, and Emma and the kids. I know it seems ridiculous to have so much of myself invested in Christmas baubles . . ."

"No, it's not ridiculous. I get it."

"What about your decorations?" she asked, picturing his sleek apartment.

"Mine?" He rubbed the back of his neck.

"Yeah. Do you have any favorites?"

"Truth be told, I've always paid someone to come in and decorate my apartment for me. I tell them the esthetic I want, and they create it."

"Seriously?"

He looked embarrassed.

"I guess I don't have as much history wrapped up in my Christmases as you do. I mean, I've enjoyed the holidays as much as anyone, but I don't have *those* kinds of memories associated with them. I've attended a lot of Christmas parties, eaten at a lot of fine restaurants, I've had skiing Christmases and sunbathing Christmases . . ."

"That sounds pretty memorable, if you ask me. If you want me to feel sorry for you, you're going to have to try harder."

"And," he said, cutting her off. "Though I appreciate that these are privileges not available to everyone, none of them are the kind of remembrances that I could summon up to keep me warm on a cold night. You have sentimental history; I have party anecdotes. It's not the same. Up until recently I was more than content with my lot. And now I find myself in my late forties, wondering what I may have missed. My situation in life has been enviable, but perhaps the grass on my side is not as green as I once thought."

She hadn't thought about it like that. She had a vast stash of happy memories and though they smarted right now, she was glad she had them.

"If it's any consolation, my 'sentimental history' is only highlighting how empty my nest is going to be and how lost I am with no one to fuss over."

"But would you change it? Would you trade your family Christmases for ones that didn't leave a mark?"

"No," she said honestly. "I wouldn't change a thing."

"Well, there you are. Your Christmas decorations are not your enemy. Maybe this is the year you lean into some new traditions, just for you."

She had imagined it would be painful to revisit all those cherished moments without the prospect of making new ones this year. In fact, the opposite was true; it was cathartic, and she felt comforted having them swirling around her. With so many wonderful memories with her daughter in the bank, perhaps she *could* afford to invest in some just for herself.

"Maybe you're right," she said. "What about you? It's not too late for you to make Christmases that you'd care to remember."

His answering smile was so sad that her heart squeezed. She had that feeling again that he was holding something back. What could be so big or so bad that he couldn't find his way to confiding in her, even after she had laid herself bare to him?

"Maybe," he said quietly. "I hope so."

....

James stayed until every surface glittered, and when at last he flicked the switch, the tree lit up with hundreds of golden fairy lights wound round and round it, making the baubles of her life twinkle on the laden branches.

"What's the verdict?" he asked, coming to stand beside her.

"It's beautiful."

It was.

"No regrets?" he asked cautiously.

"None. Thank you for making me do it, I wouldn't have done it myself."

"I figured as much."

"I feel like I owe you a dinner or something. You've brought me gifts." She gestured to the nutcrackers. She'd positioned the musical snow globe on the hall table, so that she could wind it up each time she came in out of the cold. "And you've helped decorate my home and forced me out of my slump, and you have very graciously listened while I rambled on about my daughter for the last two hours."

He chuckled, and she liked the low vibration of it.

"Microwave lasagna for two?" he suggested.

"Contrary to the contents of my fridge, I can actually cook."

He smiled. "You don't owe me anything. I've had a lovely evening."

And just like that the mood changed. The air was suddenly charged with an end-of-date energy, only this hadn't been a date and James was already standing in her sitting room. What were the rules here? Were they casual smoochers? Should she kiss him on his way out? Shake hands? What? She settled for complete avoidance by trying to delay his departure.

"Would you like a decaf tea for the road?"

James looked at his watch. "I'd better not, it's late."

He made his way out to the hall and unhooked his coat from the coat stand and she followed.

"I guess I'll see you tomorrow night at the theater," she said, for want of anything to fill the quiet tension in the air.

"You will indeed."

James opened the front door and stepped out onto the welcome mat in the communal hall. "Well," he said.

"Hmm," she replied. Her heart was hammering in her chest.

James opened his mouth as though he was going to say something and then changed his mind.

"Thank you again." Harriet smiled.

"Don't mention it."

If this went on too much longer, she was going to have full-on palpitations. Ten more seconds passed. Did he want to kiss her? If she leaned in, would he reject her?

"I want to kiss you." James kept his voice low, a deep frown upon his brow. "But I don't want to complicate things."

Don't worry about all that, just kiss me already!

"I shouldn't have kissed you earlier . . ."

Oh!

"Oh."

"I mean, I wanted to, but I shouldn't have let myself get swept up in the moment. You just looked so sad and I . . ."

Embarrassment dropped over her like a bucket of ice water.

"Are you saying that you kissed me because you felt sorry for me?" Her voice was rising. "Was that a sympathy snog?"

She thought she might turn inside out with the force of her humiliation.

"No," he replied firmly. "It's like I said before, I'm trying to do better, and part of that is not acting on my every impulse. You were vulnerable, and I kissed you—"

"I kissed you back, James, I'm not some breakable damsel—"

"That isn't the point."

"Then what is?" She was exasperated now.

"My life is complicated at the moment, and I don't know how much of myself I can give over to a relationship."

"I'm not asking you for a relationship. If you recall, I was not the one who got their knickers in a twist after we spent the night together. I was perfectly happy with a one-night stand, thank you very much, but you felt like you had some sort of civic responsibility to my vagina."

"Don't be ridiculous."

"Don't you be ridiculous."

"You are infuriating."

"And you are confounding."

"Are you still sad?"

"No. Now I'm livid. Want to have sex?"

"Abso-fucking-lutely."

They collided in an explosion of hungry kisses. Harriet pulled James back in through the front door, and he kicked it shut. Fast hands pulled and pawed at clothes, tearing them off as though they were on fire.

"Jesus! How many cardigans are you wearing?" he mumbled, tugging at layer after knitted layer.

"I'm not sure Jesus is wearing any," she gasped as he kissed her throat. "But I've got three on."

"Smarty pants," he breathed, nipping at her shoulder.

She scooted the snow globe to one side as James lifted

her onto the table and she wrapped her legs around his waist, their breaths coming hard, bodies pressing and arching, their need to be joined a vital emergency.

They never made it as far as the bedroom. But that night she slept better than she had in a long time.

TWENTY-ONE

THE GALLERY TO WHICH HARRIET AND EMMA WERE HEADED was in the nearby market town of Penrith. The snow had been causing problems on some of the smaller country lanes, but luckily the roads between Little Beck Foss and Penrith were an arterial route and had been well gritted. All the same, Pete—a cluckier hen than either Emma or Harriet—had made them stow blankets, snacks, and two thermoses of hot chocolate in the back of the car just in case. It wasn't unheard of for drivers to become stranded when the Cumbrian winter weather did its worst.

"Argh, what is wrong with me! My stomach is all squiggled up about leaving the kids at the theater."

"It's not like you left them alone—they've got like fifty adults chaperoning them," said Emma. She was hugging the steering wheel, so close to the windscreen that her breath kept leaving misty circles on the glass, which Harriet would lean across and wipe away with a chamois sponge, as though she were a surgeon's assistant. "Wipe!"

Harriet leaned forward to do the honors.

"Yeah, but you know, they can be tricky."

"So can the grown-ups, from what you've said. Won't the sexy solicitor be there to referee?"

"No, he's late-night Christmas shopping, apparently."

"Speaking of the C-word, are you still set on sulking

on Christmas Day rather than spending it with us?" Emma asked. "Wipe!"

"Ah, I wanted to talk to you about that, actually."

"You've changed your mind? Seen the light? Realized that Christmas without my children fighting is no Christmas at all?"

"No."

"Bollocks."

"I still want to spend it by myself but not because I'm sulking anymore."

"So you admit that you were sulking."

"Oh yeah, one hundred percent. But now . . . I feel like I need to do this, I want to. I'm going to cook a fabulous three-course Christmas dinner for one because I deserve to make an effort for myself."

"Wow, one evening of having your brains shagged out by James and you've found inner self-appreciation. I need to meet this guy so that I can shake him by the hand."

"It wasn't the sex. At least it wasn't only the sex, I won't say it wasn't good for my ego. It was Evaline too."

"Wait, you had a threesome with Evaline? Do you want me to drive this car into a snowbank? Wipe!"

Harriet laughed and leaned forward to clear the screen again.

"No! Idiot. She was telling me the other day about her risotto and how she makes an effort for herself. And then last night, before the sex, while James was kind of forcing me to decorate the flat, I realized that I need to prove to myself that I'm enough when I'm not being a mother or a mentor or a friend. I must teach myself that I am worth creating joy for, because otherwise I'm just a vessel for holding other people's happiness . . . does that make sense?"

Emma was quiet for a moment while she absorbed Harriet's words.

"It makes perfect sense," she said finally. "And do you know what? I'm glad. I couldn't have enjoyed the day knowing that you were sobbing into a Pot Noodle and talking to the walls. But this new option, this sounds healthy."

"I only need to do it once. Next year I'll be back in the fold, quarreling kids and all. This year I need to show myself some love."

"I'm proud of you. You're showing me the way for when it's my turn. Although at this point, the idea of empty nesting sounds champagne-cork-popping fantastic. Wipe!"

Harriet chuckled.

"Trust me, you'll miss them when they're gone."

"We'll see. Anyway, how was it in the land of thespians and troublesome teens today?"

"Pretty good, actually. Not too much sniping. Miraculously the play seems to be coming together. Grace and Billy have entered into a tentative truce; she brought him in a piece of homemade flapjack wrapped in foil today."

"Awww, that's sweet, she must know that the way to any teenage boy's heart is through his stomach," said Emma. "Jordan is permanently hungry. I wondered if he had worms for a while, until someone at work told me it was normal for teenage boys to be ravenous. Now I pretty much just throw trays of cooked chicken into his bedroom at regular intervals to stop him ransacking the kitchen; it's a bit like having a pet tiger with chronically cheesy feet."

Harriet groaned and thanked her lucky stars she'd had a daughter.

....

Emma found a parking space just along the road from the venue, and they linked arms as they wandered up the pretty high street. The streetlamps were wound with evergreen garlands, and little white dots of light shone out from them. Every artisan shop window showcased its wares festively; even the hardware store had managed to make hammers and bags of nails look like worthy Christmas gifts. It had stopped snowing, but the cold was biting and under the moonlight the ground was glittering with ice. They laughed nervously, gripping tighter on to one another as their feet occasionally slipped, knowing that if one went down the other would follow.

Warm light poured out onto the pavement from the windows of the gallery. A few people loitered outside, muffled in coats, glasses of sparkling wine—presumably the one Emma was promoting—in one hand, cigarette or vape in the other, their hushed conversations blended into the louder hum of the crowd within.

"They're very popular, this mystery artist," said Harriet, peering in at the shimmering crowd made nebulous by the thick condensation on the glass panes.

"Free booze, isn't it?" Emma replied as she pushed open the door for them. "Except for me. I'm technically working, but I'm hoping to make up for the lack of booze by eating inordinate amounts of canapés."

The heat enveloped Harriet. She was already clawing at her coat buttons as a server dressed in black and white with a tight bun clinging to the top of her head handed her and Emma each a glass of wine and a program for the exhibition. Harriet placed them both on a handy white plinth and pulled her coat off.

"Here, give me that." Placing her glass on the plinth

next to Harriet's, Emma took her friend's coat and threw it over her own arm.

"Ladies," came a man's haughty voice. "Kindly desist from perching your wineglasses on the exhibits." He handed back their glasses and motioned to a printed sign in front of the plinth that read *"White Noise Hiding in Plain Sight." A statement piece by Lionel Heggard.*

"It still looks like a plinth to me," Harriet whispered.

"That's because you're a philistine," Emma hissed back, and they fell against one another laughing.

"I feel so judged. I'm afraid to touch anything."

"Just don't hang your coat up or sit down and you should be fine."

Harriet smiled and blew her hair out of her face. She looked properly at the program for the first time and her stomach dropped.

THE VALLEY GALLERY PRESENTS

Interpretive Art Works by
Lionel Heggard
and
Paintings in Oil and Acrylic by
Lyra Hope

"What?" asked Emma, seeing her friend's wide-eyed alarm.

"Look at the name!" she replied, stabbing at the program with her finger.

Emma looked confused.

"Lyra!" Harriet muttered. "The woman who was messaging James."

"It might not be the same Lyra. There must be loads of people called Lyra."

"It's not that common a name. What are the chances of coming across two people called Lyra in the same vicinity?"

"Cumbria's a big place," reasoned Emma, and then her mouth dropped open. "Shit."

"What?"

Emma leaned into Harriet and whispered, "James is here," into her ear.

"You've never met him; how do you know it's James?"

"Did you think I wouldn't google the man my best friend is having casual sex with? Trust me, it's him."

"Shiitake mushrooms! Where?"

Emma motioned with her head, and Harriet scanned the gallery in that direction. At first, she couldn't see him, but then a cluster of people shifted and there he was, looking back at her with an expression which was both surprised and slightly sickly. He half smiled and raised a hesitant hand. She waved limply back. This was it. The moment when her fragile hopes were going to be crushed. She was going to meet his significant other, or at least his more-significant-than-her other.

She turned back to face Emma. "I need to go."

Emma looked over her friend's shoulder. "Too late. He's coming over. And he's not alone. I'm so sorry, Harriet, I had no idea."

Oh god!

"It's not your fault." She closed her eyes and took a deep breath. "Do I look sweaty?"

"No, you've gone rather pale."

She tried to gather herself. "Okay, okay. I'll say hello like a grown-up and then I'll slip out and get a drink somewhere and you can come and find me when you've finished getting your photos, okay?"

"He's here." Emma was speaking without moving her

mouth, her lips held in a frozen smile, eyes wide. "Turn around, act cool, it looks weird that you've got your back to him."

"Weirder than you imitating a ventriloquist's dummy? Mothersmucker, this is a flocking nightmare."

Slowly she turned around. He'd almost reached her. A very young, very slender woman with long black ringlets and bright red lips had her arm linked through his, and Harriet wanted to cry for being so foolish, so taken in by his "wanting to do better" act.

"Harriet." He smiled, the smooth veneer of professional solicitor settling over his face. "I didn't know you were invited. And you must be Emma." He turned his attention to Emma. "Harriet has great things to say about you." His gaze settled back on Harriet.

Say something. Say anything.

"I. Emma. Carbon footprint. Work. Wine. Plinth." Why couldn't she speak? The girl on his arm—because that was about how old she looked: twenty-three at a push to James's almost fifty—was looking at her expectantly. She had a sweet, open face, heart-shaped with a smile a mile wide.

James frowned.

"Right. Well, Harriet, Emma, I'd like you both to meet Lyra. My daughter."

Daughter! Daughter?

Lyra held out her hand and gushed, "It's so lovely to meet you, Harriet!" She had a strong Scottish accent. "I've heard so much about you. Dad talks about you all the time."

He talks about me all the time? Then why is this the first time I'm hearing about you?

"Does he?" she managed to squeak out.

Lyra shook Emma's hand as well.

"And you are Harriet's best friend, married to her ex-boyfriend. I love the sound of your blended family, so cool."

"Thank you." Emma smiled. "We're very lucky."

"And Harriet." Lyra was full of wonder, like a puppy being taken outside for the first time. "Dad's told me all about the theater and the famous five and how passionate you are. I can't wait to see the play."

James shook his head. "Lyra," he said, embarrassed.

"Sorry," she laughed, gripping his arm tighter. "I'm just so excited to meet the people in your life." She turned her attention back to Harriet. "He's so cagey!"

Harriet smiled. "Isn't he just."

"Have you looked around the exhibition yet? I'm so nervous! It's the first time I've ever exhibited, well, apart from my final show at university, but that doesn't count, does it? I hope you like it. Dad convinced me to take the chance, I'm not sure I ever would have if he hadn't kept bolstering my ego. There are canapés too! Would you like some? They're delicious, I've been shoveling them in to soak up all the wine. Sorry, I know I'm talking too much; I chatter when I'm nervous. Mum says I gibber like a gibbon!" She laughed again, clutching at James's arm with her other hand too, as though she needed to hold herself down. But all Harriet heard was the word *Mum*.

A woman in an evening gown sashayed over and tapped Lyra on her spaghetti-strapped shoulder.

"I'm so sorry to interrupt," she said. "But there's a gentleman I'd like to introduce you to; he's interested in buying some of your canvases to take back to New York."

Lyra's face radiated joy. It was impossible not to feel endeared; her happiness was a tangible thing like strands of light flowing out of her. However devastated Harriet felt that James had lied to her, she wouldn't take it out on this lovely, excited girl, she wouldn't ruin her night.

"That was the gallery curator. New York!" Lyra squealed. "Oh my god! Can you believe it?" She was smiling at James with pure delight.

"I absolutely can," said James, gently removing her hands from around his arm and holding them in front of him. "You'd better go and speak to your new admirer."

Lyra gave another squeak of excitement and looked between Harriet and Emma. "Let Dad show you around. I'm so happy you came. I've been dying to meet you." Finally, she allowed herself to be drawn away but not before calling back, "Dad, can you tell Mum where I've gone? She went to see about more canapés, and I haven't seen her since."

Oh great, Mum's here!

When Lyra was out of earshot, James faced her square on and said, "I'm sorry, I didn't mean for you to find out this way." There were those pleading eyes again, just like that first time in Evaline's car. But heartfelt looks weren't going to cut it.

"Are you married?" she asked, her voice shaking with anger and hurt.

"No."

Did she believe him? Until five minutes ago she didn't even know he had a daughter; it wasn't that much of a stretch to think he'd been concealing a wife too. She couldn't believe how quickly this evening had deteriorated.

Emma's expression was pure, unadulterated rage, and Harriet knew it was taking a herculean effort for her friend not to vent her anger at James in the middle of the swanky gallery, and that the only reason that wasn't happening was out of respect for her. Harriet took a measured breath and summoned her remaining dignity.

"I'm leaving." It was hard to speak around the lump forming in her throat.

"Please don't," he implored. "I know I owe you an explanation and I promise that you'll get one. I'll tell you everything."

"You lied to me."

"I didn't. I promise you, I didn't."

"Is that some of your legal bullshit, omission not counting as a lie?" Emma asked.

James looked down at the smooth sanded floorboards. "I can't explain myself to you here, it isn't appropriate, but please give me the benefit of the doubt until I can."

Harriet almost laughed at his audacity. "Why should I?"

"I . . ." His eyes scanned the room as though he could find an answer in the crowd. "I don't have a good reason for you right now, you'll just have to trust me."

"I don't think so." Harriet made to walk away.

He didn't reach for her but moved to put himself back in her line of sight.

"Please stay. It would mean a lot to Lyra."

"I hardly think Lyra is going to care if I go," she snapped. Though from Lyra's response to her when they met, she knew that was a lie.

"Please." James's eyes were beseeching. "You can hate me; I won't blame you. You can never speak to me again, but please . . . just stay for ten minutes, look at her paintings, and then make your goodbyes. Please don't ruin her big night because of me."

Harriet wanted to turn around and walk out but she couldn't. She couldn't walk out on that sweet girl, no matter how much of a nincompoop her father was. None of this was Lyra's fault.

It took every ounce of Harriet's willpower not to cry. She wanted to scream in his face. She wanted him to see that he had stripped away her self-confidence and her trust in her own judgment. But instead, she squared her shoulders, fingers curled so tightly around the stem of her wineglass that she thought it might snap.

"I'll stay," she said. "But you keep away from me. Don't speak to me. Don't make eye contact. I don't want to see you."

As she turned away from him, Emma stepped forward and spoke close to James's face. "How dare you." Her voice was low and dangerous.

And then she felt Emma's hand in hers.

"Ten minutes," she whispered in Harriet's ear. "And then we're gone."

....

The drive home was quiet. The snow was falling like it meant it, and Emma was having to concentrate on the dark roads, her face serious, eyes squinting as she gripped the wheel like she was steering a schooner through rough seas.

Harriet was glad for the chance to not talk as her mind ran over and over it all. There was a thunderous ache roaring inside her. She didn't care that James had a daughter; she wouldn't care if he had twenty children scattered about the world. What hurt and confused her was that he hadn't told her. She had laid herself bare to him in so many ways, and all the while he had kept a huge part of himself hidden. The balance of power was off, and it made her feel vulnerable and unsteady.

The snowflakes flurried down, hitting the windscreen

like scraps of torn paper before being batted away by the wipers.

"Has he called yet?" Emma asked as they pulled up outside Harriet's building.

She checked her phone; she'd kept it on silent specifically so that she could miss his calls.

"No," she sighed.

"We left early, the party's probably still going strong."

"It would have been nice if he'd at least tried to appear desperate to make things right between us and given me the chance to ignore him."

"It's the very least he could do." Emma was thoughtful for a moment. "But then he's one of those overly rational types who probably thinks there's no point in calling someone who's clearly not going to answer."

"Do you think he's with Lyra's mum and he's just been stringing me along? Be honest."

"I don't know. It's hard to have faith in a man who neglects to mention that he has a daughter."

"It doesn't make any sense. It's not like he hasn't had ample chances to mention it. What would you do in my position?"

Emma drummed her fingers on the steering wheel as she considered her answer. "Well, if it were me, then I would probably burn his house down first and ask questions later. But that's me. If I were you, then I think maybe I'd hold judgment until he's explained his reasons. I mean, other than this admittedly major faux pas, has he given you any reason to think he might be a downright rotter?"

Harriet let out a long sigh. "No." The answer came more easily than she would have liked, given how angry she was with him, but it was true. So either that made her a really bad judge of character or he had held back for reasons that had nothing to do with being shady.

"Then hear out his explanation. And if it's a crock of shit, then we can burn his house down together."

"I'll bring the matches."

Emma stared hard at her, studying her face as closely as she had the snowy roads home.

"Seriously, on a scale of one to ten—one being disappointed but not enough to cry, and ten, likely to spend the night wailing like a banshee and/or drown in your own tears—how gutted are you? Because I can stay, Pete won't mind."

The sting of having been lied to was still acute; boulders of anger and embarrassment clanked and churned in her gut like a washing machine set on the heavy-soil function. But she managed a weak smile for her bestie.

"I'm a solid seven. But I don't need a babysitter. I need to lie in a hot bath and soak out all the poison I'm feeling so that I can sleep tonight."

"Are you actually going to treat yourself to a bubble bath?"

"Do you know, I might."

"The good stuff?"

"Yep."

"Shit, you do feel bad."

Harriet hugged Emma before she got out of the car. "You're the best," she said.

"I know."

"I'll call you in the morning."

"Call me before, if you need to."

....

When she climbed into bed, fingers and toes sufficiently pruned after a good soak—she'd wondered why it had taken her so long to use Maisy's good bubble bath—she checked her phone for messages. She had two from Maisy, alongside a picture of her and Savannah wrapped in winter woolies on an ice rink. She smiled and tapped out a reply. She'd just hit send when another message came through, this one from James.

> Harriet, I'm sorry. I understand that my actions have hurt you. Thank you for not making a scene at Lyra's exhibition, even though you would have been within your rights. If you'll let me, I'd like to explain everything but not over the phone. Breakfast tomorrow? Before you start work. 7:30 at the little café you like on the corner? I hope to see you in the morning. x

Harriet read the message three times. She sucked in a deep breath through her nose and let it out through her mouth. He still wasn't giving anything away. She didn't reply to his message. Instead, she pulled the duvet over her head, and let sleep roll over her, which it did for a full hour and a half before her body decided that was quite enough sleep for one night.

TWENTY-TWO

IT WAS THE FIRST OF DECEMBER AND THE CAFÉ ON THE COR-
ner was fully Christmas ready. The long bar that ran the
length of the window was decorated with a poinsettia
garland, the red petals pressed against the glass soaking
up the condensation as it rolled down the window. The
counter area was hung with brightly colored pompom
swags and the tree was a jazzy mix of glitter coffee cups
and cake slice decorations.

James sat at a scrubbed pine table in the corner looking conspicuous in his expensive suit. He oozed discomfort, and Harriet would have felt sorry for him if she
weren't still raw.

Her heart was beating fast, and her stomach churned
with a mixture of apprehension and hurt. She knew that
things were about to change and she wasn't confident
about which way the pendulum would swing. James
looked up and met her eyes, and she saw him swallow
before he closed the book he'd been reading and stood
up. It was a pity, she thought, that his old-fashioned
manners didn't stretch to telling the truth. He pulled out
her chair and she sat but didn't say thank you. He sat
back down. Crossed his legs and uncrossed them, laid
his hands flat on the table and then folded them in his
lap. He was uncomfortable. Good.

"I wasn't sure you'd show up," he said.

"Neither was I." Who was she kidding, she was always going to show.

"I ordered you a flat white and a few different pastries. I didn't know what you'd be in the mood for, and I know you don't tend to eat breakfast before you leave the house."

"Thank you, you didn't have to."

He shifted in his chair, crossed and uncrossed his legs again. "I suppose I'll just get on with it, then."

"That would be best," she replied in a clipped tone.

Her phone rang; it was Cornell. "I have to take this." James nodded.

"Sebastian. What can I do for you?"

"I can't find Jemima Bryce's file, where the hell is it?" he snapped down the phone.

"Go to your saved works and double-click on 'Pending Cases.' All the files will come up by name."

She could hear the clack of the keys being finger-punched beneath Cornell's grumbles.

"And where the hell are you?" he asked. "I thought we agreed that your vanity project wasn't to interfere with work."

Harriet gritted her teeth. "It isn't. I'll be in shortly. Have you found the file?"

After an ungracious thank-you, Cornell ended the call.

"Sorry," she said to James. "Please continue."

He took a deep breath, "I only—"

He was cut off by the perky waitress, who practically danced the orders to the tables, placing a tray with two coffees and a plate piled high with pastries down in front of them.

"Hi!" she addressed Harriet brightly. "Lovely to see you actually sitting in, rather than dashing in and out like the Road Runner being chased by Wile E. Coyote."

Harriet smiled at her. "I am perpetually cutting it fine."

"Nothing wrong with that!" the waitress trilled as she unloaded the breakfast things and pranced back to the counter.

The interruption seemed to have thrown James, and he cleared his throat and cleaned his glasses.

"Where was I?" he asked.

"You got as far as 'I only,'" Harriet said helpfully.

"Right." He replaced his glasses and took a breath in. "I only—"

Harriet's phone rang on the table. Ali. She picked it up without a second thought. Across the table, James's lips thinned to a flat line.

"Morning, everything all right?"

"Yeah, sorry to bother you," said Ali. "Frederick Mercer's mum wants to discuss a plan of action after his ADHD diagnosis, and she'll only speak to you. Can I book her in for ten forty a.m.? It's your only gap today."

Harriet rubbed her forehead, "Um, yeah, of course, that's fine." She ended the call and settled back in her chair expectantly.

"Do you ever not answer your phone?" James asked tightly.

"It's my job."

"It's borderline obsessive."

"We're not here to discuss my foibles," she retorted, and was pleased to see him shift in his chair with a chastened expression. He took a sip of his coffee, then cleared his throat, twice.

"I only found out about Lyra, about having a daughter, in January this year," he began. "I had absolutely no idea that there was even a chance that I might have a child somewhere in the world until she emailed me. She's been living in Edinburgh all this time."

Okay, now he had her attention.

"That . . ." She wasn't quite sure what to say. "Must have been a surprise." This put a slightly different spin on things. But she still couldn't fathom why he wouldn't have told her.

"You have no idea." He gave a nervous chuckle and rubbed his hand through his hair. There was a vulnerability in the action that she hadn't seen before. "Talk about turning life on its head."

"That's what kids generally do."

"Except normally you get a warm-up period—you know, you have nine months to get used to the idea of being a parent and then you grow with them, learn as you go along. You don't just wake up one day and find you've got a twenty-five-year-old daughter." He raised his eyes to the heavens as though looking for spiritual guidance. Harriet took a big bite of a cinnamon whirl; she needed the sugar.

"FYI," she said around a mouthful of pastry, "pregnancy and birth don't prepare you in any way for the all-encompassing hostile takeover of your life that is parenthood. I'm just saying. Knowing everything I know now, having a ready-made adult rock up at my door would be a piece of cake."

James rubbed his brow. "Not for me."

"Okay, so I appreciate it's a big adjustment, but I don't understand why you were keeping it a secret."

"I wasn't."

Harriet blustered out an indignant huff, sending pastry crumbs across the table. "I beg to differ. I told you about Maisy that first night in the bar. At any point between then and the myriad times I must have talked about her since, you could have mentioned that you had a daughter too. Instead, you've turned it into this whole big deal."

"It's a big deal to me." His petulance knocked the rise out of any sympathy she might have been feeling.

She folded her arms and leaned back in her chair. James stirred his coffee and took a sip, then placed his cup back on the saucer, turning it so that the handle was at a perfect right angle to him.

"I'm sorry I didn't tell you. The longer I left it, the worse it was going to look when I finally did tell you. I'm still getting used to being a parent; it doesn't feel natural yet to casually proclaim myself a father. I don't feel worthy of the title, for a start. And I knew I couldn't tell you that I had a daughter without telling you the whole sorry tale, about how I had been oblivious to her existence and completely absent from her life until eleven months ago."

"Why not? You could have just said 'I've got a daughter' and I wouldn't have known any different."

He laughed humorlessly. "*Why not?* Because since the moment I met you all I've wanted to do is tell you everything. Every time you pin me with one of your looks, I have an uncontrollable urge to overshare. I'm trained to play my cards close to my chest, and you make me want to blabber like some gossipy teenager. It's disconcerting."

"Oh, so it's my fault? I see."

"No, that's not it. I'm not blaming you. I simply . . ." He sighed. "Because of the way that I feel about you, I couldn't tell you part of it without telling you all of it, and if you knew all of it . . ." He fiddled with the spoon on his saucer. "I was afraid that you would judge me."

"Why would I judge you?"

"I see the standards you set for yourself, and I didn't like the idea of not measuring up."

She wasn't sure if she ought to be offended by this or not.

"I wouldn't have thought . . . I *don't* think any less of

you because you are learning how to be a father to a daughter you didn't know you had. If anything, I have more respect for you, not less."

The compliment seemed to land heavily on him. He looked around the busy café and then took another swig of his coffee, avoiding her gaze.

"I didn't expect—" He stopped and rubbed his temples. "I didn't expect all the guilt that would come with being a parent."

She huffed out a laugh at that.

"That's another secret about parenthood that nobody ever tells you; it lurks in the same vault in your mind as eternal worry and constant fear. But if it's any help at all, I always think the feelings of guilt are how you know you're probably parenting right. It's the ones who don't give a rat's cojones about how their actions will affect their kids that you've got to worry about."

"Are you speaking from experience or trying to make me feel better?"

"Both."

"I'm sorry that I hurt your feelings; that was the furthest thing from my intentions."

There was a three-way wrestling match happening inside her brain: forgive him and move forward with whatever this thing was between them, forgive him but step away, or not forgive him and cut her losses. Was she a fool to believe that he was a good guy? She didn't think so. He'd made an error of judgment and then found himself in too deep. She wasn't so naïve as to think that all apologies were genuine, but this one was from his heart, and she knew it because she felt it strike deep into her own.

She slid her hand across the table toward his, stopping just shy of his fingers tapping nervously on the wood. He looked at her, and his amber eyes were fire. Then he dropped his gaze to the table and stretched his hand out toward hers, a mere breath of space between their fingertips now.

"I've missed so much of her life." His voice was a low whisper, a rich, deep note that resonated inside her. "All the milestones. School plays, grazed knees, first steps, first smiles, it's all happened without me. I've lost so much time that I can never get back. How can I ever make up for that? And what about the debt I owe Morgan? Lyra's mum," he clarified. "How can I ever make up for not being there to support her while she raised our daughter?"

The anger she'd felt toward him dissolved, and in its place was an ache in her chest for him. When she spoke again, her voice was soft.

"Maybe instead of dwelling on the time you've lost, you should put your energies into filling the present with moments that will make future memories."

He sighed. "I know that you're right. But I'm finding it hard to let it go. All my adult life I've been career oriented, setting goals and seeing how fast I could smash them. I was my only priority because there was only me and that made me selfish in a lot of ways, but it also didn't matter. I mean, who was I hurting if I was only responsible for my own happiness?"

"That seems like a fair point."

"But now everything is different because all that time there *was* someone out there that I should have been being responsible for. And now I look at my life choices and they feel, I don't know, empty."

"Don't say that."

"Why not?"

"Because you're cheapening your achievements; all

the things you've worked hard for still count. You should be proud of the life you've created." She chose her words carefully for the next question. "Does Lyra hold resentments?"

He shook his head, smiling at the mere mention of her name, and Harriet couldn't help but want her own name to have that effect on him.

"No, none. At least none that she's shown me. She is so much more than I deserve."

"You're being very hard on yourself."

"To her credit, her mum always made it clear that I had no knowledge of her existence."

A remembrance of an elegant woman at the gallery last night, linking her arm through Lyra's, pushed itself to the front of Harriet's mind, and instinctively she pulled her hand back.

"Are you and Morgan, I mean . . ."

He read her meaning at once. "A thing? No."

"If you could go back . . ."

He shook his head, understanding the things she wanted to know. "The truth is we were never a thing, not really. Not that it's any excuse. We just weren't. We met at university and we, well, I guess we used to 'hook up,' as the kids say."

"Friends with benefits," Harriet added helpfully.

He screwed his face up. "Even that implies it being more than it was."

"Booty calls?"

He burst out a laugh and it was like the room flooded with light. She warmed herself in it.

"Really?" he asked incredulously.

His smile was an addiction, and she needed another hit.

"Ooh, wait," she said, "I've got it: Netflix and chill."

She'd learned the meaning of that last year when she'd incorrectly used it to describe her weekend plans to her tutor group.

He leaned across the table and hit her with the full force of his grin, and she wanted to smoosh his cheeks into her cleavage.

"Can you stop denigrating my past, please?"

"You started it, I'm simply trying to categorize."

"The point is, Morgan and I were never a great love story, and even if I'd known about Lyra, it wouldn't have changed anything. We're very different people."

"Is that why she didn't tell you? Because she didn't want either of you to feel obliged to try and make a relationship work?"

He drummed the fingers of both hands on the table, his brow ever so slightly creased. This, she knew, was how he weighed his options and measured his words before he spoke. Knowing his tells gave her a warm sensation.

"There were a few factors at play," he began. "For a start, I was offered the chance to work my pupillage with a big law firm in New York straight after university, and I'm ashamed to say that I left without a backward glance. Or even a goodbye. By the time Morgan found out she was pregnant, I was long gone. Even if she'd wanted to reach out, she wouldn't have known where to look."

"Surely she could have asked around, you must have had some friends in common."

"It wasn't quite that simple." He chewed his lip. "I wasn't exactly the only candidate, so to speak. Over the years they ruled out some of the others with DNA tests, and by a process of elimination, eventually there was only me left."

"Just like *Mamma Mia!*" Harriet gushed.

"It isn't. Absolutely nobody sang."

Things were slotting into place in her mind. "This is why you want to do better. It's for Lyra and Morgan. You're atoning for the women you feel you've let down in your past."

He held her gaze and she could read it all in his eyes. "I don't know if it's atonement exactly," he said. "But I had a realization, and I want to do things differently going forward. There are disruptors and instigators of change, and I'm not one of them; I accept my limitations. You, on the other hand, are someone who leads the charge; you want to save everyone! I can't change the world, but I can change me and be one better man in it. I can move through life in a more thoughtful and respectful way."

"Changing the world one kind act at a time." She smiled at him. "That's why you suggested to Evaline that it would be a good idea to let me use the theater. It wasn't only about staging it for sale, was it?"

The left side of his mouth quirked upward. "Like I said, I'm not a disruptor, I'm a realist. I wanted to help you, but I wasn't about to piss off my firm's biggest client. I work within my limitations."

"You started a ripple," she said, smiling at him.

"Because I knew you could turn it into a wave."

Neither of them spoke for a moment as they looked at each other, the noisy café falling away. His faith in her was a gift, but it was too precious, breakable, easily crushed by her fear of failure. She was a fraud. She wasn't the instigator he believed her to be; her motives were driven by guilt, just like his. As if on cue, her phone rang.

"I need to take this," she said.

"You always need to take it."

She ignored him and went outside, returning five minutes later to find him still sat there, stewing.

"It was a student's parent. It was work," she said, though no explanation was required.

"Your commitment to your work is admirable, but surely you can't be expected to be on call twenty-four-seven."

"My job can be intense; it doesn't always keep regular hours."

"To be honest, it isn't only your job that's the issue. You are always available to everyone, always, which in a weird way makes you wholly unavailable to any one person ever. I don't think we've had a single conversation day or night that hasn't been interrupted by your phone in some way; if it's not a call, it's a message or voice note. I realize that given my recent behavior, I'm in no position to make demands, but if we are going to venture forward with this thing between us, I'd like to occasionally come higher on your list of priorities than your phone."

She sucked in a breath. He was right, of course. She'd once left a church in the middle of a wedding to take a work call.

"I have"—she fumbled for the right words—"phone issues."

James sat back, hands in his lap, giving her space to continue. Needing something to do with her hands, she took another pastry from the plate and began to carefully unroll it. If she was going to tell him, there would be no better time.

"I didn't always work in pastoral care. Until eight years ago I taught English literature."

She swallowed and began to peel apart the flaky layers of the croissant.

"There was a girl in my class, Zoe. One of those exceptionally bright students who just hoovers up information, full of potential." Her fingers were sticky, but she continued to dismantle the pastry. "She had a troubled home life. Neglect, substance abuse; none of it considered dangerous enough to remove the children, but her family was well known to social services. I knew how hard it was for her to keep up with her studies and not to get sucked into the life that seemed hell-bent on swallowing her up. I did my best to keep an eye on her, but I had sixty students in my cohort: fifty-nine other humans that also needed my attention."

The croissant lay in shreds on the plate, and she stared at her deconstruction as she forced her words out of a throat that felt as though it wanted to clam shut.

"When she started missing lessons, I alerted the relevant people at the ends of the lists; I even called at her house, multiple times. But I was so busy, I had other students, assignments to mark, and Maisy was still little . . ."

She arranged the pastry into small, neat mounds on her plate.

"Then one night I had a missed call from her; I'd fallen asleep on the sofa while marking assignments. When I woke up and saw it, I called her back, but it rang out. The next day I discovered she'd been arrested for possession of an illegal weapon and Class A drugs with intent to sell. The phone call had come two hours before her arrest. She'd reached out to me, and I hadn't been there. I went to see her at the police station. It was clear she'd been doing more than simply running the drugs. The way she looked at me . . ." Her mind threw up the image that would haunt her forever: black hollows under her eyes, lips cracked and bleeding, matted hair, and an accusing expression that asked, *Where were you? Why didn't you save me?*

"What happened to her?" James asked gently.

"She was sent to a juvenile detention center and after

that, I don't know. I don't think she wants to be found. I'm pretty sure she changed her name, certainly on social media. Her brothers and sisters were taken into care and her parents moved away. That was the end of the line."

"None of that was your fault. You understand that, don't you?"

"I let her down. She was vulnerable and I didn't see her fall because I was *too busy*. You know people always talk about 'breaking the cycle' like it's easy, like you just have to make the choice to live a different kind of life, but they don't see the jaws of that life snapping at the heels of the person trying to escape it, waiting for one small slip that will give its teeth the purchase they need to drag them in."

She picked up a napkin and began wiping her hands roughly, repeatedly, but they still felt sticky. James reached over and placed his hands over hers to still them.

"You did what you could."

"It wasn't enough. I wasn't there."

"Do you honestly think that if you'd taken that call, things would have been different? From what you've said, she was already on a rocky path."

"I'll never know, will I?"

"You can't be forever on some sort of reparations mission. You gave up a career that you loved to make sure something like that doesn't happen again; nobody can say that you haven't done enough. I'd like to meet any person who had the audacity to suggest it."

"How do you know I loved my old career?

"Any idiot can see it. I've seen how discussing Dickens with the famous five lights you up from the inside out. I've watched the text come alive for them when they see it through your eyes. Your job title may be different, but in your heart you're still a teacher."

Her mouth worked a small smile.

He kept hold of her hands.

"Well, now you know. I'm not the 'disruptor' that you think I am. I'm like you, just trying to do better," she said.

"Oh, I don't know, you've managed to completely disrupt my life." He gave her a crooked smile. "And every day I'm gladder about it."

"Your charm will be my undoing."

"Does that mean I'm forgiven?"

"I'll give a tentative yes." She smiled at him.

"I'll take that. I was going out of my mind worrying that I'd blown things with you. I hardly slept last night, just kept going over and over it in my head. The look on your face when you thought I . . . well, I don't exactly know what you thought, but it was bad. Your expression damn near broke me. I don't ever want to be the cause of that expression again."

"And I will try not to be quite such a hostage to my phone. You're right, it has become an obsession. It started with my work, but over time it's bled out into every area of my life. I need to work on that."

He rubbed his thumb over her knuckles. "I'm sorry I was harsh. I understand now where your need to be available comes from and I appreciate your willingness to try and put your phone aside for us."

They ate their breakfast together in the noisy café, the pastries that Harriet hadn't shredded, at least. Something had shifted between them, like a sky left clear and bright after a storm has wrung itself out. Last night she wasn't sure that there was a way back for them and yet here they were, in a better place than they had begun.

TWENTY-THREE

IT HAD BEEN A WEEK AND A DAY SINCE THE GREAT FOSS PLAY-ers joined the production and despite the inevitable teething problems, they were beginning to feel like a cohesive team. The famous five had managed to switch shifts at their various weekend jobs so that the cast could have their first full run-through. Harriet and James sat at the end of a row near the middle of the stalls as the actors onstage ran their lines. Although everyone still hugged their scripts tightly, they were relying on them a little less each day. Gideon stood in the central aisle, a clipboard hugged to his chest, shouting helpful things: "More projection, Ahmed!" "Sid, imagine you are speaking to the person in the very back row." "Eye contact, Isabel!"

Outside, the town was heaving as the first Saturday in December sparked a frenzied countdown to Christmas, but inside the theater the atmosphere was determinedly calm. On the stage, Ahmed as Ebenezer Scrooge was tearing a strip off Ricco, his nephew, and Gideon was in raptures.

Billy appeared beside Harriet. "Miss, have you seen Grace this morning?"

"Grace? Um, no, I don't think so. Why?"

He bit his lip.

"I can't find her."

"Why do you need her?"

"I've got a book for her. It's nothing, it doesn't matter, the point is she's not here."

"Maybe she's coming in later today?"

"She wouldn't miss a rehearsal," Billy pressed.

"Well, ask Gideon. She might have called in sick."

Billy grimaced and went over to Gideon.

If she was honest, Harriet didn't pay much attention to the older players' whereabouts; her ducks consisted of the famous five and Sid, and she made sure she kept them in a row at all times. But his concern made her wonder. Last night, when Grace was struggling to get the top off her thermos, Billy had crossed the stage to loosen it for her. And when Billy had forgotten his lines in the kitchen scene with Isabel, Grace had discreetly acted as his prompter. Small acts which showed the other they were seen. If anyone were to notice Grace's absence, it would be Billy.

Gideon clapped his hands loudly.

"Okay, everybody, good work. Let's take five and then regroup for Act One, Scene Seven. Now has anybody heard from Grace today? Billy has alerted me to her absence."

There were mumbles on the stage as people looked about them, only just now realizing that Grace wasn't with them.

"Does anyone have her mobile number?" Billy called out. Mutters in the negative and shaking heads were his answer.

"I do!" Mallory piped up. "As secretary and treasurer, I have everyone's details on file."

Harriet and James walked over to where Billy and

Gideon were standing. Mallory held her phone to her ear, frowning.

"Her mobile's going straight to answer machine. I'll try her landline." She pursed her lips. "It's just ringing and ringing."

"We need her address," said Billy. Sid had come to stand by his side, his eyes wide as he picked up on his big brother's concern.

"Do you think that's really necessary?" asked Gideon condescendingly. "She's probably stopped off to do some Christmas shopping."

"Not when she's expected here, you know what she's like about bad manners."

He had a point. Mallory dug about in her carpetbag and pulled out a brown folder.

"It'll be in here," she said, flicking through the pages. "Ah, here it is." She held out the page with Grace's details and Billy—quick as a flash—snapped a photograph of it on his phone.

"I'm going over there to check," he said.

James glanced over the file. "That's the other end of town. If you're really that concerned, I'll drive you."

"I'll come too," added Harriet.

"Can I come?" asked Sid.

Billy ruffled his brother's hair. "Not this time, buddy, you need to stay here and practice with the others." He looked over to the other members of the famous five and gave them a nod. They returned it and hurried over.

Sid, crestfallen at being left behind, was about to argue when Ricco said, "Do you know what would help you learn your lines, Sid? Maccy-D fries and a chocolate milkshake."

"Yep, that's what it is!" agreed Isabel.

"Mind if we join you, Sid?" asked Carly.

"Honest?" Sid asked, his grin returned. "Can we, really?"

"Really truly," Leo confirmed. "Chocolate milkshake is famous for helping actors remember their lines."

With Sid's bribery in place, Harriet, James, and Billy exited the theater. The town was busy, but soon they had left the main roads behind and were driving up and down quiet residential streets.

"Can I ask why you're so worried?" asked James.

"It's just a feeling," Billy said, chewing on his thumbnail. "Last night she said, 'See you tomorrow'—why would she have said that if she wasn't going to be there?"

"Isn't that just a figure of speech? Like 'see you later'?" James suggested.

"Not for her. She's . . ."

"Exacting?" Harriet offered.

"Yeah. That."

"Of course, she could simply be running late?" Harriet added.

"Nah. You've heard her moaning on about 'tardiness.' If she was gonna be late, she'd have sent an official telegram or something."

After another five minutes, which seemed to have shredded Billy's very last nerve, they pulled up outside a three-up-two-down terraced house, with a neat front garden and a holly wreath on the front door. The street was lined both sides with cars parked bumper to bumper.

"You two jump out, and I'll try and find a place to park," said James.

Billy was out of the car before James had finished speaking. Harriet followed him down the path to Grace's house as he began ringing the doorbell and calling through the letterbox.

"Maybe she simply forgot there was a rehearsal to-day," Harriet offered hopefully. Billy's nerves were rub-bing off on her.

He shook his head. "No. I'm going round the back."

Before Harriet could stop him, he tore off down a narrow alleyway. All she could do was follow. Another alleyway, overgrown with weeds, ran behind the gar-dens. Billy looked along the rows of back gates.

"Which one is Grace's?" he asked in frustration.

Puffing to catch her breath, Harriet counted along from the end.

"This one," she said, walking over to a rickety wooden gate and opening the latch.

Like the front garden, the back garden was small and neat, with a square of lawn surrounded by flowerbeds and a brick path leading to the back door. Billy ran ahead down the path and pressed his face to the kitchen window.

"She's here!" he shouted back. "She's on the floor! Grace!" he yelled, banging on the window.

Harriet rushed to the window while Billy began try-ing the handle of the door, but it was locked. Grace lay crumpled in a heap on the kitchen floor, her eyes flutter-ing. A glass bottle was smashed nearby one of her slip-pered feet, and a puddle of milk pooled around her. A bag of flour on the table had been upset and some had spilled like a layer of snow.

"We're here now, Grace," she shouted through the glass as she dialed 999. "I'm going to call for help."

James arrived on the scene just as Harriet was finish-ing up the call. At his expression, she turned from the window to see that Billy had begun to scale the drain-pipe. Harriet's heart gave a lurch of alarm.

"Billy! What are you . . . ? Come down! I don't want

to have to order two ambulances!" Under her breath, she whispered, "For flock's sake!"

"She's all alone!" Billy shouted back.

They stood at the base of the drainpipe looking up. Billy was too high up even for James to grab him.

"That looks dangerous, mate," James reasoned. "The ambulance will be here soon, why don't you leave it to them?"

"I'm not leaving her!" Billy panted. His foot slipped on the pipe, sending rusted paint flecks fluttering down.

"Son of a biscuit!" she swore. "Please be careful!" To James, she added, "Oh my god, this kid's going to give me a heart attack. I think I'm going to puke."

But Billy had already reached his destination. He swung his feet onto a ledge, grabbed hold of the wooden window frame, and posted himself through the open window of the upstairs bathroom. A loud bump, then some after-clatters and the sound of things rolling around on a linoleum floor, and then Billy's voice shouted, "I'm okay!"

"Oh, sweet baby cheeses." Harriet let out a breath and bent her head to her knees to try and get some blood back into her brain.

James moved back to the window, and Harriet stood up in time to see Billy enter the kitchen and kneel at Grace's head. They couldn't hear what he was saying, but the wan smile on Grace's face made them both puff out sighs of relief. Billy stroked the hair away from her face and gave her hand a squeeze before jumping up to unlock the back door.

A bowl sat on the kitchen table half-filled with flour and sugar. Next to it was a pot of ground ginger.

"I was making gingerbread men for Sid," Grace mumbled. "And then I came over dizzy. I must have fallen. I need to get up."

Billy, who was kneeling back beside her, rested his hand on her shoulder. "Just stay there for the moment, yeah? Let the paramedics check you over first."

"Fuss and nonsense," she argued, but her heart wasn't in it, and she stayed where she was. "How did you get in?"

"I climbed up the drainpipe and in through the bathroom window."

She gave a snort and patted his hand with her own, which still trembled from the shock of her fall.

"Stupid boy. I suppose you think you're Spider-Man now."

"Little bit," Billy smirked.

....

Several hours later they were all back at Grace's house again to settle her in. The doctor at the hospital had diagnosed an inner ear infection, which had caused her to lose her balance. It was plain bad luck that her head had met with the corner of the dining table as she'd gone down. Aside from a few bumps and bruises, she had been declared fit as a fiddle.

"The biggest bruises are to my ego," Grace complained as James and Harriet fussed around her small sitting room, plumping cushions and keeping up a steady stream of tea. "D'oh, just stop it, I'm not an invalid. I'm sixty-five, not a hundred!" she snapped, flapping her hands at James as he pushed a footstool toward her, though she did grudgingly plop her slippered feet up on it.

"You gave us all a scare," Harriet called from the kitchen as she unpacked the foodie gifts that had been arriving at the house for the last hour.

Word of Grace's fall had quickly spread around the theater. Anousheh and Sana—from the women's group—had dropped in stuffed flatbreads and enough biryani to last a week, while Mallory had brought fondant fancies, mini Scotch eggs, and other such picnic foods from the Great Foss Players. Even the maintenance teams had sent over flowers and chocolates.

Tess and Arthur had dropped round with Sid so that he could give Grace a tin of Christmas biscuits and then taken him home for some dinner. Arthur had lost weight, Harriet thought, since she'd last seen him, but she tucked that niggle away for this evening. Somewhat surprisingly, given he'd already spent the whole day with Grace, Billy didn't go home with them; Harriet wondered if it had anything to do with the giant pan of biryani in the kitchen.

"I had no idea I was so popular." Grace's tone was cynical. She made a big show of being suspicious of the plentiful kindnesses and pooh-poohed the notion that today's events had left her shaken. But in a moment that she was now blaming on the effects of painkillers, she had confessed to Billy that she'd thought she was going to die alone on the kitchen floor and that no one would find her body until it began to smell.

"Well, it turns out that despite your best efforts at cantankerousness, people still like you, so deal with it," Harriet retorted, drying her hands on a tea towel printed with a faded recipe for Cornish pasties as she came back into the sitting room. "Now, the doctor has said that you need someone to stay with you tonight just in case you have a concussion. It's simply a precaution . . ."

"Bunkum!" Grace blustered. "I don't need a babysitter."

"You do tonight," said James smoothly.

"I don't mind staying over, you've got a bed made up in the spare room," said Harriet. "I can sleep in there."

"Been snooping, have you?"

"I had to go upstairs to find the things you needed for the hospital, remember?"

Grace made a grumbling noise not unlike the dissenting sounds made by MPs during Prime Minister's Question Time.

"I'll stay," said Billy.

"Certainly not!" Grace protested.

"Afraid I might steal all your worldly belongings?" he asked, smiling sardonically.

"I'm more concerned you'll scoff my biryani," she snapped.

"Now that is a possibility," he replied.

I knew it! Harriet smiled to herself.

"I don't need looking after," Grace insisted.

"Which is why I'm perfect for the job," argued Billy. "'Cause I have no intention of looking after you. I'm only offering to stay because you've got Sky Movies."

"Well." Grace gave the impression of mulling it over. "All right, then. But I choose the movie and I want all the pink fondant fancies."

"Fair enough," said Billy, shrugging. "I'll go and dish myself up some grub, I'm starving."

He turned abruptly and walked into the kitchen.

"Little shit," Grace muttered under her breath, but the smile in her eyes was undeniable.

....

With Grace and Billy settled in front of the TV and a smorgasbord of delights laid out on the coffee table, Harriet and James made their exit.

"Do you think she'll be all right?" James asked as he parked outside Harriet's building.

"Grace? Yeah. She's made of tough stuff. She might murder Billy, though."

"They're a funny pair, aren't they? A week ago, they couldn't stand each other."

"I think maybe they see themselves reflected in each other."

"You always see the good in people, don't you?" said James.

"It's not about the good or bad, sometimes it's just about the seeing."

He looked out of the window, which was beginning to steam up, nodding slowly.

"I think I'm starting to get that. What are you up to tomorrow?" he asked.

She stretched contentedly like a cat as she thought about her Sunday plans. "Lazy morning, lunch at Emma and Pete's, FaceTime with Maisy, lazy evening. You?"

"Brunch with Lyra, catch up on some paperwork, watch the footie."

"You're into football?"

He laughed at her surprise. "Is that so unusual?"

She shrugged. "I guess I had you down for following something like fencing, or televised chess championships."

He shook his head, smiling.

They were quiet for a moment, each of them not quite ready to burst the little bubble of harmony they'd found inside the car. Harriet considered inviting him in but after the commotion of today, she was looking forward to getting into her pj's and watching a movie.

"Who knew there'd be so much drama outside of the play?" she said, yawning.

"I had an inkling the moment Gideon showed up," James replied dryly, and Harriet laughed. "So much for the first official run-through. I hope it's not an omen."

"Oh, there's plenty of time yet." Harriet laid her head back against the headrest.

"You've changed your tune." James smiled. "A couple of weeks ago, you were panicking that we'd never pull it together and now you're Little Miss Chillaxed."

She turned her head to face him. "I wouldn't go that far. But maybe I'm starting to realize that I can't control everything and that's okay. Schnitzel's going to happen whether I worry myself stupid or not, so I may as well go with the flow."

"Have you been at Grace's sherry?"

She pressed her forefinger and thumb together in the universal sign for *a little bit* and giggled. "She kept offering me 'snifters.'"

"Tess and Arthur seem nice," James said.

"They're lovely. They've been so good for Billy. And Sid." She smiled, thinking about the many changes she'd seen in Billy over the years. "You should have seen him when he first started at Foss Independent. Lordy, I thought for sure he'd be expelled before the end of year seven. It was like he'd been raised by wolves. I am so proud of that kid."

"You really care about them, don't you?"

"I really do. They've got so much potential; they could change the world. You've got to know them a bit by now—you must see it too?"

"I do. I've been thinking . . ."

"Uh-oh!" She smirked in his direction.

"I could start a legal surgery at the theater, a couple of evenings a week. You know, pro bono, offer advice to people who couldn't otherwise afford it. I think there's a need for it. Well, I know there is, even just in our own little expanding community. And I could help people like Farahnoush and Ava with their documents, that sort of thing. What do you think?"

Harriet unclipped her seat belt and with little to no grace at all climbed over the gear stick and hand brake to straddle James's lap. The steering wheel bit into the base of her back, and the cup holder was definitely going to leave a ring on her right knee, but she didn't care.

"This is what I think," she whispered as she pressed her lips to his, her hands cupping his face. She felt his arms snake around her back, pulling her down onto him.

"Now I wish I'd mentioned it sooner," he growled into her mouth. His hands fumbled with her layers. "How many cardigans are you wearing this time?"

"Wouldn't you like to know!"

Her phone rang and they both froze. This was when she would usually be compelled to answer no matter what she was in the middle of, but a quick glance at the screen showed her it wasn't a number that she recognized and she breathed out her worry and let it ring, and James's kisses became even more fervent as a reward.

The snow had picked up again, and the street was quiet. The windows of James's car were opaque with condensation, and anyone who was brave enough to be outside didn't bother knocking.

TWENTY-FOUR

SATURDAY'S FULL RUN-THROUGH HAD BEEN RESCHEDULED for Monday afternoon. Billy had just picked Sid up from school. Sid's cheeks were two red apples, and his gloves were caked in snow. Billy pulled them off him and took them outside to beat off the excess ice.

"Ah good, we have our Tiny Tim at last. Now we can begin. Places, please, everybody! Spit spot!" Gideon ordered.

People began hurrying in different directions. Ahmed took to the stage, as did the narrators: Carly, Hiroshi, Ricco, Winston, and Ernest (the Lonely Farts had been roped into playing bit parts because no one was safe from Gideon's monomania for casting). Ricco and Isabel—aka Scrooge's nephew and Roberta Cratchit—waited in the wings for the start of Scene 2. Hesther and Kingsley shuffled up beside them dragging Scrooge's front door, which had been made to stand up by itself by wooden struts nailed into the framework at the back.

Harriet was in the opposite stage wing on her hands and knees, with her phone clasped to her ear as she held a meeting with the Special Educational Needs Coordinator at Foss Independent while trying to make sense of the black sacks of costumes Mallory had brought from the Great Foss Players archives and the donations from the public, which had been steadily growing since Gideon had given a shout-out from the local radio station asking for vintage Victoriana.

By the time the meeting had ended, she had separated the clothes into piles. The costumes left over from the Great Foss Players' production of *Little Women* the year before last would come in most handy, while their outfits from *Starlight Express* and *Cats* were less useful. She had a call with a parent in an hour and a stack of emails from Cornell that had come through so thick and fast that for a moment she thought her account had been hacked. She was coming to the conclusion that something was going to have to give, but she didn't know which ball she could afford to drop.

"Miss?"

Harriet looked up, feeling dazed by her monumental to-do list, to find Billy standing above her. "Billy." She smiled, mentally compartmentalizing her life. "How can I help?"

"There's some people want to see you," he said, jerking his head backward.

She looked around his legs to see a group of people dressed in combats and camouflage standing in the opposite wing. She gave them a wave and they waved back enthusiastically.

"Righty-ho," she said, groaning as she got up off the floor. "I noticed you picked Sid up from after-school club again today. Are Tess and Arthur okay?"

"They're fine. Stop asking."

Hmmmm. Tell that to the nagging feeling in her stomach.

"Did I see Grace leave with you?" she asked.

"Yeah, she wanted to surprise Sid—she took us to the café on the corner for cake."

"That was very kind of her."

Billy shrugged.

"You would tell me if there was something wrong, wouldn't you?"

Her phone blipped with a text, and in the short time it took her to check it, Billy had slipped away, no doubt to steel himself for his appearance as Roberta Cratchit's careworn husband.

"Chains!" Gideon's voice rang out. "Destiny, my sweet jewel, where are your chains? What is Jacob Marley without his chains?"

Harriet cast a glance across the way to see Leo and Sid sat on chairs on either side of Dhruv, a mass of gray paper chains draped across all three of them and snaking along the floor.

"We're working as fast as we can, Captain!" Dhruv shouted in a Scottish accent. "But we're running out of spit!"

Harriet sniggered as she slipped behind the stage on her way to meet the newcomers.

"Hello, I'm Harriet," she said, smiling when she reached them.

A woman about her age with her hair pulled back in a high ponytail and a distinct air of the Tomb Raider about her stepped forward, smiling and holding out her hand for Harriet to shake.

"Hi! I'm Cassidy. We're the Relic Hunters."

Did not see that coming!

Cassidy must have seen her quizzical expression as she shook her hand because she added, "We're detectorists. You know, metal detectors?"

"Oh, I see." Harriet took her hand back. "Good to meet you. Are you detectoring around these parts?" She thought of the basement and what could be lurking under that dirt floor.

"No, well, yes, we are, but not here in this theater. We used to meet once a week at the community center—"

"Ah, say no more. This is pretty much the new clubhouse for community center evictees." Harriet smiled warmly at the new group.

"I did recognize quite a few faces on my way through," said Cassidy. "Anyway, we heard about what you were doing here, and we thought maybe we could help each other out. If we could borrow a quiet corner to hold our Relic Hunter meetings, we'd be happy to offer our services toward your play."

"You know about our production of *A Christmas Carol*?"

"Everybody does," said a grinning man with the hair on either side of his head shaved off and a tattoo of what Harriet presumed was the Holy Grail on his neck. Another man, with a handlebar mustache, stepped forward and shook Harriet's hand, his other hand clasped with that of a petite woman with long rainbow plaits who singsonged, "Hello!" in a tiny voice.

"You're the talk of the town," added a man with eyes the color of periwinkles behind his small round glasses. "Literally. It's all over the Little Beck Foss socials."

"Some of us are into medieval reenactment," said Cassidy, "and we know our way around a sewing machine. We bumped into a couple of the Lonely Farts in the foyer, and they said it was going to be all hands to the thread to get the costumes ready in time. So put us to work!"

"Seamsters!" Harriet clasped her hands below her

chin in wonder. "I feel like you guys were sent here by Father Christmas. We are in dire need of people who can make alterations. But just so you know, I would have let you have your meetings here regardless of whether you'd offered to help out or not. This is a community space for as long as we have it, and you are all very welcome. Make yourselves at home. There's usually a steady stream of baked goods coming out of the kitchen that you are welcome to partake of; we only ask that everyone pitches in with a couple of quid, if you can spare it. In fact, I do believe Prescilla and Ernest have been baking batches of mince pies up there this afternoon."

As she said this, a whoop went up from the auditorium, and she heard Hiroshi shout, "Here they are!" followed by a stampede of feet across the stage.

"Players! Players, please!" Gideon's impassioned plea cut through the noise. "The mince pies will still be there after the run-through!"

"They won't be hot, though!" returned Destiny. "Don't you worry yourself, Gideon, I can eat and act, I'm a professional."

Harriet left the Relic Hunters to settle in and stole around to the front of the stage to watch the run-through. She spotted James sitting in the stalls a few rows back and made her way over to him. On the stage, Destiny aka Jacob Marley was wailing, *"Mankind was my business!"*

"It's a pity Evaline isn't here to see this," Harriet whispered in James's ear. "She could learn a lesson or two from Jacob Marley."

He smiled. "She's not so bad."

"Your loyalty to her is rather touching. I'm not sure she deserves it."

"I understand her, that's all. If I were truly loyal, I probably would have tried to stop you from inviting every displaced club within a ten-mile radius into the theater."

"Do you really think you could have stopped me?" she challenged.

His chuckle was low and rumbling. "No. I don't think I could."

"Will you tell Evaline about your legal surgery?"

"Perhaps."

"What about your practice?"

"I spoke to my partners this afternoon, and they've given their blessing."

"Do you think Lyra will come to the performance?"

She felt his shoulders stiffen.

"I'd like to ask her to," he said cautiously.

"I'd like that too." She took his hand and felt his shoulders relax. "James?" She wasn't sure how to broach this subject, or if it even needed a label, but the part of her that liked things in their places had been poised with a Post-it note and pen ever since their heart-to-heart on Friday.

"Yes?" He cocked his head to one side when she didn't say anything.

Heavens to Betsy, what am I? Thirteen? Just ask him already!

"I was just wondering, um. Are we a thing?"

He quirked an eyebrow.

"After our behavior in my car on Saturday night, do you even need to ask?"

She flushed at the remembrance of her wantonness. She'd already had one run-in with the police recently; she didn't need to risk being charged with outraging public decency. He was rubbing circles over her palm with his thumb now. She cleared her throat.

"Yes, but we've engaged in a couple of encounters previous to the car and that didn't make us a thing."

"Didn't it?"

Oh!

"Did it?" she asked. "That night at my flat, you know, before the table incident, you'd said you kissed me and shouldn't have done."

"Yes. I did say that. I didn't want to be that man who takes advantage of a woman when she's in a vulnerable state, and you were feeling vulnerable when I kissed you. Less so when you started shouting at me." He gave her a wry smile, and she remembered their argument that had led to christening her hall table. "And it didn't seem fair of me to start something with you when I wasn't being completely up-front about my situation. I guess you could say I was suffering from conflicting emotions."

She bit her lip. "Right. So you wanted us to be a thing but not just then?"

"That's about the size of it. I was never interested in a throwaway encounter with you. From the moment I met you, I knew I wanted more." He turned in his chair to face her, and she inhaled sharply at the intensity of his gaze. "And I realize that my surprise daughter wasn't exactly in keeping with pursuing an open and honest dialogue," he went on. "If anything could throw you off the scent of my desire for a relationship, it would be that. But I am learning quickly from my mistakes because I meant what I said: I want something meaningful. With you. If you'd like that too?"

There's that word again! Meaningful. She could feel her heart pounding hard and fast. *Cripes! That was very romantic!* She was experiencing sensations of extreme excitement, exhilaration, and fear, like she was about to be hit by a bus driven by George Clooney blowing kisses at her. *Are relationships supposed to make you feel like you're about to be hit by a bus? He's waiting for an answer.*

"I'd kind of thought you'd meant in a generalized sense." Her voice came out squeaky.

"A *generalized meaningfulness*?" He was looking at her with amusement in his eyes. "Isn't that a bit of an oxymoron?"

"Oh god! Why am I such a tit?" she wondered out loud.

James burst out a laugh that was incongruous with Grace's onstage performance as the Ghost of Christmas Past escorting Scrooge back to his childhood. Gideon swiveled on his Cuban heels and glared at them.

"Is there something funny about a man confronting the aching sadness of his past?" he demanded.

Harriet and James slipped down in their seats.

"Would you like to share the joke with everyone?" Gideon continued.

"Oh, um, no, thank you," said James, offering a surrendering wave.

"Sorry," Harriet offered at the same time.

With a final death stare in their direction, Gideon turned back to the stage. "From the top of Act One, Scene Eight, if you please, Grace and Ahmed," he instructed, and the action on the stage began again.

In the darkness, still slunk down in their seats, James took Harriet's hand.

"Would you like to be officially in a thing with me?" he asked.

She smiled so hard she could feel her cheeks stretching. "Yes, please."

He squeezed her hand, and she leaned her head on his shoulder. On the stage, Ahmed and Grace continued in their parts while all around the Winter Theater, people were making new connections, breaking down barriers, and sealing friendships. The theater was becoming a living, breathing ark, picking up survivors and rescuing them from loneliness.

....

On Wednesday afternoon another group made homeless by budget cuts joined the merry band of misfits at the theater. Harriet had settled the new arrivals—the Under-Fives Story-Timers—on the newly varnished parquet dance floor in the cocktail lounge, away from the colorful language of the Lonely Farts Club and Relic Hunters members, who were working on the set building under the careful direction of Farahnoush and Hesther.

"Josef, may I have a word?" Harriet called him away from painting a papier-mâché goose for the Cratchits' dinner table.

He ambled over, smiling as always.

"Hello, my dear, how may I be of service?"

Harriet pulled an electric menorah from her bag and handed it to him.

"I wanted to give you this. It's almost Hanukkah, and I thought it would be nice to have something to mark the occasion here at the theater. Especially since you're very kindly helping us with our Christmas production. I know it's not got real candles," she said apologetically. "But I didn't want to risk burning the theater down."

Josef's face was luminescent. "It's wonderful!" he said. "How thoughtful."

"And if you'd like, we—that is to say, us lot"—she waved her hand around the auditorium—"thought it would be nice to hold a celebratory Hanukkah meal for you, here on the fifteenth with everyone."

"I would love that more than you know!" He beamed, his hands clasped in front of his face.

"I'm glad." She couldn't help but mirror his smile. "We have so many people of different faiths here, it makes my heart happy. If we get to keep our community space after the theater is sold, I would like to celebrate them all if we can; Eid, Diwali, we've got a couple of Pagans in the Relic Hunters . . ."

"Ooh, winter and summer solstices, I'll be in charge of the wassail," put in Josef. "I have a fabulous recipe from a good friend down in Rowan Thorp. And Eid will give me the chance to perfect my gulab jamun."

Harriet laughed. "Sounds like a plan," she said.

Josef left to find a street-facing windowsill for his menorah, and Harriet went to see Leo, who was nervously pacing the stage while Ken and his mighty maintenance crew affixed the first backcloth to the track system that would allow the backdrops to be raised and dropped during the show.

"Do you feel proud?" Harriet asked him. She was certainly proud. If anyone prodded her, she had the feeling that she'd burst like a glitter piñata.

"Kinda, I guess," Leo replied shyly.

"Ready, Leo, my boy?" came Ken's sonorous voice from behind the stage curtains. Really, with a voice that resounding, it was a waste that he hadn't pursued a career on the stage.

Everyone stopped what they were doing and came to gather in the middle aisle, shuffling left and right along the stalls to get a good view. Billy and Ricco had sprinted out of the auditorium moments earlier to gather the rest of the maintenance team, who now trickled onto the balcony and into the royal boxes to watch.

"Ready!" Leo called back, his voice small in the sudden

and unusual silence. Ricco scooted back and wriggled in beside him just in time.

The first backcloth dropped down at the back of the stage, and a gasp of appreciation rippled through the theater. It was Scrooge's office, with two large leaded windows drawing the eye out onto the snowy street beyond. Images of ragged children, snowballs poised for flight in raised hands, and carol singers in bright bonnets were lit by gas lamps. Inside, the office wall was cracked and peeling, a shelf with one candle and one book hung between the windows, a mouse hole in the skirting board below. After a few moments of stunned silence as the audience took it all in, a round of appreciative applause went up.

Ken stomped along the stage and down the steps to join the crowd in the aisle.

"Aye, you've done a grand job, lad," he said, rubbing at his eye with a meaty hand as the clapping died down. "Bloody hell, son, I think you've brought a tear to me eye."

"You're not the only one," said Odette, sniffing.

In fact, there were multiple sniffles rising out of the auditorium. Harriet's eyes were so clouded by tears that the backcloth had gone into soft focus. She felt James's arm around her, and he pulled her close. She stiffened and then relaxed into his embrace. This was a public declaration to match the one they had made privately to each other. People would talk. The famous five would definitely talk. *Let them*, she thought. She sniffed and surreptitiously wiped her face on James's jumper.

"Did you just wipe your nose on my sweater?" he whispered.

"Little bit," she replied, laughing wetly into her sleeve.

"I'll allow it," he said, squeezing her closer.

"You have a rare talent, Leo," James observed. It was a sentiment that was echoed about the space.

Leo shrugged and made a sort of grunting noise. "Thanks," he said self-consciously. "But I had a lot of help."

"Which you managed expertly," Farahnoush said, smiling. "Take the compliment. You deserve it. I worked in design for twenty years before I arrived in Britain; I know an artist when I see one."

"See!" said Ricco, who was squeezing Leo tightly around the waist. "I told you; you were brilliant." He kissed his cheek, and Leo smiled bashfully.

"Right!" said Ken, making everyone jump. "Let's get the next one rigged up. How many will there be altogether, Leo?"

"Fifteen. We've got four more to finish painting."

"Bloody hell, lad, it's like the Oscars of backcloths!"

Leo laughed, his blush visible even in the dark of the auditorium. Ken strode back behind the stage, shouting orders as he stomped.

"We need to take photographs of every backcloth in situ," said Harriet, pulling out her phone and beginning to snap pictures. "I've managed to get quite a few of you while you've been working on them."

"Why?" he asked.

"For your portfolio. This is amazing stuff, Leo. Imagine how impressive this will be if you want to apply for art colleges."

"Which you definitely should," added James.

James's encouragement of her kids threw another log on her already smoldering feelings toward him. He was so far from the cold fish she had encountered that day in the police station.

"Yeah, but I've had loads of help painting them," Leo objected.

"To be fair, babe, it's practically been painting by numbers," said Carly. "I love you and everything, but you are a classic micromanager."

"You are very particular with your vision," said Ava delicately.

"Like Steve Jobs with a paintbrush," added Hiroshi, and everybody sniggered.

"This is exactly the kind of project that art colleges would be wetting their pants over," said Harriet, getting the conversation back on track. "So, anyone who can, get pictures of the artist at work, and we'll start putting together a portfolio." If this didn't instill the boy with some confidence in his talent, nothing would.

People began to drift back to what they'd been doing before.

James had to leave for a meeting with some of Evaline's financial advisors, but he drew Harriet into one of the dark corners of the theater first to steal a kiss. He smelled like bergamot shower gel, sandalwood, and freshly ironed cotton, and she breathed him in as their lips pressed together, one kiss leading to another, then another. His low moan sent a spike of pleasure down her stomach, making her breath hitch and her grip on his back tighten.

"Kissing you is my new favorite pastime." He smiled against her mouth, his voice raspy with desire.

"It's good to have hobbies," she answered breathlessly.

"It could become an obsession."

"We can but hope."

"I have to go."

"Yes, you do."

"I'll come back later to walk you home."

"You don't need to do that."

"I know."

After one last kiss goodbye, James left for his meeting. She hid in the corner for a few minutes longer, fanning her face and rearranging her pinafore, which had become rucked up during some very unprofessional bottom grabbing. Kissing James always left her breathless and wanting more. Every kiss felt like a small promise. She didn't need extravagant declarations of forever. She was a practical, independent woman of a certain age, and what she wanted was this, one small daily promise which said, *Today I am yours, today we promise to be each other's.* Maybe they would make that one small promise to each other every day for the rest of their lives, or maybe they wouldn't. For now, she couldn't think of anything better than committing wholeheartedly to one day at a time.

TWENTY-FIVE

TWO MORE WAIF AND STRAY COMMUNITY GROUPS HAD ARrived and been quickly assimilated into the theater. They were followed by a single-parents coffee group who, once they'd finished their meeting, were eager to help with painting the last of the backcloths. The buzz in the theater was so intoxicating that almost everyone who'd arrived ended up offering their services in some way to the production.

Harriet and Gideon stayed at the theater late that night drawing up volunteer sheets with jobs that needed doing. By late Friday afternoon, most of the sheets had the names of willing participants scribbled beside their chosen tasks. *A Christmas Carol* now had a full quota of stagehands and lighting and sound engineers.

"Harriet!"

She heard her name whisper-hissed and turned in her seat, from where she had been half watching the rehearsals onstage, as she tried to file reports ready for Monday morning's department meeting. Mallory was beckoning her furiously from the middle aisle. Harriet shimmied along the row toward her.

"Hey, Mallory, have you seen the sign-up sheets? They're almost full."

"Never mind that. Evaline is in the foyer!" Mallory exclaimed.

"What? She wasn't due to visit today."

"Well, she's here and she looks pissed. And she's asking for you."

"Oh, cripes! Okay, let's go see what she wants." Harriet gestured toward the lift.

"Oh no, not me. You're on your own!" Mallory swiveled, cackling wickedly, and zipped off down the aisle toward the orchestra pit, where the final touches were being made to the window from which Scrooge would call out to a street urchin near the end of the play.

Harriet found Evaline in the middle of the foyer, sitting like a queen in a wheelchair with red velvet cushions, her expression radiating *I am not amused*. Austin, in his chauffeur's cap and suit, stood behind her chair like a bodyguard, poised to push when the order was given.

Harriet was surprised to see her in a wheelchair, but she made no mention of it.

"Evaline." Harriet smiled. "How lovely to see you. We weren't expecting you today."

"So I see!"

The doors to the building next door opened and James appeared, allowing the cacophony of the five-to-elevens music club—Sonja's Semibreves—to flood into the already noisy foyer. Clearly, he had been alerted to the grande dame's arrival too.

"Evaline!" he called jovially over the sound of cymbals crashing and a rubber mallet streaking enthusiastically along a xylophone. The old woman looked him up and down, taking in his jeans and knitted sweater, the corners of her mouth twisting downward in displeasure. "What a lovely surprise," he continued. Harriet could tell that he was caught off guard, but he was covering it well.

"A *surprise*, I am sure, though I doubt you find my

presence *lovely*. I seem to have found you in the middle of a chaotic episode."

"Oh, good lord no, it's always like this!" trilled Priscilla, floating through the foyer at speed, flapping a book of sheet music. "You should see it when it's busy! Snacks are on the way, chaps and chapesses!" she called, taking the grand staircase two steps at a time.

Evaline had the look of a woman being silently electrocuted.

"Who are all these *people* in my theater?" she demanded.

Harriet chanced a glance at James, who seemed to have decided to embrace the situation rather than manage it. He grinned mischievously as he made his way to her side and said through gritted teeth: "I think the jig is up, we may as well come clean."

Oh my god, he's going to get himself fired! Her mind spun wildly as she tried to think of ways that she could explain all of this and paint James as a hapless victim of her overzealous community spirit.

But before she could articulate her excuses, he took hold of her hand and with the other made a wide arc of the foyer, and said, "Welcome to your community hub, Evaline!"

Evaline's eyes squinted like she'd just bitten down on a Sour Patch sweet. Her nostrils flared as she sucked in a deep breath, but James didn't give her a chance to speak.

"Over here, we have the Relic Hunters." He gestured toward them, deep in discussion about the items on their finds table, and waved. "Can you talk us through what you're doing today please, guys?"

Cassidy, who had been sitting with a long cream petticoat spilling out over her lap as she sewed, stood.

"Sure. So, we're detectorists, and usually once every

couple of weeks we get together and show our finds and discuss them, but since we've joined the theater, we've pretty much become part of the furniture."

"A very welcome and vital part of the furniture," Harriet added, smiling.

"Thanks," said Cassidy. "I think we've found our kin among the folks here. You're welcome to come over and have a look at our most recent finds, if you like."

"What I would like—" Evaline began, but Harriet, seeing that she was about to say something disagreeable, cut her off.

"And because we're all multitaskers here, they are also lending a hand to *your* production by knocking up some costumes, alongside the Lonely Farts and some of the women in Hesther's group. Josef and Dhruv are up in the kitchen now, baking snacks to keep us all going for practice tonight. It's all hands on deck if we are to meet *your* tight deadline."

"The Lonely *what* did you say?" Evaline spluttered.

"Farts!" James grinned. "Okay, then; thanks, guys!" James gave the Relic Hunters a thumbs-up, and they went back to their artifacts and their needles and thread. "And over here . . ." He motioned to the area near the old box office, which had been set up with a trestle table and chairs. "We have some more of our Lonely Farts Club members."

Winston looked up and smiled. His beard and hair were a mass of tight gray curls and his eyes always twinkled with merriment.

"Excuse us," he said. "We are in the midst of a rather thrilling game of dominoes."

Kingsley waved one of the cream tiles. "Ernest is painting backcloths with Farahnoush, and the last time I saw Harry he was helping to stop the wobble on Scrooge's bedroom window. We're rather scattered about the place at present."

"The Lonely Farts are invaluable members of the team," said Harriet, smiling fondly at Kingsley. "The youngsters in particular have really benefited from their wisdom."

"People are always saying that you can't teach old dogs new tricks, but they never take into account the old tricks that we can teach the new dogs." Winston winked at her.

"Quite right," said Harriet. She turned to Evaline, still sitting monarchlike on her throne. "This experience is beneficial in so many ways to all of us."

"I'm sure I'm delighted to be accommodating a huge portion of the proletarian populace in my theater so that they can *find* themselves," Evaline snipped.

Harriet felt her cheeks redden with embarrassment. James looked equally mortified.

"I think you've been living up in your high tower for too long," Kingsley said calmly. "You seem to have forgotten your manners."

Evaline's eyes grew so wide with outrage that Harriet feared they might pop right out like two hard-boiled eggs. The old woman pushed on the arms of her chair, hands shaking as she made to stand. Austin immediately moved to one side of her and James to the other, like sentries.

Any great declarations she might have been about to make were swallowed by the swing doors opening— pushing in the sounds of a trombone and trumpet being played badly—and several joyful humans carrying trays of hot snacks.

"Right, nosh is up, people!" Josef called. "To the auditorium!"

At this, dominoes and historical artifacts were discarded as everyone followed the Pied Pipers up the grand staircase.

"Evaline, perhaps you'd like to try the new lift to take us down to the auditorium?" Harriet asked. "I'm sure you'd like to see how the production is coming along."

Evaline gave her a cold, hard stare.

"Very well. Since it pertains to my reason for being here, I may as well."

She allowed herself to be gingerly lowered back into her wheelchair and did her utmost not to show that she was impressed by the restoration of the beautiful Art Deco interior of the lift.

As the doors swished closed Harriet began, "I don't want to sound rude, but why are you here?"

"I came to inform you that as of tomorrow the box office will be open."

"I'd thought the production was going to be free—why do people need tickets?" Harriet queried.

"It's a fire safety thing," James answered. "Legally we can only have a certain number of bodies in the building. It makes sense to ticket the event, so that we can be sure we are meeting fire safety standards."

"Oh, okay. But the tickets are still free, right?"

"Almost. There is a two-pound charge, one hundred percent of which goes to the local food bank," said James. Evaline sniffed disdainfully. Harriet wanted to press herself against James and tell him he was wonderful.

"It would appear that your obsessive do-gooding has rubbed off on my solicitor and made him soft in the head. You are like a snowball, Ms. Smith, rolling downhill, gathering up waifs and strays as you go before thundering like an avalanche into *my* theater."

"Ummm, thank you?" Harriet said.

"Be quiet! I am not finished."

Harriet bit her lip and stared down at the carpet.

"However," Evaline continued, "my accountant will

see that my generosity to local charities works favorably on my tax return."

The lift opened and despite being in her chair, Evaline used her stick to hit at the ankles of anyone who got in her way. When they reached the front row of the dress circle, Austin helped Evaline to a seat in the center. Harriet seated herself beside Evaline, with James on her other side. Austin settled in a few rows behind.

Smells of hot mince pies and gingerbread mixed and mingled with honey-sweet and cumin-savory pastries laid out on tables below the stage. All over the theater, people stopped what they were doing to grab a hot morsel or three and got comfortable in the stalls while they ate. Under the stage lights, Ahmed as Scrooge and Odette as the Ghost of Christmas Present played out their roles.

"*Spirit! Are they yours?*" Ahmed fell to his knees, hands clasped in supplication, looking up at Odette.

"*They are man's,*" Odette replied.

As the scene came to its dramatic end, a bell rang twelve times and a shiver ran down Harriet's spine. Then the theater erupted into rapturous applause. Harriet joined in, but it didn't surprise her to note that Evaline's gloved hands remained folded in her lap. She found herself reciting one of the lines she had helped Carly to learn in her role as Belle. *You fear the world too much. All your other hopes have merged into the hope of being beyond the chance of its sordid reproach.* Without turning fully, she cast her eyes sideways at Evaline in time to see a single tear run down the old woman's softly crumpled cheek and drip down onto the fur collar of her coat.

TWENTY-SIX

HARRIET AND JAMES SAT ON HER SOFA, A SCENTED CANDLE burning, the nutcrackers standing sentinel on the fireplace and *Love Actually* playing on the TV above it. She'd cooked them a meal, from scratch. It felt very decadent for a Monday. She felt contented, with his arm draped loosely around her, her head resting on his chest.

"I should go soon," James said, kissing the top of her head.

"Oh." She snuggled in deeper. "Stay to the end of the film."

"It's already half past eleven."

"Did you always want to be a solicitor?"

"Don't change the subject."

"It seems like a strange thing for a child to aspire to. Surely you must have wanted to be an astronaut or a firefighter before a solicitor?"

He sighed, chuckling. "Not if you grew up with parents who avidly watched *L.A. Law*, *Hill Street Blues*, and *Cagney and Lacey*," he said.

"Wouldn't that have made you want to join the police?"

"No way! In all of those shows, the people who had the power to make the bad guys go away were the lawyers. Plus, they got to wear nice suits and talk fast.

Although I hadn't realized that practicing law in England meant I'd have to wear a wig."

She laughed.

"So that's why you wanted to go to America, you didn't want to ruin your hair."

"It's great hair."

She could feel him smiling and reached up to run her fingers through his great hair.

"What about you? Did you always want to be a teacher?"

"Always. I mean, of course I wanted to be a pop star and a member of a famous dance troupe and a fashion designer, but mostly I wanted to be a teacher. I had a couple of amazing teachers at primary school and obviously there was Miss Honey from *Matilda*."

"Obviously," James parroted. "Who is Miss Honey?"

She sat up.

"Seriously? You never read *Matilda*? We might have to break up."

Her phone rang from where she'd left it in the kitchen and she stiffened, her contented drowsiness evaporating. *Everything's okay, you just talked to Maisy a couple of hours ago, it's fine, it's fine. Even Cornell wouldn't call you at this hour, would he?*

"Do you need to get that?" James asked. "I can see you freaking out a little bit."

She bit her lip. Alarm bells were clanging in her head.

"It's just, it's so late . . ."

"Answer it." He gave her hand a squeeze.

She bounced off the sofa and dashed to the kitchen in time for the ringing to stop and a notification to pop up.

MISSED CALL: TESS ARMITAGE.

Oh god! Her heart hammered as she hit redial.

"Tess, is everything all right?"

On the other end of the phone, Tess's voice quivered as she swallowed a sob. "Billy and Sid have gone." Her voice broke. "They've run away."

Harriet felt light-headed. She gripped the worktop with her free hand. *Not again. Please not again.* James had muted the TV and joined her in the kitchen, concern etched on his face. Harriet put the phone on speaker and took a breath, swallowing down her panic.

"Tell me what happened," she said calmly. Her hands shook.

A shuddering sigh on the other end of the phone. "Arthur had heart bypass surgery a few weeks back."

"Oh my god!"

"He's fine. We didn't tell anyone because we worried that if social services found out, they'd take the boys into respite care while Arthur recovered, but at our age, we knew there was a chance that we might not get them back. Billy didn't want to take the risk, and neither did we."

"Oh, Tess."

"We made it work. Billy did the school runs so that I could look after Arthur. We just wanted to keep the boys with us until Billy turned eighteen. They've had such upheaval in their lives."

"What changed? Why did they run?"

"Arthur had a small turn yesterday, nothing major, just some medication hiccups. The surgery must have contacted social services. They came this evening when the boys were at the theater. They've arranged for a respite placement starting tomorrow. It was out of our hands." She sobbed. "We broke it to them when they got home, but when Arthur went to check on them before bed . . . they were gone."

Harriet closed her eyes.

"Tess." James spoke into the phone. "It's James Knight, we met at Grace's house. What time did you realize that they'd gone?"

"Um." Her voice was very small. "About half an hour ago. We've been calling their phones. We went out looking for them. We don't know what time they left. Billy put Sid to bed at about nine o'clock and then he didn't come back downstairs. We knew he was upset, we just assumed he wanted some alone time."

"You stay put," said Harriet. "You need to be home in case they come back. I'll find them."

"Please," Tess sobbed.

"I'll find them." She was already grabbing her coat off the hook and pushing her feet into her boots. "I'll find them, Tess, I promise."

Hanging up, Harriet rushed to the bathroom to throw up, then splashed water on her face, grabbed a scarf from the coat stand, and wrapped it around her neck.

"I'll drive," said James, pulling his coat on. "You contact the famous five."

She nodded, grateful that James was here. Her hands trembled so violently she could barely type.

The roads were quiet, the pavements empty. The night sky was eerily pale, with clouds the color of split pea soup, a promise of more snow. But for now, the air was still, as though time had stopped, and Harriet thought that was what this diabolical uncertainty felt like, like the real world had abandoned them and left them sealed in a nightmarish snow globe.

Any hopes she'd had that Billy might have holed up with one of the famous five had been dashed early on. But her phone pinged relentlessly with suggestions of places Billy might go. She'd contacted Mallory and Hesther, and they'd spread the word among the rest of the community groups. The theater security guard confirmed that no one was in the theater. Those with cars drove around the town, checking in frequently with Grace—who had appointed herself search-and-rescue coordinator—so that time wasn't wasted searching areas already covered.

Harriet was still nauseous. The uncertainty was a dull agony that dragged through her body, a dread so heavy it was an effort to move. But move she did. They'd combed the park, torches swinging in wide arcs, frozen leaves crunching beneath their boots. Every now and again one of their beams would illuminate a pair of gleaming eyes in the darkness: foxes and badgers, fellow prowlers in the freezing night. The air was sharp with cold, making her ears ache and the tips of her fingers tingle.

At the bus station they scanned every booth, shelter, and bench, thinking maybe Billy and Sid had decided to wait it out and catch the first bus out of Little Beck Foss in the morning. But the boys weren't there, and the rough sleepers they approached hadn't seen anyone matching their description.

When they reached the train station and found that it too was empty, Harriet sat on a bench with her head in her hands.

"Where are they?" she called out in frustration.

"We'll find them," said James.

"Will we?"

It was almost two a.m. Deep night. Frigid cold. That was what killed her, thinking about the two of them shivering together somewhere, frightened and alone. James put his arm around her. The station clock ticked loud on the deserted platform.

"I dropped the ball," she said. "I knew it. I knew in my

gut that something wasn't right. I should've pushed Billy. I knew it when he kept picking Sid up from school. I let it slide. I let all the other things I had on my mind push it to one side."

"But he told you everything was fine. How were you to know he wasn't telling the truth?"

"Because that's my job, James." She rounded on him. "I'm supposed to know." She shook her head and looked up at the sky glowing tawny in the hazy light cast by the station lamps. "It's happening again."

"No." James's voice was firm. "This isn't Zoe. It wasn't your fault then, and it isn't now. We're going to find them. They're going to be okay."

She wondered if the conviction in his voice was to keep her sane or himself.

"Where would they go?" She'd lost count of how many times she'd asked that question over the last two hours; it was going around in a loop inside her head.

James rubbed his chin. "Billy wouldn't do anything that would put Sid in danger," he said.

"No." She sniffed and wiped her nose. It was so cold that it felt like it was running even when it wasn't. "He wouldn't."

"It's a long shot, but do you think he might have checked them into a hotel overnight?" he asked.

"Maybe. I mean, he's got a job; he could have money stashed. I don't know."

"Does he have any other friends? Outside of the famous five?"

"Not really. No one he would trust enough to ask for help."

"Okay. Okay. So we've called all the taxi ranks in town and none of the drivers have picked anyone up matching his description . . ."

"They could have caught a bus or a train hours before we even knew they were missing," said Harriet.

"But to go where? Where do desperate sixteen-year-olds go to escape?"

Harriet stood abruptly.

"I know where he is," she said, wiping her nose again, even though she couldn't feel it.

"Where?"

She laughed, borderline hysterically.

"He's at the theater," she said, throwing her arms in the air in exasperation at Billy Matlin.

James was looking at her with concern.

"The security guard searched all over, there was no sign of them."

"That's because they're hiding in the flunking basement!"

....

Twenty minutes later, they stood outside the Winter Theater, waiting for Ken to unlock the door.

"Are you sure about this?" Ken asked, pushing the doors open. "I mean, how would they even have got in? All the doors are locked by nine p.m. And we've got a security guard doing the rounds."

"I'm sure," Harriet replied. "I can't tell you exactly how he did it. But that kid can climb a drainpipe. He was coming here by himself long before he inducted the rest of the famous five into breaking in."

They stood in the silent foyer. It had been a long time since she'd seen the place empty, not since she'd first followed Leo here. It had undergone quite the transformation. But even though it was shiny again, in the dark, its ghosts could be felt.

"Quiet. I don't want to spook them," Harriet whispered. "Torches only."

The men nodded and followed Harriet through one of the side doors and down the long passages that snaked through the back of the theater. Past dressing rooms and storage cupboards until they came up behind the stage, to the hidden flight of stairs leading to the basement.

"You stay here, I'll go down," she whispered. James made to protest but she stopped him with a finger to her lips. "I'll be fine. Wait here."

She tiptoed as quietly as she could down the rickety stairs and pushed the door open at the bottom. It was deathly quiet and for a moment she wondered if perhaps she'd been mistaken. But then she saw them. A camping light gently illuminating two sleeping figures, curled up together in sleeping bags on a bed of old blankets on the dirt floor. Sandwich wrappers, a thermos with two plastic cups, and a copy of the second *Percy Jackson & the Olympians* book lay on the floor beside them. She wept tears of silent relief, allowing herself to exhale for what felt like the first time in hours. She hadn't been able to save Zoe, but she could make things right for Billy and Sid.

....

While James notified first Tess and Arthur and then all the other folks who had been out searching or simply sitting up in dressing gowns awaiting news, Harriet had gently woken the lost and found boys.

Billy had just ended an emotional call with Tess and Arthur when Grace arrived at the theater, dressed as usual as though she was ready to take some corgis for a trot around the Balmoral Castle grounds.

"What in god's own name were you thinking?" she scolded.

There was an air of defeat about Billy that Harriet had never seen before. He'd admitted to her, down in the basement, that his sudden decision to run away had been driven by pure panic. He had no plan other than a determination not to be separated from Sid. It happened sometimes, in emergency situations; siblings got split up in the system. It had already happened to them once before, and he couldn't risk it happening again.

"I didn't know what else to do," he said simply. The fight had gone out of his voice and the crack in Harriet's heart broke a little wider.

Grace took him by the shoulders.

"Look at me," she demanded. Dejectedly, he did as he was told. "If ever you don't know what to do, you come to me," she said. Her voice was soft yet firm. "If you're worried, or sad or scared, you come to me, and I will move bloody heaven and earth to make things right. You and Sid are not alone. Do you understand?"

Billy's eyes were tired and glistened with tears he refused to shed, but when he nodded, one dislodged itself and rolled down his cheek.

"Good," she said. Then she turned to Harriet, James, and Ken. "They can stay with me for what's left of tonight," she said with authority. "And we'll decide on next steps tomorrow when everyone's had some rest. Billy? Sid? Is that okay with you?"

Sid nodded, trying to rub the sleep out of his eyes, and shivered.

"If that's all right," said Billy.

"Of course it's all right. Do you think I would have offered were it not?" She smiled. "You looked after me when I needed it. Now it's my turn."

"That's very kind of you, Grace, so long as you're sure. I don't mind having them to stay with me tonight either," said Harriet.

"Or they could stay at mine," offered James. "I've got space."

"No, that makes no sense," she snapped. "I've got two spare bedrooms and Billy's stayed before, he knows his way around the place, particularly the fridge. No, it's the only sensible solution, the boys are coming home with me."

....

The dawn chorus had already begun by the time James pulled up outside Harriet's building, though the sun wouldn't rise for another couple of hours yet.

"You could call in sick," James suggested. "I'm sure Ali could hold the fort for one day. I'm certainly taking the morning off."

She yawned and rubbed her eyes. She felt as though she could sleep for a week.

"No, I need to see Cornell. I've made a decision."

"Oh?"

"I'm going to ask to take some leave."

"That's a bold move. I mean, I agree with it whole-heartedly, but are you sure? You are a person who likes to be in control."

"But I'm not in control. I dropped the ball once with catastrophic results, and tonight history almost repeated itself."

"Harriet, you have got to stop taking responsibility for other people's actions—

"No." She put a hand up to stop him. "I know that. *Now*, I know that. In my head I've always thought that if I take charge of it—doesn't matter what 'it' is—at least I know it'll get done. But all that ends up happening is that I'm doing so many things that I miss the very signs that I took charge to make sure didn't get missed in the first place."

"You're being very hard on yourself."

"No, I'm being kind to myself by accepting that I'm not She-Ra, and it's taken me a while to get here. You were right, I did love teaching and I gave it up because I thought I could stop more kids from falling through the cracks if I was in pastoral care. But since being at the theater . . . I don't know, I guess I feel like I'm making more of a difference, or at least a different difference? I think maybe I'm drunk with tiredness." She rubbed her face and was pleased that James didn't try to fill the silence. "If I can make Evaline see how vital a community space is to the people in this town, I know it could help so many people. It could give *all* the kids on the list, and even those not on the list, a safe place where they could meet other people and learn new skills and . . ." She threw her hands in the air. "I don't even know. I literally don't know. And I won't know if I don't give myself the chance to find out. All I do know is that by trying to straddle my job at the school and my role at the theater I'm doing them both a disservice. Ali's always telling me about his PhD; well, I'm going to give him the chance to put his money where his mouth is."

She looked at James, giving him the go-ahead to respond at last.

"I think taking some time off is a sound idea," he said carefully. "And it sounds like you don't have a plan at all."

She laughed. "Absolutely none. Isn't that brilliant? My only plan is to work out what the hell my plan is."

TWENTY-SEVEN

SEBASTIAN CORNELL'S FACE WAS A MIXTURE OF OUTRAGE and fear as he sat behind his vast desk on Tuesday morning, eyeing Harriet with what could only be described as contempt. For her part, she'd let herself sleep for an hour when she'd got home, and then set about making sure she'd dealt with everything in her inbox and drawn up a detailed plan of action to see Ali through the next week—not that he'd need it. At seven a.m., she'd called him and briefed him on the situation. When she momentarily lost her confidence in her plan-not-plan, Ali asked, "Have I ever told you about my PhD?"

She'd laughed. "You may have mentioned it two or three hundred times."

"Then for the love of god, Harriet, I beg you to let me make use of it. I know what I'm doing. The whole team does. Give us our time to shine."

By eight forty-five, she had briefed the rest of the team in her office and handed over what amounted to a "how-to" guide that they could refer to should they need it and assured them that she was available for answering questions at any time. At this, Susan had asked, "Doesn't you being available to solve our problems twenty-four-seven defeat the purpose of you taking time off?"

Harriet scratched her head. "You make a good point. That is something for me to work on."

And so, by nine fifteen, having just consumed her third coffee, she was sat opposite Cornell, feeling very much like she'd been up all night, which of course she had.

"How much *leave*?" he asked. The disgust in his voice was so thick one would think she had asked him if she could do a wee in his wastepaper basket. "Effective from when?"

"Effective from now, up until the Christmas holidays begin. Term ends on Friday anyway, so technically I'm only asking for less than a week to begin with."

"And what about your workload?"

"To be shared equally between Ali and the rest of the team. You will, of course, have to take back the work that you delegated to me, but I've already done most of it, so it shouldn't keep you up at night."

He leaned back in his chair and squinted his eyes at her.

"Harriet," he said, giving her a killer-clown smile, "I would hate for a student to slip through the net because of your irresponsibility. Think of the effect that might have on your mental health. Remember Zoe?"

She almost couldn't breathe. He wasn't usually so blatant, but she figured that was because she'd taken him by surprise. *You can only do the best you can.* She repeated it. *You can only do the best you can.* And then something occurred to her.

"But provided I've performed my due diligence with regards to my handover, which I absolutely have, then the responsibility ceases to be mine and becomes the team's, and ultimately—as head of pastoral care— yours."

The space between Cornell's eyebrows turned a blotchy red.

"I don't know what's come over you, or who you think you are, but you cannot simply waltz in here and ask to take leave in the middle of a term," he spluttered.

She took a breath and gathered herself. This was the right thing; she was sure of it.

"Firstly, it's the end of term, not the middle. Secondly, I am entitled to take unpaid leave for personal reasons provided that provision has been made, which it has, but I will gladly take it as holiday if you'd prefer. And thirdly, what's come over me is the realization that I can't do everything, no matter how much I'd like to. You know how Zoe's case affected me and you've used it to your own advantage for years; to say that's unethical would be an understatement." She stood, making herself as tall as she could and hoping that she didn't look as frazzled as she felt. "I'm leaving now. I've sent a copy of my request to the dean. And if you don't like it, then . . . then duck you!"

She slammed out of his office, feeling exultant and dizzy from lack of sleep, and went straight home to bed.

....

When Harriet arrived at the theater that afternoon, the box office was open and the queue for tickets reached to the door.

She found James at a desk in a corner of the lower cocktail lounge, ready to start his first legal surgery. Above their heads, the ceiling rumbled with the sounds of many toddlers dancing to "If You're Happy and You Know It." Smells of orange, cinnamon, and buttery pastry wafted in from the kitchens. Usually, Harriet arrived after the school day had ended, and it warmed her heart to see so many of the groups using the space earlier in the day too. The theater might have been sleeping for fifty years, but it was alive and kicking now.

James walked around to the other side of his desk and folded her into a hug. He was big and warm, and he smelled good, and she yawned loudly and snuggled into him like a cat.

"Since you're here, I presume your plan to take leave worked out."

"It did. I'll tell you about it over a coffee when you're free. Do you have appointments booked in?"

"I have my first one with Ava in forty-five minutes; I've just finished going over her case notes."

"After that, then." She pulled back to look up at him and smiled.

He cupped her face in his hands, his amber eyes full of warmth, and then he bent to kiss her.

"Ahem, is this a bad time? I was under the impression that this was where you held your legal surgery, not a nooky shop."

"Good afternoon to you too, Grace," said James in a consummately professional voice. Harriet turned to smile at the woman in tweed.

"Hi, Grace. How are Billy and Sid?"

"They are well rested and unharmed after their adventures."

"Good. Is Billy here?"

"In the theater, with Gideon. They both are. I thought Sid would benefit from a day with his brother. I phoned his school this morning and excused him under the guise of a nasty bout of diarrhea."

"I'm surprised you condone lying to the school authorities," Harriet teased.

"I wasn't lying, I was acting. It's quite different."

Harriet frowned.

"I suppose we need to decide what to do next." A dull headache was forming above her eyebrows. Billy and Sid's situation was unchanged; social services would be arriving at Tess and Arthur's home later in the day to remove them.

"That's why I'm here," said Grace. "James, I need you to represent me. I intend to become the boys' guardian."

Harriet was stunned.

"Are you sure?" James asked. "Have you thought this through?"

"Yes, yes. I'm sure. It makes sense. I have a three-bedroom house with a garden big enough for a child to kick a ball about in. I am physically fit, notwithstanding the inner ear infection, which has since departed. Most importantly, if they're with me they can stay together and they can visit Tess and Arthur whenever they like. And down the line, if Arthur's health improves, maybe they could even move back in with them if they wish, or we could work out some sort of joint custody situation, you know the sort of thing."

"Have you discussed this with Tess and Arthur?" asked James.

"Of course. I took the boys round there this morning, Billy was desperate to apologize, terribly worried his actions might have strained Arthur's heart. We all had a jolly good discussion. They don't want to lose contact with the boys, and this way would work perfectly for everyone."

"It's such a lot to take on, Grace. Have you had much experience with children?" Harriet asked.

"I'll learn as I go along. Billy's pretty vocal, I've no doubt he'll point out any errors I make along the way. Don't keep gawping at me like I've just grown a new head. The simple fact is, I want to give them a home and I know that I can make it a happy one." Her voice softened. "You know I'm not one for great shows of emotion, but this feels right. I feel like I've been given a second chance at having a family." She cleared her throat loudly and continued in her usual headmistress tone. "Now are you going to help me or not? Hmm?"

"And the boys want this? You've talked it all through with them properly?" Harriet asked.

"Well of course I have, foolish girl. Do you think I'd be here if I didn't have their approval? Go and ask them if you like."

Harriet looked at James and a laugh bubbled out of her. Grace was right, it was the perfect solution. Her relief felt like floating. "Can you help make it happen?" she asked James.

He looked from Harriet to Grace, nodding slowly, his solicitor mask making his expression inscrutable. Finally, he said, "Yes. Yes, I believe I can. Or at least I can represent you, Grace, and put forward your case for guardianship. If you're available now, we can make a start."

"I've got time," said Grace, looking at her watch. "I'm not due to haunt Scrooge until three forty-five."

....

It was a long time since Harriet had had anyone else in her bed. But it didn't feel odd to have James beside her. She liked feeling the heat radiating off his skin, and how her head fit perfectly in the space below his shoulder, his arm slung loosely around her, his fingers lazily drawing up and down her side, tracing the dip of her waist and the rise of her rib cage.

The last couple of days, they had been like ships passing. She had been tied up with organizing the space in the theater to fit the multiple groups that had made it their home and helping with rehearsals and getting the production ready as the date for the performance marched ever closer. And James had been consumed with the requirements of the legal surgery, in particular the urgent liaising between Grace, Tess, and Arthur and social services to ensure that Billy and Sid were not placed elsewhere while the legalities for their new joint guardianship were put in place.

On Thursday night they had gone out for dinner after rehearsals to catch up with each other properly, and one thing had very much led to another . . .

"Tell me about your childhood," James said, pulling the duvet up around them.

"What do you want to know?"

"How did you end up in the system?"

Oh, that. Of course. People always wanted to know. She supposed it was human nature to be curious about origin stories, especially those of the people with whom they were intimate. But to her it always felt weighted, as though her stock was automatically lowered because of her upbringing.

"I was taken away from my parents when I was three years old. I don't remember them. At all. I don't have any real memories until I was five; I think that was probably my brain's way of protecting me."

"Your parents never tried to get you back?" he asked gently.

"They never came for me. I guess that's what hurt the most. That they never fought for me. I waited and waited, but they never showed up."

"That must have been hard."

"As a little kid it was. A lot of parents, like Pete's mum, they came for their children when they could, you know?

People in general don't simply give up their kids; there are extenuating, heartbreaking circumstances that lead up to that point, and it is *always* a last resort. Which leaves the ones who are left behind to wonder, 'What's wrong with me? What did I do wrong?' Because nobody's going to tell a three-year-old that she had to be taken away from her parents because they hurt her; all you know is that you got dumped and you don't know why."

James sucked in a breath and her head rose up as his chest filled with air. He brought his other arm across her so that she was encircled by him. "I'm so sorry. Did you ever try to find them?"

"When I was older. It wasn't easy, there was no Internet back then, but I found them."

"And?"

"And that's when I changed my surname by deed poll to Smith, the most common surname in the UK. My foster parents helped me do it. The daydream I had for all those years that my parents—who I imagined were royalty from some small faraway country—would swoop in and claim me suddenly became my worst nightmare; I didn't want to take the chance that those people would *ever* find me."

"I'm so sorry."

"Don't be, it gave me closure. Seriously, I dodged a bullet. I thank my lucky stars they never came for me."

"Was it tough?" he ventured.

"I was lucky, I was placed with nice foster families. When the system works, it works brilliantly. And then when I was eight, I went to live with Sue and Gil, and they fostered me until I left for university. It was like being part of a regular family, really, except ours had a lot of moving parts. Some kids stayed for a few months, some a few years. Some, like Pete, were respite kids. That's how we met. He started coming to stay with Sue and Gil when we were ten; he'd stay for a few weeks and then go back to his mum."

"How come?"

"Pete's mum suffered with depression. Sometimes her depression got really dark and when that happened, Pete would come and stay with us until his mum was well again. She was a lovely person, but her wiring was messed up. He was in and out of my life like a kind of cousin, really."

"A kissing cousin," said James dryly.

She laughed. "Our shared experiences meant that we understood one another in ways that other people didn't, and I think we fell in together because it was easier than taking the risk of making new connections. In the end, though, we had to admit that we were settling. We'd thought we were saving each other from heartache, but the truth was, we were denying each other the chance to find real love."

"I can see how you got there, though. I mean, in theory your decision to be together made perfect sense," said James.

"Except love is perfectly nonsensical."

"Until you find the right person."

"Until then."

"Did you? Ever?"

"I've been in love a couple of times. But I never found anyone I would walk barefoot through the snow for," she said honestly.

His chuckle was a low hum that vibrated through her. "Is that your mark of true love?" he asked, amused.

"Isn't it everyone's? How about you? Apart from your wife, of course."

"I thought I was in love once, and it felt like the real deal, but now that I look back on it, I think I loved her mostly because she didn't love me back."

"Unrequited love or masochism?"

"Is there a difference?"

"Good point."

They lay quietly in each other's arms while the snowflakes brushed past the windows. She didn't want to label the things she was feeling for James, but she couldn't deny that they felt significant.

"Your turn," she said. "Tell me about your childhood."

"Very normal," he replied.

"There's no such thing."

He sighed. "My parents were good people trapped in a bad marriage. Time spent alone with each of them was wonderful, but together they were a nightmare."

"They never divorced?" she asked.

"Eventually, but not until they'd wasted the best years of their lives trying to force the wrong person into being the right one."

"That's sad."

"I promised myself that when I grew up, I'd do things differently. And yet here I am with a failed marriage and a surprise daughter who I have more than likely emotionally damaged by my absence. I've managed to make the same mistakes as my parents and a bunch of new ones too."

"You can't hold yourself accountable for things you weren't aware of."

"It feels like I'll never be done trying to backfill the dad-shaped hole in her life. I don't know. Sometimes I think it's hereditary, like it's in my DNA to screw things up and I should just make my peace with it."

"That's such a cop-out." Her voice came out more clipped than she'd intended.

"How so?"

"It removes any personal responsibility for your own life. It's how people excuse themselves for giving up when things get tough."

"Harsh."

She smiled and laid a kiss on his chest. "I'm sorry. Inherited dispositions are a touchy subject for me."

"No. I'm sorry, that was a stupid, insensitive thing to say."

James ran his fingers lightly up and down her arm and then lifted her wrist to his lips and laid a tender kiss at her pulse.

"I would fight for you, Harriet." He whispered it like a promise into the spot where her blood ran closest to the surface and sealed it with another kiss. "I *will* fight for you." He pressed his lips to her pulse again. "I will always show up for you."

Her breath hitched. He couldn't know that, of all the words in the world, those were the ones she had longed most to hear. She was no damsel in distress. She didn't need a prince to save her. She simply needed him to show up, to hold her trust like the precious thing it was, and if the chips were down, to fight for her. Something inside her broke free, a dam bursting its banks, sweeping through her like whitewater rapids, a crescendo of emotions that were everything all at once. It was like being hungry and thirsty and too hot and too cold and craving a cigarette or a drink or to dance or to scream or to laugh or to cry, it was all need and want and the only thing that would sate her was having him as close to her as was humanly possible.

TWENTY-EIGHT

ON THE EVENING OF FRIDAY, THE FIFTEENTH OF DECEMBER, Harriet met Josef crossing the foyer on his way up to the restaurant, where the tables and chairs had recently been reconfigured to form a large square.

"Happy Hanukkah, Josef!" she said, smiling. "I would hug you, but I'm weighed down with fish and chips." She leaned in and kissed him on either cheek instead.

"Thank you!" he replied, beaming. "I've been looking forward to this all week."

"Come on, then, everyone's waiting for you."

She ushered him through the doors and up the stairs to the restaurant.

A cheer went up when Josef entered with greetings of "Shabbat Shalom" and "Happy Hanukkah." Everyone stood as he lit all eight candles on the menorah he had brought from home and offered a blessing. Harriet did indeed feel blessed, ever more so.

It was noisy as food parcels were passed around the table, a great crinkling of paper as everyone unwrapped their fish and chips. And when Farahnoush and Carly came in carrying plates of plaited babka they'd ordered from the local bakery, Josef almost jumped out of his seat.

"Well, one thing's for sure," said Destiny, "we'll all be high on carbs tonight!"

"We've got doughnuts yet!" Ricco called across the table.

"I'm only glad I had my cholesterol test before this feast!" Kingsley joked.

"I wish we could have parties every night," said Sid.

Harriet took a moment to soak it all in, this marvelously colorful gathering. Every person here held a story and a strength within them, and when they mixed and mingled all together, their stories became an epic tale and their combined strengths bloomed into a force to be reckoned with. Humans had such a propensity for love and kindness, and here in this room, in this theater, it seemed to explode out in hearts and stars; she could feel the warmth of it fluttering around her like snowflakes.

"That chip has been dangling from your fingers for the last two minutes. What thoughts have you so engrossed in them that they are surpassing the allure of classic British cuisine?" James asked, taking the seat beside her.

She looked at him.

"I love it here," she said, almost dreamily. "Don't you?"

"I do." He mirrored her smile.

"I mean, I didn't love it at first and I still hide in the toilet when everyone wants a piece of me at once. But I feel like, I don't know, like I've grown into the space or maybe like it's grown around me. Have you ever seen the way a tree can grow around and through iron railings? I'm not making sense. Ignore me."

"You are making sense," he said, looking into her eyes. "I understand you completely. In fact, what you've just described is rather how I have come to feel about you."

She swallowed. Her heartbeat was very loud in her ears. There was so much she wanted to say to him, but all her words had fallen into a massive black hole.

"That's nice," she said weakly.

He raised an eyebrow. "Nice? I just told you that I no longer know where I end and you begin, and your response is 'that's nice.'"

She cupped his face in her hands.

"No, no, it's so much more than nice. It's all the very best words. If you were inside my body right now, you would know how you make me feel."

"Well, that's a very saucy invitation." He grinned mischievously.

She flushed instantly, realizing what she'd said, and dropped her hands, snorty-laughing as she did so.

"Oh gosh," she said, flustered. "What I meant was . . ."

He kissed her, and she could feel the smile on his lips. "I know what you meant; I'm only teasing."

"Let's keep it clean at the dinner table, shall we?" Grace called.

....

The call came through just after six a.m. on Saturday morning. As with any call that came in late at night or early in the morning, Harriet's mind immediately flew to bad news. *Oh god, Maisy!* She swallowed down the adrenaline as she snatched up her phone.

"Hello?" Her voice was gravelly with sleep and trepidation.

"It's Ken. Sorry to wake you so early."

Not Maisy! The relief was dizzying, and she flopped back onto the bed, taking a couple of deep breaths, one arm draped over her face.

"Are you still there?" Ken's voice broke through the sound of blood rushing in her ears.

"Yep. Here. What's up, Ken?"

"We've got a problem."

She sat up again. Alert. "What kind of a problem?"

She knew he would be rubbing the back of his neck with one of his giant hands.

"Some of the pipes froze overnight."

"Okay."

"And burst."

"Where?"

"Over the stage."

"How bad is it?"

"Bad."

....

Forty minutes later, having waded through last night's fresh snowfall in the dark—her car was snowed into its parking space—she arrived at the theater. James was waiting for her on the path just outside the main doors, stamping his feet against the cold.

"How bad?" she asked.

He screwed his face up in answer.

"Fixable?" she asked.

"So Ken says. I guess he would know." But he didn't look convinced. "My phone's been pinging like a pinball machine since you messaged the group chat."

She sighed. "I figured they had a right to know."

James held the door for her, and they went inside, the lights bright after the darkness. Shouts and ominous crunching sounds poured down the grand staircase to the auditorium. She looked up and sighed again.

"I guess there's no point putting it off any longer. Better go see what the damage is."

Their feet squeaked on the thick plastic protecting the carpet. Together they pushed through the swing doors at the top of the stairs and headed straight to the edge of the balcony.

It was worse than she'd imagined. A huge chunk of ceiling flapped down from the joists above, like the lid of a grand piano hanging in midair. The sounds of wood straining creaked ominously around the theater like a portent of doom, and stagnant water dripped from the massive hole onto the stage below. The stage itself was a swamp. The trickle must have been a torrent before the water was switched off. The curtains hung heavy, saturated both from the waterfall above and then drinking in the flood from the hems up. Jagged fragments of old plasterboard littered the stage, and clumps of plaster hung down in wet clags from the horsehair they were originally mixed with. It smelled earthy, like chalk cliffs after a heavy rainfall. Inside the hole were bundles of wires, layers of old wet newspaper, and the bottoms of the floorboards that lined the attic space.

"Flapping fudge nuggets," she breathed.

"Yeah," James agreed.

"Frozen pipes did all this?"

"Ken thinks they probably had hairline cracks from winters before and were leaking so slowly that nobody noticed. Each year they weakened a bit further until this year's big freeze—"

"Finished them off," she concluded.

"Yeah."

"Crikey. Thank god no one was here."

She looked at the heavy chunks of plaster that had smashed down onto the stage, fragmenting into sprays of white shingle. "If anyone had been under there when it collapsed . . ." She shuddered.

James put his arm around her. "I know," he said. "I keep thinking the same thing."

Ken was directing the positioning of a skip being maneuvered by a heavy-duty forklift to rest beneath the island of swinging ceiling. To the side of it, a scaffold tower was being hastily erected. Ken looked up and saw Harriet and James watching.

"Right, people, keep going, I'll be back in a mo," he shouted to his team, and disappeared out of the auditorium, reappearing moments later by their side. "You got here quick," he said.

"It didn't seem like a time to dawdle," she replied. "What's the plan?"

Ken rubbed his chin, the sound of his stubble like sandpaper.

"Well, first off, we need to cut that lump of ceiling down before it flattens someone. Then we'll make the area safe. And then we can start on a proper cleanup."

"What about the show?" she asked.

He sucked in air through his teeth, the universal signifier of bad news.

"You've got two options. The first is to postpone the performance until after we've replastered and made everything good. Realistically you're looking at the middle of January."

"And the second?" asked James.

"We make it safe. Clean everything up and cover the hole with a strong waterproof tarp. It won't look pretty, it'll likely be drafty, but you can have your show as planned. We can get it into working order in a couple of days. Quicker if we have help with the surface cleanup."

Harriet looked at James and could see him weighing the two choices in his mind. For her, though, there was only ever one course of action.

"Let's do option two; not pretty with a tarp," she said with conviction.

"Are you sure?" James asked. "I could speak to Evaline—"

"I'm sure. Too many people have worked too hard on this. If we postpone, we lose the momentum. This whole production has been created by determination and good-will. We've built it on make do and mend, and I can't think of a more fitting way to showcase our hard work in the face of adversity than to do it despite a massive hole in the ceiling."

James smiled at her. "You're right," he said. "This has us written all over it."

"Brava!" Gideon boomed, surprising them all. "I came as soon as I could. Of course, the show must go on, that is the cornerstone of every creative's belief. The gods may rain their trials and tribulations down upon us, but we will rise to the occasion!" He swooped his arms into the air as though he intended to take off from the balcony and fly around the auditorium.

"Right you are, then," said Ken, wholly unimpressed by Gideon's outbursts. "I'll crack on. Nobody's to go down there until I say it's safe. Understood?" They all nodded. "If you need to practice, do it in the cocktail lounges."

And with that he was gone. The scaffold tower was almost complete, and at its base three members of the maintenance team were clambering into safety harnesses while others gave their chain saws a quick once-over.

"Rather them than me," said James just as his phone began to ring. He pulled it from his coat pocket, frowning when he saw the name of the caller. "Lyra. Is everything all right?" His expression was serious and growing more so by the second. "Is she okay?" A beat as he listened. Harriet could hear crying down the phone. "All right, I'll come up. No, it's fine, nothing that can't wait. I'll be there as soon as I can." More talking on the other end.

"You too. Bye." He slipped the phone back into his pocket, not making eye contact with Harriet as he took two steadying breaths, seemingly making decisions and locking them into place in his mind. "I have to go," he said finally, meeting her eyes.

"Go where? Is Lyra okay?" she asked. Her stomach was sinking.

"She's fine. I mean, she's physically fine but she's upset. I have to go to Edinburgh. Morgan was in a car accident this morning on her way to work."

"Oh my god. Um, okay." Her mind was scrabbling around trying to put everything together. "Is it serious? Morgan, I mean, is she seriously hurt?"

"Lyra says not. She's just a bit shaken up. The paramedics assessed her on the scene and said she was fine to go home. They suggested she rest up for the day."

"Right. So, Morgan's okay and Lyra's okay?" Harriet clarified.

"Yes. Both are fine. But Lyra is upset, and I said I'd go up there for moral support."

"Does she need you to?" Harriet asked.

"What do you mean?"

"Well, only that she's an adult and Morgan is clearly unhurt and what with all this going on . . ." She gestured to the mess down below.

"She was crying down the phone! She needs me!" His usual cool air had evaporated.

"There's no need to raise your voice. I'm simply pointing out that we need you too. I need you."

"I'm sorry Morgan didn't time her road traffic accident better."

"Don't be a bum-wipe. You said Morgan is fine. You're going to drive three hours in the snow because you feel guilty."

"Why are you being like this?" he demanded.

She looked out toward the scaffold now being scaled by maintenance workers lugging chain saws.

"You asked me to put you first, to put down my phone and choose you instead, and I did. Now I'm asking you to put me first. Please. They are okay. Lyra is fine, you said so yourself, she's a bit tearful, but surely it isn't anything that can't be soothed by a FaceTime?"

"I need to be there."

"And I need you to be here. I haven't asked you for anything. You have had to make exactly zero concessions for me. I am asking you for this one thing."

He looked at her for a long moment.

"No, I'm sorry. I can't."

The words hit like a slap.

The swing doors swished closed behind him, and Harriet was left feeling more alone than she had in a long time.

"He is a man of passions," said Gideon gently. She'd forgotten he was there.

"Yes," Harriet replied absently. How quickly she had allowed herself to fall. A lifetime of caution thrown to the wind for a handsome face and some pretty words.

"Come now, my dear. We have play business to discuss. It's early still, let us go to the little café on the corner and I'll buy you breakfast, what do you say?"

Harriet looked down at the stage. Gideon touched her shoulder.

"I believe our Mr. Knight needs to deal with his ghosts, as we must ours, though of a Dickensian kind."

She looked at him then, in his green corduroy cape.

"That's very astute of you," she said.

"People often mistake my flamboyance for narcissism.

It's a useful tool, people drop their guard under the presumption that I am a brick wall, when in fact I am a keen observer of the human condition." He winked at her and tapped his nose.

"Blimey," she said.

"We have hours before the hordes arrive for practice, and I don't believe you want to spend the intervening time with nothing but your own thoughts for company."

That was probably true.

"And I have heard tell that the café offers a festive pancake stack, which I am most interested to sample." He tapped his forefinger to his lips thoughtfully. "Surely you won't make me eat alone?"

She smiled at him, grateful.

"Thanks, Gideon."

He flapped his cape over one shoulder and put an arm around her. "Now, my dear, riddle me this, have I yet regaled you with tales from my time at a little theater you may have heard of called Shakespeare's Globe?"

"No," she said warily, as they left the theater.

"Then you are in for a treat!"

....

Harriet had spent most of Sunday lying on the sofa in her sitting room alternating between watching holiday movies and reading; some might call it moping. James hadn't called her, but neither had she called him. Actually, that wasn't strictly true; he had phoned her twice on Saturday and left messages, both of which she had ignored—he had asked her to spend less time beholden to her phone, after all—but by Sunday he seemed to have got the message and for the first time in years, she wished her phone weren't so quiet. She was sad that their spark hadn't had the chance to become a flame, but she reasoned that it was better to know where she stood now rather than later.

James might not have been her favorite person right then, but she was grateful that he had made her decorate her home for Christmas. Her festive space would keep her warm now that it seemed likely that James would not. Really, she should thank him; he and his dreadful boss had helped her to see the value of self-care . . . and it looked like now she'd have plenty of time to practice it.

"Explain it to me again," Maisy asked. Her phone was propped up on a dressing table while she packed her suitcase, ready for when she and Savannah's family drove up to their cabin in the mountains for Christmas. She kept wandering back and forth across the screen while she talked. "He wouldn't stay because his daughter was upset and you wanted him to stay, and then he called you and you didn't respond."

"I mean, yes, that's the nutshell version, but it isn't the whole nut tree. What about your fleece hoodie? A mountain cabin sounds cold to me."

Harriet was eating a bowl of vegetable noodles that she had made from scratch, and it felt like a big win for her personal growth. She watched Maisy pull her fleece out of a hamper and add it to her pile.

"But you like him. I mean, you must really like him to have told me about him, you're normally well cagey about your boyfriends."

"I'm not cagey, I'm selective."

"Yeah, whatever," said Maisy, flinging a pair of bed socks over her shoulder. "My point is, if everybody decided not to get together with the person they fancy on the chance that one day that person might let them down, then nobody would ever get together with anybody."

"You have managed to both overdramatize and oversimplify the situation in one fell swoop. Don't forget to pack gloves and a hat."

On another pass by the dressing table, with several pairs of knickers scrunched up into balls in her hand, Maisy stopped and bent to the phone screen. "Love is all about taking risks, isn't it?"

"Who mentioned love?"

"All right, then, falling in 'like' is all about taking a risk because nobody knows what the future is, do they?"

"That's a calculated risk, based on there being no obvious glaring red flags. And James is currently waving a big red flag at me. At any given moment Lyra or Morgan could break a nail, and he'll go scuttling off to Scotland with an emergency emery board."

"Now who's overdramatizing? Striped scarf or checked scarf?"

"Striped."

"The thing is, Mum, she's his daughter and he put her first. Isn't that exactly what you would do with me?"

"Yes, of course. But this was different. If the situation had been reversed and I knew that you were perfectly fine aside from being a bit upset then I would have talked you through it until you felt better; I wouldn't have driven a hundred miles to help you blow your nose."

"But that's because you know me. You know how I tick; you know what I need when I need it because you're my mum and you've always been there. James is a proper novice. He barely knows his daughter—for all he knows, she could've been having a full-on meltdown."

Harriet slurped up a noodle as she both marveled at her daughter's emotional intelligence and wished she weren't quite so perceptive.

"Okay, you make a good point."

"I know."

"But what about Morgan?"

"You think there's something going on between them?" Maisy asked.

"No," she conceded. "But I don't know how far he'll go to make amends."

Maisy held up two oversized chunky knit cardigans.

"Both, obviously," said Harriet.

"It sounds to me like he's still working out how to navigate having a surprise family."

"Well, maybe I don't want to invest in somebody who doesn't have their ducks in a row yet."

"Sheesh! You and your ducks!" Maisy exclaimed.

"What? You leave my ducks alone. Anyway, even if nothing romantic ever happens between him and Morgan, I could still be setting myself up to get left in the lurch a lot."

"Or maybe Lyra and Morgan are the perfect excuse for someone as risk-averse as you not to put yourself out there?"

"I am not risk-averse!"

"Mum, you choose exactly the same curry, side dish, and naan bread every single time we go to the Everest Inn."

"That's just being sensible, I know that I like their vegetable bhuna, aloo gobi saag, and peshwari naan and if I ordered something different and I didn't like it I'd be disappointed, which would be a waste of money."

Maisy laughed and lobbed a bottle of perfume across

the room, where it landed on top of the pile of clothes in her case.

"Now play that back in your head and tell me that's not risk-averse."

Harriet narrowed her eyes. "Choosing a curry is not the same as committing to a relationship."

"Well, that's just a matter of perspective," Maisy said smugly.

Harriet chuckled at being outpsyched by her seventeen-year-old daughter.

"Well, you're no help. Don't roll your dress like that, you'll never get the creases out."

"There!" Maisy said, leaning bodily on her suitcase to click it shut. "I'm packed."

Harriet was suddenly flooded with the knowledge that for the next few years her relationship with her daughter would revolve around suitcases being packed and unpacked as she traveled back and forth between home and university, until one day she would pack up her suitcase and leave to find a place of her own to call home.

"Mum?" Maisy was studying her with a concerned look on her face. "You all right?"

"I'm fine, darling." She swallowed hard. "You know that I love you more than the sun and the moon and all the stars put together, don't you?"

Maisy smiled. "I love you too."

With a knock at the door, Savannah stepped into her room.

"Hi, Harriet!" she said brightly. "We're going to see the living nativity on the corner of Main Street, do you mind if I steal your daughter away?"

"No, not at all. Go, have fun!"

She managed not to cry until after Maisy had hung up.

....

Later, as she lay in bed, pondering Maisy's words, she wondered if her daughter might be onto something. Was James the king prawn rogan josh, Bombay aloo, and keema naan that she'd always wanted to try but had never dared? Sure, the vegetable bhuna had never let her down, there was safety in the bhuna and that was not to be sniffed at, but might the rogan josh be an even better fit for her if she only gave it the chance? "Ugh!" she groaned, flinging the duvet off. "Now I've made myself hungry!" And she padded out to the kitchen in search of crackers, cheese, and mango chutney.

TWENTY-NINE

ANYONE EVEN REMOTELY INVOLVED WITH THE WINTER THE-ater had been invited, via the now gigantic WhatsApp group, to meet on Monday morning at nine a.m. to help with the cleanup.

When Harriet arrived, there were already dozens of mop-wielding volunteers in Wellington boots waiting in the foyer. A line of yellow tape strung between the two wooden newel posts at the bottom of the main staircase had a paper sign hanging from it that read *DO NOT CROSS THIS LINE UNTIL YOU'VE SEEN KEN!*

"Harriet!" Hesther waved her over.

"Good morning! It's great to see so many people here already."

As she said this the famous five and Sid arrived, suited and booted for the occasion since school had now officially broken up for the holidays. Grace came in behind them, carrying a bucket filled with bottles of disinfectant, rubber gloves, and dishcloths.

"I heard about James having to rush off," said Hesther. *Bad news travels fast!*

"Yes. Well, there are plenty of us here, I'm sure we can make up for his absence."

"Not really what I meant. Are you okay?"

"Why wouldn't I be? It isn't like we were a thing." She tried to brush it off.

"Weren't you?" Hesther's expression was skeptical.

Hesther was someone who paid close attention. Despite all Harriet's sensible self-pep-talks, her disappointment with James dragged like one of Jacob Marley's chains clanking along behind her.

"I thought we were becoming something. But I guess I was wrong. I don't know."

"Have you spoken to him?"

"He called, but I let it go to voice mail."

"Mature."

Harriet cracked a smile, but her gaze wandered idly toward her students. As she watched, they separated like cells dividing and drifted toward other people. Billy joined Josef and Ahmed in conversation, while Leo and Farahnoush had their noses thrust into a sketchbook. Carly chatted animatedly with Winston, while Isabel sat on one of the sofas helping Paksima with some of the English words in her book, and Ricco appeared to be being taught how to jive dance by Destiny. Three weeks ago, these kids clung to each other like a life raft, willfully shunning anyone who floated too near and regarding anyone who offered rescue with mistrust.

"It warms the heart, doesn't it?" Hesther said, following her gaze. "So many souls finding a safe harbor here in this theater."

"It does," she agreed. *This is a good thing, even without James.* She looked up at the beautifully reconstructed stuccoed ceiling and the gleam of dark wood that paneled the walls. And then at the sea of people in the grand foyer, people who never would have come together in this way anywhere else. This building had done something to her, a bewitchment of sorts; she suspected it charmed everyone who entered. It beckoned you in and whispered its secrets and made you love it. She wished

Evaline could let go of her animosity long enough to feel the magic singing in the walls.

Ken trudged down the staircase and stopped just shy of the yellow tape.

"Right, you 'orrible lot," he began. "We've made the ceiling safe, but it took us all bloomin' weekend to do and we haven't had time to clean the place up yet, as you've clearly been informed." He cast his eye around the mops and buckets ready for action. "But I am told we've got plenty of willing bodies to help us with the task."

Rather surprisingly a cheer went up, possibly started by Mallory.

"Put us to work, old man!" shouted Carly.

Ken beamed. "Cheeky mare! Your wish is my command. Everybody—and I mean everybody—needs to wear a hard hat." He pointed to two large waste bags at the top of the stairs, bulging with yellow helmets.

"Why do we have to wear hard hats if it's safe?" asked Grace, pulling Sid protectively into her side.

"It's purely precautionary while we make sure that nothing else is likely to spring a leak or drop out of the sky. But you have my assurances that we don't anticipate anything of the like. You don't wear a seat belt because you expect to crash every time you get in a car, do you?"

In response, Grace gave a satisfied nod and ruffled Sid's hair. Sid gave a Cheshire cat grin, and Harriet spotted Billy watching him out the side of his eye, the smallest twitch of a smile on his lips.

"That's going to ruin my hair," said Odette, her hand raised in the air, and everybody laughed.

"No hard hat, no entry, I'm afraid," Ken chuckled. "We'll all have helmet hair together. I've lived with it for forty years; it's done nowt to dampen my sex appeal."

More chuckles rippled around the foyer. Harriet

watched a few people worrying at their carefully crafted coiffures, mostly the men.

"I see some of you have brought your own mops, and more power to you," Ken continued. "We've got tools of the trade you can use as well, and Ms. Winter has paid for some industrial dehumidifiers, which will be delivered later." He found Harriet in the crowd and gave her a conspiratorial wink.

Ken cut the tape like he was opening a shopping center, and the various groups and clubs climbed the stairs, stopping to take a hard hat before swarming into the auditorium.

A thick layer of turquoise tarpaulin covered the ceiling, sucking in and out like the belly of some mythical monster. It didn't look pretty, but when Harriet compared it to the overall desolation of the place a few weeks previous, it wasn't so bad. This building had become an echo of the good people who frequented its halls, humans sculpted by trials and tribulations, cracks and scars chiseled onto their hearts making each one a unique and beautiful survivor. Somehow this disparate assembly had become a family, and this old theater had become its home, and Harriet would fight with everything she had to hold on to it.

Later, Evaline paid a surprise visit, and Harriet had to stifle a snigger when she entered the elderly woman's favored royal box and found her looking resplendent in a fur coat, pearls, and a hard hat.

"Evaline, how lovely to see you," she said.

Evaline looked Harriet up and down and presumably found her wanting, judging by the way in which she screwed her nose up ever so slightly. "You seem to have everything in hand. The play will go ahead as planned, I presume?"

"Yes," Harriet replied.

"Good. All the activity in the theater has stirred up media interest; I wouldn't like to be embarrassed."

"I thought you'd enjoy watching us fail."

"Why ever would you think that? Foolish girl. Your success is my success. I want the whole of Cumbria to see the theater thriving. It will drive the price up."

"Why not simply open the place back up yourself? You don't need to sell, it's not like you're strapped for cash. You were featured in *Forbes* magazine twice last year."

"Someone's been doing her homework." Evaline looked impressed.

"Just returning the compliment." Harriet held the old woman's gaze.

Evaline gave a wry smile in appreciation. "This theater was God to my father; he was devoted to it, it was everything to him. I was expected to show it the same level of devotion."

"So, leaving it to rot was your revenge?"

Evaline flashed a wicked smile.

"You are finding your teeth, Ms. Smith. Yes, I believe it was. And now selling it is keeping a promise I made to myself to have all association with this theater severed before I die."

"And yet you've kept it all this time." Harriet hesitated before sharing her next thought. "I think, despite your neglect of it, a part of you doesn't *want* to let this place go. Maybe because the Winter Theater is the only piece of your father that you have left?"

"Don't be ridiculous," Evaline bit back in response.

"More ridiculous than taking revenge on an inanimate object like, say, a theater?"

Evaline pointedly ignored her, taking a sip from her

cup and then leaning forward in her seat, looking down her nose at the people below.

"Are they doing all this for free?" she asked.

"Yes."

"Why?"

Harriet thought for a moment. She hadn't really considered the *why*; she had only been certain that they would.

"Well, I suppose because they're invested in this theater and the people in it. They, like me, are hoping that you'll keep your promise and insert a caveat into the deeds so that the future owners have to provide space for the community."

"I agreed to consider that concession before I realized how much community there was!"

Harriet tried to quash the nagging feeling that Evaline was looking for ways to renege on their agreement.

There was a shuffling from outside the curtained royal box, and then "Knock, knock," said a small voice.

Harriet pulled back the curtain to find Ava and Josef, one holding a plate of little pastry parcels giving off a deliciously spicy aroma, and the other with a stack of napkins.

"Hello." Ava smiled. "We wondered if Ms. Winter would like to try a samosa?"

"Come on through, you can ask her yourself." Harriet beckoned them in, hoping Evaline would be civil.

"Ms. Winter, it's lovely to meet you," said Josef. He gestured to Ava, who held out the plate of samosas. "A few of us like to get baking in the kitchen, especially when it's so busy."

"It feels good to have people to cook for," Ava added in halting English.

Evaline eyed the morsels and then chose the fattest triangle on the plate. Ava beamed, and Josef handed Evaline a napkin.

"Our elves are just waiting for the knafeh to finish baking." Josef grinned.

"And Grace and Sid are making 'melting moments' if Sid can stop eating the biscuit dough." Ava chuckled.

"Good luck with that," said Harriet.

"I understand you do this often?" Evaline asked, taking a bite of samosa. Her eyes glinted and she sighed with pleasure.

"When we can," Ava replied.

"Last week, Ricco made us his grandma's famous cannoli and Odette taught us how to make vegetable curry patties," said Josef.

"Oh my god, they were so good!" said Harriet.

"We've started a recipe board," said Josef. "People write the things they'd like to make, and the ingredients needed, and everyone chips in with cash or donates ingredients. Spread between us, it costs less than a takeaway coffee each per week."

"We are very grateful to you." Ava smiled at Harriet and Evaline.

"Indeed, we are," said Josef. "Right, we'd best be off, we need to feed the workers before they begin to revolt."

Ava and Josef excused themselves, and Austin swiped two more samosas off the plate as he held the curtain aside for them to leave.

"You seem to have incited quite a cooperative, Ms. Smith," Evaline said, dabbing at the corners of her mouth with the napkin. She had evidently enjoyed her samosa.

"Not really. I simply offered them a space in which to meet. They've done the rest."

"Hmmm. Austin!" She snapped her fingers and her chauffeur jumped to attention, swallowing the last mouthful of samosa he'd been savoring and crossing immediately to Evaline, where he stood motionless, arm out so that she could pull herself up using him as a human handrail. "No Mr. Knight today, I see."

"He had some personal business to attend to."

"Did he?" Gripping tightly onto Austin, she took shuffling steps out of the royal box, with Harriet following behind. It was hard to tell while she was holding court—her snippy remarks and supercilious air made her a formidable force—but watching her now, Harriet could see how her fur coat hung from her thin shoulders, her spine bent and crooked as a windblown tree, and her legs were spindly twigs with her tights wrinkled at her ankles. Evaline Winter was not a well woman.

....

The stage was cleared of debris, and the water had been pumped out of the orchestra pit. It was unfortunate that the nice new varnish on the fresh floorboards of the stage had turned a ghostly gray, but the carpenters had assured them that as it dried out properly the patina would fade. The main thing was that they had a working stage again, almost. The new curtains had soaked up a good deal of the floodwater and now Harriet joined her fellow cleaner-uppers in twisting the huge drapes as tightly as they would go to squeeze out the excess water. As Ken had quite rightly said, "The dehumidifiers will do their job, but they're not miracle workers." And so here they were, essentially milking three massive sets of stage curtains into rows and rows of buckets. Her hands were cold to the point of pain, every fingertip pale and pruned; she wished she'd taken Mateo's offer of rubber gloves.

Gideon—in yellow mackintosh and galoshes—had taken on the role of cheerleader and morale booster, which also meant he didn't have to get his hands dirty.

"That's it, you've got this, guys! I think that one can stand another twist. Harry, that's the way. Isabel, darling, don't pat at it, get your arms around it and squeeze!"

"I'm gonna twist and squeeze *him* if he keeps this up," Billy growled.

"I'll hold him still," said Grace; her expression suggested she was only half joking.

Sid and some of the other children were running back and forth from the toilet block emptying the buckets and delivering them back to catch more water. Harriet twirled one of the cross-stage curtains with Mallory, twisting the fabric round and round and trying to ignore the freezing dribbles that ran up her forearms to her elbows, soaking into the pulled-up sleeves of both her cardigans. Her back was to the auditorium when she heard Carly call out, "Oi, James! Nice of you to show, finally!"

Harriet froze momentarily, then continued to twist the curtain, refusing to turn around. Mallory glanced at her but she pretended not to notice. Anger and embarrassment were doing the tango in her stomach, and now inexplicably she felt tears pricking at her eyes. *Don't cry, don't cry, don't cry.*

"You've missed all the fun!" Gideon called, which earned him some groans.

"So it would seem." James's voice was smooth and calm. Harriet seethed. *How dare he be calm!*

More people called out to him in greeting. *Well, isn't he just Mr. Popular!* Mallory caught her eye and nodded slightly, but she didn't need that to make her aware that James was right behind her. She could feel his presence. She had known that he would make a beeline for her, and she hadn't yet decided what she should do about it. Left to her own devices she would like to walk away without acknowledging him; actually, she would probably run. But her students were here and they believed her to be a grown-up, even though she felt like a girl who'd been stood up at the school disco. The insinuation that one day all the chaos and confusion of the teen years would melt away to be replaced by a sage state of adulthood was possibly the biggest mutual lie of adult humans the world over, but it wasn't her place to shatter the illusions of the young, not today.

"Harriet, could I possibly have a word?"

I can think of at least seventeen—let's start with "armpit fungus" and work our way through the alphabet!

She turned to him, forcing a smile and trying to ignore the hammering of her heart and the way his eyes looked like they held sentiments that she didn't know if she was ready to hear.

"Of course." She turned back to Mallory. "Excuse me, Mallory, I'll be back in a moment."

Without looking at him, she began walking toward the backstage, stepping gingerly around the buckets and wet towels dotted all over the place and making sure not to slip. She knew he was following her. Once they'd left the noise of the auditorium behind, she carried on past the makeshift coffee area and let herself into another dressing room, farther along the corridor where she was sure they wouldn't be disturbed.

Once inside, she closed the door. Instinctively she folded her arms across her chest and then unfolded them, forcing herself to keep an open posture; she didn't want him to think that she was protecting herself, even if that was exactly what she wanted to do. She wanted to armor up and save the soft parts of herself from being pierced, but she'd be damned if she'd let him know it.

She lifted her chin and pulled her shoulders back.

"How is Morgan?"

James, usually so buttoned up and ready to argue his case, seemed at sixes and sevens. "She's fine. A touch of whiplash, perhaps."

"And Lyra?"

"Also fine. Relieved that her mum's okay."

"Excellent. Well then, I'd better get back, lots to do to make the place shipshape again. Though as I'm sure you can see, we've made inroads since you left. Turns out we were just fine without you." *So much for taking the high ground!* "I'm sorry, that was mean of me, can we strike that from the record?"

"Sustained," he said.

"Thanks."

She shook her head at her idiot self and made to leave.

"I made a mistake," he said, stopping her in her tracks. "All my priorities were suddenly standing in line and glaring me in the face, and I panicked and went with the one that was shouting the loudest."

Oh, for cluck's sake! How could she argue with that?

"No," she sighed, and looked to the ceiling. "You didn't do anything wrong. Your priority should always be your daughter."

"My presence was very much surplus to requirements, a fact which was obvious when I turned up at the door on my white steed and found them eating popcorn and watching movies."

"You didn't know that when you left. For all you knew she might have been putting on a brave face. You did the right thing for Lyra. But Lyra isn't the issue."

"I know what you're going to say." He looked down at his shoes.

"But I'm going to say it anyway. I understand that you have all kinds of guilt around Lyra and Morgan. And I fully expect and accept that Lyra comes first for you, that's a given, I wouldn't want it any other way. But I was angry and hurt at the way you cut and ran when the sky in the theater was literally falling and tried to make *me* feel bad about it. I'm happy to play second fiddle to Lyra, but not to Morgan."

He rubbed his hand over his unshaven face; it suited him but was a testament to his distraction.

"I was an arsehole and I tried to turn my guilt around onto you and I'm sorry, really I am, that was inexcusable behavior and you deserved better."

She sighed. He was making this very hard for her. "It doesn't change our situation."

"I don't want to be with Morgan," he said.

That didn't exactly answer her question.

"But I owe her so much. She brought up my child," he said.

"*Her* child," Harriet corrected. "She didn't bring her up as a favor to you. She raised Lyra for Lyra's sake alone because she's a parent and that's what we do."

"Of course, you're right. You are absolutely right. I worded that badly. It's just that I have so much to make up for, I feel like I'm in her debt and I've got no way of repaying her."

"And therein lies the problem, because I don't know to what lengths you might go to assuage your guilt. And I get it, I honestly do. But I'm not going to put myself in a situation where I might be cast aside at any moment. That's not going to be good for my mental health."

He nodded, his expression grave, his eyes so sad that she wanted to swallow back all her words.

"What does that mean for us?" he asked.

She fought against the hopeful romantic in her head and the ache in her heart. Instead, she chose safety.

"It means I want to be your friend and I want to be a part of your life, but I can't commit to more than that while Morgan is your priority. I have to choose to put me first."

THIRTY

IT WAS TWO DAYS BEFORE CURTAIN UP, AND NERVOUS ENergy crackled in the air like static. They had lost a whole day's worth of rehearsals to the cleanup, and even with the eight industrial dehumidifiers roaring at full pelt the stage curtains were still wet. It didn't help that the auditorium was only ever a few degrees above fridge temperature when all the heaters were on. Still, the stage had dried out remarkably well and the blue-whale-belly tarpaulin was holding fast.

By eleven o'clock the final backcloths had been rigged up and the stagehands knew exactly which one to drop for which scene. James was demonstrably absent, but thankfully Harriet didn't have time to dwell on where he might be. Being "just" friends with James was proving to be infinitely harder than being lovers. Apparently, her heart hadn't got the memo that they were now simply platonic because it still leaped every time he walked into a room. Her hands betrayed her too, twitching with a want to hold his whenever he was near. He had accepted her decision with good grace. He had been consummately respectful. And her irrational, traitorous heart yearned for him to fight for her like he'd promised he would.

Backstage was frenzied as people shimmied into costume and makeup. For the people playing more than one part there would be quick costume changes between scenes, and Harriet, Hesther, and Farahnoush oversaw making sure these were readily available when the time came.

Gideon's words of rousing encouragement carried all the way to where Harriet and Farahnoush were trying to do up Carly's corset, which wasn't easy with cold fingers.

"Players all! Hear me now! This will be our only full dress rehearsal, so let us make it count. We go live in two days. This is the quickest production I have ever worked on, but it has also been my greatest pleasure. You are all stars of the stage! Let us glisten like the celestial beings that we are! Everybody, stand by and take your places, please!"

There was a beat of almost total silence, bar the nervous breathing and the rustling of crinoline dresses, and then Prescilla's piano playing began, and the first wave of actors and narrators took to the stage.

Backstage became a place of hushed frenetic business. Harriet grabbed her script and hurried into the wing, ready to prompt anyone who might need it.

"Miss," Billy whispered.

"Yes," she whispered back, not taking her eyes off the stage. "Are you ready? Is Sid okay? Not too nervous?"

"Nah, it's not about that. It's James, he wants to see you."

She ignored the way her heart skipped a beat. "Well, I'm a bit busy, tell him to come here if he needs me."

"Right. He said you'd say that, and he told me to tell you that he needs to show you something and he can only do it outside."

"What?"

"Shhhhhhh!" Destiny hissed from across the stage. She was in the other wing—wound round in several meters of silver paper chains—and was making furious "fingers on lips" actions at her.

Sorry! Harriet mouthed back.

"I can take this over until you get back. He's waiting out front for you."

She harrumphed as quietly as she could, acutely aware of Destiny eyeing her from across the stage.

"All right, I'll be as quick as I can," she said grudgingly and handed Billy her copy of the play.

As she came down the main staircase, she saw people waiting to buy tickets at the box office in a queue that snaked around the foyer and out the door, letting in the fearful icy wind from outside. At least they were guaranteed an audience for their efforts.

Harriet pulled cardigans one, two, and three together and headed out into the snow. It was falling heavily; the head of white on the wall had grown four inches since she'd arrived that morning.

The Christmas tree looked resplendent, and the Salvation Army band played "Good King Wenceslas" despite the mounds of white covering their shoulders. A small boy stood with his face to the gunmetal sky catching large snowflakes on his tongue while his mother fished in her purse for a coin to drop into the charity bucket.

Harriet looked around and saw James stood in the small garden area of the theater, next to a trough filled with hellebores peeking their heads above the snow. His back was to her; he was wearing his long black woolen coat and hugging his arms around himself. She wanted to run to him. She longed to tell him that she wanted to be more than just friends, that she'd been hasty, that life was too short not to try the rogan josh. But maybe she was too late; maybe taking a step back had made him realize he had feelings for Morgan after all. The thought of it made her want to cry with frustration at her own stupid cautiousness.

Her top cardigan was growing a snowy crust. She needed to do something before they both became snowmen.

"James. I'm here."

He turned and smiled at her.

"Ah, good. Right, here goes!" He bent down and rolled up each of his trouser legs and then began to untie one of his shoes, pushing his foot out of it with the toes of his other shoe and hopping as he slipped off his sock and poked it into the empty shoe. He grinned at her and placed his naked foot down on to the ground, where it instantly sank into the snow.

"All the holy saints! That's cold!" he yelled, before bending down and repeating the process with the other shoe and sock. "Christ on a bike!" he shouted, hopping from one naked foot to the other and getting some unusual looks from the trombone section of the band. He began to walk backward and forward in front of her, his hands flexing open and shut as he went.

"What are you doing?" she asked incredulously.

"I'm glad you asked." His voice was halting from the cold. "You once told me that you'd never loved anyone enough to walk barefoot in the snow. So, this is me, walking barefoot in the snow for you, to prove how much I think I love you. I can't promise that I won't make mistakes, but I can promise that you are the only woman that I will ever walk barefoot in the snow for."

"You silly ass!" she laughed. "You're going to get frostbite!"

"It'll be worth it if you admit that you think you love me too." His teeth were chattering loudly.

In a moment of rebellion against every risk-averse instinct, she reached under her long needlecord tunic and wriggled her tights down as far as the tops of her boots, noticing the cymbal player miss his cue as he watched her with a frown on his face. Then she unzipped her boots and stepped out of both them and her tights. James burst out a shivery laugh.

"Mother Smucker Gloriana ballbags!" she screeched as her feet sank into the snow. The trumpet player played a bum note in surprise. She began to move about with James in a sort of exaggerated pony trot, hopping from foot to foot as she went, so that the two of them looked like they were performing the weirdest ever "Dance of the Sugar Plum Fairy." "You are the rogan josh I've always wanted but been too afraid to try!" she said breathlessly.

"That's wonderful, I think?" James said, his voice shaking. "What does that actually mean?"

"It means I think I love you too!"

"Thank flock for that!" he said, pulling her into his arms and lifting her off the ground as he kissed her.

The Salvation Army band began an impromptu rendition of "All I Want for Christmas."

"For the love of all things holy!" shouted Grace, standing in the doorway dressed in robes of gray flowing chiffon as the Ghost of Christmas Past. "Have you lost your senses? Get in here at once!"

Still hopping from foot to foot, they did as they were told, sheepishly picking up their discarded footwear and following Grace back into the theater, where she made them both sit in the wings with their feet in bowls of warm water and forced them to drink cups of hot sweet tea laced with brandy even though it wasn't even lunchtime.

....

The theater was filling up fast. Harriet had managed a quick hello to Emma and Pete when they'd arrived but had no time to chat. Evaline—who was seated in her royal box, a picture of austere glamour in evening gown, pearls, and a tiara with Austin by her side—had informed her that the show was sold out, though she'd shown no pleasure in the news. Also in the box with her were two stiffly suited men that Evaline had introduced as the representatives of the theater groups interested in purchasing the Winter Theater. The tarp ceiling was undoubtedly an eyesore, but Harriet surmised it was unlikely to be a dealbreaker when the rest of the theater was so utterly majestic. She had quashed the theatrical urge to hiss and boo when she shook the representatives' hands. All she could do now was hope that Evaline wouldn't go back on her word.

Backstage, the frantic energy was palpable, pulsing down corridors and into dressing rooms like shock waves. Nerves were stretched thin, but the camaraderie was strong, and inevitable snaps prompted fits of giggles rather than scoldings. The bonhomie was infectious, and it infused every soul behind the scenes.

The corridors leading off each wing were lined with clothing rails ready for swift costume changes. Orchestral Christmas carols floated out through speakers fixed high up on the walls, piped down from a sound system that would complement Prescilla's piano playing throughout the show. There were two states of motion backstage: running full pelt or standing stock-still. It was as though every person in the production had woken that morning having forgotten how to walk at a reasonable pace.

"Come, come, good people, places, please!" Gideon implored. "The lights go down in one short minute, and then it is curtain up! This company is ready to give the town of Little Beck Foss the greatest show in its history! So without further ado I say to you all, break a leg! Break all your legs! And give this town something to remember!"

The cheers may have been muted by nerves, but wide smiles said that his words had done their job.

"Okay, places, everyone!" said Harriet. Her heart was beating wildly. She hadn't felt this jittery since two pink lines had indicated she was pregnant with Maisy. With every fiber of her being she wanted this production to go well for the famous five and all the people who had given their time and positive energy to the cause.

Ahmed and the narrators and townspeople who would be opening with him lined up in the wing beside Harriet. The curtains obscured the audience, but the low rumble of voices vibrated the boards beneath their feet. They knew the lights had gone down when an excited ripple of sound spiked in the auditorium and then grew quiet.

"Okay," said Harriet, offering them one final thumbs-up and a maniacal smile. "On you go, you'll be amazing, you've got this!" She ushered them onto the stage and watched Ahmed's chest fill with a deep breath before the curtains were drawn up.

"Marley was dead: to begin with . . ."

....

The next two and a half hours were a blur of frantic costume changes, makeup touch-ups, and hissed encouragements and congratulations. Harriet was stationed in the left wing and James the right, their eyes meeting fleetingly and often before their focus was redirected to their duties.

Carly and Ricco—as Belle and young Scrooge—sang "What If" to a rapt audience while behind the curtain the stage was readied with swift precision for the next scene. When they'd finished, bowing their heads and moving back away from one another as though pulled asunder by the hands of time, the sudden quiet left by their voices was filled with sniffs and hiccups before applause rolled through the theater like thunder.

Harriet grabbed them as they left the stage and hugged them tight.

"Amazing! You were even better than in the dress rehearsal."

"Do you think so, miss?" asked Carly, still trying to catch her breath.

James bounded across the still-curtained stage to them.

"That was incredible, you two!" he said, shaking each of them enthusiastically by the hand. "I'm so proud of you. You've got half the audience sobbing into their finery out there."

Harriet watched the easy way they were around each other, so at odds with when they had first met.

The curtains opened again, and Scrooge was back in his bed while the narrators stood around his sleeping form, chronicling the tale until Odette, in green robes, took to the stage as the Ghost of Christmas Present to wake him for further lessons.

"I can't do it, miss." Billy was standing before her, dressed as a Victorian house husband, shaking his head and chewing the skin on the side of his thumb.

"Yes, you can. Billy, you've got this."

"I can't. It's such a big scene. All those people . . ."

"Listen, all your scenes are with either Sid or Isabel, so just focus on them, don't look at the audience. Pretend it's simply another rehearsal, you're with your brother and your mates just messing about."

Sid came to join them. "I can hold your hand the whole time, Billy, if you like," he said. "Gideon won't mind, will he?"

"No, he won't mind at all. And the audience won't be any the wiser," said Harriet.

Isabel came up beside them, smiling once at Billy before taking Sid's hand.

"Ready, Sid?" she said, bending to his height.

"Ready!" He grinned back.

"Then let's go!"

Isabel and Sid took to the stage. Somewhere along the last few weeks Isabel had developed a newfound confidence that Harriet was happy to see. Billy watched his little brother skip onto the stage and then remember his hobble. The audience tittered delightedly.

"What if I mess it up? Or forget my lines?" Billy's eyes were wide with panic when he turned back to Harriet.

Harriet waved her printout of the play.

"That's what I'm here for. How about this, while you're on the stage I won't do anything else except stand in the wing where you can see me, following your lines, so that if you stumble, I can whisper them straight to you. We can do the whole scene with me feeding you your lines if need be. Okay?"

Billy took a second to think about it and then nodded.

"Yeah, okay." His voice was hesitant. "And you'll stand where I can see you?" He could have been six instead of sixteen in that moment, his shell of self-contained capability temporarily shucked. "The whole time?"

"Yes. I will always be in your line of sight. I promise."

He nodded again and took a deep breath. On the stage, the Ghost of Christmas Present was directing Scrooge to peek in at the Cratchits' Christmas.

"It's time," said Harriet, taking Billy by the shoulders. "You can do this. I know you can."

Hesitantly and somewhat stiffly, Billy took to the stage. Harriet positioned herself where he could easily see her. He glanced at her once before beginning.

"What has ever got your precious mother, then? And Tiny Tim! And Martha warn't as late last Christmas Day by half an hour!"

Harriet followed his lines, shifting her position as he moved about the stage to stay in his eyeline.

"He's doing really well," said Hesther, watching Billy bustle about the stage kitchen. "I wasn't sure he'd go on at all."

"Sometimes you just need to know that there's a safety net before you jump," said Harriet, her eyes flicking between Billy and his lines on her printout.

"Never was a truer word spoken, my friend." Hesther squeezed her shoulder and melted back into the melee backstage.

Sid of course managed to woo the entire theater, and Ricco was all affable charm as Scrooge's nephew. Hiroshi terrified his audience as he danced malevolently around the stage as the Ghost of Christmas Yet to Come. And when it came time for Scrooge to look upon the people selling his still-warm belongings after his death, Harriet couldn't help but feel sorry for him. She craned her neck to steal a glance up at Evaline in her box but jumped back and hid in the shadows when it seemed as though Evaline had at that moment trained her opera glasses directly upon her. *Surely not?* But later again, when Scrooge witnessed his own name upon the tombstone in the churchyard, she dared another peek, and this time Evaline not only had her in her sights but nodded once to acknowledge that she had indeed seen her. Harriet suppressed a squeak just as Scrooge cried out: *"No, Spirit! Oh no, no! Spirit! Hear me! I am not the man I was."*

The final scenes were the busiest of them all as they required almost all the cast and bit players to be on the stage in some capacity or another. Two of the Relic Hunters stood behind the set of Scrooge's house and held the frame firm as Ahmed climbed the box stairs and pushed open the window to speak to Sid on the stage below.

"What's today, my fine fellow?"

"Today!" called up Sid, disguised in a cap and thick scarf. *"Why, CHRISTMAS DAY."*

The audience roared their approval.

The end of the play was near, and the collective tension was relaxing into the euphoria of knowing that something terrifying was almost over. The cast were enjoying themselves; even Billy had a genuine spring in his step when he took to the stage for his final scene. At the very last moment Ahmed scooped Sid up off the floor—which hadn't been part of the plan because of his hip replacement last year—and Sid laughed joyfully and shouted, *"God bless us, every one!"*

There was a standing ovation as everyone involved in the production, even Ken and the maintenance crew, took to the stage in a messy, joyous muddle. Harriet could see Emma jumping up and down in the stalls, waving her arms above her head and whooping. Gideon was in raptures, bouncing from one end of the stage to the other, his cape flying out behind him. For a few moments, the audience was forgotten, despite their riotous applause and foot stamping, as new and old friends slammed together in hugs, swung each other round by the hands, landed kisses on cheeks, heads, lips. James found Harriet in the bustle and swept her into his arms so that her feet left the floor as he kissed her. The sound of Prescilla's piano playing finally broke through their rhapsodies, and as one they turned to the audience, taking the hand of the person beside them as they joined in singing "Put a Little Love in Your Heart." The audience went wild.

Gideon made his way to the front of the stage, bringing with him a microphone and stand, tapping it loudly so that the boom shocked stage and audience alike into quiet.

"Greetings and salutations to the town of Little Beck Foss!" he bellowed. "If I might invite Harriet and James to stand beside me?"

Harriet gulped and went to his side. James, looking equally uneasy, went to his other side.

"When these good people called upon my expertise for their small production of a Dickens classic . . ."

Here we go, Harriet thought keeping the rictus grin plastered to her face.

"My expectations were far from great!" He stopped and waited for people to get his joke. There was a smattering of polite laughter. "I thought, how shall I ever be able to mold this ragtag group into a cohesive production crew, with no budget and little experience between them?"

Bit rude.

"But I was wrong. As it turned out, they molded me."

Didn't see that coming!

"I have borne witness to a group of disparate humans coming together to form friendships and bonds that will stretch far beyond this production. It has been my honor to work with them all. And I am a better person for having met all of you."

With that, he bent into a deep bow, forcing James and Harriet to bow with him since he had a tight grip on their hands. The cheering took up again both in the stalls and on the stage.

A sharp rap-rap-rapping noise reverberated through the theater, and one by one people stopped clapping and fell quiet to watch as Evaline Winter hobbled onto the stage, her stick tapping with every step, Austin walking respectfully beside her. The theater became so hushed that even the scratch across the boards of the beads at the hem of her gown was audible.

She made a slow beeline for the microphone stand, and James quickly altered the height for her. A gold-tasseled evening bag with a beaded chain hung from her arm. When she reached the stand, her labored breaths sounded loud through the microphone. She didn't rush. Harriet wasn't sure she could have if she'd wanted to. Every person in the theater held their breath, and then she began to speak.

"This theater has been in my family for generations. For almost half of my life, it has lain forgotten, harboring all the ghosts of my father's disappointment and my ill will. I wanted shot of it, but that was mere emotion speaking, and I am a businesswoman first and foremost. I was not about to part with this place until the price was right. Tonight, thanks to the refurbishment of this old place and in no small part to this production, I am finally being offered what this building is worth."

Harriet had to keep reminding herself to breathe. Her

fists were curled into balls as she waited to see if Evaline would screw her over, when they had gone to all this effort to do her bidding just for a small corner of her empire that they could use for the community. It seemed cruel that during this journey her modest hopes had grown so much bigger, and the disappointment would be so much greater for the number of people who would be let down if Evaline went back on her word.

"My father was a snob. You may be saying to yourselves, 'Like father, like daughter.' I cannot defend myself on that score. The Winter Theater failed because instead of allowing the real people of Little Beck Foss to enjoy it, my father put his pride and his pretensions and his profits above all else. Now I see that by ignoring this community, by denying the good people of this town the simple resource of a space in which to form connections, I was indeed built in his image. But as we have seen here tonight, even the hardest heart can be softened. Perhaps there is time for my soul to be saved after all. And so, I hereby politely decline the generous offers from all interested parties, and instead pledge the Winter Theater to the community, under the careful and watchful regard of Ms. Harriet Smith and Mr. James Knight. I wish you all a merry Christmas."

Harriet's mouth dropped open. The theater remained quietly stunned. She looked up at the royal box in time to see the theater group representatives stand to leave, each with a phone to his ear. Evaline turned, leaning more heavily on her stick now, Austin close in beside her and James placing himself on her other side. She made her way painfully slowly toward the stage wing. She locked eyes with Harriet and nodded once.

"I don't know what to say." Harriet scrambled for anything that would convey her gratitude and shock.

Sid ran to the front of the stage and grabbed the microphone. "And God bless us, every one!" he shouted into it.

Evaline cracked the smallest of smiles as the audience found their voices.

"Then let him say it for us," she croaked. "I shall leave quietly through the back door. Don't follow me. I'm tired and I don't want to talk to anyone, least of all the unwashed masses. My solicitor can sort out the mess I've made, that's what I pay him for," she cackled, glancing at James, and Harriet was almost glad to see that the old woman hadn't undergone a complete personality transformation.

Gideon, sensing an opening for an encore, nodded to Prescilla, who played the opening bars of their final number, and the audience got to their feet in readiness. Sid was out front and center, showing off his breakdancing skills, and Gideon joined him. Harriet allowed herself to be pushed back as the rest of the cast surged forward. Her eyes roved over the stage counting her ducks as was her habit—Ricco, Carly, Leo—and she gave a little hiccup when she spotted Billy and Isabel locking lips in the wings.

"Looks like it's not only us who got a dream come true tonight," James said into her ear, his arm snaking around her waist and pulling her close into his side as they swayed together to the music.

THIRTY-ONE

IT WAS FINALLY HERE, THE DAY HARRIET HAD BEEN DREADING, even more than putting on a play in front of the entire town. Christmas Day. And now that she was in it, she found she didn't mind it all.

She had begun her morning early with a hot, deep bath heady with exquisite English rose bath oil and slathered herself afterward in the matching body butter; had there been anyone around to hug her she would have swished out of their embrace like a garden-scented soap bar.

When she was dressed—in her very favorite navy blue tunic dress with deep pockets and favorite cardigans one and two—she unboxed the orange-and-cinnamon candles and lit them in the sitting room. Then she warmed up a plate of raspberry-and-dark-chocolate rugelach that she'd stashed in the freezer after Josef's Hanukkah feast and ate them for breakfast, feet up on the coffee table, a giant mug of coffee beside them while a black-and-white Alastair Sim Scrooged it up on the TV.

By eleven o'clock, the smallest turkey she could find—which would still feed her for a week—was stuffed and smothered in streaky bacon, butter, and sprigs of thyme. She covered it over with foil and had just slipped it into the oven when her phone rang with a FaceTime.

"Merry Christmas!" blared out when she answered it as Emma, Pete, and their three kids all yelled at once. Emma's hair was a bird's nest and all of them were still in their pajamas.

Harriet laughed. "Merry Christmas to you too!"

"Now you've proved that you can do Christmas all by your own self, will you please get your arse over here?" Emma begged. "I'll come and get you."

"She hasn't hit the booze yet," Pete chimed in. "But the clock is ticking."

Emma elbowed him out of the frame only for Taylor to muscle in.

"Harriet, please don't leave us here with Mum's cooking!"

"Taylor! You traitor, what's wrong with my cooking?" Emma addressed her daughter.

"It's fine for everyday, but it's not Christmas-worthy, not like Harriet's. Harriet uses goose fat for the roast potatoes, you put yours in the air fryer."

"Harriet, we miss you!" called Phoebe from under a blanket on the sofa.

"Yeah, come on, Harriet," added Jordan. "It's bad enough Maisy's not here without you splitting the family up."

"I'll be with you all day tomorrow." Harriet managed to get a word in edgewise.

"It's not the same, we always have Christmas together!" whined Phoebe.

Emma put her face up close to the screen. "Can I come over to you, then? I'll leave this lot here, just let *me* come, as your faithful bestie."

"If Mum ditches to go to Harriet's, I'm going too!" shouted Taylor.

"Nobody's ditching Christmas!" Pete called jovially,

pouring himself a glass of Buck's fizz. "You're all stuck here for the duration, mwahahahaha!"

A small pang of longing tugged inside Harriet's chest, which she acknowledged and then quieted. She needed this day to be hers alone. What had started as a glorified sulk had morphed into something she had planned for and looked forward to. Next year, like all the years before, and probably forever after, she would do the big family Christmas, with or without Maisy. But this Christmas Day was her gift to herself, and she deserved every moment of it to be her own version of perfection.

"Seriously, though." Emma cocked her head to one side. "If you want to join us, any time of the day, just get in a taxi and come on over."

"Thanks, Em. But I won't. I think I really need this."

Her friend smiled at her. "I think you do too. Enjoy your day and we'll catch up tomorrow. I love you."

"I love you too." It was a good feeling, to know that she was loved enough that she could be alone and never be lonely.

A loud unharmonious chorus went up of "We love you, Harriet!" from her family on the screen. "And your goose-fat roast potatoes!" yelled Taylor.

Harriet laughed when Emma's face loomed up close again and whispered, "Give me strength!" before the screen went black and the call ended.

She looked with satisfaction at her neat piles of vegetables for one, ready to be prepped—plus extra for bubble and squeak to go with the leftovers, of course—and got to work.

At midday, just as she'd tipped the parboiled potatoes, hissing and spitting, into a tray of hot goose fat, her phone rang again. She pressed answer as she slid the tray into the hot oven.

Hic—"Merry"—*sniff*—"Christmas"—*sob*—"Mum."

Harriet looked into the red-rimmed eyes of her daughter, a messy bun piled on top of her head and the collar of her Rudolph pajamas just visible in the frame. Her heart squeezed like someone was using it as a stress ball.

"Maisy, sweetheart, what's the matter?"

"Nothing." Another sob escaped. "I just miss you. I miss everyone. I think this was a terrible mistake."

"Oh, my darling girl, I thought you were having a wonderful time."

Already her brain was calculating how much it would cost to get her daughter home on Christmas Day from upstate New York.

"I am," she sniffed. "I'm having the best time. It's amazing here." Another huge tear rolled down her flushed cheek. "But I woke up this morning, and you weren't here. And Savannah and her family are great, and they've been so kind to me, but they aren't *my* family and I miss you, Mum, and it hurts, it hurts really bad. I feel like I can't breathe, and I've left you all alone, and you won't go to Dad and Emma's, and it's all my fault for being so selfish."

"Okay, let's just calm it down, shall we? Now I want you to take some deep, calming breaths for me. Can you do that?"

"Uh-huh." Maisy sniffed again but did as she was told and began to take deep, shaky breaths in and out.

"That's great, my love, now you keep breathing and I'll do some talking. All right?"

"All right."

Harriet could hear her breathing calming already.

"This is simply a spot of homesickness, nothing more, and it will pass, my love, I promise. It's okay to miss your family, that's completely normal. You'll have loads more years to spend Christmas with us. But this might be your only chance to spend Christmas in a cabin in the mountains. How amazing! And I miss you too, my darling, of course I do, but you'll be home soon enough, and I'm having a gorgeous Christmas, I promise, so don't waste your time thinking about me when you need to soak up every fabulous moment with Savannah. My love is wide enough to reach all the way to New York and back again, Maisy my darling."

"But. You're all. Alone," Maisy hiccupped.

"I am choosing to be by myself today because I want to be. But I'm not lonely. I am spending some quality time with me. I've never done that before. I am on my own personal journey this Christmas."

Maisy laughed snottily. "You sound like a self-help book."

"I do a bit, don't I?"

"Don't enjoy yourself too much, or you won't want me back next Christmas."

"Oh, there will always be room for you in my Christmases."

"Thanks, Mum. Sorry I blubbed."

Her voice was still a bit shaky, but Harriet could tell that the storm had mostly passed.

"You don't need to apologize. Now, what are your plans today?"

Maisy blew her nose. "Um, well, after presents, we've got a champagne breakfast. Then we're going to walk down to this little hotel that's got an ice rink on a lake, and we'll do skating and have drinks and dinner and then come back for candlelit fondue and Christmas movies."

"Eugh! That sounds awful. No wonder you miss me."

That made Maisy laugh. "I love you, Mum."

"I love you too, sweetheart. Will you be okay now?"

A big sniff. "Yeah. I'm good."

"Call me later?"

"I will. I'll call you before you go to bed."

"Okay, love. Merry Christmas! Have the best day ever!"

"Merry Christmas, Mum."

The call ended, and Harriet had a little sob into one of her Christmas tea towels, but it was only brief, and in another moment, she was back to basting her parsnips.

....

By four p.m., she was nodding off on the sofa, the remnants of a most delicious dinner cleared away and the dishes drying on the drainer.

She had eaten her three-course dinner—pan-fried scallops to start, full turkey dinner with all the trimmings for main, and Christmas pudding with brandy butter and clotted cream ice cream for dessert—on a tray, on the sofa, with her feet up and *Die Hard 2* on the TV. She had never before eaten Christmas dinner in front of the telly.

Today had been decadent: decadent because she had permitted herself to accept that she, Harriet Smith, all by herself, was worthy of good things. Next year, bedlam would reign once again as their two households collided, and maybe James would even join them. Maybe. She had no expectations on that front, she was simply happy to see where life might lead them.

But today she had celebrated her own Christmas, just for herself, and it had been good.

THIRTY-TWO

AT HALF PAST FOUR, THE DOOR BUZZER JERKED HER OUT OF A snooze. She wiped the dribble off her chin, checked her face in the hall mirror, and answered the intercom.

"It's James. Merry Christmas. Now if you're about done doing Christmas for yourself, get your coat on and come down here." His voice was fuzzy through the speaker.

She wasn't done, really, but her heart had skipped several beats at the sound of his voice and she always got excited when he used his most stern voice on her.

"Merry Christmas to you too. Why do you need me to come down there?"

"I have a surprise for you."

If he wanted her to come downstairs, it was unlikely that he had postprandial ravishing in mind. *More's the pity.*

"Could you bring the surprise up here?"

"Afraid not," came the crackling response.

She sighed, but aside from binge-watching *Downton Abbey* and eating her own weight in honey-roasted cashew nuts, her plans this evening were pretty fluid, so she pressed the speak button on the intercom and said, "Give me three minutes."

"Roger that."

I wish you'd roger me! she thought, but then her stomach gurgled; she'd take coitus off the menu for today.

Five minutes later—scented candles snuffed and hair zhooshed—she was sat in the passenger side of James's car. He leaned over and kissed her, and she wished she'd been less liberal with the garlic in her stuffing.

"You smell good enough to eat," he said.

"Garlic. Sorry about that."

"No, that's not it, you smell like cinnamon buns."

"Ah, that'll be my Christmas candles."

"You mean you finally unboxed the fanciest candles?" He pulled a shocked face.

"And lit them."

"Now that's a Christmas miracle!" He smiled.

After stealing another kiss that made her rethink her sex embargo, James started the engine, and they pulled out onto the empty road.

"Where are we going?"

"You'll see," he said, smiling smugly. "Did you enjoy your day of solitary decadence?"

She sighed contentedly. "I certainly did."

"I'm glad."

"You know, I have you to thank for that. If you hadn't forced me to put up my decorations and Evaline hadn't kept going on about self-love, I would have spent the whole day sulking in my bauble-barren apartment, eating dry instant noodles and hating Christmas."

"A veritable Harriet Scrooge."

"Exactly."

"I suppose that makes me one of the ghosts of Christmas."

"The ghost of pain in the bum," she goaded.

He smiled but didn't take his eyes off the snowy road.

"Was it nice to spend Christmas morning with Lyra?" she asked.

"It was. I dropped her at the hotel where Morgan is staying just before lunch."

"You didn't eat with them?"

"No, I had somewhere else to be, and as much as I respect Morgan, she is not the person that I wanted to spend my day with."

He gave her a quick, meaningful glance that left her in no doubt that it was *her* that he wanted to spend his day with, and she closed her eyes to enjoy the warm sensation as it flooded through her.

....

"Here?" she exclaimed as they pulled up outside the theater.

"Here," he confirmed.

She couldn't imagine why James would bring her to the theater on Christmas Day. The snow had lain thickly on the empty pavements of the town and banked up around the trunk of the Christmas tree, but as she walked up the path to the theater entrance, she noted that it had seen a lot of traffic; all kinds of footprints traveling up and down the path were freezing in place as the late-afternoon temperature dropped, ready for what promised to be another snowy night.

When she pushed open the doors she was hit with scents of fresh coriander, cinnamon, fried onions, and garlic. Despite her gigantic festive lunch, her stomach growled loudly. James eyed her stomach, smiling knowingly.

"It's after five o'clock!" she said indignantly. "Dinner was four hours ago."

She didn't mention that dinner in its entirety had taken her two hours to consume.

"I didn't say a thing." He grinned. "Come on."

He jogged up the stairs, and Harriet followed behind at a pace befitting a woman who had recently eaten her own weight in Christmas pudding.

As she neared the top of the staircase, she could hear voices coming from within the auditorium. She was briefly transported back to when she'd first ventured inside the theater in search of her truanting students. *And look at the old girl now*, she thought lovingly as she ran her hand up the newly varnished handrail and felt the bounce of thick carpet beneath her boots. She wasn't sure if buildings had souls, but if they did, she felt connected to the Winter Theater's. It had ceased to be merely bricks and mortar to her and had become a refuge, and a sanctuary to all those it welcomed through its doors.

"Are you ready?" James asked as they stood at the top of the staircase, outside the doors to the auditorium. He was smiling like someone who was very pleased with himself.

"I think so?" She frowned.

"Good."

They pushed the doors open, and a wave of noise and aromas washed over her. Down below, the stage had been set with many trestle tables laid out in a large U formation, with chairs on both sides. A few seats were taken, but mostly people were zipping back and forth delivering trays piled mountainously high with food to the tables. Steam curled above smorgasbords of pastries, pakoras, falafel, sausage rolls, and that was just what Harriet could identify from her vantage point. Josef climbed onto the stage, and Billy rushed to take the enormous chocolate Yule log from him and laid it on the table. Carly and Leo followed behind with two more plates. Everywhere she looked, she saw the brightly colored hijabs belonging to the women of Hesther's refugee group as they chatted with friends and helped to ferry the trays of food.

"What. I. What is all this?" she finally managed to stammer.

"Merry Christmas, Harriet," said James.

"I don't understand."

"Don't you? Take a closer look."

She reached the bottom of the stairs and walked slowly down the middle aisle, taking in the familiar—and some not so familiar—faces of the bustling crowd that was filling the tables with food and taking seats around them. The Lonely Farts Club was in full attendance, as were the Great Foss Players—Gideon leading the charge of filling glasses from a bottle with a homemade label. Grace was chatting with Tess and Arthur while Sid sat on her other side, his head resting on her shoulder, as he read from the open book on his lap.

Someone waved at Harriet from the stage, and she recognized Ricco's parents, and with them Isabel's mum and siblings. Carly and Isabel were herding a dozen or so little kids as they sprinted in and out of the wings. Farahnoush and Mallory pulled a Christmas cracker that made a loud pop, and everyone mingled with everyone.

As she reached the orchestra pit, Hesther came over to greet her.

"Merry Christmas," Hesther said, smiling.

"You don't celebrate Christmas," laughed Harriet.

"But you do. And besides, this isn't a Christmas party per se; it's a nonspecific winter party that happens to fall on December the twenty-fifth."

"I love a nonspecific winter party!" Harriet gushed.

"This is wonderful! How did you get everyone together? On Christmas Day! And how did I not know about this?"

Hesther nodded in James's direction. "James did most of the organizing, and everyone chipped in where they could. We wanted to get you a thank-you gift for facilitating our gatherings, but nothing seemed to measure up."

"And then Billy suggested that maybe the best gift we could give you was to throw a party that you didn't have to organize," James chimed in.

Harriet laughed at that. "This was your idea, Billy?"

Billy shrugged. "No big deal."

"It was unanimously agreed that you deserved to just turn up and enjoy something for once, and after that it was easy to keep it a secret," Hesther finished.

From nowhere, tears pricked at Harriet's eyes.

"Okay, I have to go back and supervise the kitchen, so I'll leave you to mingle." Hesther pulled Harriet into a hug. "Enjoy," she whispered into her ear. "And thank you."

"Are you all right?" James handed her a tissue and she wiped her eyes and blew her nose.

"I am so much more than all right."

....

It was loud. It was chaotic. And it was wonderful. It was family. Harriet hadn't thought she'd be able to eat another morsel, but it turned out there was always room for one more tempura king prawn and a baklava bite to finish it off.

After a while, the children left the grown-ups to sit around the tables chatting and went off to play tag in the stalls. People leaned back in their chairs, belts and buttons undone, while still picking at their plates. There was so much laughter, Harriet wished she could bottle it.

"So, talk us through your meeting with Evaline," Gideon asked. "What's the plan going forward? I've asked James, but you know what solicitors are like, cagey bunch."

James laughed. "Allow me to protest," he said. "All I said was, let's wait until we're all together and Harriet's here too, since it is she who will be affected the most by all of this."

"Like I said, cagey." Gideon folded his arms. Today his waistcoat bore one blue and one red nutcracker soldier down each panel.

Evaline's announcement after the play had taken everyone by surprise and left Harriet with some careful thinking to do. Of course, Gideon would be interested; as far as he was concerned, having Harriet and James at the helm was practically being gifted his own theater.

Harriet was aware that many pairs of eyes were now directed at her.

"Well, obviously it means all the groups who have found their home at the theater can remain here."

Exclamations of relief went up around the table.

"And we'll hold meetings to make sure we are doing the best that we can for people and also to plan for the future. This is such an incredible opportunity, we really need to ensure we get the most out of it, and of course this is a community theater and space, so we need to find a way to be self-sufficient. I have a few ideas of my own on that score and I'll be asking all of you for your thoughts too."

"I have a lot of thoughts," said Josef.

"Good. Start making notes, because I'm scheduling

our inaugural meeting for the first week in January," Harriet replied.

"I'll be suggesting more productions," said Gideon.

"Of course you will." Ken winked. Beside him his wife smacked his arm playfully. "You're not going to be driving yourself into the ground for free, I hope, Harriet?"

"Evaline has offered to take me on as a permanent member of staff." She wasn't sure why she felt so self-conscious saying it.

"She's offered you the role of chief executive of the Winter Theater," James corrected. "And Evaline is going to change her will. The theater will be held in trust for the community, with Harriet and me as the trustees. We will be looking to form a board of directors going forward."

"Harriet! That's fantastic!" Hesther gushed.

"You're going to leave the school?" asked Leo's mum.

"I don't know yet. I need to think about it. I guess I need to decide where I'm most useful."

"Here at the theater, of course!" Gideon exclaimed. The sentiment echoed around the table.

"I have responsibilities at the school too," Harriet replied.

"Maybe you could incorporate the two, somehow?" suggested Hesther. "Work here but liaise with Foss and maybe even other schools."

"Yes," agreed Grace. "A place for youngsters like the famous five."

"Which is how it all began in the first place." James smiled. "With that first meeting in Evaline's car when you suggested creating a safe space for the young people of Little Beck Foss."

How could I forget! She smiled back at him.

"Does everyone automatically refer to us as the famous five now?" huffed Carly.

"*Yes!*" came the unanimous response followed by an explosion of laughter.

"Well, I have faith that whatever you decide will be for the best," said Odette to nods and noises of agreement. "A very merry Nonspecific Winter Christmas Party to you all!"

....

It was late by the time James drove Harriet back to her flat, her plate of leftovers on her lap, his in the back seat. The snow was gentle, as though cherubs on fluffy clouds were blowing white feathers off their palms.

They parked outside the library. The street was deserted, though windows glowed with life behind the curtains.

"What are your plans tomorrow?" he asked.

"A quiet morning and then I'll be going over to Emma and Pete's for the afternoon. You?"

"Brunch with Lyra and then a quiet afternoon."

"Sounds lovely."

"I wondered if you'd like to join us for brunch. I know Lyra would love to have you there. And Morgan is keen to meet you. If that wouldn't be too weird?"

She smiled.

"I think we are way past weird. In fact, I was going to ask if you'd like to join me at Emma and Pete's for the afternoon. Their kids basically want to grill you."

He chuckled. "Checking I'm good enough for you?"

"One hundred percent. Maybe I could brunch with you and then you could afternoon with me?" she wondered. "Then we'll have properly met each other's people. Aside from Maisy, of course—you have that pleasure to come."

"I'd like that," he said, taking her hand. "Very much."

They sat quietly, gazing at one another. Harriet felt blessed not only for having met James but for all the people who had found their way to the theater. They made for a loud, messy, imperfect kind of gang, but she knew she could count on them to show up for each other on the bad days as well as the good and that if one in their number should stumble, many hands would shoot out to catch them. The knowledge was a warm, bone-deep comfort.

"On any other day I would invite you up," she said finally. "But I think I'd like to finish this Christmas off in my own company, if you don't mind?"

"Not one bit. You deserve some quality time with yourself. And tomorrow we'll enjoy each other's company even more for it."

"Perfect."

James walked her to her door, and they kissed beneath the cottony moon. Her flat was warm and cozy, and it welcomed her in. She changed into fleecy pajamas, poured herself a generous glass of chocolate Baileys, and piled a plate with leftovers to pick at. Then she snuggled under a blanket on her sofa, with only the twinkle lights from the tree and her reading lamp to light the room. The fire flickered in the hearth, and she sighed with contentment as she opened a book and began to read.

EPILOGUE

Four Months Later

HARRIET PULLED OPEN THE ORNATE GLASS-AND-GILT DOORS of the theater and breathed in the heady scent of hyacinths carried on the fresh spring breeze. The long winter had hung around like a guest who'd outstayed their welcome, but this morning the sun was out, and the daffodils and tulips planted in the theater garden shone iridescent in its golden beams. She fastened the doors open to let the air through and made her way into the auditorium.

Dress rehearsals were well under way for the Easter performance of *The Sound of Music*, and the energy was the kind of pure unadulterated chaos that only the Winter Players could encompass.

As part of her mission to make the Winter Theater not only vital again in its own right but also a valuable local resource, Harriet had liaised with schools and community groups, and now the stage was in almost constant use for everything from debate teams to music and dance clubs, design technology apprenticeship schemes, and of course theater groups. Ticketed performances were booked in every two weeks almost until December, showcasing ballet recitals, jazz nights, and all things in between. All of which brought in a healthy revenue that could be plowed back into community projects.

Harriet still had to pinch herself that this was her job now: chief executive of the Winter Theater. It was a lot of responsibility, but she relished being in control of the theater's destiny and her own. And thanks to a very generous trust fund left by Evaline in her will, she didn't need to skimp on the infrastructure that would make the theater a safe space for anyone who needed it, which had included opening it up as an emergency winter shelter during the coldest February in decades.

She had worried at first about leaving the kids on the "list" back at the school, but she needn't have. Via one route or another, almost all of them ended up spending time at the theater, where she could keep an eye on them, and when they were at school, Ali—who had taken over her role in pastoral care—was their fierce protector. She wasn't good at relinquishing control, but she trusted Ali implicitly, and he reminded her constantly that she needed to calm the flock down, which helped enormously.

She had a lovely spacious office in the attic with a window overlooking the high street, but most often she brought her work and a small reading lamp down with her and settled at the back of the auditorium, just in case anyone needed her.

....

The Sound of Music was the first production by the Winter Players since *A Christmas Carol*, and anticipation was high; tickets had sold out in the first week of sale.

Backstage, actors and stagehands bustled to and fro in preparation. Out in the auditorium, Gideon—in a cape lined in a tulip-patterned fabric—bellowed the ten-minute call until curtain up.

Grace emerged from her dressing room wearing a dirndl and a cropped blond wig. Even the astonishingly thick stage makeup couldn't hide the fact that at sixty-five Grace made for a somewhat mature Maria, but then Josef was no spring chicken as Captain Von Trapp either. Sid—cast as little Kurt Von Trapp—walked beside her chattering.

"And Tess said the holiday house looks over the sea and that they have palm trees everywhere in Torquay. I'll share a room with Billy, which he's well cross about, but you get your own room, Grace, and we can all have breakfast together every morning. Arthur is going to teach me how to catch crabs with a bucket on a line. Have you been to Torquay before?"

"A long time ago, when I was about your age. I'm looking forward to going back. Now where is your brother?"

"He's still helping Hesther in the cocktail lounge."

Grace nodded. "Well, you'd best go retrieve him before Gideon bursts a blood vessel."

With James's help, Tess, Arthur, and Grace had been awarded joint guardianship of Billy and Sid. The boys spent half the week at each house, and once a week they all had family dinner together.

Gideon's voice echoed around the backstage corridors. "For the love of Shakespeare, I need my script writer! Where in Chaucer's name is Billy? Could we have the orchestra settled, please. Mallory, where is my Austrian dancing troupe? This is a professional theater, people, let's shake a tail feather!"

Ricco was seething in the left wing in a brown waistcoat and lederhosen, and Carly, who was playing Liesl, couldn't stop laughing at him.

"I look ridiculous!" he complained.

"I think it's cute," Leo offered, earning himself a scowl.

"Hold still!" Isabel admonished as she tried to adjust his braces.

"Seriously, you chose this month to start hitting the gym?" asked Carly, laughing.

"Excuse me for wanting to be buff!" Ricco replied testily.

"I like it," said Leo dreamily, and Carly rolled her eyes.

"What time did we say for dinner tonight?" Lyra called across to Maisy as she attached ropes to the pulley on one end of a backcloth depicting Austrian hills. Working on the same task at the other end of the backcloth, Maisy replied, "I think Mum said she'd booked the bistro for seven p.m."

The two had become easy friends, and Lyra had quickly been assimilated into their family and into the theater as a guest set designer, helping Leo and Farahnoush to bring their creative visions to fruition. Maisy would be leaving for university in September, and, though the thought of it still speared Harriet's chest with shards of melancholy, she was ready to embrace this next stage of her life. She would ensure that she nurtured herself and cherished her time alone and would then be fully ready to celebrate the long holidays with Maisy.

Harriet looked up as Billy strode—head down, hands in pockets as was his way—down the middle aisle to where Gideon was expostulating loudly about the tightness of Douglas's trousers.

"Kingsley, my dear man, is there anything we can do about those lederhosen? I don't think we need to assault our audience with quite such a vivid outline of Douglas's bratwurst!" Kingsley scurried onto the stage with a tape measure dangling over his shoulder and shuffled a rather proud-looking Douglas into the wings. "Billy, my boy!"

Gideon beamed. "Do you have the latest rewrites for the party scene?"

"Yep," said Billy, handing over two sheets of printed paper.

Gideon took them greedily, his eyes darting left to right as he scanned the page, a smile growing across his face. "Marvelous, simply marvelous, we will miss your writing talents when you leave us for the bright lights of London."

Billy was the first recipient of the Evaline Winter Playwriting Scholarship. He would be heading off to Goldsmiths next year.

"Cheers," said Billy, shrugging.

"It never ceases to amaze me how one so taciturn in real life can be so unreserved on the page."

Billy shrugged again and said dryly, "I'm an enigma."

Harriet bobbed her head down to hide her giggle.

"I thought I'd find you here," said James, moseying his way along the seats to reach her.

"It's too quiet in my office."

"Is that code for you don't want to miss anything that's going on down here?" he asked. He bent to kiss her before shifting some of her papers to the free seat on the other side of her and sitting down.

She smiled. "You seem to have the measure of me."

"Intimately." He waggled his eyebrows at her.

"I still have a few secrets," she said archly.

"Which I'm sure I'll wheedle out of you once you move in with me." He grinned.

"Er, you mean when you move in with me," she countered.

"My flat is bigger."

"My flat is more conveniently situated and infinitely cozier."

"Hey, I like my flat."

"I like your flat too, but I like mine more."

"You are unconscionably stubborn."

Variations on this discussion had been ongoing since February and went round in a complete circle, neither of them budging an inch.

Harriet laughed.

"I guess we've both been set in our own ways for too long."

"Perhaps we need to employ an intermediate phase to ease our transition from stubborn independence to—"

Harriet held up a finger to interject. "If you're going to say 'dependence' you can stop right there. I will never be dependent on anyone."

"If you'll allow me to finish," he said, a knowing smile tugging his mouth. "I was going to say to ease our transition from stubborn independence to mutual independence."

She narrowed her eyes and chewed the inside of her cheek, wondering if this was a trap.

"Okay, I'm listening."

"Let's become neighbors."

"You're bananas." She burst out laughing, earning herself a disapproving glare from Gideon.

"I'm serious." James shifted to face her, taking one of her hands in his. "Let's wait for two neighboring cottages or two flats in the same building to come up for rent and . . . see what happens. We get to be close and have our own space."

Harriet considered. It did seem like a good idea. "Neighbors with benefits," she said, chewing the tip of her pen.

"Exactly."

"You know." Harriet was thoughtful. "Mr. Parker in flat two was telling me that he might be relocating to Dubai with work in the autumn."

James's eyes twinkled in the light of her reading lamp as he leaned in close to kiss her.

"Then I guess I've got till autumn to pack," he whispered against her lips.

The introduction to "The Lonely Goatherd" song plink-plonked on the piano by Prescilla broke their kiss and made them look at the stage. Isabel, playing the puppet of the "girl in the pale pink coat," and Ricco, playing the goatherd, danced jerkily on the stage, while the rest of the cast sang and yodeled the lyrics in the wings. They were soon joined onstage by Destiny and the Lonely Farts Club, who unwittingly resembled demonic ventriloquist dummies with their puppet makeup and moved haltingly about the stage like the dead girl climbing out of the well in *The Ring*.

"That's going to scare small children," said James, as Destiny, with two red circles for cheeks, grinned maniacally out at the stalls and Winston sneezed his false teeth out onto the stage.

Harriet winced and nodded. "I'll have a word with Gideon," she said.

"What I would have given for a haven like this when I was a horrible teenager." James's tone was thoughtful.

"Me too," she laughed. "Maybe we would have been less horrible if we'd had one."

James quirked his head to one side. "No," he concluded. "I'd still have been horrible. Come on." He took her hand and brought it his lips, laying a kiss across her knuckles. "I'll treat you to a coffee in the cocktail lounge. The chef is making mini simnel cakes; I reckon we could bargain ourselves a couple of testers." He flashed her a devilish grin, and Harriet wondered how any woman could deny him anything ever.

"In that case, lead the way," she said, discarding her work for the moment. She could allow herself a coffee break.

Holding hands, they made their way down the grand staircase into the bustling foyer. Sunlight flooded in through the open doors as members of the various community groups scurried to and from meetings held in the many spaces within the theater buildings.

Harriet and James crossed the foyer and pulled open the double doors that led up to the restaurant and cocktail lounges. A familiar explosion of noise and smells spilled over them in a bright wave of nursery rhymes and pealing laughter, all wrapped neatly in scents of mixed spice. They smiled at one another as they surrendered themselves to the tide of mayhem.

Hanging above the door in a gilt frame was the portrait of Evaline Winter that had been completed just before her death. Her smile was comfortingly wry, and her straight-backed posture attested to her matriarchal status. But in her eyes the artist had captured what only those closest to her would have witnessed in those last few months of her life: mischief, of course, but also a twinkle of contentment that told of a woman who had found a way to free herself at last from the ghosts that had haunted her.

Harriet hoped the same freedom waited for every soul who walked through the doors of the Winter Theater.

ACKNOWLEDGMENTS

Kiss Me at Christmas is my fifth novel, and truth be told I still haven't got my head around having even one book published. But I think it's okay to still be in awe, to still have massive imposter syndrome, and to be constantly bedazzled by the notion, because it means I will never take any of it for granted and I will always be brimming over with gratitude. And feeling gratitude daily is a gift, to be sure.

With that in mind, here are some of the people for whom I am deeply thankful. Without them there simply wouldn't be a book. It takes a lot of talented people with a heavy dose of goodwill to turn my gigantic, messy Word document into the book you're holding.

To my agent, Hayley Steed, at Janklow & Nesbit, I will follow anywhere you lead. Thank you for believing in me, for your good advice and enthusiasm when I am bouncing ideas around, and for being an absolute force of nature. I can't believe I got so lucky. And thank you, lovely Mina Yakinya, agent's assistant, for keeping me organized. I am thankful too for the rights team at J&N for working hard to get this book into as many hands as possible: Nathaniel Alcaraz-Stapleton, Mairi Friesen-Escandell, Ellis Hazelgrove, Maimy Suleiman, Janet Covindassamy, and Ren Balcombe.

And now to give my thanks to the team at Putnam in the U.S.; there may be an ocean between us, but my love for you all easily stretches the distance. Kate Dresser, my glorious editor, you are as mighty as you are hilarious. Being told off by you for killing off one of my characters was one of my favorite moments ever! I adore our editorial meetings; I love bouncing ideas around with you, and afterward I always feel fit to burst with inspiration. You are the spell to my wand, the stick to my piñata!

Dear Tarini Sipahimalani, editorial assistant and so much more besides, thank you for calmly steering me through the editing process and for your patience when faced with my many—frankly bananas—questions and panics; you are lovely. And to Amy Schneider, copyeditor, and Claire Sullivan, production editor, your hard work to make my manuscript make sense is so appreciated. I live for the phrases that get lost in translation; I'm still chuckling about my misuse of "landing strip!"

Thank heavens for proofreaders! Seriously, Courtney Vincento and Leah Marsh, thank you; I have a skill for omitting important words and punctuation, but thankfully your keen skill for spotting my errors is greater.

Sanny Chiu, I am consistently awed by your jacket designs and this one is no exception. I am so thankful for your talent; you make my books shine out from the shelves. Thank you also to Shannon Plunkett, interior designer, for making this book a pleasure for the eyes of its readers.

To Shina Patel, marketer; Kristen Bianco, publicist; Jessenia Lopez, publicity assistant; and Alexis Welby, publicity director, thank you all for your tireless efforts to get my books seen by as many people as possible. When I start getting emails from you, I know it's that time of year again when things are going to get exciting!

You are all so very appreciated. My heartfelt thanks go to Maija Baldauf, managing editor; Emily Mileham, senior managing editor; Ashley McClay, marketing director; and Erin Byrne, production manager. Without the marvelous publishing team there simply wouldn't be a book. I hope I haven't left anyone out, but if I have it is because I am a dipstick and not because you aren't appreciated.

Thank you, lovely Hannah Smith at Penguin Michael Joseph, for making me feel so welcome in my new UK publishing home; I feel very lucky. And huge thanks to Sarah Bance for being a brilliant copyeditor; it has been a pleasure to work with you.

Of course, enormous, stupendous amounts of my gratitude go to you, dear reader. Thank you for reading my book; I can't express what it means to me to know that you took a chance on me. Thank you to all the booksellers, the small indie shops and the big chains; I am grateful to you all for stocking my book and for recommending it to readers. I always trust a bookseller. I am so lucky to belong to the book community. I am especially talking about Instagram; you took this scatty, nerdy, anxious little writer into your booky hearts and I am so happy to be there. I love chatting about books with you. Thank you to all those who take the time to write kind words about my books in their reviews; reviews are incredibly important to authors, and they are so appreciated. I have made some incredible friends in the online book community; I chat with some of you daily! Lauren Garcia and the members of the Read Rovers Book Club, you are like sunshine on my news feed. And where would I be without my book club, the Bayou Book Babes! Lauren Bethancourt, you and the BBBs make my heart glad.

To my family and friends outside of the interweb, I am blessed indeed to have you in my life. Thank you, Mum and Dad, for being my biggest cheerleaders, and for reading everything I've ever written. I love our weekly beach coffees, whatever the weather! To my siblings, Linzi and Simon, no one makes me snorty-laugh like you guys. Thank you, Aileen, for waiting patiently for me to be free for lunch dates. Jack and Will, you are my everything; good gracious, you two make me proud. I cherish the times you come back to visit the nest. And Dom, thank you for loving me at my best and my worst; you are always just what I need.

My heart is full and overflowing with love and gratitude.

DISCUSSION GUIDE

1. *Kiss Me at Christmas* is set in the charming English countryside. Discuss which setting—suburban or city—you tend to associate with the holidays.

2. Harriet would rather forget the holidays altogether when her daughter doesn't come home for the season, because "Christmas [feels] pointless without someone to make Christmas for" (p. 13). Discuss what "making Christmas" looks like for you. To what extent is there pressure to feel "bright and merry" during the holidays?

3. According to Harriet's students, Harriet has gone "rogue," something she might agree with after her out-of-character one-night stand. To what extent can making bad decisions sometimes lead to the best outcomes?

4. Harriet takes the fall for her students who trespass on the town's old Winter Theater. Do you think she would have behaved similarly if her daughter was home for the holidays? Where does Harriet derive her sense of purpose from?

5. After Harriet's exciting night with James, she's surprised to meet him again at the police station. How would you react if one of your exes didn't acknowledge your shared history? How would you discern which version of them was authentic?

6. After Harriet gets caught for trespassing, she is tasked with fixing up the old town theater. Discuss how this act of reconstruction might be symbolic of the "new beginnings" often associated with the new year. By the end of the novel, what would you identify as Harriet's "new beginning"?

7. Evaline and James are two characters who might, on the surface, be perceived as selfish. Despite this, discuss how they play a part in Harriet's embracing of self-care. Similarly, how do Harriet's efforts with the theater foster Evaline's and James's growth?

8. From assembling tricky costumes together to engaging in cheeky audition banter, Harriet and James's initially rigid relationship slowly deepens. Describe your favorite "Jarriet" moment. Which romance tropes did you observe of them?

9. Harriet's decision to put on a Christmas performance fosters great community and holiday cheer. What is it about the theater that fosters liveliness and connection?

10. Have you ever cooked yourself a three-course meal, or taken yourself out to dinner, simply for your own pleasure? Why or why not? Why do you think women especially feel guilty with the idea of treating themselves?

11. *Kiss Me at Christmas* is full of winter charm and old-town nostalgia. Discuss the fond wintertime memories this story might have sparked.

12. *Kiss Me at Christmas* illustrates love in all its forms. Even without the presence of her daughter, Harriet finds a way to surround herself with love and affection. Discuss how and where Harriet will spend her holidays next year.

ABOUT THE AUTHOR

A former professional cake baker, **JENNY BAYLISS** lives in a small seaside town in the UK with her husband, their children having left home for big adventures. She is also the author of *The Twelve Dates of Christmas, A Season for Second Chances, Meet Me Under the Mistletoe,* and *A December to Remember.*

JenniBayliss

BaylissJenni